LINE OF BATTLE

No. 2

Outpost

BY W.P. BROTHERS

Outpost

Line of Battle No. 2

Published by Alena Publishing, 2017

Cover Design by Brutal Disorder Logos

ISBN 10: 0-9977394-3-6

ISBN 13: 978-0-9977394-3-5

Acknowledgements

The expression goes that it takes a village to raise a child. I think the same could be said for supporting a writer. I'd like to give my heartfelt thanks to everyone who helped me through this project:

Jenna Christophersen, Ben and Taylor Smith, Sebastian Morrisseau, and Pierre Néri for encouraging me to keep going through some very difficult times.

Christopher Wu, for his help with military procedure and protocol; and Benjamin Collins, for his engineering and physics knowledge. If this book manages to seem realistic, it is thanks in no small part to these two gentlemen. Their unwavering friendship has been a wonderful gift to me through the years.

Merry Cutler, for her helpful feedback and suggestions on the very first draft of this manuscript.

My parents, Vincent and Pamela. Your advice has always been invaluable, and I can't imagine where I'd be if you both had not nurtured my love of reading and learning. Thank you for always pushing me to take risks and be my best self.

My family, above all. Without you, what's the point?

DEDICATION

To Grandma Rachel, who did not live long enough to see this book completed. Wherever you are, I hope you can read a copy.

CHAPTER 1

Aboard the RAS Barracuda

Wet-docked at Kensington Station

It was a measure of how far Captain Jordan Edwards had fallen that even the warmth of real sunshine couldn't improve his mood. Then again, shining a light into a hole didn't make it any prettier. Jordan shielded his eyes from the sun's glare and scanned the coastline spread out in front of him.

Endless blue-grey docks, washed with rust, lined the beach to the horizon, small cargo tenders bobbing in the surf in front of them. The still forms of cranes bristled from the metal platforms, their cables smacking their lift arms in the breeze. Behind them, bulky warehouses and maintenance bays glowered, their camouflage paint bleached from the sun. A crescent of dark green forest stretched to the horizon, hugging the sides of jagged hills, blue in the distance.

Jordan had visited Kensington Station once before, a few months after the war. The dockyards had been crowded then. Army units waiting to catch the next transport to their home worlds, Navy personnel loading supplies amidst the blue-white flicker of repair teams and their welding torches. Jordan had been a lieutenant, and he'd been glad to be moving on. He'd known as soon as peacetime came and the politicians got their hands on the national budget, stations like this would be a dead end. He'd wanted to keep moving fast, and he'd looked at the station personnel with pity. A few months, and they'd be sitting on their thumbs. A year, and they'd be reassigned, long after the choice billets were taken. Jordan had been right — these old wartime stations were practically abandoned now, staffed and protected by a handful of units that serviced the odd ship on patrol.

Ships like the *Barracuda*, Jordan's ship.

Jordan turned to look down the length of the hull, the reflection of the sun off the superstructure's view ports like beams from a magnifying glass. He'd accepted the command of the destroyer with joy. Finally, he'd had his own captaincy. It was only after the first few months of duty in this backwater sector that he'd realized the trap he'd fallen into. He was far away from the action, stuck on an old tub endlessly patrolling supply lines.

A dumpy, insignificant ship.

His ship.

Andrew had told him it was part of paying his dues. Everyone started with a boring, easy command. But Andrew, a captain only three years his senior, had already moved on to a cruiser.

Despite his mood, Jordan couldn't help but smile at the sight of his crew. Some of them were slogging through their planetside work details, inspecting the hull, cleaning the gun turrets, and assembling air-capturing units. But others were sprawled out in the sun, their heads thrown back, their dark blue uniform shirts unbuttoned in the heat. Jordan would reprimand them in a minute. Even if the *Barracuda* was only a destroyer, she was *his* destroyer, and he would keep her in order.

But not right away.

"No contact with the supply teams since touchdown, sir."

Jordan jumped at the sound of Commander Agrum's voice and turned to see his second-in-command standing in the hatch behind him, the inside of the launch control room black next to the blinding light of the Kensington sun.

"We expected as much." Jordan shook his head.

Indeed, dealing with the station had been one disappointment after another. First, they hadn't been able to make contact until the *Barracuda* had landed in the water. No doubt a malfunctioning communications relay somewhere in the solar system or in orbit was to blame, a clear sign of neglect. Second, when they'd finally caught the station on the radio, the operator on the other side of the line had made it clear that the *Barracuda* would wait.

"We're loading the trains now," she'd said. "You can expect them to reach the docks within an hour of splashdown."

"We're not here for shore leave," Jordan had said, leaning beside his radio operator. "Expedite your operations."

"We have limited staff here. Within an hour." She'd ended the exchange before Jordan could respond. Apparently, the yokels manning the station had forgotten they were in the military.

"Shall I deploy the marines? Secure the shore?" Agrum's brown eyes flicked to the coastline, his mouth pressed into a frown.

"No need, Commander." If the situation hadn't been pathetic, Jordan would have laughed. Here they were, far from any enemy and in the middle of nowhere, and Agrum wanted to send the marines to run around in the woods looking for someone to shoot. More than likely, they'd just harass the wildlife. Besides, Jordan could see the entire detachment of marines sunbathing near turret two, their cool grey uniforms contrasting with the dark blue of the rest of the crew.

"Very good, sir." Agrum's frown deepened. He'd had multiple deployments during the war, some of them quite harsh. Jordan had been jealous when he'd read his service record before taking command. Jordan had missed most of the action, and if his current career path was any indicator, he'd never get any.

Jordan turned back to survey the landscape. "If they don't arrive soon, we'll raise the fort again. Until then, relax." Jordan pointed to the jade-colored water below. "Organize a swimming detail."

"Sir?"

Jordan turned to face Agrum again. "You're supposed to laugh, commander. It was a joke."

Agrum grimaced, though Jordan supposed it was a smile. "Yes, sir. A joke, sir. Very funny."

Jordan clapped Agrum on the shoulder. "If you'd like to go by the book, take a stroll on the deck and maintain the uniform standard." Jordan pointed to the crewmembers below, who had completely removed their uniform shirts now, their white undershirts blinding in the sunlight.

Agrum nodded, saluting stiffly before disappearing inside the landing bay. Jordan turned back to the coastline. He supposed he ought to enjoy the sunlight while he could. In a few hours, they'd all be on patrol again, and he'd be stuck with artificial light and recycled air for another three months.

Jordan's eyes caught movement, and he watched as swarms of people filtered between the warehouses and onto the docks. About time.

"Button up your jackets and get the tenders moving!" Agrum had appeared on the deck below, shouting orders to the lounging crew. "Let's get these supplies loaded."

Crewmembers rushed into the lower landing bay entrance, directly below Jordan. He heard the bark and whine of a fusion drive starting up, and a second later, the *Barracuda's* five cargo tenders flew out of the bay door. Jordan held his cap on his head as the hot backwash from their engines whipped over him. The tenders circled the ship, then hovered in place as they began to lower themselves one by one into the water.

Jordan looked at the docks again and saw the people climbing into the numerous cargo tenders. It seemed like the station was going the extra mile after all the delays. They must have pre-loaded the tenders with supplies, because the people at the docks were already starting their engines. With that many rigs, perhaps sixty in all, the *Barracuda* would be re-supplied within the hour.

Jordan turned and walked through the hatch into the flight control room, blinking to adjust to the sudden darkness. Several crewmen were arranged in front of glowing, green scanner screens while Ensign Hong, the flight control officer on duty, looked out the windows with his binoculars.

"Call our tenders back in," Jordan said, leaning over one of the scanning screens. "I think the station's crew has it handled."

"Aye, sir." The shipman closest to Jordan nodded and picked up the radio handset. "Baker units, Launch control. Standby for new instructions."

A second later, the sound of a radio squelch signaled that the tenders had heard and were ready for new orders.

"Baker units," the shipman continued. "Cancel shore operations. Station personnel are handling supplies."

Another squelch confirmed reception.

"They're in one hell of a hurry."

Jordan turned to look at Hong, who was looking out the door. "They ought to be, after making us sit on our hands."

"Just as long as they don't crash into anything."

Jordan walked back outside to the railing, holding a hand in front of his eyes to block the sun. The last of the *Barracuda's* tenders was lifting out of the water while the others rumbled back into the landing bay. The station's craft were only a hundred yards away now, leaving white foam behind them as they raced toward the *Barracuda*. Jordan was just about to shout to Hong to raise the station's craft and instruct them to slow down when he saw flashes erupt down the length of the approaching fleet. Half an instant later, something thwacked into the hull behind him and searing pain lanced through Jordan's neck.

"Son of a bitch!" He cupped his neck as the crackling boom rolled over the water from the station's tenders. Jordan looked at his hand and saw blood. *Bullet fragments.*

"General quarters! Take cover!" Below, Agrum was running along the deck, shouting at the confused crewmembers, who ran for the nearest access hatches, their unbuttoned shirts billowing behind them. Jordan heard screams, saw a red mist burst from a woman's chest as she fell. Bullets scythed among the frantic crew, dropping them here and there. The marines were scrambling behind the turret for cover.

"Sir, get down!" Hong was squatting behind Jordan.

"They're firing at us!" Jordan gaped at Hong, his mind spinning.

Who the hell would do this?

"Down!" Hong dragged his captain to the metal grille of the deck and started pulling him toward the hatch.

Jordan turned to see the *Barracuda's* tender, hovering now, turn to face the firing craft. Its heavy machine gun ripped into action, two rockets screaming from its launcher ports. One of the station's craft exploded. Jordan smashed his hands against his ears, trying to stop the deafening noise.

"Sir, we need to get you inside—" An ear-splitting blast interrupted Hong.

Jordan looked in time to see the *Barracuda's* tender shudder as rockets struck it. A wave of heat washed over Jordan, his sinuses compressing painfully. He blinked, realized that he was lying on his back a few feet from the hatch. The tender was gone. Had it exploded? Jordan tried to roll over and get to Hong, couldn't get his leg to move. He looked down and saw a jagged piece of metal embedded in his left shin. He dragged himself backward as more explosions blossomed over the hull of the *Barracuda*. The station's tenders were right against the hull now, their top gun turrets ripping through the people still on the deck, bunched around the access hatches. Jordan touched Hong's hand, but Hong didn't seem to realize it.

"Take hold of me!" Jordan shouted. He turned to see Hong leaning against the frame of the doorway, several massive shrapnel splinters protruding from his chest. He stared at Hong's empty eyes. The hull shuddered with another terrific explosion. Jordan covered his head, and peered through his fingers at a massive plume of smoke and fire that unfolded into the air from the ship's side. The lift thrusters. The *Barracuda* would be trapped planetside without them. He heard shouts and saw people climbing up mesh ladders from the enemy tenders to the deck of the destroyer, rifles on their backs.

Jordan dragged himself over Hong's limp legs and into the control room. The crewmembers were shouting into their radios over the wail of the alert klaxon.

"Baker units, lift off and engage enemy units. Fighters prep for launch!"

One of them — his name patch read Owens — turned and saw Jordan. The young man ran over to him, dragged him to his feet, and kicked the hatch controls. Hong's body toppled outside as the hatch clanged shut.

"They're boarding," Jordan panted, his leg suddenly hurting. "Deploy counter-boarding parties and seal all hatches."

Jordan heard the shipman Williams, manning the radio, pass on the orders to the bridge. The deck lurched, and Jordan felt his insides shift as the ship began to lift.

"Get me to the bridge," Jordan shouted.

Owens nodded, and Jordan had to suppress a groan as the shipman carried him toward the hatch to the corridor.

Another explosion, and the deck rocked beneath them. Jordan and Owens crashed to the ground and rolled across the floor, smacking into the bulkhead below the windows.

"Sir, they've destroyed all our starboard launch thrusters," Williams shouted from somewhere. "We're in the water again."

Jordan felt Owens dragging him to his feet. He looked out the window. Another wave of tenders was headed toward the *Barracuda* from the shore. At least two hundred enemy soldiers were on top of the ship. Many more were splashing in the water, no doubt thrown clear in the ship's attempt to lift off.

He squinted at them, trying to identify the attackers, unable to get a clear view through the smoke and confusion.

Could the Milipa have made it this deep into the Alliance?

Some of the ship's defense emplacements spun around and began firing at the enemy tenders. Explosions peppered up and down the line of the approaching craft as the turrets hit their mark. With a throaty rumble, the *Barracuda's* tenders flew from the landing deck below, over the heads of the attackers. Jordan saw one of the hostiles point a rocket launcher in the direction of the bay. A missile burst from the weapon and streaked toward the bay, colliding with one of the tenders as it emerged. The craft burst into flames as it flew over the hull in a great arc. It crashed into turret four, and the ship rocked again as a massive explosion raced toward the sky. The attackers were pushed flat onto the deck, and some, set on fire by the blast, ran frantically toward the water.

The lights flickered out, and the defense emplacements outside sputtered to a halt.

"Sir, I've lost communications!" Williams' voice cracked with what could only be panic.

Below, groups of attackers were rushing into the open landing bay. Jordan turned to face Owens.

"Are there sidearms here?"

Owens nodded, and ran to a locked cabinet in the corner. The clank of boots on stairs echoed from below. Williams and Jordan looked out the hatch toward the corridor.

"Shit!" The color drained from Williams' face, and he tore off his radio headset. "Shit!"

He ran to the open hatch, Jordan limping after him. They pushed the door shut together and grabbed hold of the manual lock wheel. Jordan heard a bang behind him, and turned to see Owens throwing chairs into a barricade. Pain sliced through Jordan's leg again, and he'd have fallen to the deck had Williams not caught him. They shuffled together around the end of the barricades to where Owens knelt. Williams eased Jordan to the ground.

"They haven't changed the issue sidearm since I was your age, have they?" Jordan held out his hand to accept the pistol that Owens thrust toward him.

"No, sir. M7A1, forty-five caliber." Owens' voice shook with fear.

"Just like old times, then." Jordan tried to smile. He hadn't touched a pistol since basic training, but they didn't need to know that.

The thunder of boots on metal crescendoed, and something hard began to pound on the hatch. A second later, Jordan heard the hiss of a welding torch biting metal. Whoever was out there must have come prepared — or raided the tool shop on their way up.

Jordan slapped a magazine home, racked the slide, saw Owens and Williams do the same. A white-hot glow appeared near the door's locking mechanism. It wouldn't be long now.

Jordan wiped the cold sweat from his forehead. Spots danced before his eyes. He looked and saw a puddle of blood under his wounded leg. It figured he'd get mangled in his first real fight. That was his luck. He fought away the dizziness and trained his sights on the hatch.

The locking clamps began to flex and give way, and Jordan rested his finger on the trigger. He'd be damned before he'd let them have his ship. And as the hatch gave way and he opened fire, he repeated the words in his head with each shot.

My ship. My ship. My ship.

CHAPTER 2

Lieutenant Christine Flores peered through her binoculars toward the harbor, careful to keep the lenses shaded by the fat leaves of the bush she was lying beneath. A huge column of smoke was still rising over the water, the occasional muffled boom breaking through the air like a distant firework.

Air hissed from between Christine's teeth. They'd first heard the sound of explosions a half hour ago, when the trail had crested the saddle between two hills and come into view of the dockyards. Christine had ordered the platoon off the road, and they'd contoured around the reverse slope of the taller hill. Then she'd taken half of Sergeant Meyer's rifle squad — Corporal Lazaar, Privates Clos, Miller, Harris, and Henrikson — and crept to the shoulder of the hill, leaving Sergeant Néri to set up positions overlooking the trail and the road beyond. She'd been pleased to see her platoon operate so smoothly and so quietly. Kensington may be the middle of nowhere, but they were still rangers, and she'd made sure they learned how to act the part.

It hadn't been easy.

The imbecile who'd commanded her platoon before her had let them get lazy, ignoring protocol, sticking to vehicles and roads and ignoring facilities that could only be reached by foot patrol. Christine had arrived with a batch of fresh officers Major Parks had chosen to "tidy up" the unit before he'd been transferred, and that's exactly what they'd done. Extra patrols, early morning PT, and a merciless emphasis on technique and procedure had honed the entire company quickly. Her satisfaction at seeing her own platoon patrol had almost made up for being stuck on Kensington. Becoming a ranger officer was a ruthless ordeal. Brutal physical fitness regimens, medical screenings and vaccinations to make sure she wouldn't get sick in the wilderness too easily, endless marksmanship training and weapons drills. She'd been as proud of the ranger badge on her sleeve as she was of anything else she'd ever done. It had almost made up for everything she'd lost that year.

When she'd received her commission, she'd hoped to be stationed somewhere close to Ryan. He was all she'd had left, and she hadn't wanted to be so far away that she couldn't visit him on leave. But then her assignment came — a three-year billet on Kensington. She and Ryan had agreed to postpone the wedding until she was back. With Ryan's income from the academy and the extra stipend Christine would receive for being assigned a "difficult" billet, they'd actually have money for a real party by then. Waiting sucked, but she owed the rangers everything. They had saved her, given her a purpose and a job to do. No matter where the rangers asked her to go, Christine would give them her best.

Still, saying goodbye to Ryan had been hard.

Christine shook her head, tapped her engagement ring against the barrel of the binoculars. No time for that now. She raised the lenses to her eyes again. An enormous tan shape seemed to be hovering over the smoke, although at this distance, it was hard to tell.

Could it be part of the smoke plume?

She blinked, and the shape was gone. Christine heard a rustle behind her. She turned her head to see Corporal Lazaar crawl up beside her, the long-range radio unit on his back, carbine in hand.

"Ma'am, the platoon is holding position. We've contacted the rest of the company. Everyone's checked in."

"Good." Christine nodded. "What are they saying at the fort?"

"They're having trouble with communications. The relay network seems to be out of order."

"Of course, it is." Christine rolled onto her side, slid the binoculars back into their leather case. Nothing surprised her where the fort was concerned, not since Major Parks had been transferred. Parks, the commanding officer of the Third Ranger Company, had been an excellent soldier, and the perfect counterweight to Colonel Neville, the fort garrison's do-nothing leader. Neville was great with paperwork and organizing supplies. Word was he'd been a logistics officer for a long time. But he was not a leader. He didn't know when to take charge and when not to micromanage. Worse, Neville's career was his one real concern. Christine had no doubt he'd throw any of them under the bus without a second thought to advance himself. Christine had seen where that kind of attitude led, in uniform and out. She knew the price leaders like Neville exacted on those around them, and that made her hate the colonel more than anyone else on Kensington.

While Major Parks had still been around, things had been okay. Parks had taken charge more than once to make up for the inadequacies of Neville, working hard to keep the aging Kensington facility in operational condition and the bored garrison motivated. Everyone, even the fort staff, had viewed him as the real leader on the planet. Unfortunately, someone further up had noticed the major's skills and decided to transfer him and his command platoon to a "more urgent" billet. Apparently, the military needed the more experienced officers and staff closer to the border with the Milipa to form a new ranger unit. As usual, Kensington personnel were left to do more with less while they waited for a replacement officer and staff for the ranger company. Christine's heart had sunk when she'd heard that Neville would act as the rangers' CO in the meantime. As the senior officer among the fresh batch, Christine had been forced to be the liaison between the colonel and the rest of the rangers, a position she loathed because it meant talking to Neville on a regular basis.

"What are their orders?" Christine slung the binocular case around her neck.

"They think the train to the docks may have derailed and exploded. They want us to meet Third Platoon and investigate."

"Get them back on the line and tell them the smoke is coming from the water—"

Another distant explosion interrupted Christine. They both turned their heads toward the harbor as a rapid series of booms broke through the air.

"Damn." Christine shook her head. Something was wrong, but somehow, she couldn't believe it was a train wreck. She looked back at Lazaar. "Tell them we think it may be coming from the destroyer that was due today, and the explosions sound like weapons fire."

"Yes, ma'am." Lazaar dragged himself backward through the bushes.

Christine took one more look toward the harbor before crawling after Lazaar. After a few meters, the dense brush opened onto a small glade. Clos, Harris, and Miller knelt around the perimeter of the clearing, their carbines trained into the woods. Henrikson and Meyer were helping Lazaar to his feet.

Christine stood and dusted the dirt and twigs off her olive-green uniform. She nodded at Lazaar, who activated his handset.

"King One, Raven Five-Six, we've got eyes on the source of the smoke, break."

As Lazaar exchanged information with the fort, Christine crossed the clearing to where she'd left her patrol pack. She hauled the pack onto her knee, adjusted the weight, and slipped one arm through the strap. The helmet and body armor strapped onto the pack's exterior clanked as she hefted the pack onto her back. It only took a few days in the blazing sun of Kensington to realize that wearing armor while on patrol was a fast track to dehydration and heat exhaustion. Christine pulled her carbine from where it hung by its sling on her shoulder, then turned to face Lazaar, who was stowing his handset.

"The rest of the company is pulling back to occupy bunkers one through ten." Ali's voice strained slightly as he adjusted the weight of his transmitter pack. "We're to continue and investigate with Third Platoon at the rail line, as before."

"Finally getting some exercise!" Clos flashed a smile toward Christine. They'd already patrolled close to seven miles with full combat loads.

"The rail line?" Sergeant Meyer shook his head. "Why don't we bring a marching band with us as well?" Following the low-lying riverbed and cleared of all brush for two hundred yards on either side, the rail line was the perfect place to meet — if you wanted to be seen from every hilltop within several miles. Rangers knew better.

Christine nodded. "I agree. Corporal?"

She turned to Lazaar. "Get Third on the line and tell them to rendezvous at Bunker Fifty." The approach to the overlook would allow them to keep to the forest trails and steep ravines, concealing their location. Something was not right, and the last thing Christine was about to do was risk her platoon's safety by using shit tactics.

After Lazaar relayed the information, the group hiked back down the hillside toward the rest of the platoon. The sun was directly overhead now, and Christine could smell the sweet odor of grasses and plants curing. The monsoon season was coming. How anything survived on Kensington long enough to reach it was a mystery to Christine. The dossier she'd been given when she'd been assigned to the planet had explained that it was close to its sun, just barely within a habitable zone for humans. Christine had found that fact interesting, but it wasn't until she'd stepped off the troopship and the heat had smacked her in the face that she'd realized what it meant.

They reached the spot where the platoon had been and came to a halt. The unit had done a good job hiding itself. They were absolutely improving. Christine scanned the woods, taking the opportunity to run her troops through the familiar test. She'd never failed to find them, but hopefully the day would come when she couldn't.

"You, Salzman!" Christine pointed to a glint in the bushes twenty meters from her. "Cut the reflection on that scope if you don't want a bullet through it!"

Frustrated groans issued from all around them, and one by one the members of the platoon melted from the woods and assembled around Christine. Sergeant Néri stepped forward. A foot taller than Christine and built like the mountains they patrolled, Néri had been in the Ranger Corps longer than anyone there. It never ceased to impress Christine that he could move his bulk through brush without making a sound.

"No movement on the rail line or any of the roads we can see," Néri murmured. "If anyone's out there, they're still at the docks."

Christine nodded. "If we pick up our rear ends and get down there fast enough, we'll catch them before they leave."

Bunker Fifty was about six miles away. The platoon would need to hike quickly.

"Ma'am," One of the soldiers craned his head over the other rangers. "Are we assuming there's a hostile presence on Kensington?"

"Hope for the best, Francis," Christine said, making eye contact with each of her rangers. "Assume the worst. That's what they told me in basic, and it's never led me wrong."

Actually, Ryan had been the one who always said that, but Christine wasn't about to talk about her fiancé with these guys. It was better that she keep her own vulnerabilities to herself. When she was with her rangers, she was a commanding officer first and a human being second.

Christine explained their destination, and in short order the platoon had gathered their gear and was ready to march. They contoured the hill back to where they'd left the road and crossed to the other side. Before them, the ground rose sharply to another hilltop before plunging down to a gorge with a fast, shallow river cutting through it. The platoon skirted the hill's summit, and then followed its shoulder as it blended into the lip of the gorge. Keeping just below the crest of the ridge, they paralleled it, the rush of the river drowning out all other sounds. Christine watched as the ranger to her left stumbled, his khaki gaiter caught by a thorny bush. She pushed herself to keep up the pace, not let any of her fatigue show. Somehow, knowing she had to act a certain way in front of her troops made physical exertion easier. The pain just didn't seem important when she had a platoon to run.

As the gorge curved northward, the rail bridge spanning it came into view. The rangers found the familiar trail that cut down the gorge to the river, and followed it. The trees in the bottom of the gorge were immensely tall and close together, their silvery bark and shaggy, blue-green foliage clumps reaching for the sunlight. It had taken the rangers several months of trial and error and consulting old maps to find a quick way through. An old road snaked beside the river, no doubt constructed when the bridge was built to allow access to the pilings. Overgrown and hidden from view, it provided the perfect conduit to cross the rail line undetected.

The rangers passed under the bridge and along the access road until it started climbing back up the side of the gorge. They left the road, but paralleled it up the side of the gorge, stopping for a few minutes to take water. Christine peered between the trees at the sun. They were making good time and had many hours of daylight left. If their pace held, they'd be with Third Platoon in an hour and in position to overlook the docks within four, giving them plenty of time to find a defensible position to make camp before nightfall.

After a mile, the gorge deepened and the noise of the creek increased as the water sped faster downward. Where the creek emptied into the main river, the platoon cut over the crest of the ridge and toward a broad hill, its summit a cap of lighter blue-green, cleared of trees. Christine strained to hear any sounds from the dockyards, which lay only a half mile beyond the hill, but the air was silent, other than the footsteps and breathing of her own troops. Whatever had been happening at the docks had ended in the hours since they'd started their journey.

At the base of the hill, the rangers came to a halt.

"Tell third we've arrived," Christine said, wiped sweat from her forehead.

While Lazaar keyed his handset, Christine leaned back against a tree. She remembered when her father would drag her along on his "wilderness" hikes in the recreation parks back home on Artemis. He was always so happy to leave the factories for a day, and Christine never made it easy on him. She'd never seen the point of walking around in the woods. She couldn't help but smile, considering how ironic it was that she worked in the wilderness for a living.

If Dad were here, he'd point that out.

The voice of Lieutenant Squires in her radio headset broke through Christine's thoughts.

Third Platoon was on the other side of the hill. Lazaar looked to her for a response.

She keyed her shoulder mic. "Raven Three-Six, Raven Five-Six Actual, copy. We'll meet you on the east side at the tree line."

Christine faced her troops and motioned them to follow. They moved quickly up the hill and established a position right below the edge of the summit clearing. In the middle of the clearing sat Bunker Fifty, its reinforced concrete walls stained with streaks of black. The artillery pits next to the bunker were filled with water, which reflected the sunlight as it rippled slightly in the breeze. Christine made a mental note that they would need to empty the pits before they moved on.

Each platoon worked facility maintenance into their patrol schedules, but with so many emplacements to worry about — some two hundred bunkers, shelters, redoubts, and gun pits — there was very little they could actually do but slow the rate of decay. Christine guessed that, in ten years, without real renovations by the Army Engineers, many of the bunkers, already leaking and beginning to crumble, would be unusable. She tried to imagine what it must have been like during the war, each bunker armed and manned to capacity with howitzers mounted in the pits, a full regiment garrisoned at the fort. So much effort had gone into building fortifications for only a few years' use before letting them fall apart.

Christine's eyes caught movement, and she recognized the slender, lanky form of Lieutenant Squires walking toward her, his platoon in tow.

"Have a pleasant trip up?" Squires smiled and held out a hand.

Christine took Squires' hand and shook it impatiently. The lieutenant always seemed to be extra nice to her. Even mentioning Ryan hadn't kept him from trying to flirt. She didn't have time for bullshit. "What have you managed to see?"

"Nothing yet. We came up the ravine to the north. This is our first chance to look."

Christine slung her carbine over her shoulder. "Lazaar, Harris, you're with me and the lieutenant. Sergeant Néri, set up the platoon to cover the spur from the rail line."

"Third Platoon, cover the ravine and the road," Squires added, turning to his troops. At least he knew how to do his job, even if he couldn't take a hint.

Squires led the way around the clearing, Christine a few steps behind with Lazaar and Harris. Christine heard Squires sniffing the air.

"Someone leave the turkey in the oven too long?" Squires coughed.

Christine wrinkled her nose as the smell hit her. Melted electrical cables, burning industrial lubricants — and the unmistakable odor of scorched flesh.

Harris raised his hand, and they dropped to their knees. Christine tilted her head slightly, and caught the muffled sound of raised voices. Whoever it was out there was only a couple hundred yards away at most. Christine unslung her carbine from over her shoulder again and pulled the bolt back slightly to make sure it was loaded. Seeing the base of a bullet in the chamber, she locked the bolt closed and positioned her finger near safety, ready to click it off. She made eye contact with Harris and Lazaar, then drew her bayonet from its scabbard on her belt and slid it into place at the muzzle of her weapon with a soft metallic click. Every ranger knew that, in dense wilderness, where good guys and assholes sometimes stumbled upon each other with only a few yards between them, close quarters fighting was not only possible — it was the norm.

The four rangers continued on, skirting the clearing, their eyes scanning the woods. The voices faded away as they reached the side of the hill opposite where they'd left the two platoons. As the harbor came into view, Christine expected to see the destroyer burning in the water but instead she saw—

Where the hell did it go?

The harbor was empty, and except for the smoke that hung in the air like an acrid mist, there was nothing that made the scene look out of the ordinary. The rangers moved into the clearing just high enough to see over the tops of the trees, then took cover behind a clump of bushes and looked down toward the water. The docks were mostly hidden from view by a line of huge, rusty warehouses that stood a hundred yards beyond the base of the hill, across a narrow dirt road and a branch of the rail line that ran right up to the warehouses. One of the cargo doors on the closest warehouse was open.

"Looks like nobody's home," Squires whispered.

"Should we go knock on the—"

Christine raised a hand, cutting off Lazaar mid-sentence. The sound of voices was growing louder again. A second later, a group of six figures appeared around the corner of the warehouse, arranged in pairs carrying between them what looked like —

Bodies.

Christine could just make out the dark blue of Navy uniforms on the corpses before they were chucked one by one into the warehouse. Another group rounded the corner, their backs weighed down by bundles of what looked like debris, which were also thrown into the warehouse.

"Definitely bipedal," Squires said. "I don't think we're dealing with Frontin."

At least that was a relief.

Harris cursed under his breath. "Milipa bastards! How'd they get here?"

Christine had fought the Milipa before she'd gone to OCS. She would never forget the horror of her first combat against them. The first time she'd killed another being up close had been in a skirmish to secure an important ridgeline on Annecy Major, an "unofficial" action that politicians on either side would never acknowledge or admit to. Her platoon had occupied the ridge ahead of the main advance and kept the bastards away with precise gunfire. But one of them had slipped through the line, appearing from around a boulder a few yards to Christine's left. With a burst from his weapon, the Milipa soldier had cut down the man next to Christine. A ball of fear driven by anger and training, Christine had rushed forward, punching the tip of her bayonet through the base of the bastard's neck. As the Milipa fell to the ground, she couldn't stop stabbing it again and again.

But the creatures at the warehouse were different somehow. The skin was the wrong color, and they weren't nearly tall enough. The distant roar of a fusion motor carried from the harbor, and two small craft — they looked like standard Navy cargo tenders — pushed out into the harbor. As the rangers watched, they came to stop, then started again, seeming to scoot in short bursts.

Christine drew her binoculars from their case and peered out toward the closest tender. It growled forward fifty feet and then stopped. A figure emerged from the open side hatch and hauled aboard another body. Christine swallowed, and trained her binoculars on the water. What she hadn't seen before suddenly came into sharp focus — the water was full of floating bodies.

Christine shifted the binoculars back to the closest warehouse. She wanted to know whose ass she needed to kick, and she wanted to know now. She focused her binoculars on the face of the nearest enemy.

"Oh, my god." Christine's pulse pounded in her ears. She blinked and looked again. "This is impossible."

"If we are facing a Milipa attack, this could mean all-out war." Squires sounded tenser than Christine had ever heard him.

"I don't think we're dealing with Milipa here." Christine turned to face the others, who looked back at her, confused. "They're human."

CHAPTER 3

Captain Kim Morden stared at the blank computer screen in front of her. Of all the paperwork a commanding officer had to do after a battle, this was her least favorite. Repairs, damage assessments, and preparing casualty lists were bad. But condolence letters? Post-action reports? Each was an opportunity to reconsider every decision, second-guess every fact, think about the possibilities or outcomes she'd missed in the moment. Somehow, seeing other versions of events made the ones she was stuck with seem worse.

Kim sighed and drummed her fingers beside her keyboard. How could this be so hard? Condolence letters ought to be simple, a series of facts about a good person who died doing something important. There was something beautiful about honoring the dead, finding every reason to praise them and then expressing them all. And yet each one felt like a trial. The people who would soon discover that their loved ones were gone forever would want to know how and why their father, mother, husband, wife, son, daughter had died. Could anything have prevented it? Did it have to be that way? Hell, Kim couldn't answer those questions for herself, much less the grieving families of the honored dead.

Kim had done her best to complete the last of them back-to-back this week, cloistering herself in her room and emerging only to eat and take the occasional tour of the bridge. She was reaching the end now. Only the official post-action report for her superiors, the ultimate judges of her actions, remained. Given what she'd already made it through — the digital mountain of letters she'd written — this should be easy.

Yeah. Easy as pulling teeth.

"Regulations state that all crewmembers must behave in such a manner as to be conducive to good health and top performance," Lieutenant Commander Wilcox had said. He'd come to bring her coffee at the end of today's main shift, an exaggerated, disapproving look on his face. Old spit-and-polish Jack. Leave it to him to use rules as a way to show concern.

"You have no reason to fear for regulations, Mr. Wilcox." Kim had imitated a grin, not wanting Wilcox to see how much the letters had affected her, but he hadn't bought it.

"Have you even been back there?" He'd pointed at the door to the bedroom, on the opposite end of the foyer from the desk.

"Thank you for the coffee, Commander."

Wilcox had simply shaken his head and held out the steaming mug. Kim had accepted it and drunk it without tasting, not even noticing when Wilcox had left the room. After finishing her condolence letters, she had gone straight into her action report. She'd stopped and started again and again, writing and erasing. She'd only realized she'd been awake all night when she'd heard the chime for the morning shift an hour ago.

Kim stood from her desk and paced around her foyer, looking at her feet and threading a hand through her hair. She ignored the twinge in her shoulder. It always seemed to come back when she worked out or didn't take care of herself. Slumping in a chair for eighteen hours certainly hadn't helped. Kim looked at the room, half expecting to see Captain Knight's furniture there. She still wasn't used to being in the captain's suite. When Knight had been there, antique weapons and paintings had decorated the walls, and sculptures and plants had shared the built-in wooden shelves with books. A large couch with a coffee table had sat in the center of the room, giving officers and crew somewhere comfortable to sit. Everything had been tasteful, cozy, and bright.

Kim preferred to stick to the essentials. It made things easier to manage. She'd left the shelves and walls empty, and other than the regulation work desk, chair, computer terminal, and a small refrigerator tucked into the wall under the shelves, there was nothing else in the room. Kim suddenly wished she had something, *anything* to look at beside blank walls, blank pages, and the blank expanse of space displayed on the holoports. Fighting her rising irritation, she sighed and rubbed her eyes.

"Isabelle, if I paid you, would you finish this for me?"

"Good morning, Captain." Isabelle's voice chimed from the computer, her light French accent a balm on Kim's nerves. "I can provide you with records of all the scanning data collected during the engagement as well as transcripts of when all commands were given, if that is helpful." The artificial intelligence avatar of the *Verdun*, Isabelle didn't miss anything the ship experienced.

"I don't think the admiral will want to read that," Kim dropped back into her desk chair, facing the image of Isabelle that had appeared on her computer screen. "But thanks anyway."

"Did you sleep well?"

Kim rolled her eyes. "Like a rock."

Isabelle raised an eyebrow. "Do you lie like this on your reports, Captain?"

"Do you always ask questions you know the answers to?"

Neither of them spoke for a minute. Finally, Isabelle crossed her arms.

"Are you sure the sensor data would not be helpful?"

Kim smiled in spite of her fatigue. "Go ahead and send it to this terminal. I'll attach it as a reference."

"Very good. I'll check in shortly if you need anything else."

"Thanks."

Isabelle nodded, and her image vanished from the computer screen.

Kim typed out a sentence, erased it. She did the same, trying to stick only to the facts. At just past 1700 hours, Kim had ordered the *Verdun* to move in and neutralize the enemy station. At 1712, several Frontin warships had appeared from hiding and converged on the *Verdun*. Kim shuddered, remembering the thunder of explosions as enemy munitions had curved around the ship's magnetic ordnance shield and detonated.

Kim stood again, and turned around just as a knock came at her door. Kim looked down at her disheveled uniform, ran a hand over her hair, which she could tell was a frizzy mess.

"In a moment!" Kim quickly undid her bun and retied it, walking over to the door. She tucked her light blue uniform shirt back into her dark blue trousers, realized she'd taken her tie off somewhere. Not seeing it, she crossed the room again, picked up her dark blue jacket from where it was draped on her chair. Her hands flying over the jacket's buttons, she jogged to the door. She hadn't exactly been available to the crew for the last few days during her paperwork exile. The least she could do is try to look professional when they came to her. Kim put on a neutral face, reached for the latch, and opened the door to see —

"Commander?"

Commander Emma Holsey stood in the corridor, a computer pad in her hand.

Kim felt her insides tense. For a second, they only stared at each other.

Holsey raised her chin slightly. "May I come in, Captain?"

Kim stepped aside and gestured for Holsey to enter. Holsey strode into the foyer, her eyes fixed on her computer pad.

"How are repairs?" Kim followed after Holsey as she walked to the desk.

"We've done as much as we can without landing. As you know, there's a lot of work to do."

"Very good." Kim figured she should probably offer Holsey something to drink, but she wasn't in the mood for verbal sparring. The sooner Holsey left, the better.

Holsey had never forgiven Kim for a boarding mission that had gone bad under her command ten years ago. Kim had taken a chance and ignored safety protocols, resulting in the death of everyone on the team, except for the two of them. Holsey's fiancé, Glen Brevel, had been among the fallen.

When Holsey reached the desk, she turned and thrust the pad toward Kim. "Here is the list of all munitions and supplies we'll need. Wilcox has already signed it, but we wanted your approval before we transmit it to the station."

Kim took the list and sat down while Holsey stood at attention. Shells, torpedoes, deck plating, assorted repair components… The list was many pages long. Kim had almost forgotten about Kensington Station. After a battle, it was standard procedure for Navy ships to land, re-supply, and have thorough repairs and inspections undertaken by ground personnel. It was always a long and tedious process, and the stations in this part of the galaxy, a backwater since the end of the last war, were usually isolated dumps run by frustrated, bored officers counting down the days until they could receive a new billet.

"Thank you, Commander." Kim returned the list to Holsey and turned back to the blank screen in front of her, expecting Holsey to leave. When she didn't, Kim looked up to find the commander watching her.

"You haven't been on the bridge in two days, Captain." Holsey's voice was flat, her eyes like barricades. Was she trying to give Kim a reprimand?

Holsey had made it clear on multiple occasions that she had no problem telling Kim exactly what she thought of her decisions.

"As you probably learned in training, dealing with post-action functions is a captain's priority after combat."

"Yes, ma'am."

"I'll be at my normal duties before they'll be neglected. Until, then, carry on."

"Yes, ma'am." Holsey didn't budge.

Kim sighed, looked back at her computer screen. "I'm having trouble with the last part of the report, that's all."

Kim heard Holsey turn to leave, but only heard a couple footsteps before they stopped.

"Regrets?"

Kim turned in her chair to square herself with Holsey. She wasn't about to have her decisions questioned again. "Should I have said this instead of that, seen something sooner, fired to port instead of starboard — What would that accomplish? But when I write these damn reports—"

"You can't help but see the possibilities." Holsey finished Kim's sentence, looked at the floor.

Kim studied Holsey's stone face. Was that sympathy or a criticism?

"I can't change any of it," Kim said.

Holsey met her gaze, and for a second, they said nothing. A soft chime called the change of the hour.

"No, you can't," Holsey said. "But right now, this crew is asking themselves the same kind of questions, and they need to see their CO."

Kim nodded. "I'll finish this as soon as I can, Commander. Dismissed."

Holsey saluted, then turned on her heel and walked toward the door.

"Thank you for these reports," Kim called after her.

Holsey opened the door, looked back at Kim, who pointed to the pad Holsey had brought.

"I'm glad they're what you needed." Holsey stepped out of the room and closed the door behind her.

Kim stared after Holsey for a long time. Then she turned around in her chair, took a deep breath, and started typing.

"That's the last one." Lieutenant Commander Jack Wilcox made notes on his computer pad as Ensign Morris propped the rifle back into the gun rack.

"Sure as hell took long enough." Morris shook his head, reached up, and pulled the heavy metal door closed over the rack, its automatic lock engaging with an electric whine.

Jack grunted his agreement. Morris and his armory staff had been working almost non-stop ever since the battle with the Frontin to locate, repair, refurbish, and inventory the ship's small arms. It had been a monumental task. The fighting had destroyed or damaged more than half of the ship's stock of weapons. Losses like that were more than just a logistical headache — they hinted at the extreme violence of the combat that had raged in the *Verdun's* corridors.

The high casualties among the crew — Morris' section had lost more than its share — hadn't made the job any easier. Normally, Lieutenant Voth, the ship's master at arms, would be the one to supervise Morris and his crew, but Doctor Cadogan had only just released him from light duty. Jack was happy to do something, anything to help.

It was the least he owed the crew, after what he'd done — or, rather, not done. Jack had missed the fighting aboard the Verdun. He'd been sent to safety aboard another ship and made to stand by while so many of the crew had suffered and died. In a pinch, the captain hadn't trusted him, had thought he couldn't handle real combat. Now, he'd probably never have a chance to prove her wrong.

Jack put his signature on the pad, handed it over to Morris, who added his own, tapped the button to send it to Voth.

"Glad to have that out of the way." Morris yawned, handed the pad back to Jack.

"Don't celebrate yet." He slid the pad into his jacket pocket. "Voth wants to keep the armory running until we've built up the regulation stockpile of spares again." It was a good idea, given the number of weapons that had been destroyed beyond repair.

Morris' face fell. "Oh. Yes, that."

Jack couldn't help by grin at the man's obvious disappointment. "When it rains, Ensign…"

"We appreciate the help, sir."

"You'll have Mr. Voth back soon enough." Jack gestured toward the door, and they started down the corridor that split the long, double row of numerous sealed gun racks and ammunition cabinets.

"We'll put him right back to work." Morris stopped as they entered the guardroom outside, turned to close and lock the access door, its surface pitted where bullets and Frontin claws had torn at it. He yawned again, shook his head. "I've got some coffee on the drip in the workshop. Care for some, sir?"

Jack shook his head. "Why don't you take a break and get some from the galley instead. You deserve it."

Morris chuckled. "You mean I can sit down? At an actual table? Do those exist anymore?"

"With all the powdered creamer and sugar you like."

"Hallelujah!" Morris wiped his hands on his work coveralls. "Care to join, sir?"

"No, thanks." Jack tapped the pocket that held the computer pad. "I'll get over to the workshop and give them the bad news to keep working." Jack could keep the ball rolling while Morris had a break.

"You don't have to tell me twice." Morris strode toward the door.

Jack hadn't been in the workshop since… ever, really. He tried to remember the name of the person in charge there. "Hold on a second, Ensign. Who's the chief armorer over there? Chief Ruiz?"

Morris stopped in his tracks, looked over his shoulder, a pinched expression on his face. "Ruiz got killed, sir."

The air left Jack's lungs, and heat rushed to his face. "Oh."

"I don't expect you'd have had a chance to know that." Morris pursed his lips together. "You don't work down there, I mean."

It was kind of Morris to add the last part, but Jack knew what he really meant. "I see."

"Petty Officer Hundegger is filling in for the moment."

"Right." Jack forced a pleasant expression onto his face. "Enjoy your break, Ensign."

Morris tilted his head in acknowledgement and walked out the door, leaving Jack alone, all too aware of the scars of battle on the walls around him.

CHAPTER 4

Lieutenant Marcus Hillman ignored the stares of the ground crew techs as he walked across the hanger, stepped over wires and spare parts laid out on the floor. Why did people still look?

He took a deep breath, walked faster, his eyes focused on his destination, the door to the flight deck office.

"*That's* Bug Stomper Hillman?" One of the techs whispered a bit too loudly to her friend.

"Yeah. They say he killed every one of the Frontin on that ship," another voice answered.

Bug Stomper Hillman. The idiot name that had followed Marcus ever since the battle. He ignored the all-too-audible whispers, relieved to reach the door. He pulled it open, jogged up the narrow metal staircase, and emerged on a small landing. Offices and crew rooms opened up on the right, a closed door to his left with the words "Air Wing Commander" above it. Marcus knocked.

"Come in."

Marcus swung the door open, stepped inside, and closed it behind him. He turned in time to see Commander Frost lifting his tall, muscular frame from the chair behind his desk. Marcus realized Frost was waiting and saluted.

Frost returned the salute, then leaned across his desk and offered his hand. "Nice to see you, Lieutenant."

Marcus took Frost's hand, shook it. "Thank you, sir."

"Sit down." Frost gestured to the seat opposite his, and sat down.

"Thank you, sir," Marcus repeated, pulling his own chair out and easing himself into it.

Frost turned to the computer, seemed to be looking for something. Marcus drummed his fingers on his thighs, took in the perfect cleanliness of Frost's office, everything stacked, neat, immaculate. There were hardly any of the personal signs that a living man worked there. A framed certificate with the Royal Marine crest and a second lieutenant's silver shield pins attached to it was on the wall behind Frost. On the desk was a picture of a young woman, who looked to be about eighteen.

Marcus looked to Frost, whose pale blue eyes were moving back and forth, reading the screen in front of him.

He cleared his throat, pointed at the picture. "Your daughter, sir?"

Frost looked over at the picture, and his expression tightened ever so slightly. "No."

"Ah." Marcus looked away, not sure what he'd done to bother the man. They sat there in silence for what felt like an hour before Frost cleared his voice.

"I don't understand your request, Lieutenant. Frankly, I don't know why you didn't handle this with Mr. Blake."

"Mr. Blake isn't on duty right now, sir, and I wanted this resolved quickly." Marcus paused. "As for the other matter, I think it's clear enough in my report."

Frost massaged his temple. "Blake's off, eh? I've got everyone working around the clock on repairing our embarked craft, and he—" Frost interrupted himself. "Blake's my problem to deal with, Lieutenant. Forget about it." He pointed at his screen. "I understand *what* your request is. I just don't understand *why*."

"I'd like to get back out there. I want to be useful." It was the only explanation anyone needed to hear. Frost didn't need to know about the gossip, the hero worship among the crew — or the sleepless nights spent reliving that battle, the sight of every one of his squadmates incinerating under the hail of enemy fire.

Frost shook his head. "I'm sorry, Mr. Hillman. Regulations are very clear here. Someone who dealt with your situation is to be on rest leave for a full ninety days while we evaluate your emotional condition." He leaned back in his chair. "Besides, we're going to be in repairs at Kensington for a good long while. I doubt we'll have any need for you."

"If it's all the same to you, I'd like to be back on active duty. Doctor Cadogan—"

"Yes, yes, I see here he cleared you, and it's not the same to me." He raised an eyebrow. "This isn't some kind of tough-guy act is it? Has all that Bug Stomper nonsense got to your head?"

Marcus had to keep himself from wincing at the sound of his unfortunate title. He hadn't realized the stories had made it up to the command officers. "No, sir." He squirmed, not sure how much to say. "To be honest, I don't much care for it. I'd like to get back out there, if I can. I don't want to let my skills get rusty, and…" He trailed off, the next bit a little too close to the truth.

"And?"

Marcus kept his voice neutral, refused to look away. "And I'd like to get to know the pilots I'll be squadded with sooner rather than later. Now that Raptor Squad is gone, I mean."

"I see." Frost stared at him for a few seconds, seemed to be studying him. "You know, Lieutenant, Raptor Squad is not really gone. We'll bring the name out again as soon as we have pilots to fill it. You'll still have your position as squadron leader, assuming brass don't promote you."

"Yes, sir. All the same, I'd like to stay active."

Frost sighed, chuckled. "I wish I could put your motivation in a bottle and slip some of it to Lieutenant Blake."

"Sir?" It was more or less an open secret onboard the *Verdun* that Frost, all rules and discipline and drive, was not pleased with his easygoing deck officer. Marcus hadn't realized Frost's disappointment was so acute.

"Forget about it." Frost picked up a stylus, ran it over the touchpad beside his keyboard. "There, you have my approval. I'll have Mr. Blake pass down some shift rotations tomorrow. But don't expect anything too substantial. We'll start you off on half duty, and I still expect you to check in with Doctor Cadogan. Am I clear?"

"Yes, sir." Marcus' spirits rose. He was getting back in the cockpit, away from the exaggerated chatter of his shipmates.

"Anything else?"

Marcus got to his feet. "No, sir. Thank you, sir." Marcus saluted.

Frost saluted back. "Dismissed."

Marcus turned on his heels and left the room, the Commander's voice following him as he walked.

"And if you see Blake, tell him to get his ass in here."

Kim finished the report and sent it on to Wilcox and Holsey for their signatures. She called in a breakfast order to the galley and then walked into her bedroom. She sat on her bed to wait for the meal, grateful to sit on a surface softer than her work chair. When she started to fall asleep sitting up, she undressed and slipped into the shower. Leaning her head against the cold tile, she let the warm water wash over her aching shoulder.

Breakfast arrived right as she finished putting on a fresh uniform. Kim thanked the shipman who brought her tray, then shoveled the food down. Standard-issue bacon with powdered scrambled eggs, a section of baguette, a cake of butter, a small container of jam, and some canned fruit with a cup of coffee. While part of it may have been the caffeine, Kim felt like a new woman when she emerged from her quarters fifteen minutes later, carrying her empty tray between one arm and her hip.

Kim walked toward the officer's mess, returning the salutes of crewmembers and officers she passed as she walked. Work crews moved up and down the corridors, carrying all manner of tools, replacement parts, pieces of new bulkhead plating. The ship was in much better condition than the last time she had emerged a few days ago. Hell, compared to the mess it has been when they'd left Derek's Triangle three months ago, it looked practically brand new. None of the lights were flickering, all the damaged sections had been cleared of debris, and the gentle thrumming that carried through the deck told Kim that the engines were fully operational again. The crew was clearly swamped with activity, and Kim felt a pang of regret that she had stayed in her room so long.

When she reached the wooden double doors to the officer's mess, Kim stopped. She was tempted to turn around and drop the tray outside her room, where someone from the galley would pick it up. Kim took a deep breath, raised her head high, and entered.

Two dozen or so officers were clumped here and there, sitting and finishing breakfast. A couple marine officers in service dress reds were leaning near the hot bar. They all looked up at her and stood.

"As you were." Kim walked over to the window to the dish room and passed her tray through, then turned and walked over to the closest group of officers. Everyone's eyes followed her, even though they had continued their conversations. Captain Knight had always made this seem so easy.

She cleared her throat. "Lieutenant Kepperling, how is fire control?"

Kepperling, a tall woman with dark skin and black hair, looked nervously up at her. "Quite well, ma'am."

"You have reason to be proud. You all did wonderfully." Kim tried to fill her voice with booming confidence she didn't feel.

"Yes, ma'am. Thank you, ma'am."

Kim moved about the room, saying a few words to each of the officers there. When at last she was in the corridor again, Kim breathed a sigh of relief — though she couldn't help but grin. Being a pep-talker was never her skill set. She'd been the organizer, the executor, the right arm of the captain. But she was learning.

A few minutes later, Kim stepped onto the bridge and felt the last trace of tension leave her. This was her place. She surveyed the room, gathering an idea of her crew's activities by their distribution around it. The bridge was a rectangular room, brightly lit by small circular lamps, caged in metal wire, spaced around the high ceiling. The holoports, long rectangular screens running the circumference of the room around the top of the wall, were working again and showed the star-streaked void outside the *Verdun*. To the left of the door was the holographic action table, in pieces and surrounded by a repair crew. In the center of the room was Kim's chair and foldaway computer terminal, set on a raised platform. Lieutenants Urquhart and Stetler were talking to each other at the helm, set in a lowered pit forward of Kim's chair. Holsey and Lieutenant Voth were standing next to Holsey's computer, to the left and behind the command platform. Several crewmembers were clustered around the radio communications station set against the wall to Kim's right. Across the room from them was Wilcox's operations station. Wilcox himself was bent over his computer, concentrating hard on his damage control panel. With all the various repair crews to coordinate, the man had been more than busy, pulling extra weight to keep the ship running.

Stetler glanced over, saw Kim. "Captain on the bridge." Everyone looked at Kim, then went back to work, except for Urquhart, who smiled at her.

"Good morning, Captain."

Kim returned the smile. "Thank you, Lieutenant. As you were." The bridge was about business, not ceremony. Kim liked that. But she was always grateful for Callista's sunny disposition.

Kim settled herself into the command chair and folded down her computer terminal. The screen flashed blue and turned on, showing an exterior camera view that angled toward the front of the ship and the expanse of space beyond. Kim looked over at Holsey, catching her eye.

"Commander, what is our status?"

"We'll be arriving at Kensington Station in five hours, ma'am."

"Excellent," Kim swiveled her chair to face the communications console. "Has the station confirmed they have what we need?"

The radio operator turned, frowned. "No, ma'am. We haven't been able reach them at all. Even accounting for the time delay from our transmission, the communication relay doesn't seem to be functioning."

Kim drummed her fingers on the chair's armrest. It was bad enough that the *Verdun* was not part of Kensington's schedule, but being unable to give the station time to prepare was worse. It would take that much longer to get supplies ready and coordinate work crews with the station personnel.

"Captain," Voth stepped forward. "Suggest we put fighter squadrons on standby."

"Who's going to attack us here?" Urquhart piped up. "We're in friendly space."

Voth shrugged. "I'd rather be overcautious than be ambushed in our current state."

Kim felt Holsey's gaze boring into her, but she kept her eyes fixed on Voth and nodded her head. Prepping fighters when communications were down was standard procedure. "Agreed. Mr. Voth, inform Commander Frost."

Voth tilted his head in acknowledgement and walked out of the bridge. Kim looked at Holsey, who nodded slightly before returning to her work. Kim felt a rush of satisfaction. She wouldn't make the same mistakes again, regardless of what Holsey thought of her. Besides, after this morning, it seemed like she and Holsey might be able to coexist. Not as friends, perhaps, but at least not as open enemies.

"We're entering Kensington's solar system," Urquhart called out.

"Slowing for approach," Stetler added. "We'll go sub-light near the outer planet."

"A nice gas giant by the looks of it," Wilcox added.

Now it would just be a few hours' cruise toward Kensington itself.

"Mr. Wilcox," Kim said, raising her voice over the whirr of a tool buzzing from the work crew behind her.

"Yes, ma'am?" He turned in his chair to face her.

"Begin assembling teams to load supplies. If we're not expected, their crews aren't going to be ready. We'll want to speed things up."

"Yes, ma'am."

"Commander?" Kim looked back at Holsey. "Have Major Osterman assemble a marine escort for the work crews. Let them have some fresh air."

Holsey nodded, and both she and Wilcox strode out of the bridge. The marines had suffered particularly heavy losses in the Triangle. Giving them some exercise under real sun and non-recycled atmosphere would no doubt help boost their morale. Kim knew that Major Osterman, finally cleared by the infirmary for light duty, was chomping at the bit to get out and do something.

Kim stood and walked around the room. Looking at the smooth efficiency of her crew, she couldn't imagine how she'd started the day so low. This would be the tone of things from now on, Kim decided. No more hesitation. No more nervousness. Moving forward, everything would be by the book and everything, every detail, would go smoothly.

CHAPTER 5

"Son of a bitch!" Christine swore under her breath as she lay prone, carbine in front of her, and watched the cargo tender take off. She looked to her left, down the line of rangers kneeling behind trees, bushes and fallen logs at the edge of the woods. Several troops were still rushing into position, and one of the machine gun teams was fitting the gun to its tripod. At this rate, they'd be lucky to have anyone to attack by the time they were ready. She looked in front her toward the warehouses, only a hundred yards away across the road and the rail line, and counted how many of the enemy soldiers were left.

After identifying the enemy as human, Christine and Squires had quickly surveyed the dockyards through their binoculars, counting the combatants, trying to assess their abilities. Whoever they were, they weren't lacking for weaponry. They seemed to have standard-issue Alliance Mk3A2 Enfield rifles, machine guns, and even a few handheld rocket launchers. Worse, the troops on the beach had been taken away one cargo load at a time, the small ships flying in a great arc over the bay before heading east and back inland about a mile north of where the rangers were. With no idea where the enemy was going, the possibility of being flanked or cut off from the fort had suddenly become real.

Christine and Squires had made their way back around the hill to their platoons, shifted their defenses to counter any attack from the northeast, and contacted the fort with their findings, using Lazaar's long-range radio pack to repeat the signal from Christine's headset.

"We need an immediate counter-attack," Colonel Neville's voice had crackled over the radio. "Seize the docks and take prisoners."

"But we don't know where they're going to or coming from," Christine had explained, her hands pressing her headset to her ear, Squires kneeling next to her. "If there are more of them somewhere in the woods, we can't ensure our flank."

"You have your orders." Neville hadn't wanted to listen.

"Colonel," Christine had persisted, trying to keep her voice even. "The enemy is leaving the docks of his own accord. We need to secure the northeast perimeter to be sure they're not mounting an attack there or occupying some other part of the station, like the warehouses or barracks—"

Neville had cut Christine off. "If you do not attack, I will relieve you of duty and place Lieutenant Squires in command of both platoons."

Christine had looked at Squires, who had merely rolled his eyes and flipped a middle finger at the radio pack. Lazaar had bitten his lip not to laugh.

"Copy. We'll organize the attack immediately."

Neville had gone on to insist that the rangers wait for Lieutenant Ames' platoon to drive the pack howitzers from the fort to Bunker Fifty. If Christine were going to make a stupid attack, she at least wanted to do it quickly and efficiently. While they'd waited for the guns to arrive and be hauled up the hill and assembled, the number of combatants — there'd been three hundred to start with — had dwindled. Now there were only some one hundred left, sitting around the warehouses, smoking and talking among themselves as they waited for the tender to return.

Christine glanced to the empty woods to the north, looking for any sign of movement. There were two hundred of the bastards out there, likely more — after all, the rangers had arrived *after* the fighting in the harbor had ended — and here they were turning a blind eye to the enemy's movements and rushing into an attack.

At least the plan was simple. Squires' platoon would fix the enemy position with fire, drawing them out of the warehouse complex and to the left. Then Christine's platoon would move forward and around to the right, using the rail line and its gravel bed as cover. They would destroy the enemy with closer-ranged flanking fire, then rush forward to take any survivors prisoner once the enemy force had been reduced. The pack howitzers would target any pockets of stiff resistance. If the bad guys wouldn't surrender, well... Christine's eyes flicked to the warehouse's open cargo door, where the bodies of Navy men and women had been thrown like garbage. Her grip tightened on the fore stock of her carbine.

Christine looked back down the line and saw that her troops were in position, their eyes on her. The late afternoon light filtered through the trees and glinted faintly off the metal of the rangers' carbines and bayonets. A cool breeze blew steadily from the direction of the water, the whisper of air through foliage the only sound other than the murmur of the enemy soldiers below. Christine raised a hand, palm forward, into the air, saw the NCOs down the line do the same. They were ready. Shifting her body slightly, she looked over her shoulder and up the hill, where Squires' platoon was stationed on their left. Squires gave a thumbs-up.

Christine turned to her weapon, aimed her sights at a man sitting near the cargo door, and waited for the explosion of gunfire from Third Platoon. The enemy soldiers jumped to their feet and looked up the hill, and for one moment Christine thought they'd seen Squires' troops. Then she heard it — a deep, growing roar coming from... where?

Christine waved a palm-out hand in front of her face, signaling the group to hold fire, saw Squires repeat the gesture out of the corner of her eye. The sound grew louder and louder, filling the air and making the ground vibrate beneath her. Christine realized what it was a second before she was cast in shadow. She instinctively flinched as a massive shape flew high overhead. A ship was landing.

Christine blinked as the vessel moved out of the sun and the hot gust of its lift thrusters whipped through the trees. The enemy soldiers were frantically grabbing their weapons and disappearing around the warehouses toward the docks.

Good God! Was this their ship?

Christine motioned her troops to stay put and lifted herself off the ground. She dashed up the hill, her feet maneuvering through the roots and branches. She saw Squires run up the hill, too, and adjusted the angle of her climb to meet him. They ran on together, their breath coming fast as they fought the grade of the hill. When they'd climbed high enough to see over the warehouses, they stopped, looking out toward the water through a gap in the tree canopy. The ship was hovering a few hundred feet above the water.

"Is that a cruiser?" Squires panted.

"No." Christine slung her carbine over her shoulder. "It's too big." She reached for her binoculars.

"Did we have another ship due in?"

Christine thought for a second as she withdrew the binoculars from their case. "No, not for three weeks."

"Christ." The fear in Squires' voice was obvious. With the communication relays out and no chance of help from any ship but the scheduled patrol destroyers each month, a warship that size could dominate the system.

Christine steadied her breathing and trained her binoculars on the ship. Blue-grey Alliance paint scheme with standard red and royal blue trim. The ship started to descend toward the water, and she refocused her binoculars on small black letters near its bow. Christine could barely make out the words.

RAS VERDUN.

"Three hundred feet… Two fifty!" Stetler called out the dropping altitude from the helm as the deck vibrated and shook.

Kim gripped the armrests of her chair, trying to ignore the feeling in her stomach. She'd never liked roller coasters, the sensation of falling. Landing operations ranked among her least favorite aboard a space vessel.

"Gently, Mr. Stetler," Kim called out, trying to sound casual.

"One hundred feet," Stetler continued. "Firing final thruster sequence."

Kim felt the rate of descent slow, heard the faint roar of the lift thrusters from outside.

"Touchdown," Stetler said, bending over his controls.

The hull lurched, bumped, and then was still. The thrusters whined and faded into silence. Kim breathed a sigh of relief, took a deep breath to chase away her lingering nausea.

"Chief Baudouin, announce secure from landing stations, and then try to get Kensington on the line again." Kim called out to the communications operator, a tall woman with green eyes and blond hair done into a regulation bun.

"Aye, ma'am." Baudouin repeated the command on the ship's intercom.

"Chief Hatfield." Kim turned toward the shipman manning Wilcox's station, a thin man with dark brown hair and a mustache. "Call the launch bay and tell Mr. Wilcox and Major Osterman to deploy their supply crews. Tell Commander Frost to stand down the fighters."

"Yes, ma'am." Hatfield turned to his controls.

Kim stood, shook her head, her stomach still protesting the rapid descent to the planet. She walked forward and leaned next to Stetler, placing one hand on the back of his chair.

"Mr. Stetler, you and I are going to define the word 'gently' sometime."

Stetler looked up at her, the corners of his frown tugging upward slightly. "Yes, ma'am."

"I'll bring the dictionary." Holsey's voice sounded from her booth.

"Captain?" Baudouin's voice held a note of concern.

"Yes, Chief?"

"We're receiving a transmission from the station." Baudouin looked up from her computer screen and over at Kim, her forehead scrunched in confusion. "They're asking us to verify our identity."

"What?" Holsey crossed the bridge to stand next to Baudouin. "Did you not identify us when you called out?"

"Yes, ma'am, I did. They want full confirmation tones, and they want the captain's authorization."

Kim frowned and rounded the helm console to stand beside Holsey.

"Did they give any reason?"

Baudouin picked up her handset and keyed the button. "Kensington, Victor One-Five-Five, please explain request for identification."

Holsey reached out and flicked a switch, piping the communications chatter onto the overhead speakers.

"Victor One-Five-Five, Kensington." A man's voice, colored with more than a hint of annoyance, rang from the speakers. "Submit to identity check to ensure friendly status."

Baudouin shrugged and looked up at Kim and Holsey.

"Isabelle, lock in and transmit the ID code." Kim said.

"Right away," Isabelle's disembodied voice responded. The ID code, kept only by the AI officers, was a series of tones assigned to each ship used to identify it at long range.

"Tones received," the voice said. "Standby."

"Kensington, Victor One-Five-Five, will you now identify reason for this procedure," Baudouin said.

"Victor One-Five-Five, Kensington, negative." The irritation in the voice was becoming more obvious. "Cannot identify reason until we have cleared you."

Holsey looked at Kim, concern written on her face. "If there's something going on here, we need to know."

"I'll start by finding out who the hell this idiot is," Kim said, grabbing a spare hand mic, her patience gone. "Kensington, Victor One-Five-Five Actual, this is Captain Kim Morden, commanding officer of the Verdun. You will specify exact reason for identity check."

There was a long pause. "Kensington, Victor One-Five-Five, there has been an attack at the docks in your area by an unknown enemy force. We are checking your identity to ensure you're not—"

Fear bolted through her as she flicked the speaker switch, cutting off the voice. "Baudouin, deal with that idiot."

She turned to Hatfield. "Chief, are Wilcox and Osterman's tenders in the water yet?"

"They're already on the shore, ma'am."

"And the fighters?"

Hatfield looked at his computer screen. "They've started stand-down procedures. It'll take few minutes to get them up."

Holsey swore under her breath.

Kim suppressed her mounting fear, kept her voice calm. "Call the crew back immediately!"

CHAPTER 6

Jack stepped out of the crowded interior of the tender and into the blinding sunlight. The late afternoon heat hit him like a wave as the craft's engine spluttered and shut off. Jack loosened his tie and stepped out of the way as Major Osterman the six marines he'd brought as escort filed off the transport. Jack watched as Osterman blinked in the light, sweat beading on his forehead.

"Didn't dress for the weather, did we?" Jack grinned, pointing at Osterman's body armor.

Osterman fixed Jack with a gaze that clearly said, "Shut up," and turned to the other marines. "Secure the docks!"

The marines scrambled up the dock toward the shoreline, Osterman jogging behind. It was good to see Gordon out and about again, if it was for a simple exercise like this. His wounds from the battle with the Frontin had been so severe that it had seemed the infirmary would never let him go. Osterman's charming, levelheaded presence had been keenly missed at staff meetings, and Jack for one was happy the man was back with his marines again.

Jack turned and watched as the second tender grumbled to a halt behind the first. The hatch opened, and another six marines emerged from inside, running to catch up with the first group, their rifles reflecting the withering sunshine, their grey uniforms and armor a perfect match for the faded paint of the silent cranes and machinery up and down the dockyards.

"I think we've had the day saved for us," Jack said, bending to look back inside the tender. The dozen crewmembers buckled inside laughed and began to extricate themselves from their seats. One by one, they stepped past Jack and out of the craft, which was opening its cargo bay. The top of the tender's blocky rear section opened like a book, a small crane unfolding automatically.

When Jack saw that the other tender had done the same, he turned to check on the marines, who had reached the juncture of the dock and the shoreline now, about a hundred yards away, and were setting up behind a tarp-covered pile of crates.

Jack squinted down the shoreline at the endless expanse of the dockyards, shimmering in the heat. He frowned, looking for any sign of movement. The lift cranes were still, like skeletal fingers jutting up here and there from the clutter of crates, parked trucks, and palette lifters arranged along the docks. The long line of tall warehouses glowered back at him, their front cargo doors closed. Behind the warehouses, the steep-sided hills, one of them with what looked like a bunker sitting atop its cleared summit, were like silent, blue-green sentries.

Where the hell is everyone?

Jack started after the two work crews, who were walking together in a clump toward the marines, when he heard the pilot call out from inside the tender.

"Commander?"

Wilcox ducked inside, grateful for the coolness of the air-conditioned crew compartment.

"Yes, Mr. Piskorz, what is it?"

Piskorz, a muscular man with dark stubble on his square jaw, turned around in his chair to look at Jack, one eyebrow raised. "Commander, I'm getting a call from the Verdun. We're to return immediately."

"Are they worried we'll get heatstroke?" Jack chuckled.

"No, sir. We have a report of enemy activity in the area."

Jack's humor evaporated in an instant. "Get the engines started." He ran back out onto the dock, cupped his hands over his mouth and shouted to the rest of the group. "Pack it up!"

The sound of the tender's engines drowned out Jack's shout. One of the marines turned to look at Jack, who raised both arms and waved them toward himself. The marine nodded and turned to the other troops and the personnel gathered around him. A second later, Jack saw him stand up, then fall to the ground, clutching his arm. For half an instant, Jack wondered what had happened. Then the boom of a rifle shot carried over to him.

A crewmember jerked and fell as the rest of the group hit the deck. Jack did the same, dropping to the hot metal surface of the dock as the roar of gunfire split the air.

"Verdun, we're taking fire from shore!"

Jack heard the pilot calling out over the smack of bullets on the tender. Ahead of him, the marines at the barricade were returning fire. Jack followed the direction of their rifles and glimpsed the forms of people spread out behind various vehicles and crates along the dock. They were popping out from behind a crate, firing toward the Alliance personnel, then ducking back into cover. Jack spotted an enemy trooper pointing a long tube toward his direction. It was only when the rocket burst from the front of the tube that Jack realized what it was.

"Christ!"

The rocket missed the tender by a few feet, exploding in the water. Droplets showered Jack, who covered his face and head protectively.

"Sir! I need to lift off!" Piskorz called from inside the tender.

"Not without them!" Jack pointed to the *Verdun* teams at the barricade.

"Then get them here!"

Jack looked toward the barricade, then back at the pilot. "You're crazy!"

"Sir! I need to go!"

Jack nodded, his mouth going dry. He took a deep breath, then stood. He dashed forward, but dove onto his stomach again as the crushing roar of machine guns erupted from behind him. Jack looked and saw that the tenders had opened fire at the enemy positions with their machine gun turrets. On the shore, the enemies scrambled for cover. Jack took the opportunity to launch himself to his feet and sprint to the pinned-down work crews.

Jack slid to a stop next to Major Osterman, ducking behind a cement barrier.

"You've got to get them up!" Osterman was fitting a rifle grenade to his weapon's muzzle. "We're stuck here until they move!"

Jack looked at the crewmembers plastered to the deck, covering their heads, shouting. Somewhere, someone was screaming. Most of them had never seen ground combat. Neither had Jack, for that matter. The other marines popped over the barricade and fired in staccato bursts.

Jack winced as a bullet sizzled over the barricade.

"We'll cover you," Osterman shouted. "Get them up." Osterman turned around, aimed his rifle toward the closest enemy barricade and touched off the grenade. The barricade exploded, and Jack saw several bodies — or at least parts of them — thrown clear. His stomach turned.

"Get them up!" Osterman kicked Jack, who lurched forward and onto his feet.

Not wanting to be hit, he stumbled forward toward the crewmembers.

"We're getting out of here!" Jack shouted, but none of them seemed to hear. He grabbed the collar of the nearest crewmember and hauled him to his feet. Somehow this broke the spell, and the rest followed, standing up to a low crouch. Jack heard the marines launch another grenade, another explosion. Jack glanced over his shoulder. Between the fire of the marines and the tenders, the enemies seemed to be pinned down.

Jack led the crewmembers back down the dock toward the tenders. They were fifty yards away when a jet of fire and smoke streaked by, striking Piskorz's tender full on. The craft rocked backward and exploded, ripping the dock apart next to it. Jack tasted blood, realized he had dropped to the dock again. He forced himself to his feet, dragging the crewmembers with him. But the fire from the shore had increased again, and a woman to Jack's left pitched to the ground, then a man just ahead of him fell limp. Jack stepped over the body and kept running, pushing the rest of the group ahead of him.

Marcus lowered himself into the cockpit of the Stallion he'd been given, pulled his helmet and air mask closed.

He was getting back to work sooner than he'd thought.

The cockpit slid shut, muffling the noise of the klaxons blaring on the launch deck, the rumble of the other fighters' engines spooling up.

His hands moved to the controls, punching in the settings for planetary flight mode, and an underwater launch. He hadn't done this sort of thing in a while, his mind racing back to the endless times they'd practiced this in flight school.

The bay door opened in front of him, and water flooded upward, swirled around his craft.

"Water equilibrium in twenty seconds. Standby." The computer's pleasant, relaxed voice spoke to him.

"Come on. Come on." He activated the holodisplay, every nerve aching to get going. People — their people — were being attacked out there. Damned if Marcus was going to allow some other asshole to take more of the *Verdun's* crew.

"Equilibrium achieved," the computer said.

Marcus pushed the control stick forward, his body thrown backward in his seat as the Stallion shot downward and into the inky green water.

J ack was almost to the remaining tender, was starting to reach for the door.

"Shit!"

Another rocket surged past and exploded beside the craft, which started backing away from the dock.

"No, damn you!" Jack tried to wave for the tender to stop, but it was turning, picking up speed, and surging for the *Verdun.* Another crewmember fell, holding his leg. Bullets whistled and thwacked around them. Jack pulled his people back down flat against the pier. He looked back at the marines at the barricade. No longer held back by machine gun fire, enemy soldiers — at least a hundred — were closing in, moving from cover to cover. One of the marines fired toward the oncoming group, dropping two of his targets, but the surge of attackers continued unabated.

Jack saw an enemy soldier aim a rocket launcher for the marine barricade, was about to tell the group around him to swim for it. The man with the rocket pitched forward, then several more attackers around him fell as gunfire crackled from further down the docks to the left.

Jack shifted where he lay to get a look, half expecting to see more enemies. Instead, he watched as olive-green soldiers poured from between two of the warehouses and onto the docks. Relief surged through Jack as the newcomers moved behind cover and blasted toward the enemy attackers.

Thank God for the Army!

The marines, no longer pinned down, launched another salvo of grenades. Caught between the fire of the marines and the newcomers, the enemy ranks withered. Jack saw a pair of green-clad soldiers drop a machine gun into its tripod and then open fire on the confused hostiles. As many as a hundred of the newcomers were on the waterfront now, some of them surging forward in short rushes to the marine positions while others ripped the enemies apart with machine gun and rifle fire. A rocket from one of the newcomers detonated among the ranks of the enemies, who turned and fled up the docks, only a few pockets of them remaining, firing blindly.

As Jack watched, a short, dark woman at the head of the group — an officer maybe — jumped over a pile of crates concealing two of the remaining enemies. She shot one of them at point blank range, and when the other swung his rifle at her, she ducked and drove the point of her bayonet through his chest. The marines were up and out from behind the barricade now, joining the charge forward after the fleeing enemies, who were two hundred yards up the dock, tossing their rifles aside and running as hard as they could.

Suddenly, the woman — yes, she had to be an officer — held up her hand. The charging soldiers stopped in their tracks and went to cover. A heartbeat later, Jack heard a sound that almost made him want to cry. It was the boom of approaching fighters.

The docks where the enemy soldiers were running were ripped to pieces in a hail of gunfire. Three enormous explosions obscured the enemies in flames, and a fourth a second later blasted the section of shoreline where they stood into fragments. Jack heard cheers and looked over at the marines and newcomers, who raised their rifles as a squadron of Stallions and Sparrowhawk fighters from the *Verdun* screamed overhead, their graceful forms catching the dying sunlight.

Jack stood, helped his crewmembers to their feet. They were in one piece, mostly. Cuts, a minor bullet wound, very afraid. Nothing serious. Jack glanced back up the dock, saw the bodies of the three crewmembers who'd been shot during the dash for the tenders. One was still clutching his leg, but the other two — and some of the marines at the barricade...

A pair of brown boots and khaki gaiters entered Jack's field of vision. "Are you in charge here?"

Jack looked up to see the woman who had led the counterattack walking toward him, her rifle canted toward the ground, Major Osterman and another officer from the newcomers, lanky and tall, a few steps behind her.

"Yes," Jack said, straightening up, his voice tight from the smoke drifting from the obliterated docks. Realizing he'd only croaked the word, Jack fought the stinging smoke and shouted. "Yes, I'm in command."

"I'm Lieutenant Christine Flores."

Jack held out his hand. The woman looked at it for a moment before taking it and shaking roughly.

"We owe you infantry our thanks," Jack said.

"We're not infantry. We're rangers. Third Company, Fifth and Third Platoons."

"Whoever you are," Jack said, taken aback by Flores' abrupt response, "we have a problem."

Lieutenant Flores pursed her lips, nodded. "That's the first smart thing I've heard all day."

CHAPTER 7

"Your inaction nearly cost these people their entire landing party!" Colonel Neville stood from his spot at the *Verdun's* briefing room table, wishing he could jump over it and backhand the two rangers across from him. Instead, he leaned forward, working every ounce of rage he felt into his voice. "What is your excuse for delaying so long?"

Lieutenant Flores and Lieutenant Squires, standing at attention near at the head of the table, next to the captain, Morden, looked straight ahead into space, but said nothing.

"Well?" Neville asked.

"Sir," Squires began. "We broke from our position on the hill and engaged as soon as we determined that the enemy force intended to attack the landing party and that the two forces were not in collusion. We—"

"Wrong answer!" Neville slammed his fist on the table, making everyone in the room jump. Everyone except for Lieutenant Flores, who tensed her jaw slightly, but remained still. "You were hesitant and incompetent. Had you struck *before* the Verdun landed, you would not have needed to determine anything."

"No, sir," Flores said, meeting Neville's gaze. The look in her eyes, of defiance and open disgust, made Neville even angrier, if that was possible.

"No?" Neville crossed his arms.

"No. We waited until the pack howitzers, which you ordered us to use, were in place. We couldn't attack before the Verdun's arrival—"

"How dare you blame me?" Neville spat, interrupting Flores. He wanted to throw something at her, kick her, hell, *shoot* her. "Do not implicate me in your failure to—"

"—Because of the nature of the orders we received from you." Flores finished her sentence, her voice rising to match Neville's. "We attacked as soon as we were able to."

Neville bit his lip, fought to keep his breathing down. "You acted like a coward and disgraced the uniform you wear." Neville saw something flash in Flores' eyes, and a shiver of fear streaked through him.

"Control yourselves." Captain Morden stood. "In case you've forgotten, this is my briefing room. You two will comport yourselves appropriately." Morden fixed Neville with a frown. He wanted to laugh. Who did she think she was? Kensington was his station, an Army station. Besides, this Kim Morden was just a pretty little girl. Dark hair with big brown eyes, creamy pale skin, and curves in all the right places that showed even through her uniform jacket as she sat back in her chair. Unfortunately, regulations gave ranking naval officers operational command, even if they were little trollops.

Neville forced his face into a smile. "Of course, Captain. My apologies if the conduct of my officers offends you." Neville sat down, folded his hands in front of him. "I assure you their incompetence will not go unpunished."

"Frankly, Colonel," the Commander seated to Morden's right spoke up. "If we're punishing incompetence, we're going to start with you and your staff at the fort, not the lieutenants here."

"Commander... Hansen, is it?" Neville softened his voice, tried to make it as friendly as he could. She wasn't bad looking, either.

"Holsey," the woman replied flatly, pointing to where her name was embroidered over her jacket pocket.

"Holsey," Neville continued. "On what basis do you make this accusation?"

This was not going as Neville had planned. As soon as the *Verdun* had radioed the news of the ambush to the fort, Neville had ordered a jeep to drive him to the docks immediately. He'd known the rangers would blame it all on him. It was no secret that they didn't appreciate his being in command of them while they waited for a new officer. Flores in particular had mouthed off to him more than once in the past, and he hadn't wanted her to poison the opinion of *Verdun's* crew against him. When Squires and Flores had tried to keep him from coming to the docks by saying it might not be safe to drive there after nightfall, Neville had known they were definitely trying to undermine him.

He'd ordered his driver to push through anyway, glowering at the dark walls of forest on either side of the main road paralleling the rail line to the docks. When he'd finally arrived at the dockyards — unharmed, exactly as he'd known he would — some ranger private had held his jeep back. He'd had to wait an hour while the rangers and *Verdun* marines secured the dockland and checked over the supply train to make sure bad guys weren't hiding in it, or something like that. They'd found the bodies of the dockworkers and the train's crew, but no enemies. Sure, it had been frightening seeing the rangers carry the corpses off the train, but not worth wasting his time. When he'd finally made it aboard the *Verdun*, he'd found Flores and Squires exactly where he'd known they would be, talking up the command staff with their version of events.

Neville was the same as any other officer. He wanted to earn a living and advance in rank. He'd worked hard after the academy, moving up in rank as a supply officer during the war. But peacetime had wrecked his ambitions. The Army had chosen a trash dump like Kensington for him to command, but Neville was determined to get away from it. He wouldn't let some dirt-covered, unbathed ranger and Captain Tits ruin his chances and blame him for something that wasn't his fault.

"Your station did not inform us there was a danger present until after wasting time on an identification procedure."

"By which time we were already on the shore," added the lieutenant commander. Wilcox was his name.

The tall marine, a Major Osterman, who was seated between Wilcox and Lieutenant Voth, the *Verdun's* master-at-arms, nodded. "And under fire."

Neville's head buzzed. He swallowed hard to suppress his rising annoyance. "We followed standard identification procedures, which—"

"Which still allow you to divulge the existence of a potential danger so long as the details given do not compromise your own safety or strategic interests," Holsey said.

Neville couldn't help but sneer. "I've read the regulation, Commander."

Holsey looked like she was about to say more, but Morden interrupted. "Good. Then it should be obvious to you why we should have known about the enemy presence sooner."

They had already judged him. Neville could see it in their eyes. "What you are missing, Captain, is that your crew would not have needed rescuing if the lieutenants here had done their job earlier and attacked."

"Which we were delayed in doing because of your orders to wait for the howitzers," Flores said, sounding almost bored.

Neville was about to stand up again, but Major Osterman beat him to it.

"As far as I'm concerned," Osterman began, his deep voice quiet and yet somehow filling the room, "these rangers saved our lives today. Since the ambush, I've seen the area they ran from, the woods behind the warehouses and the hill beyond." Osterman turned to Morden. "We were under fire on the beach for only a couple minutes. For the rangers to pack up, maneuver into position, and then attack in that time was a fine display of skill."

"I'd say," Voth raised a cup of coffee in the direction of the rangers. "A damn fine show."

"Thank you, sir." Squires piped up, sounding more than a little nervous.

Osterman took a seat, nodding over at Squires and Flores, whose face remained hard and unreadable. Or was that satisfaction?

Neville's disgust rose in his throat. Flores was winning. In her sweat-stained uniform and mud-caked boots, she was winning. Neville's eyes caught movement at Flores' side, from her left hand. Was she flipping him off? He stared at her hand, and saw her pressing her thumb against something on her left ring finger, before Morden's voice brought his focus back to the meeting.

"It is my judgment that the lieutenants here acted as they should have. We lost four good people today, and it would have been more had they not intervened." Morden fixed Neville with a hard glare. "Now, we have a lot of work to do here, and trying to assign blame is a waste of our time."

Neville grit his teeth, looking for a way out, and found one. He split his face into a smile. "Of course, Captain. You have my apologies for the unpleasant afternoon. I will work with my staff at the fort to correct their error in protocol. They should have warned you sooner, and they will be made aware of their mistake."

From the other side of the table, he thought he heard Holsey scoff.

"Please continue with the meeting," Neville finished, averting his eyes from Morden's glare and pretending to examine something on his screen.

No, this hadn't gone well at all.

CHAPTER 8

"Let's run through this again." Lt. Commander Wilcox stood at the head of the table beside Captain Morden, pointing at a view screen built into the wall that displayed an overhead map of the Kensington complex.

Christine examined the map from where she sat, between Commander Holsey and Squires. Anything to not look at Neville, who was all smiles where he was seated on the other end of the table. Christine noted that many of the patrol trails were missing from the map, but she doubted whoever had drawn it had known about them. Probably some survey crew who hadn't climbed a mountain in their lives. Still, all the other details were there. The dark U of the dockyards lining the harbor and the primary warehouses directly behind them; the rugged hills rising almost from the shore, the couple hundred or so bunkers and infantry shelters capping their summits; the web of small roads and narrow-gauge rail lines connecting them together and to the fort; the massive secondary warehouse complex, midway between the dockyards and the fort along the main line; the old barracks, off by itself several miles north of the secondary warehouses; and the fort, a huge pentagon shape some twenty miles east of the docks and perched atop a plateau just to the west of the jagged mountain range, where communications antennas bristled and another set of bunkers guarded the fort's rear.

Combined with the air-to-space missile silos that dotted the complex and the rest of the planet, it was a formidable network of fortifications. Or at least it had been twenty years ago, before most the weapons had been stripped from the bunkers and the fort, and almost all the silos had been removed, leaving deep pits scattered through the forest.

"At approximately oh-nine-hundred hours," Wilcox said, his voice bringing Christine's attention back to the meeting. "The RAS Barracuda, the destroyer scheduled for service today, lands in the harbor."

"We didn't know it was there until it had already landed," Neville chimed in. "We're experiencing issues with our communications relay."

"We know," Holsey muttered under her breath. She gave Christine a small smile, and Christine realized she'd been the only one Holsey had intended to hear. Christine gave Holsey a slight nod, sensing that, under the desk officer's uniform, there was a real warrior.

"Until it's repaired, we have a serious problem," Voth was saying. "We can't relay a radio message for help, and the nearest working post is a few days away at top speed."

The group was silent for a moment as they considered it. Christine hadn't known this. Guilt tugged at her. She was still working on her latest letter to Ryan. If the relays were down, it may be a while before she could send it, assuming she got the chance. Kensington was far off the beaten path. Without communication relays, they might as well be totally alone.

Wilcox cleared his throat. "At oh-nine-fifteen, the fort orders the train from the secondary warehouses to the docks. It arrives sometime later, but the crew is attacked and killed."

"Or they were killed at the secondary warehouses. We won't know until we check them." Major Osterman leaned back in his chair, his face grim. "It was very dangerous for you to drive by that area tonight, Colonel."

Neville's face reddened, but his composure didn't break. "I'm beginning to understand that."

Christine doubted it.

"The attackers hijack the cargo tenders docked at the port, and at approximately ten-thirty hours, they attack the Barracuda." Wilcox pointed at the harbor on the map, his voice tinged with anger.

"How do we know they stole the tenders and didn't bring them from elsewhere?" Holsey crossed her arms, raised an eyebrow.

"The station's compliment is missing, for one thing," Wilcox answered.

Squires nodded. "And we saw them transporting the enemies off the beach when we arrived."

"A cargo tender has limited weapons," Lieutenant Voth said, taking a sip of his coffee. "But they do have air-to-air and air-to-ground rockets that could damage a small ship's more vulnerable systems."

Wilcox pointed on the map to the saddle between the two hills where Christine had first heard the explosions. "They certainly did enough damage to the destroyer that Lieutenant Flores sees the smoke plume from her position with Fifth Platoon, about ten miles inland, here, at around...." Wilcox looked over at Christine.

"Eleven hundred, sir."

"However," Wilcox went on. "By the time Fifth Platoon meets Third near the dockyards at around fifteen hundred, the destroyer is completely gone, and only three hundred combatants are still occupying the area."

"Could it have exploded?" Neville rested his elbows on the table.

"An explosion from the fusion reactor on a ship that size would have incinerated everything for miles," Morden said, shaking her head. "Maybe it just sank."

"Possibly," Wilcox agreed, eyeing the harbor on the map, as if he was trying to see through it. "We'll need to sonar map the seafloor to be certain."

"What if someone carried if off?" Christine felt all eyes turn toward her.

"Do you think they packed it through the bush, Lieutenant?" Neville smirked at her.

Christine ignored him and looked at Morden instead. "I... saw something through my binoculars. Something hovering in the smoke."

"Something?" Morden's brow furrowed.

"It was very far away and the smoke was pretty thick." Christine closed her eyes, trying to picture what she'd seen. "It was very large, tan in color. It held position in the smoke cloud. I could barely see it."

Morden turned to Neville. "Would the fort have detected a space vessel entering the atmosphere?"

Neville turned red again. "Unfortunately, no. We don't have a planetary scanning grid."

"You don't have one?" Holsey crossed her arms. "Why? Have you not repaired it, either?"

Neville shook his head. "I guess they didn't install one."

Christine felt her nose wrinkle slightly. The man was in charge of the fort and he didn't know a thing about the station. She suppressed her disgusted snort by speaking instead. "It had one, but a lot of the planet's scanning hardware was dismantled after the war for use on the Milipa frontier. There are big gaps in the system now, especially on the side of the planet opposite the fort."

Neville glared at Christine. She knew she had embarrassed him, but she wasn't going to leave out details to spare his ego.

Wilcox sighed. "And so, this something the lieutenant saw could have entered the atmosphere somewhere else and flown low enough to approach the Barracuda undetected."

"Yes, sir," Christine said.

"If they've got a warship out there..." Voth's voice trailed off, his gaze meeting Morden's.

"Why didn't you mention this *something* you saw earlier, Lieutenant?" The disgust in Neville's voice was obvious, all sugar coating gone.

Christine met his gaze, refused to blink. Under the table, she pressed her thumb against her engagement ring, keeping an image of Ryan in her head. "I thought it was the smoke playing tricks on me. It was there, then gone a second later."

Morden's frown deepened. "Do these facilities still have any way to defend themselves against space vessels?"

"Yes, ma'am," Christine replied. "The fort still controls a couple dozen or so ground-to-space silos."

"We're not totally desolate, you see." Neville raised his chin. "The fort has a sufficient armament to even destroy a carrier."

"If it can see them," Christine said.

Morden leaned forward, cutting off whatever Neville was about to say. "After you left the hill to meet Third Platoon, were you ever in view of the harbor?"

"No, ma'am," Christine replied. "We stuck to the ravines and the forest. We didn't want to be spotted approaching the area."

"If there had been a ship, that would have given them ample time to lift off the destroyer." Voth squinted at the map, clearly deep in thought.

"Which means the group that ambushed us really was just the cleaning crew," said Osterman. "I knew there were too few to have attacked a destroyer."

"Some cleaning crew." Wilcox frowned. "And when Fifth and Third Platoons arrived at Bunker Fifty, they saw the cargo tenders taking this group away one load at a time and heading somewhere to the northeast—"

"Which means they're still out there." Osterman finished Wilcox's sentence.

"So," Holsey said, laying her hands flat on the table. "We have a missing destroyer, a possible enemy warship with at least enough infantry on board to assault said destroyer, and no idea who these people are."

There was silence for a moment.

Finally, Morden spoke, looking at Neville. "Colonel, if they're hiding somewhere, it's probably fairly close by. Are there any areas outside the complex where they could stage an attack?"

Neville shook his head. "I—I don't think so, Captain. I can't think of anywhere they would be other than in the forest. These woods are quite dense, you know."

Morden raised an eyebrow and looked over at Christine. "Flores, Squires, you spend a lot of time on foot throughout this area. Is there anywhere close to the complex they could be hiding a warship?"

"A warship, no," Squires said. "The terrain is too hilly for hundreds of miles, and they'd need to clear the forest. We'd have noticed that."

"Not a warship," Christine said, studying the map. "But infantry? Yes."

"Where?" Wilcox gestured at the map.

Christine stood, rounded the end of the table, and stood next to the display screen. "The trees north of here are very thick, like the colonel said. If they wanted to hide under the canopy, they could have parked their space ship somewhere and hiked overland." Christine drew an imaginary line with her finger from the northern coast, about sixty miles from the harbor, down toward the Kensington complex. "But I don't think they'd be too comfortable for long."

"Comfortable?" Neville scoffed, but no one looked at him.

"If I wanted to hide soldiers and shelter them, I'd put them here." Christine pointed at the block on the map that represented the old barracks complex.

"But that's part of your own facility," Osterman said. "How could they hide there?"

"It's easy." Christine turned to face the group, feeling suddenly very out of place. Except for Squires, everyone was neat and spotless, like the room itself. She raised her chin slightly. Daddy had always told her a working person's got nothing to be ashamed of. "This area used to house regiments being staged here before going to the front. It's the most isolated spot Kensington has. Given all the other bunkers and facilities we have to patrol and maintain, we only get to any one of them a couple times per year.

Especially since we're… discouraged to waste time on it, since it's the farthest facility out." Christine avoided Neville's gaze, but she could see him shifting uncomfortably out of the corners of her eyes.

"When was the last time you patrolled this area?" Morden looked up at Christine, a trace of worry on her face.

"I think Third hit it last." Christine looked over at Squires.

Squires closed his eyes, seemed to be thinking hard. "Yeah, I think we were out there about two months ago."

"Then we know where to start." Morden turned to face the rest of the group. "First and foremost, I want re-supplying and repairing the Verdun to be a top priority for both crews. I want this ship prepared for a fight. Once the Verdun is ready, I want us out of the water, where we are vulnerable, and in space to investigate and repair the damage to the relay system. Second, we need to secure all parts of Kensington Station. Major Osterman, coordinate with Colonel Neville to combine your marines with ranger platoons. I want every bunker and redoubt searched to make sure they're not using any of them. Once we've checked the smaller facilities, I want a combined force to move in strength on the barracks."

"Why not send a fighter escort?" The air commander, Frost, raised an eyebrow.

Morden swiveled to look at him. "We only have tatters of our fighter compliment left after the Triangle. I'd rather have them in the air and screening us here than spread out elsewhere. Once the Verdun is in shape again, we'll use them to do all the scouting we need."

Morden paused, looking around the table. "No further, questions? Get to it."

There was a general chorus of "Yes, ma'am" from everyone at the table, everyone except Neville, who stared in front of him.

"We'll issue woodland uniforms and armor." Osterman shifted in his seat to face Christine and Squires. "It will make our operations with the rangers go more smoothly."

Christine returned Osterman's gaze and nodded.

Good call.

The marines would blend in much better in their ODs. To a ranger, approaching the enemy unseen was a necessity.

"You have complete discretion, Major. Dismissed." Morden stood and walked out of the room, and her officers filed behind her. Christine stood and turned to follow them.

"Squires, Flores!" Neville's bark stopped Christine in her tracks.

She turned. Neville, his fists clenched at his side, strode toward her and Squires. She wondered if he was going to punch her, hoped he would give her an excuse to wipe the floor with his pudgy ass, but he stopped a few inches in front of them. She stood at attention, looking into Neville's eyes. He was so close she could see the pores on his nose.

"I suppose you think I'm going to pin medals on you because you won today," Neville said, spraying Christine's face with spit. He turned to look at Squires, who stood as straight as a rifle barrel.

"But remember, once Captain Ooh-la-la is gone, I'm still in command. You damn well never forget it."

"Yes, sir," Squires said, though Christine knew he didn't mean it.

Neville turned to her again, his nostrils flaring.

"Yes, sir," Christine said.

Neville grinned at her, clearly satisfied. Then his nose wrinkled. "And take a bath, you two. You're an embarrassment to me like that." He pushed past them and out the door.

Squires chuckled. "Hike your ass off, risk your life, save the day—"

"And get reamed," Christine finished. "C'mon. Let's see if they have any food on this thing."

Christine nudged Squires with her elbow, and they walked out the door together.

CHAPTER 9

Tom Petrarcha strode through the endless rows of barracks, his head bent low against the strong wind that was blowing in from the harbor. The weather had begun to change not long after nightfall. Soon, it would be raining, a relief on this sunbaked planet. Even at night, this place never cooled down.

Tom glanced to either side of him, checking on his people as he passed. They huddled in groups in front of their barracks buildings, talking to one another in low voices, cleaning their rifles, repairing clothing, the glow of cooking fires peeking out through the heavy blankets they'd nailed over the barracks' doors. They couldn't risk being discovered, though now Tom supposed it didn't matter. With the arrival of the warship, everything was different.

The re-appropriation of the destroyer had gone well enough, better than Tom could have imagined. They'd lost relatively few people in the attack and taken many prisoners. More importantly, they had the ship, the first prize of their campaign. But the bigger warship had surprised them, and now more than a hundred of his people had been slaughtered. Yes, nothing was the same, and Tom expected that was why the Supervisor had called him to talk so late.

Supervisor.

The title was vague enough and impressive enough that everyone knew to fear the people who carried it. They made the decisions, everyone followed. Tom supposed the progress they'd made so far proved the Supervisors really were the rightful leaders of the Legion, but, to be honest, he missed the days before they had come.

In the beginning, the United Worker's Legion had been a movement of ideas. Meetings held in the dust and filth of the living quarter, speeches and debates about just systems of power and the rights of individuals. The last election had energized the Legion, and where the meetings had once been the secret of a few individuals, they became enormous assemblies with hundreds of people who came to listen, to speak their minds. Then the meetings became networks that helped each other, supported each other. Tom had become the leader of one of them, coordinating its activities. He'd had every member give whatever they could — spare rations, blankets, medicines smuggled from outside the company stores — and whenever someone became ill or was in want of anything, they'd use the supplies to see that person through. The companies had learned of the groups and banned them instantly, and the government had looked the other way, ignoring the laws they had promised to strengthen and enforce during the election. It hadn't been the first time a political party had disappointed Tom, but after raising his hopes so high? He knew now there could be no compromise. Only action would change things. Only fighting would make people see.

Then the Supervisors had come, contacting the networks with offers of weapons and supplies. Tom hadn't trusted them, especially when they'd started taking the role of leaders. He wouldn't put it beyond the companies to infiltrate the networks and expose them from the inside. But the people had loved them. They'd brought medicines and foods in quantities people had never seen before. When the companies had issued warrants for their arrest, Tom had set aside his misgivings and accepted them. The Supervisors may not have suffered on the production lines, but the actions of the companies had driven them to seek justice, too. Or at least that's what Tom had told himself.

The Supervisors had turned the Legion into a crusade, unifying the networks, arming them, pushing them to train and to prepare. They'd even used their connections to steal warships of their own. Tom had felt a rush of exhilaration, knowing that they would soon have the spotlight of the entire Alliance on them and their cause. That was when the Supervisors had pushed to attack the way stations. More strategic targets, they'd said, more likely to draw attention. They selected Kensington as the first, though Tom had yet to see what was strategic about this place. An opportunity to test their strength, his Supervisor had said.

But something about their mission here was not what Tom had planned for. He had no problem with killing the guilty. He'd seen enough suffering in squalid tenant housing and on the assembly lines to justify a thousand executions. But these Navy men and women — they were not the enemy. Talking to them, it was clear that some of them had lived the same life he had lived. They served the enemy's interests, indirectly, but they were not guilty. Still, for the cause…

If it meant justice, Tom would do what he had to.

Tom met the eyes of a group of his people as he passed them, sipping broth from steaming cups.

"Good evening, Tom."

"Step carefully, leader."

Tom nodded back at them. They looked stronger now, their bodies fuller under the stained rags and work coveralls they still wore. These barracks had been a blessing. When the Supervisor had said they might have to live in the forest, Tom had worried his people didn't have the strength. But the barracks had provided shelter. Hell, even though it was clear they'd been unoccupied and only occasionally maintained for some time, they were far safer than any of the units in the living quarter back home. And they'd held old crates of military rations, which had done wonders for their health, even if they'd been partially gnawed by vermin.

Tom reached the end of the row of barracks, turned toward the smaller outbuilding that the Supervisor had taken for his post. It was a small square building, made of the same corrugated metal as the others. Outside stood two guards at attention, rifles held in front of them with their butts on the ground. As Tom reached them, they raised their rifles and shouldered them in exact synchronization, an impressive — and unnecessary — display. But then again, the Supervisor had a flair for showmanship.

Tom nodded to the guards and entered, ducking his tall frame through the door. The smell of roasted meat and toasted ration biscuits hit him in the face, made his mouth water. The room was small, with a cot pushed to one side and a desk with a small battery lamp on the other. A young woman sat on the cot. She looked up, caught Tom's gaze, and blushed. Somehow the Supervisor never lacked for company. But the Legion was built on the ideals of freedom, and Tom wouldn't tell any man or woman how to spend their time, even if he disapproved of a leader mingling with those under him.

Tom diverted his eyes to the Supervisor, who was sitting behind his desk next to the pile of trophies he'd had brought to him from the destroyer. Rifles, bayonets, body armor, and the ship's ceremonial ensign, a bright blue and white flag with a long, jagged-toothed fish embroidered on it in gold. The Supervisor was bent over slightly, running his hands over a pistol, and Tom realized with a jolt that he had put on one of the Navy uniform jackets, this one with the four bars and one star of a captain on its shoulder boards, the name *Edwards* embroidered over one of the breast pockets.

Tom cleared his throat. "Supervisor, you called for me?"

The Supervisor looked up, his face splitting into a grin. He was a slender man, just a bit shorter than Tom, with a weak chin covered with blond stubble, and a shaved head. He placed the pistol on the desk, stood, and walked to Tom, holding out his arms, no doubt to show off his new uniform.

"What do you think, *Commander* Petrarcha?" He turned in place, his face beaming in the dim light of the desk lamp.

"Supervisor?" Tom did his best to hide his annoyance. If he were only here to witness a fashion display, he would be very disappointed.

"See," the Supervisor said, pushing a shoulder toward Tom to show off his shoulder boards. "I'm a captain. That makes you a commander."

"The movement doesn't recognize ranks of this type, Supervisor. You know that."

The Supervisor worked his face into a pouty frown. "Serious Tom, as always. And I have a name. Smith. Trenton Smith."

"Yes Supervisor… Smith." Tom held the man's gaze. "What did you call me here to discuss?"

The Supervisor turned to the young woman on his cot, and waved his hands at her. "Shoo, my dear. We'll see each other later."

The woman stood and walked past Tom, her gaze on her feet as she passed him.

The Supervisor walked back to his desk, flopped down in his chair, his face transforming to the image of concern.

"We have a problem, Tom."

Tom held back a snort. That much was obvious. "Yes, we've suffered higher losses than expected."

The Supervisor shook his head, flicked a hand as if to scare away a fly. "No, not that. I think we need to move to a better place."

Tom nodded. "I agree. This Kensington mission has failed."

The Supervisor chuckled. "That's what I love about you, Tom. Always so absolute, so honest with your opinions."

Tom said nothing.

"No," the Supervisor continued. "Our project here has just begun."

"Supervisor—"

"—Smith!" The Supervisor interrupted, smiling again.

"Smith," Tom said. "More than a hundred people won't be returning to their families. Add that to those we lost taking the destroyer. We've made our point. We have the destroyer, and we should go before we waste any more people." Tom didn't consider himself a smart man, but he wasn't dumb either. He'd worked hard in the factories, moving from the assembly line to working in the machining room with the CNC equipment. When he'd been younger, he'd even taken pride in helping to make the finest atmospheric compressors in the sector.

"Correction!" The Supervisor pointed a finger toward the ceiling. "We've seized the destroyer but don't yet *have* it. Not until we can hack the AI matrix."

"Forget the matrix. We can tow it out of here and go back into hiding before we provoke a battle we can't win."

"Don't you see? The war *is* here." The Supervisor stood so suddenly that Tom took a step back. "And besides," he continued. "We have a greater prize to win now."

Tom stared at the Supervisor, his mind blank. Then comprehension dawned and he wondered if the man had gone insane. "The warship that came today?" Tom shook his head violently. "No. No way."

"Why?"

Tom was tempted to slap the grin off Smith's face. "That is a capital ship. There is no way we can take it, and if we tried, we would all die."

The Supervisor laughed, an exaggerated, high sound. "My dear Tom! You underestimate our strength. With the fleet we have here and the additional warriors who have arrived, there is nothing on this planet to oppose us. Besides, there are other weapons here you have not considered."

Tom wasn't in the mood for guessing games. "What weapons?"

The Supervisor grinned. "Bring the other leaders here. It's time we planned for our next operation."

Tom crossed his arms. "So, we're going to sit here and talk while the military comes to crucify us? They've likely figured out where we are by now and are sure to attack soon."

"So impatient! That's another thing I love about you, Tom."

His smile faded when Tom didn't respond.

"We will let the military come. Let them come and find exactly what they want to find."

Tom rolled his eyes. Clearly the Supervisor wasn't going to tell him everything until everyone was there and he had a bigger audience.

"Fetch the leaders, Tom. And give the order to begin using... harder methods to persuade the destroyer's crew to help us crack the AI matrix."

Tom took a step toward the Supervisor, anger suddenly tearing through him. "We are crusaders. You've said that yourself. We're not murderers or cowards who torture prisoners."

The Supervisor's grin drooped slightly, but did not disappear. "Perhaps. But if you're going to be a crusader, you must become much more comfortable with bloodshed. You want to free the oppressed, punish the guilty? You've already killed for it."

Tom looked at the floor. "Yes, I want to punish the guilty."

"Then give the order. The Legion can't afford to lose this great, strategic outpost. Everything depends on it."

His feet heavy, Tom turned to leave, but the voice of the Supervisor stopped him.

"Make sure to let my lady friend back in on your way out. And give us a little time."

"Yes, Supervisor."

Tom stepped out into the cool breeze, the young woman brushing past him as he left. As he walked back down the rows of barracks, he wondered if he'd have joined the Legion if he'd been told it would come to this. War? Torture? Tom shook the slimy feeling in his chest, thought of the millions he was trying to save, the millions for whom life itself was torture, torture for the greed of the few.

No. There was no time for guilt. He'd come too far for that, and there was still too much to do.

CHAPTER 10

Christine steadied her carbine, listened to the plinking of rain falling on her body armor. Just like home. Daddy setting out bowls and pots to catch the drops leaking from the roof. Mom complaining about how the company representative had promised to fix it months ago. Daddy laughing and saying it was a free shower.

"At least it gets the dust off," he'd said, drying himself with a ratty towel.

Christine had stared at the metal bowls, which caught the orange glare of the sodium lamps on the outside of the food dispensary across the road as they filled with raindrops. Fire and water together.

Christine chased the image from her mind, focused on the present.

She looked across at Sergeant Néri, who held the butt of his submachine gun in his shoulder, the barrel tilted toward the ground, his back against the doorframe of the warehouse. Lined up next to Néri, scrunched against the corrugated steel walls of the warehouse were a dozen other soldiers — a mix of rangers and the marines from the *Verdun*. They held absolutely still, their faces tight. The only sound was the patter of rain on armor and the breathing of the troops lined up behind Christine.

Christine met Néri's eyes. He nodded, and stepped in front of the closed access door. As Néri placed small breaching charges on the door hinges and locking mechanism, Christine shifted her carbine into the crook of her arm and pulled a heavy, round stun grenade attached to a long, thin steel shaft from the pouch at her side. She fitted the shaft onto the end of her carbine, minding the point of the bayonet as her hands worked near the muzzle. She double-checked to make sure the carbine was unloaded, then positioned the pointer finger of her support hand over the flashlight activation button built into the carbine's fore stock. It would likely be dim in there, and with the prospect of finding wounded or captured friendlies in her line of fire, Christine wouldn't risk shooting until she could illuminate her target.

Néri stepped back, holding a small black remote, his eyes fixed on Christine.

Christine slowed her breathing, felt the slight vibration of raindrops on her helmet. "Go, go, go!"

The door vanished in a cloud of smoke as it was blasted inwards, the force of the breaching charges pressing against Christine's sinuses. She aimed her carbine into the warehouse and pulled the trigger. She heard the whine of the rail mechanism cycling and then the dull thunk of the grenade flying off the carbine's muzzle. She stepped back into cover, looked away from the door. An earsplitting bang echoed from inside the warehouse, and Christine imagined the flash of light that came with it.

She racked her carbine's bolt and surged forward into the warehouse through the open door.

"Get down! Put your hands up!" Christine shouted, her troops repeating the command. Even if she couldn't see anyone, she wouldn't risk shooting any friendlies that might be holed up in here. She blinked as her eyes adjusted to the blackness and filed to the left, heard Néri move the other way. She swept the vast interior with her carbine, her eyes searching for movement. Endless rows of stacked boxes stacked in thick steel racks fifty feet tall. A fork lift. The rusty control box for a ceiling crane. A stack of empty wooden crates, soaked from a leak in the roof. The smell of rot, of dust and stale air mixed with the acrid smoke of the grenade. The footfalls of the soldiers behind her echoed off the metal walls.

Christine trained her weapon down each row as she passed. Something dark jumped off the side of the crates and ran toward the back of the room. Christine raised her carbine, clicked the flashlight button and released it. A beam of white light knifed into the darkness for an instant from the bayonet ring stud on the front of her weapon before switching off automatically.

Just a pack of rodents.

Christine let out a small sigh and kept moving to the left. She reached the last row, turned right, and moved down it. The wall formed by the towering stacks of boxes pressed in on her, made her feel like she was in a tunnel. She reached the end of the row, turned right to enter the back aisle, and her gaze fell upon what looked like a person sitting with his back against a crate.

Christine shouldered her weapon, ready to fire, and clicked on her flashlight.

For a split second, her light fell upon—

"Bodies." The soldier behind her murmured the word.

The horrible scene in front of Christine fell back into darkness as her weapon light switched off. She stepped cautiously toward the pile of corpses in front of her. She counted five, all in the green work coveralls of TLS planet staff, one of them leaned against a crate in a sitting position. Their uniforms and the floor around them was caked black with dried blood. The smell of decomposing flesh made Christine gag, stung her eyes. She fought back her body's reaction and moved slowly toward the corpses, her rifle trained on them. She'd learned from fighting the Milipa that it wasn't beyond an enemy to use bodies as a means to kill, either by hiding living soldiers among the dead or by using the cadavers as the lure for a booby trap.

Christine reached the body sitting against the crate, avoided looking at its face, and kicked it hard in the shoulder. Stiff and still bent at the waist, it fell with a thud that made Christine shudder. As she passed each body, she poked it with the tip of her bayonet, concentrating only on the press of her ring against the carbine's fore stock. Christine stepped over the last body, and continued along the rear aisle, grateful as the smell diminished. She heard Henrikson cussing as he passed the corpses.

Christine saw movement at the end of the aisle, recognized the silhouette of Néri. They moved toward each other and met in the middle of the back aisle.

"Clear," Néri said.

"Clear," Christine repeated. "Except for some former tenants back there."

Néri nodded gravely. "Two more in the second-to-last row."

"Let's mark it and move on." Christine raised her voice. "Alright people, check your shit and stay alert. We've got four more to do."

Jack watched as marines and rangers filed out of warehouse G20, already knowing by the looks on their faces what Lieutenant Flores would do before she emerged, turned, and sprayed a red X next to the breached door.

"Damn," Jack said, talking more to himself than to Major Osterman, who stood next to him on the small rise overlooking the bunkers, just under the branches of the nearest tree. He didn't feel like looking at Osterman about now. "Team six found more bodies."

Osterman remained silent. The day had already been quite sobering. They'd started searching the secondary warehouse complex at daybreak, having hiked in via a set of winding, muddy trails at the insistence of the ranger officers. So far, the eight groups searching the buildings had found six bodies, not including the ones Flores' team had just discovered. With only a few more warehouses to search, Jack was beginning to think that most of the sixty personnel who Colonel Neville had said were assigned to the warehouses would not be found. That meant prisoners, and prisoners meant leverage for the enemy to use against them. Chills ran down Jack's spine at the thought of what might be happening to those people now.

Jack had been happy to lead the search teams. After yesterday, it seemed like a nice break in routine. The rangers and the *Verdun* marines had spent the previous day frantically securing every single bunker in the greater Kensington complex. They'd used the station's supply of jeeps — old, clunky things covered with splotches of green, khaki, brown, and black paint — to ferry the different teams, formed by squads of rangers and marines working together, to the various facilities. The effort had dragged on for what had seemed like forever but had gone smoothly. Jack wasn't certain whether he felt relieved or concerned that the enemy combatants hadn't revealed themselves. On the one hand, the day had passed without casualties. On the other, it meant the bad guys were still out there somewhere, and part of Jack just wanted it to be over with.

Nonetheless, watching the marine and ranger search teams secure the warehouses one by one had proved more difficult than Jack had anticipated as the number of bodies had increased. There was something about this place — a planet where servicemembers ought to be safe turned into a battlefield — that left Jack feeling unsettled. But he supposed he couldn't complain. His job had certainly been better than what Commander Cadogan, the *Verdun's* senior medical officer, had to do, identifying and seeing to the burial of the *Barracuda* crewmembers whose bodies — some seventy in all — had been found in a warehouse at the dockyards. And it wasn't as if Jack had to see the bodies his teams were finding today himself, thanks to Major Osterman.

Jack had wanted to help lead the teams, but Osterman had objected.

"During the ambush, you choked," Osterman had said, peering at him from under his helmet.

"What exactly do you mean?" Jack's head had spun, his friends' reproach a slap in the face.

"You hesitated. Fear got the better of you."

"I acted as anyone would have in that situation," Jack had said, his face flushing hot.

"No, sir. You acted like someone who hasn't seen combat."

Jack hadn't believed what he'd been hearing. He'd been in more than few battles while on the *Verdun*. Perhaps he'd never been in a firefight like that, but his life had been in danger before, and he'd never lost his cool.

There's a first time for everything.

"This wouldn't have anything to do with the Triangle, would it?"

Osterman had stared back at him for just a second too long. "I don't know what you mean, sir."

Jack had escaped the brutal, close-quarters fighting against the Frontin in their last mission in Derek's Triangle by virtue of not having been aboard the *Verdun* when it had happened. Ever since he'd returned to the ship and learned how many of the crew had been killed, he'd felt overwhelmed by ... Guilt? Shame? He couldn't help but wonder...

No, it wasn't worth going there. He'd had a different job to do, one that had taken him away from the ship. What had happened onboard was not his fault. He couldn't have changed it by being on the *Verdun*, no matter how much he wanted to.

Keep telling yourself that.

And now this recent fight at the dock... He *had* hesitated. But wouldn't anybody do the same in an ambush like that? The enemy had come from nowhere. There was nothing Jack could have done differently, nothing he could have done to save those crewmembers.

Yeah, right.

"Are you suggesting I am unfit to command our efforts here?" Jack had clenched his fists at his side.

Osterman had shaken his head. "No, sir. But frontline operations should be left to ranger and marine personnel. People who have experience with ground combat."

As commander of the *Verdun's* marine contingent, Osterman's opinion carried weight. Even though Jack was the ranking officer, he had chosen to follow Osterman's suggestion, although he hadn't liked it. Jack was a lieutenant commander after all, not some damn greenhorn. More than that, he and Osterman had served together a long time. He considered the marine a colleague, a friend. To think that maybe Osterman considered him incompetent… An image of Colonel Neville leapt into his mind. Jack shook it off and looked through his binoculars again.

Team Four, commanded by Lieutenant Squires, was preparing to breach one of the buildings. Jack saw the door blast inward, saw a flash as the grenade exploded inside the warehouse, then watched the team move into the dark doorway, two sharp cracks carrying over to where Jack stood a half second later.

The details of the attack here were starting to clear themselves in Jack's mind. Whoever their enemy was had struck at the secondary warehouses first, killing some of the TLS workers and the few soldiers stationed here, then taken the freight train down to the docks and set up an ambush. What troubled Jack is that he couldn't imagine why. There hadn't been conflict like this between humans in… Jack couldn't remember the last time.

The enemies were normally so clear. The Frontin, Milipa, and all the other adversaries of the Alliance were as different from humans as they could be, and there was something simple about fighting them. But to think that enemies could come from within the Alliance itself. Jack shuddered, and not because of the chilly rain.

He lowered his binoculars and nearly jumped out of his skin when he saw Lieutenant Flores, followed closely by one of the ranger sergeants — Néri was his name, Jack thought — and Lieutenant Arnot, one of the marine officers from the *Verdun*, walking toward him from only a few feet away to his right.

Covering his surprise, he turned to face them and was about to open his mouth to ask for a report of their progress, but Flores walked instead to Osterman.

"Sir, all the other teams except Squires' have finished."

"What's the final tally?" Osterman asked.

Jack crossed his arms, his bile rising in his mouth. Arnot eyed him nervously, clearly aware of the break in protocol that was happening.

"Seventeen total," Flores replied. "Plus whatever Squires finds."

Osterman nodded gravely. "Get started on—"

Jack cleared his throat. "I am in command here, Lieutenant Flores. Please direct your report to me."

The officers looked at him, and Jack saw Flores stiffen slightly. She nonetheless squared herself toward him and met his eyes.

"Yes, sir. The area is secure. I recommend we leave immediately and take up positions in the woods just north of here in case any enemy forces come from the barracks. We're visible from high ground while we're in this complex."

"Recommendation noted," Jack said. "But I'd like to hold position here until we can radio in to the Verdun and receive new orders."

Flores shifted slightly where she stood. "Yes, sir."

Jack held Flores' gaze. "Form a perimeter around the northern part of the warehouse complex and stay alert."

"Yes, sir." Flores repeated. She turned on her heel and jogged down the hill.

Jack watched Flores go, Néri, Squires, and Arnot a few paces behind her.

"I'm sorry," Osterman said. "I should have deferred to you."

"Yes." Jack turned to look Osterman in the eyes, his anger mounting again. "You should have. Regardless of what you may think, I earned these." Jack pointed to the gold fleur-de-lis rank pin on his collar. "And I'm still wearing them. Captain Morden put me in charge of these operations, and I won't sit back and do nothing just because you don't respect my experience. Do I make myself clear?"

Osterman's face hardened. "I won't make the same mistake again."

"Good." Jack turned to the radio pack sitting next to him, shiny with rainwater. He hauled it up and onto his back, adjusting his stance as the weight sank onto his shoulders. He picked up his binoculars and looked through them in time to see Squires emerging from the warehouse with his team. Jack sighed with relief when they did not stop to paint an X.

Unhooking the radio handset from its shoulder clip, he depressed the side button.

"Victor One-Five-Five, Victor Six, come in."

The radio fizzled, and the voice of Chief Baudouin responded. "Victor Six, Victor One-Five-Five, go ahead."

"We've cleared the secondary warehouses. Seventeen bodies accounted for. Please advise."

There was a long pause. Jack listened to the sound of raindrops plopping into mud, plinking off Osterman's armor, and smacking against his raincoat. Then the radio crackled again.

"Victor Six, Victor One-Five-Five. Hold position until other units can join you, break."

Wilcox keyed the handset again. "Go ahead."

"The captain and Colonel Neville are sending the rest of the combined force to your position for an immediate attack on the barracks."

Surprise bolted through his chest, and Osterman pursed his lips tighter. Jack raised the handset to his mouth. "Copy, out."

"At least they're moving fast," Osterman said as Jack tucked away the handset. "I'd like for this to be done with."

"You and me both." Jack started down the hill toward where he could make out Lieutenant Flores directing troops into position, the squish of Osterman's boots on soaked grass following him.

Jack tried not to think of the possibilities of an approaching battle, focused instead on an odd sense of excitement. It wasn't that he wanted to be in another firefight. But he did want Osterman to see him in one. This time would be different. Osterman would see what Jack was made of.

CHAPTER 11

Kim watched as Chief Baudouin turned from the communications station and looked in her direction, acutely aware of Colonel Neville's eyes on her. She'd caught him looking somewhat below her collar a few times, and she was rapidly losing patience.

"Ma'am," Baudouin stowed her handset. "Commander Wilcox confirms. All other units en route."

"Good." Kim willed herself to look at Neville, whose eyes flicked up to hers from southward. "Colonel, I'm concerned that committing all of our forces to the attack will leave the rest of the complex unsecured and undefended in case of a counterattack."

Neville smirked. "Trust me, Captain, we're plenty secure. You have the rest of your marines here on the Verdun, and I have the garrison at the fort, a whole platoon."

Morden shook her head. She'd agreed to an immediate attack because she'd wanted to strike before the enemy force had a chance to react. If they were at the barracks, she wanted to catch them before they could disappear into the forest. But Neville had insisted that the rest of the ranger company, including the artillery section, join in the assault, and despite his confidence, Kim doubted that a platoon was an adequate defense for the fort.

"A proper attack, with proper force behind it, will ensure all of our safety. We wouldn't want the operation to fail for lack of numbers."

Kim couldn't argue with that. And since the *Verdun's* marine compliment was so reduced after the battle in Derek's Triangle, it wasn't far from the truth that the entire ranger company was necessary for the attack.

"Of course," Neville was saying. "You could spare more marines from the Verdun…"

No way in hell. Kim had seen the bodies of the *Barracuda* crew being carried to the ship's morgue. She wasn't about to let the same happen to the *Verdun,* and so long as they were in the water and vulnerable, the ship would stay at security alert with enough marines on board to repel an assault.

"Colonel, now that the Verdun has been re-stocked, I'd like you to return the fort to manage station operations. I need someone in charge over there."

Neville's face worked into an exaggerated frown. "And here I was hoping I'd be aboard for dinner with you."

Kim raised an eyebrow.

"And your officers," Neville added.

Kim saw Holsey look toward Neville from her station and roll her eyes.

"I'm afraid not, Colonel. There's work to do. We still have extensive repairs to complete, communication relays that need to be looked at, and you have a station to repair and put back in order."

Neville shook his head. "You Navy types have no sense of fun. Very well."

Neville walked toward the door, clicking his tongue like he was scolding a child. "But you must let me entertain all of you while you're still at port."

"Possibly. Good afternoon, Colonel."

Neville exited, and Kim sensed a collective relaxing of tension in the room.

"He likes to talk, doesn't he?" Stetler called from the helm station.

"He's probably just lonely," Urquhart answered. "But I guess… Yeah, he does. It's nice that he wants to get to know us better."

Leave it to Callista to find something positive about everyone — and miss Neville's ulterior motives. "Yes, very nice, Lieutenant."

Holsey's scoffing sound made Kim turn around.

"He's an idiot. I think you're wasting your own time being diplomatic with him and not telling him to shove off."

"You're absolutely right, Commander."

"Good." Holsey said, looking back down at her work. "I'm glad we agree."

Kim smiled, and for a split second, she thought she saw Holsey do the same.

Neville stepped into the jeep, slamming the door behind him. "Be quick about it, Corporal."

"Yes, sir." The driver looked back at him from the front seat then bent forward to push the ignition. A second later, the vehicle's battery kicked in, and the jeep grumbled forward.

Neville twisted in his seat to look out the small back window. The tender that had brought him to shore was backing out into the dark green water, turning slowly back toward the *Verdun*, which looked huge compared to the dockyards.

"Cold bitch," Neville murmured.

"Sir?" The driver's voice came from the front seat over the hum of wheels on asphalt and the patter of rain on the roof.

"Just drive." Neville didn't feel like explaining. Besides, it wasn't the business of some corporal.

Neville had spent the day trying to let Captain Morden know he was interested in her, and she'd all but thrown him off the ship. He'd thought she'd appreciate the attention. After all, command could be lonely. Rules forbade commanding officers from romancing their subordinates, no matter how appealing they might be. A fellow leader provided a rare opportunity to have some fun. Then again, Neville had met plenty of women who just didn't seem to like it when men were nice to them. A peculiarity of the species, he supposed.

Neville looked to his right out the window at the ruined section of docks that the *Verdun* fighters had obliterated. The least Morden could do would be to pay for the damage her people had done with a friendly dinner. It would take months to get the facility fully operational again. Then again, there were miles of undamaged docks to use and only a few destroyers per month to use them on. There would probably be no need to repair the damage. Clean it up a bit, salvage what could be salvaged, and move on. Neville had learned to economize where he could. The fools who had stuck him here gave him few resources, and he was savvy enough to know that the less he bothered them, the more likely they'd let him out.

The view of the docks gave way to big, blocky warehouses and then the shaggy, blue-green wall of the forest as the jeep left the dockyards and followed the road paralleling the rail line. Neville looked out the windshield at the far-off mountains, their rounded peaks gleaming with a thick coat of snow. Below them was a broad hill, its summit a long, flat line, bare of trees. He could just make out the green bump of the fort's superstructure and the road leading up to the front gate. Neville scowled. It might as well be a prison.

Neville saw three jeeps ahead, heading in the same direction, the pack howitzers loaded into their rear cargo beds. Behind them marched a platoon of rangers — Lieutenant Ames' artillery section and Lieutenant Mahoney's heavy weapons platoon by the looks of them — with some of the *Verdun* marines. They were moving slowly, and Neville figured they were probably on their way to meet the rest of the attack force. Just like the rangers to drag their feet.

"Pass them," Neville barked.

"Yes, sir."

The driver cranked the wheel over to the right, and the vehicle surged past the marching soldiers, whose heads were bent forward under their armor and rain jackets. No doubt seeing the gold lion's head he knew was painted on the outside of his vehicle, they watched him drive past. Neville was tempted to flip them the bird. The rangers had been a problem for him since Major Parks, their old commanding officer, had left and Neville had been given temporary charge of them. They'd made it clear they didn't think he was able to lead them, especially Flores. Had he not needed every officer he could get, and had he thought Command would back him up, he'd have sent Flores packing as soon as Parks' desk was emptied out. As it was, he could only hope she'd catch a stray bullet and be sent home with a medical discharge. At least then she wouldn't have a chance to contribute anything unfriendly to him in the incident report.

Damn! He'd almost forgotten all about that. Neville put his face in his hands. He'd wasted so much time on Morden, he'd neglected to begin working on the report. It absolutely had to come from him. It was the only way to make sure the report reflected the truth and no one's personal vendettas or judgments. But since Morden had operational command, writing the report would fall to her, and she seemed to be on Lieutenant Flores' side.

A damn female conspiracy.

Neville pondered the possibilities as the jeep climbed above the surrounding hills and up the slope to the fort. By the time they crested the hill, Neville had formed a plan. He'd return to the *Verdun* tomorrow, apologize to Morden for having apparently made her uncomfortable, and offer to take the report off her hands. She had so much to do with repairing her ship. Neville couldn't help but smile. It would be so easy.

Neville looked ahead at the fort, its dreary details thrown into bright relief by the late afternoon sun. It was a huge, steel-reinforced concrete maze, three stories tall, covered with eighteen feet of sand, another twenty-four feet of concrete scree, and then capped with thirty feet of dirt. Tunnels joined the main superstructure of the fort, which contained the barracks, powder magazines, main gun turrets, kitchens, galleys, armories, workshops, power generators, communication machinery, lavatories, and infirmaries, to the front entrance, counterscarp galleries, and the small, armored hanger in back. All but impenetrable, even from orbital bombardment — or that's what he'd been told when he'd arrived.

The outer wall, its earthen shell covered with grass, sloped up in front of them. On the other side, Neville knew, the walls dropped into a ditch running around the fort's superstructure. Counterscarp galleries built into the wall and facing into the fort defended the ditch with interlocking fields of fire. The superstructure rose fifty feet, its top dotted with five machine gun turrets and four larger artillery turrets, each with twin 155mm guns and each with its own smaller observation dome, and four artillery casemates protruded from its sides. Crowning the superstructure was the flag of the Royal Alliance, fluttering in the soggy breeze, a communications tower, and the truly massive heavy artillery turret, twice as big as any of the others, with its two 400mm guns.

Old junk on an ugly pile of dirt, in his opinion.

He'd found it impressive at first, but when he'd learned the counterscarp galleries had been stripped of their machine guns and that the supporting artillery pits on either side of the fort had been emptied, he'd known he was truly in a backwater. At the very least, the missile batteries were intact, their metal hatches flush with the sheer rock wall of the mountainside a half mile behind the fort.

The jeep pulled into the gate, and a soldier peered through the empty machine gun ports of the outer guardhouse, built into the wall of the entrance tunnel. The soldier saw the painted lion's head, and disappeared. A second later, Neville heard a buzzing sound, and the massive metal gate retracted to the left, a second gate retracting to the right just behind it. The driver pulled the vehicle forward, and the hum of the jeep's motor became a fierce growl as it echoed off the walls. Immediately inside the gate was a second set of machine gun ports — these ones actually had weapons in them — and the door leading into the guardhouse. The soldier emerged from the door and saluted again. Neville waved him off.

A minute later, the jeep was parked in the fort's garage and Neville was climbing the stairs to the second level, his eyes adjusting to the dimness of the fort's interior. The walls were smooth concrete, painted with directional signs, a red line running at chest level indicating that the area was bombardment-proof. Light bulbs, covered with steel cages, were spaced along the ceilings of the narrow corridors, joined by the nest of cables and wires that linked the fort's electrical and information systems together.

The corridors were empty, as usual. The staff of a dozen and garrison of fifty were a token compared to the two thousand the fort was designed to accommodate. Even with the full ranger company present, the fort didn't feel full. Neville reached the end of the corridor, turned left, returning the salute of the soldier walking from the direction of the south artillery turret, and stepped into his office, shutting the door behind him. He'd no sooner stepped to his desk than a knock sounded behind him.

"Come in!" Neville plopped down into the seat behind his desk, which was covered with stacks of paper and empty coffee cups.

Captain Sam Holden, a short, strongly built man with thinning hair, perfect posture, and boots that could be used as mirrors stepped inside and saluted.

"Glad to see you're back, sir."

Neville doubted that. "Anything new?" He leaned back in his chair.

"Attack forces have called out that they are almost ready to move." Holden eyed the mess on Neville's desk.

"Good. Make sure the machine gun turrets are manned tonight while all the rangers are gone." Neville put his feet on the desk. He knew Holden hated it, and right now, he didn't feel like dealing with the captain's stodgy formalities.

"Yes, sir." Holden was obviously trying not to look at Neville's boots. "Shall we man the counterscarp galleries as well?"

"No need. They don't have machine guns as it is, so why bother?" Neville couldn't help but smile at Holden's discomfort.

Holden nodded, looking down at the floor. "Yes, sir. Will we expect you in the command center? We'll need you there once the attack begins."

"I'll be there momentarily. Dismissed."

Holden turned and left the room, shutting the door behind him.

Neville sat back upright, putting his feet back on the floor. He wriggled off his boots, then swiveled to face his computer terminal. As it turned on, he considered how he would phrase his incident report. There would likely still be a couple hours before the attack, and he wanted to complete a draft before then. Morden would be more willing to let him take over the report if she saw he was diligent. The command center could wait for a while. With that in mind, he started typing.

CHAPTER 12

Tom jogged the width of the barracks complex, shouting orders, inspecting the positions his warriors were setting up, and trying to ward off the feeling of guilt in his chest. Tonight, they would win a great victory for the Legion, seize a great prize, but the defenders of the barracks would pay the highest price.

People were rushing every which way, lugging machine guns, building barricades, the pale rags they were wearing fluttering behind them as they ran. They would make one hell of a fight; that was for sure. Their martyrdom was assured, and the movement would continue, thanks to what they would help it achieve tonight. Still, Tom hated what lay before them.

"Careful with that!" Tom shouted at a man and a woman jostling a crate of mortar shells between them as they ran. At least they would be well armed, even better than before. The armories of the *Barracuda* had made sure of that.

He reached the eastern edge of the complex, saw the outlines of a few final stragglers heading into the woods in front of him. Most of the strike force had already left hours ago with the Supervisor. Only the ones who had stayed to help set up had remained. Tom had waited until the last moment, but it was time to go. He turned around, took one last look at the barracks. The rain had cleared, and the last rays of the sun raked the top of the treetops, throwing all the colors into saturated relief, and dyeing the dull metal of the bunkers bright red. Compared to the ash and decay of his home world, it was staggeringly beautiful.

Tom couldn't help but shake his head and smile. How putrid a galaxy it was that a decaying military camp in the forest on a backwater outpost should be an improvement to anyone. To some of Tom's people, this was probably the nicest place they'd ever lived. This thought cut the last chains of guilt from his chest.

The Supervisor was right. The movement required sacrifice, and it was a gift to die in a place like this rather than live back home. What they did here, the lives they would take, the people they were losing, were necessary, every one of them.

Feeling suddenly light despite the weight of the rifle on his back, Tom turned and walked into the woods. Tonight would be the best night of his life.

Christine reached the edge of the trees, dropped to a knee, and signaled with one arm for the rest of the platoon to do the same, her other arm cradling her weapon. They came to a halt, their eyes fixed on her. Down the line, Christine could barely make out Squires, Garrett, and Rankin doing the same with their platoons, the marine platoons immediately behind them following suit, moonlight glinting off bayonets and gunmetal. She looked ahead at the dark shapes of the barracks, trying to catch any movement, but the buildings merely frowned back at her, silent and still.

"Dammit!" Christine swore under her breath. The assholes were going to make the attack force pry them out of the buildings one by one, and that was going to take some time. There were at least two hundred buildings, all of them long, low-slung metal structures with little access paths running between them and two larger roads, one running north to south and the other east to west, cutting the complex into quarters.

The combined assault team of rangers and marines — some five hundred in all — had arrived on the wooded ridge overlooking the barracks about an hour before dark, having followed the old road that ran north from the secondary warehouses. Private Henrikson had climbed into a tree to get a clear look of the barracks compound.

"I see lots of activity among the buildings," he'd called down. "Looks like a few of them are moving off into the woods on the east side of the complex."

Christine had wanted to cut around the southern edge of the complex and sweep its eastern edge to intercept whoever was leaving. After all, it could be a group preparing for a counter attack, and Christine wanted to eliminate the entire enemy threat in one action. However, Wilcox had already decided their plan. They were to strike the barracks themselves in force as soon as darkness had fallen.

"And if the people Henrikson saw leaving are setting up a counter attack?" Christine had crossed her arms, not believing they were going to just attack without securing the surrounding area first.

"We need quick, decisive action, Lieutenant," Wilcox had said. "If we spend time searching the woods, it could delay the attack or give away our position. We hit the barracks as soon as we can." Wilcox had looked at Major Osterman then, and she'd felt a tension pass between them.

When she'd tried to argue further, Osterman had interrupted her.

"Commander Wilcox is in charge here, Lieutenant. Prepare your platoon and pass the word to the other ranger units."

Christine had done as she was told, not because she'd wanted to, but because she was too pragmatic to waste her time when the issue was settled. She'd organized her platoon, made sure they got ammunition and grenades from the truck, then returned to Osterman and Wilcox to see what circus-ass strategy they'd come up with. This, at least, had not been the mess Christine had feared it would be.

Four of the ranger platoons, along with some hundred or so Marines, were to attack the compound from its southwest corner. Christine's and Squires' platoons would wrap around the left, Rankin and Garrett would come around the right, and the marines would drive up the center. Meanwhile the rest of the marines and the final ranger platoons, Mahoney's heavy weapons platoon — including six heavy machine guns and three 80mm mortars — would stay in reserve and provide suppressing fire. Ames' artillery crew and their three pack howitzers would set up a few thousand yards behind, ready to obliterate stiff resistance. It was a textbook assault on a fixed position. The only problem had been Wilcox's other order, the one saying that he would personally be at the head of the attack.

She heard the snapping of twigs behind her, and a second later Wilcox knelt down next to her, a rifle in his hands. At least he'd swapped out his Navy blues for an olive-green field uniform, a helmet, and some armor.

"Why have we stopped?" Wilcox's eyes were white circles in the darkness.

"We're observing the site for any activity, in case they've spotted us and have something planned."

"Are you certain they're still there?" Wilcox's whisper was just a little too loud for Christine's taste. He did have a point, though. Between the time Henrikson had observed the area from the tree and now, the compound had certainly calmed down. But she didn't believe for a second it was empty.

"Yes, sir."

Wilcox nodded. She couldn't make out his face in the dark in any detail, but she could tell by his breathing that he was tense.

"Let's move forward."

Christine stood and motioned her platoon to follow. They emerged from the woods and into the open ground immediately surrounding the complex. As Christine sprinted to the left and toward one of the buildings, she scanned the darkness in front of her, looking for any warning that they were going to be fired on. If they were caught without cover…

Out of the corner of her eye, she could see the other platoons moving to the right before the barracks building at the very southwestern corner of the complex blocked her view of them. Squires' platoon paralleled Christine's to the left. The sounds of equipment and uniforms shifting, of men and women breathing hard from exertion, were as loud as gunshots in the still air. Christine reached the closest barracks and stopped, putting her back against its cold metal wall. She saw Squires arrive at the next building over, and then her rangers were grouping around her, Wilcox right beside her. To her right, the gap between the barracks where Squires' platoon was gathering and where she was yawned like a great chasm.

"First Squad, Second Squad, move in!" Christine hissed the command between her teeth. While the two squads moved into the gap, two others moved along the side of the building, training carbines around the other corner. Christine, Wilcox, and the remaining squad peered around the corner and into the gap, their weapons covering the advance of the first two squads. Christine saw them stop at the barracks door, kick it in, and then disappear inside. She breathed a sigh of relief when they emerged a few moments later.

Clear.

"Next one, let's go!" Christine ran around the corner and after Squads One and Two, who had stopped at the next barracks building, their carbines pointed around its sides and into the complex, covering the advance of the rest of the platoon. Christine ran past the two squads and up to the door of the building, Wilcox and Squads Three and Five close behind, Squad Four heading to join one and two in providing cover.

Christine steadied herself and kicked in the door, the impact vibrating painfully up her leg, her body armor clanking as she moved. She leveled her carbine and stepped into the black void of the barracks' interior, her pulse kicking up as the darkness surrounded her. She pivoted to the left and Wilcox pivoted to the right. Christine hoped to God he was sweeping behind the door. The man was not the same as Neville by any means, but he was not a ranger.

Having secured the corner to the left, Christine aimed her weapon down the long building. She smelled the sweet odor of wood smoke, saw a clump of ashes and partially burned logs. A few metal plates, some with crusts of bread rations sitting on them, were piled next to the ashes. A rope ran across the room, with what looked like laundry hanging on it. Someone had clearly moved in, made herself at home, and moved right on out.

"This one's clear. Let's keep it up!" Christine turned and followed her rangers back out of the barracks. She could make out Squires' platoon clearing the barracks north of her, their rushing forms coming in and out of view through the little alleys between the buildings. She turned right, and sprinted with Squads Three and Five to the next barrack. They set up to cover the paths leading out from the center of the complex, and waited for the other squads to follow. Squads One, Two, and Four streaked silently over to them, rounded the corner of the barrack, and kicked in the door.

"This is going well," Wilcox whispered, a hint of relief showing through his voice.

"Don't count chickens yet, sir." Corporal Lazaar spoke up from Christine's left, breathing hard from the running.

Christine didn't know how long they continued like that, leap-frogging their way from barracks to barracks, moving deeper into the complex, but in the screaming silence, it felt like hours. Sweat trickled down Christine's temples and down the tip of her nose as she sprinted, stopped, kicked in doors, plunged into darkness, and sprinted again.

Maybe the enemy really had left. The thought crossed her mind, but she stuffed it away immediately. She wouldn't get sloppy, not now.

She could see the center north-south access road ahead, and the rushing figures of the marines to their right were coming into view now, clearing buildings and advancing forward with impressive efficiency. They might not be rangers, but Christine didn't mind having them at her side.

Christine led her platoon forward in one final sprint, and emerged out of the barracks and onto the main road where it intersected with the east-west road. This area was a large opening, perhaps seventy yards across, no doubt where troops would have assembled for review and physical training during the war, an old flagpole sitting in the dead center, its old rope thwacking on its metal side in the light breeze. Christine looked to her left, saw Squires' platoon emerge along the east-west road. To her right, the marines were slowing to a stop as they moved straight along the north-south road. Further still to the right were the dark forms of Garrett and Rankin's platoons as they moved onto the east-west road on the other side of the complex.

"Let's hold here." Wilcox came to stand next to Christine. He repeated the command into his radio headset, and the attack force came to a halt, crouching down to one knee. The officers from the other platoons ran over to them, circling around Wilcox, the forward observers for Ames' artillery section following behind them.

"Did you come up with anything in your sectors?" Wilcox looked around the circle.

"Not a thing," Garrett said, adjusting his helmet.

"Looks like they've been gone at least a couple hours." Lieutenant Arnot stepped forward, the other marine officers nodding in agreement.

Wilcox looked across the road, his neck craning slightly. No one spoke for a moment as he seemed to study the rest of the complex. Christine stared at her boots, hoping to God Wilcox was about to say something smart.

Wilcox turned back to the group, cleared his throat. "Okay. Okay. I don't want us getting split up again as we move forward. We're going to continue the sweep, but we're going to move together along a north-south axis of advance. We'll send one half of the force forward while the other half covers them. We'll leap-frog row to row as we've been doing."

There was a chorus of "Yes, sir," and the officers ran back to their squads while the forward observers positioned themselves next to Wilcox. Christine breathed a sigh of relief.

Not bad, Wilcox.

She turned to her platoon, who were crouching here and there around her, some of them kneeling behind a stack of metal barrels.

"Squads One, Five, Four — advance to the other side of the road. The rest of you get into position to cover us."

Her soldiers leapt into action, the squads that were to move forward organizing themselves into a serried line while the supporting squads found cover. She watched as Accardo, one of the light machine gunners, pulled out his bipod and locked it down.

"Move forward." Wilcox's voice crackled over her headset.

She stepped next to Sergeant Néri and moved forward with the attacking squads, sprinting for the other side of the crossroads. They were moving fast, but Christine felt like she was trying to run in water, acutely aware of how exposed they all were.

They were reaching the middle of the road now, only a handful of seconds to go.

Everything went white. Christine blinked, recognized the shape of a flare burning against the black sky, and then the world shattered as gunfire burst from all around her. The whizzing of bullets. A scream. She fought the instinct to hit the dirt, kept running.

"Move into cover!" She shouted, willing her voice to break over the din. "Don't stop in the open!"

Christine reached the other side of the road, throwing herself flat against the side of one of the bunkers. She peered around the barracks into the darkness to the north, trying to locate the source of the fire as her troops came to a stop next to her. Something strange was happening. Christine could still hear the rounds slicing the air close to her head. A second later, two of her troops jerked and tumbled to the ground where they stood against the barracks wall, gasping and choking as they fell.

Can they shoot us through the building?

Realization clicked just as a round thwacked into the wall beside her. She looked down the length of the east-west road, saw the muzzle flashes sparkling from the woods beyond the edge of the complex.

"They've got us in enfilading fire! Move into the complex!" Unsure whether she'd been heard, Christine grabbed the closest ranger, pulled him from the side of the barracks and launched him around the corner into cover. She waved wildly to catch their attention, watched them move around the barracks and out of sight. She looked behind her, saw the other part of the force scrambling to return fire, and then ran around the building.

Her troops were waiting there for her, flattened against the barrack, panning their carbines around, searching for targets. The blast of gunfire from behind them was deafening.

"What the hell do we do now?" The voice was Henrikson's.

"As long as they've got that road covered, we're cut off from the rest of the attack force," Christine explained, catching her breath.

"We can't move forward without them, can we?" Lazaar spoke up from somewhere.

"We're assaulting those woods." Christine squared herself to her troops, putting every bit of confidence into her voice. "It sounds like the rest of the force is already putting them under fire. All we need to do is—"

Christine cut herself off mid-sentence, her ears sifting a new sound from the roar. She looked for Néri, met his eyes, and saw the same comprehension there. The sound grew louder, clearly audible now above the exchange of fire. It was hundreds of voices screaming, getting closer. Christine turned, jogging away from the battle behind her, and peered around the corner of the next barrack. A couple hundred yards away, she could make out the shapes of people running in a mass wave toward them.

Christine turned, strained her voice to shout over the terrible roar of the attackers. "Take defensive positions! They're charging!"

The rangers filtered among the immediate buildings, scrambling to find cover and good firing positions. Néri came to stand next to Christine, his face showing the same mounting panic Christine felt. Cut off by fire on one side, attacked on the other, the rangers were going to be crushed in the middle.

CHAPTER 13

Jack looked across the crossroads and saw Lieutenant Flores vanishing around the corner of the nearest barracks building. All down the line, the advancing squads were doing the same, fleeing the open ground of the crossroads to other side of the first line of barracks.

"Dammit!" He tucked himself back behind the steel barrels he had leapt behind when the firing had started, shifting to allow the ranger next to him to pop up and fire toward the woods, each shot splitting the air and vibrating through Jack's head.

How the hell had this happened? His mind cast about frantically for the best option, found none. His heart pounded in his temples, making it impossible to concentrate. Looking back down the north-south road toward the woods where their own support platoons were, Jack saw a series of flashes erupt from the woods. Osterman's people had clearly seen the attack from their position in the rear and were firing on the enfilading attackers with machine guns, though they wouldn't use anything heavier without clear fire coordinates. Then a thought struck him. He peeked around the barrel toward where the forward observers had been when the enemy machine guns had fired — and saw the lot of them lying in a heap.

Son of a bitch!

There was only one option. Jack tapped the foot of the ranger next to him, who looked down at him.

"Sir?"

"Can you see a radio operator?" He'd need the longer range of the pack to reach the howitzers over the intervening topography.

The ranger looked about. "Twenty yards to the left. One of Squires' troops."

Jack cautiously peered over the lip of the barrel, saw the soldier with the radio pack partially behind the cover of a barrack. Jack waved and tried to get her attention, but the woman was firing her carbine out toward the woods and didn't see him.

"You'll need to run over there," the ranger next to Jack said. "I'll cover you."

Jack shook his head. There was no way he could go out there. But then the ranger was popping off shots toward the woods and shouting for Jack to get up and go. Holding tightly to the grip of his pistol, Jack stood and ran hard toward the radio operator. He heard a bullet sizzle through the air near his head, saw a couple small puffs of dirt shoot up ahead of him. He reached the barrack, dove behind it, and landed on his stomach, covering his head.

A pair of hands hauled him up. "Sir, have you been hit?"

Jack looked around to see Squires examining him, his face thrown into relief by the intermittent muzzle flashes of the rangers firing nearby. Jack shook his head, pointed at the ranger with the radio nearby, unable to make a sound.

Squires nodded, walked over to the radio operator, and tapped her on the shoulder.

"Corporal Doussouba! Get back to the commander!"

Doussouba fired one last shot toward the woods, then jogged back to Jack with Squires.

Jack shook his head, cleared his throat. "Set that thing to repeat my signal. I want Ames on the line."

"What?" The woman tilted her head toward him.

Realizing his voice had been drowned out by the gunfire, Jack balled his hands into fists and shouted. "Set your radio to repeat. I'm going to call in coordinates!"

Doussouba slung her carbine over her back and dropped to one knee. While she worked the controls on her pack, Squires walked to the corner of the bunker and peeked out. Jack pulled a map from one of his belt pouches, finding their location on it. Using it to call in fire would be relatively easy, so long as Squires could estimate the distances to the enemy accurately.

"You ready?" Squires looked back at Jack. "We'll start with the bastards on the right."

A sound, like thousands of voices screaming rolled toward them from the other side of the barracks toward the north, followed a few seconds later by a new rattle of gunfire.

"Son of a bitch," Jack said. "They're attacking from the north." A chill moved through him as he imagined a human wave bursting through the line of bunkers and carrying him away.

A frantic motion caught Jack's eyes, and he saw Squires waving at him and pointing at the radio operator.

Jack straightened his helmet, his cheeks flushing. He holstered his pistol, keyed his mic with one hand, tried to shield it from some of the noise with the other.

"Foxtrot, this is Victor Six, requesting fire support. Copy my location, break." Jack fought the urge to yell over the noise as he spoke into the radio. It had been a long time since he'd been trained to call for artillery fire. "Grid Lima-Mike-Mike-November-five-three-eight-two, over."

The radio crackled, and Jack recognized the voice of the RTO in Lieutenant Ames' artillery section. "Victor Six, this is Foxtrot. I copy your location. Grid Lima-Mike-Mike-November-five-three-eight-two. Transmit your fire mission when ready."

"Foxtrot, Victor Six, fire for effect polar, over."

While the Ames' RTO repeated the radio traffic back at him, Jack looked at Squires, who peered around the barrack.

Squires turned to face Jack again, and cupped a hand by his mouth to shout. "Looks like direction one five hundred, distance five hundred."

Jack nodded and looked down at the map. "Direction one five hundred, distance five hundred, over."

After a moment, the voice on the other side of the radio echoed the direction and distance.

"Looks like at least a company," Squires said, peeking around the corner again.

Jack mouthed the word "okay" and turned to the hand set again. "Danger-close infantry company in forest, over."

Ames' RTO restated Jack's words, and there was a long pause. Jack knew that Ames and his troops were busy working out the firing solutions, selecting the proper shells for the target and terrain. Jack took the opportunity to get Lieutenant Mahoney's heavy weapons platoon on the line. He duplicated the same radio traffic with them, except this time Squires peeked out at the enemy group to the left and gave the appropriate corrections.

Just as Jack was finished speaking with Mahoney's RTO, the first voice from Ames' section returned.

"Message to observer, Foxtrot, quick, four rounds, target number Alpha-Alpha-zero-zero-one-three, over."

Jack recited the traffic back into the radio to confirm reception. A minute later, Mahoney's platoon called in their message to observer. Then, static.

"Come on, come on, come on…" Squires was shaking his head.

Jack gritted his teeth, the back-and-forth chatter between the machine guns of the enemy and the rifles of the rangers grating on his nerves, the scream of the charging enemy troops louder every second. Jack's people were dying out there, and arty was taking its sweet time.

Hurry it up, dammit!

Finally, the radio crackled. "Shot, target Alpha-Alpha-zero-zero-one-three, over."

Jack smiled and repeated the command. The first round had left the barrel.

He crept over to stand next to Squires, careful not to expose himself too much as he looked first left and then right down the east-west road. The rangers and marines were all behind various kinds of cover, only visible in the darkness because of the muzzle flashes of their weapons. In the woods on either side of the complex, the enemy machine guns were still firing. They'd clearly had time to prepare some kind of protection if the return fire hadn't hurt them much.

A shrieking sound filled the sky, drowning out the other noises of battle.

"Here comes the—" The rest of Squires' sentence was inaudible as the woods to the east erupted into massive, red flashes, one after another in a thunder that shook the ground and rattled up Jack's legs and into his body. Jack counted twelve impacts, then activated his mic again.

"Victor Six to whichever platoon is furthest east—

"That's Garrett's rangers, sir." Squires interrupted.

"—Garrett's troops, right. Raven Four, this is Victor Six. Assault the woods on your flank and secure them. We'll be doing the same as soon as the artillery hits the west flank. All other platoons move forward and link back up with the forward part of our attack force."

No sooner had he finished speaking then the radio crackled again. This time, the voice was from Mahoney's mortars.

"Shot, target Oscar-Papa-zero-zero-two-eight, over."

The shriek of incoming shells ripped through the sky again as the woods to the west tore themselves to pieces. They were much closer to this side of the woods, and Jack pressed his helmet's headphones hard against his ears, shutting his eyes against the deafening blast. When it cleared, Jack opened his eyes, about to order the rangers to attack the woods, but Squires was already out in the crossroads yelling at his platoon.

"Now let's move before they pick themselves up!"

The rangers catapulted themselves to their feet and toward the woods at a sprint, their fearsome shouts covered by the gunfire and screams carrying from the other side of the barracks.

Jack stayed behind with Doussouba long enough to give the end-of-mission command and damage assessments to the artillery and mortars, and then ran after Squires' platoon, Doussouba's radio backpack bobbing in front of him.

The woods ahead were silent, with small fires burning here and there. Jack saw a couple of flashes and heard the crack of a few rifles firing a second later. The shots began to increase in number, and Jack saw a patch of dirt to his right pop into the air. Then one of Squires' men ahead clutched his side and fell. Jack ducked his head and put every ounce of energy he had into running. The ground rose slightly, and then they were in the woods. By the flickering firelight, Jack saw the white bark of exploded trees, what looked like a wrecked, makeshift pillbox, and several bodies, some of them missing arms or legs.

A dozen or so enemies stumbled from behind trees and ran at the rangers, shooting their rifles from the hip. The rangers stepped behind trees or dropped to a kneeling position and fired, cutting them down one by one. Jack gaped as one of the rangers knocked down a charging combatant with the butt of his carbine and then drove his bayonet into the man's prone body.

Movement caught Jack's eye, and he saw something emerge from behind a bush and run toward him. It was one of the attackers, holding a twisted and bent rifle over his head, blood soaking his clothing. Jack stumbled backward, remembered where his pistol was. He reached for it, but his boot caught on something. Jack cursed and fell to the ground, his weapon still in its holster. The enemy swung down at him, and Jack rolled to the side, hearing the impact of metal on dirt. Jack drew his pistol, and fired at the bloodied man, who stopped in his tracks. Jack emptied the magazine, watching as bloody holes appeared across the man's chest. The man gasped and collapsed. He realized the slide had locked back and that he was still pulling the trigger.

"We've got to stop meeting this way." Jack heard Squires behind him, and then strong arms hauled him to his feet.

Jack's hands shook as he put another magazine into his pistol, pushed the slide release. "W—we need to get back down there, h—help the others." Jack bit his lip, willing the shake in his voice to go away.

Squires nodded, and in a second they were moving back toward the complex. In front of and below them to their left, they could see the rangers and marines who had taken cover behind the barracks, flashes erupting along the line as they fired.

"Holy God!" The voice came from one of the rangers, but Jack was too transfixed by what he saw to pay attention to it. Visible here and there through the barracks were the running figures of hundreds of men and women, rushing toward the rangers and marines, and falling by the dozens.

"It's suicide!" Jack shook his head, watching as wave upon wave of attacking enemies were mown down.

"If they want to die, let's go help them do it." Squires' voice broke over the screams and gunshots. "Let's go."

The rangers started down the hill, when suddenly everything in front of them exploded.

Christine lined up her sights with a man's chest, fired, saw him fall, then moved them to a woman only a hundred yards away, dropping her with a single shot. As fast as she could align her sights and fire, the enemies kept coming. The rangers would mow down an entire line of attackers and another one would follow closely behind them, firing wildly from the hip as they poured from the forest to the north and ran into the complex, each group making it just a little closer than the last. She could still hear the argument raging on the other side of the crossroads between the enemy machine guns in the woods and the other half of the attack force.

Christine felt the bolt on her rifle lock back, ducked behind the corner of the barracks, detached the empty magazine, and slapped another one in place. She watched as Private Krouri, kneeling behind a pile of empty barrels, passed another belt of ammunition to Private Accardo, who placed it into the feed tray of his light machine gun. Beside Christine, Sergeant Néri fired bursts from his submachine gun toward the approaching mass.

Christine turned to Henrikson, Clos, and Miller, who were shooting past her from prone a few feet away.

"Rifle grenades! I'll cover you!" Christine aimed around the corner again, surprised to see how much closer the enemies were now. She aimed and fired, moving her sights from target to target as they came apart from her bullets. Then a terrible rushing shriek filled the air, and a series of explosions rumbled from behind Christine and toward the right.

Good. That would be the artillery she'd heard Wilcox call for over the radio. Relief loosened her chest. The pack howitzers had opened fire. If only they could call them now. Unfortunately, the attackers were so close now that an artillery strike would kill as many of her troops as it would enemies. The Alliance troops would have to make do with smaller tools. Christine ducked back into cover, shouting back at her troops.

"C'mon! Where the hell are those grenades!"

She leaned out, fired again, and heard the thunk of grenades flying off the muzzles of three rifles. The advancing enemy line disappeared in fire and smoke, but a fresh wave of attackers appeared a second later.

The scream of shells returned, and explosions roared from behind Christine and to her left. A few seconds later, marines and rangers began to appear from around the barracks between Christine and the crossroads, joining the troops already shooting at the approaching attackers.

Good.

It meant some of the others had managed to survive the enfilading fire. She scanned the faces of the arriving troops.

Where's Wilcox? Squires?

She turned and aimed at the enemies again, concentrating on breaking the wave in front of her one shot at a time. She remembered the first time she'd shot someone, during the Milipa campaign on Annecy. She'd spent that night wondering about his family, his friends, before her sergeant had told her to stop wasting her time.

"Milipa fucker'd have killed you in a second, Flores, and don't you forget it. When you're out there, you're just shooting clay pigeons. Nothing more."

Christine kept firing, seeing only targets, filtering out any recognition that she was shooting people. They were targets, and they were moving closer every second.

BOOM. A target fell, clutching the base of its neck.

BOOM. A target spun slightly as it dropped.

BOOM. Another target fell sideways, tripping the target beside it. Christine felt the heat of the barrel radiating from the front hand guard.

BOOM. A target's face disappeared, its body falling limp. Christine concentrated on the press of her ring against the growing heat of the rifle, letting her training run her body while her mind hid somewhere sunny with Ryan.

BOOM. BOOM. BOOM. The target fell and Christine realized her sights were on air. She blinked, calling herself back to the moment. The enemy line was thinning. Through their ranks, she spied the dark trees to the north, clear and unbroken, troops no longer rushing from them. Either they had run out of people to send, or they weren't sending them anymore. Christine wasn't sure which option was better. One way or another, they would have to assault through those trees. Christine was about to turn to her troops to tell them to prepare to attack when she saw a few points of light flash among the trees. Then came a horrible shriek, this one different than before.

Mortars. Good God, no!

The barracks ahead of Christine and to the right exploded, showering shrapnel over the attacking enemies. A second later, another explosion burst behind her. She heard Sergeant Néri grunt, turned to see him gritting his teeth and holding the back of his neck where a piece of shrapnel had grazed it. Another explosion ripped through the alley only twenty-five yards from Christine, and she ducked behind the barracks. Dirt and debris fell from the sky and clanked off her helmet.

"Move up!" Christine shouted, moving her arm back and forth to get her soldiers' attention. The explosions were all around them, and she realized with a jolt that the enemy was bracketing their position. In seconds, the shells would strike among them.

"Come on! Let's go!" Christine gave her soldiers a push as they ran past her, and then she followed them, moving forward toward the straggling attackers, who ran at the approaching Alliance troops, firing blindly. Christine heard an explosion behind her, kept running. She stumbled over enemy bodies, then jerked suddenly backward. Someone had grabbed her helmet, was trying to pull her back or break her neck. She hit the release buckle on her helmet with one hand, drove the butt of her carbine back behind her with the other. Her helmet fell off, rolled somewhere, and she turned, saw a man there swinging a pistol at her, blood down one side of his face. Her boot connected with the man's groin, and he fell sideways and onto his back, holding his inured anatomy. Christine bit her lip as she pushed the point of her bayonet through his ribs. She put her foot on his chest and pushed down at the same time as she pulled back on her carbine, refusing to look at the man's face.

She looked for her helmet, couldn't see it in the darkness and the chaos.

"Dammit!" The helmet had her radio in it, but she couldn't very well stand there like an idiot looking for it.

She took off running again, looking ahead as her troops burst through the line of hostiles, clubbing them with rifle butts, bayoneting them, shooting them at point-blank range.

A barracks building exploded ahead and to Christine's right, and two of her soldiers — she couldn't tell who — fell, pierced by the metal torn from the building's side. Another explosion landed behind her and to the left. Than another just ahead of the charging line, showering them all with blood and bits of their opponents. Another ranger fell, holding her shoulder. Christine ran past her where she lay, tried to ignore the woman's screaming.

They were almost to the edge of the complex, just a few yards to go. Suddenly machine guns roared to life ahead of them, their muzzle flashes dancing between the trees.

"Cover!" Christine yelled, diving behind the closest barracks. She peeked out, saw the other marines and rangers moving into safety. One of them stumbled, tried to crawl, and jerked as bullets stuck him, then lay still. Another mortar shell screamed through the sky and exploded on the other side of the barracks. More dirt showered down, but Christine ignored it, aiming around the corner of the building to sight in on a muzzle flash. She fired, saw that the flash was extinguished. She searched for another one, felt a tap on her shoulder, looked, and saw Néri, his neck dark with blood.

"We can't stay here!" His voice was barely audible over another explosion.

"We can't move forward under those machine guns." Christine flinched as a mortar whistled overhead and crashed somewhere back toward the crossroads. She glanced back out at the line of forest. It was just far enough. She turned back to Néri. "Get the artillery on the line."

Néri nodded and turned to his mic. Christine listened as he called for Lazaar to set his pack to repeat. But then a sound tortured the night sky, rising above the noise of the mortar shells.

The artillery!

Christine peeked around the edge of the bunker and watched as the forest ahead dissolved into fiery explosions. The crash of mortars around her ceased as the woods shattered, the white of naked bark popping into view as trees tore apart or fell, their trunks mangled. The bombardment seemed to last forever, and Christine tried to count the shells, but stopped at twenty. Then the impacts stopped, and the woods fell silent, save a few agonized groans.

"Charge for the woods!" Christine shouted, heard other officers giving the same command from somewhere. Christine sprinted forward, the footfalls of the men and women beside and behind her almost drowned out from the ringing in her ears. Fifty yards. Twenty. Ten. The ground sloped up, and they filtered into the trees. In front of them were the bodies of enemy troops — at least a hundred — stripped of their clothes by the blast, cut in two, draped over wrecked machine guns, dangling from the branches where the artillery had tossed them. Still others were scrambling to their feet as the rangers and marines ran toward them.

Christine locked her gaze on a group of them a few yards away, raised her carbine and fired, cutting them down as they tried to stand. She kept running, heard the chatter of Néri's sub-machine gun, saw two enemies fall. She looked right in time to see an enemy troop swing at her with something. She raised her carbine, deflected the club, then swiped across the man's face with the butt of her rifle. He toppled in front of a marine, who bayoneted him and kept moving forward. They reached the end of the area wrecked by the artillery, and Christine could see a few straggling enemies fleeing into the woods. She dropped to a kneel, added her fire to that of the other Alliance troops. The enemies fell one by one until the forest was still.

Silence assaulted Christine's ears.

"Fifth Platoon, assemble over here!" She stood, looked around for her troops. Through the woods to the left, she could see movement. She raised her carbine, but recognized Lieutenant Squires a second before he called out.

"Third Platoon here! Don't shoot!"

A few seconds later, Third Platoon was gathered beside Fifth, which had coalesced around Christine. Stray rangers and marines walked by along the line, looking for their squads.

"Holy fuck! Am I glad to see you in one piece." Squires' eyes were bright in the darkness.

Normally, Christine hated the attention from Squires, but at this moment, she thought she could kiss him. She knew Ryan would understand.

"Are we clear on that side?" Christine thrust her chin from the direction Squires' troops had come.

"We left nothing breathing." Squires said. "Damn! When we saw those mortars hit—"

"We called the artillery." Wilcox emerged from behind Squires, pistol in hand. "Did it help?"

Christine looked around her at her platoon, knew immediately that they weren't all there. "Yeah," she answered at last. "It helped."

CHAPTER 14

Tom winced where he lay in the grass as the distant thunder of explosions carried over to him from the barracks complex. From the sound of it, the military had brought artillery. It wouldn't be long now.

Seven hundred warriors...

There wasn't time for mourning now. Their deaths would buy a brighter future for his people, for all the Alliance. He couldn't waste their sacrifice now by fucking up, not when he was so close.

Tom peered up the slope of the hill, could just make out a machine gun turret traversing slowly, the muffled whirr of its motor drifting over from the fort's superstructure. He looked over his shoulder, past the tense faces of the sixty or so people with him and down into the far away woods where the rest of the force was waiting. This was a huge gamble. If they were caught, the fort's guns would shell the woods and his entire force into oblivion. The Supervisor could say what he wanted, but warships were nothing without infantry to take and hold the target.

Tom looked ahead again, then continued his crawl up the slopes of the fort's outer wall, the weight of his rifle pressing through the thin cloth of his shirt. The smell of ashes filled his nostrils, made his throat tighten. They'd taken handfuls of the stuff from their campfires in the barracks and coated themselves with it before they'd begun the crawl up to the fort. It was the best camouflage they could get.

He reached the crest of the slope, peered down into the ditch. The ditch's retaining wall, made of white stone, was a light-colored blur in the darkness. Tom could barely make out the dark shape of a counterscarp bunker in the distance and the broad outline of one directly below. Tom turned, looked at the woman who was closest.

"Rope." Tom mouthed the words.

The woman nodded, passed the message pack. In a second, the coiled end of a long rope was passed up the slope and into Tom's hands. He tossed one end over the edge, saw his comrades grab hold of the other. The machine gun turret whirred again and traversed over where they lay. Tom's insides froze as he held completely still. He looked past the turret at the observation dome, willed whoever was in there to overlook them, to turn away. If they didn't... His gaze moved farther up the fort to one of the huge artillery turrets.

Don't panic!

The turret kept traversing, and Tom breathed a sigh of relief. Grabbing hold of the rope, he slipped slowly over the edge, not wanting to catch the eye of the observer with quick motion. He dangled in space, then slid downward, the rope burning his hands. He passed in front of the face of the counterscarp bunker, pushed his feet slightly against it to swing himself to the side. If Smith's intelligence had been wrong, if the bunkers were fully armed... Tom didn't want to come down directly in front of its gun ports.

He reached the ground with a soft thump just to the right of a gun port and next to a steel access hatch. Tom let go of the rope, turned slowly to look at the other bunkers further down the ditch in either direction, expecting them to open fire. But they remained silent. Tom scooted along the outside wall of the gallery to the steel door, put his ear against it. When he heard nothing, he placed his hand against the door and pushed. Locked, as he expected. He moved back the other way, expecting to be shot any second when the other bunker spotted him. He took a grenade out of the bread sack he'd tied around his waist, then carefully bent over, peeking in through the gun port. The room inside was completely empty. He turned and looked at the other bunkers, realized that they too must be empty. He stared into it, giddy satisfaction surging through him. The Supervisor had been right. Perhaps this was not going to be the slaughter he feared.

He tugged twice on the rope, then crouched as, one by one, his people crawled over the edge and down the line, the whir of the panning machine gun turrets audible over the distant booms from the barracks compound. When the entire group had made it down into the ditch, Tom selected Theresa, a short, skinny woman, to climb through one of the gun ports. It was a tight fit, but they managed to grab hold of her legs and push her through.

Malnutrition had its upside.

How fitting that the horror Tom's people had faced before the Legion began should give them the tools they needed to bring justice.

Tom listened to Theresa scuffling around in the room, looked in, saw her searching a control panel against the wall. She pushed a button, and Tom heard an electric buzz and a soft click as the door locks disengaged. A second later, the access hatch swung open, and they were inside. The interior of the bunker was smaller than Tom expected, and there were no machine guns, empty bolt holes drilled into the concrete floor the only sign that their tripods had been here. A short corridor went off to the left, a staircase at its end.

Tom took his rifle off his back and into his hands and ran into the corridor, padding down the steps as quietly as he could, the footsteps of his people echoing softly off the walls. Tom couldn't help but think of a cave. At the bottom of the staircase, the corridor turned left again. Tom peeked around the corner with his rifle. Seeing no one, he stepped out and moved down the tunnel, ducking his head slightly to avoid scraping the ceiling. He tried to picture where they were moving in relation to what he'd seen outside the fort, figured they were walking under the ditch and toward the superstructure.

The passageway was narrow, only four feet wide, and a shade too low for Tom's tall frame. Tom glanced behind him as he ran, saw how tightly packed his team was behind him. If someone caught them like this and opened fire, it would be over in seconds.

They passed a pair of steel doors, each labeled, "AMMUNITION — COUNTERSCARP — NORTH" and then came to another staircase, at least twice as tall as the last one. Tom took the stairs two at a time, coming to a halt at the short landing. He signed for the people behind him to stop. Ahead, the corridor split three ways. Tom squinted, reading a directional sign on the wall directly ahead. One arrow pointed down the corridor ahead next to the words, "MAIN LEVEL," while another pointed left, saying, "MG TURRET 2." Still another pointed right with the words, "MG TURRET 1."

Tom held his breath, peered around the edge of the landing and into the corridor. He saw someone at the end of the hall to the right turning around a corner and out of sight. The other ways were clear. Tom moved back down the stairs, turning to face the dark, sooty faces of his group.

"Two of you with me. I need three others." Five people stepped forward — Eugene, Harold, Delphine, Peter, Jennifer, and Oliver — good warriors, all of them.

"Harold, Peter, come with me. Oliver, Delphine, and Jennifer, you will go right, to the next turret. Be silent. And remember, our goal is to take prisoners. We'll need their help to run the fort."

They nodded.

Tom led the way back up the stairs, checked again to make sure the hall was clear, then turned left and ran down the corridor. Perhaps seventy yards ahead, the hallway bent to the right, and just a few yards ahead and to the left was another junction. One way continued forward, another went left under the sign, "MG TURRET 2." Tom turned left, finding himself in a small room with an open ammunition closet, belts of bullets glinting silver from the overhead light bulb. On the other end of the room the corridor continued and turned to the right, a metal ladder leading up through the ceiling straight ahead.

The observation dome.

Tom tiptoed toward the ladder.

"Harry, did you see that?" A voice echoed down from the hole in the ceiling. Tom froze.

A speaker crackled. "No, what?"

"They're really kicking ass at the barracks," the voice continued. "Oh! There's another one. Look at that flash!"

The speaker spit and crackled again. "Bob, how about you do your job and actually observe."

Tom crept up to the ladder, considering for a moment as the conversation continued. Then he took the corridor to the right, Harold and Peter close behind. The corridor continued past more ammunition closets, then turned left again.

This is a fucking maze!

Tom's skin crawled with irritation. He was like a trapped animal in this concrete box, expected someone to burst around the corner any moment.

Thoughts on the mission, Petrarcha.

Ahead, a large room opened up. He stopped just shy of it, flattening himself against the corridor wall. The room ahead was tall and cylindrical, its walls smooth, white concrete. In the center of the room were two, circular steel platforms, one just above ground level, the other much higher. They were built around a large, vertical metal shaft with what looked like two mechanical arms at its bottom, each with a counterweight at its end. A ladder led upwards from the ground platform and through the floor of the higher platform, which was enclosed by a metal cage. Tom could see two pairs of boots and two pairs of legs up to the knee standing on the upper platform next to what looked like the base of a machine gun tripod and the legs of a stool.

Tom moved into the room, then walked carefully up the short staircase to the lower platform. A loud humming noise filled the chamber. Tom covered his ears and looked over the guardrail at the metal shaft, which went down to two huge motors in a pit in the floor. One motor, connected to a series of cranks that were in turn connected to the counterweight arms, was silent and still. The other was running a wheel that interfaced with a large metal cylinder at the bottom of the shaft, rotating it in place. Echoing off the concrete walls, the sound of the motor was deafening. Tom looked up, saw that the upper platform was rotating, and realized that the motor was what caused the turret to traverse back and forth. Silence came over the room as the rotation stopped. An idea popped into Tom's head, and he slid over to the base of the ladder to the upper platform, where he held completely still.

"Looks like it's all finished over there." The voice of one of the two soldiers in the turret carried down. That must be Harry.

A second later, a speaker crackled, and Tom heard the voice from the observation dome.

"Yeah, wish our artillery turrets had at least fired. It'd break up the incredible excitement here."

"Keep your shirt on, Bob," Harry said. "Your shift is almost up."

The loud hum of the motor filled the room again, and Tom started up the ladder, the soft metallic clank of his boots on the rungs drowned out by the mechanical noise. He emerged into the turret just as it finished turning. It was a small space, no wider than the interior of one of the factory's supply vans, and just tall enough to stand up in. The bottom half of the room was a steel cage, while the top half was solid metal, several feet thick. The ceiling was slightly concave, like a shallow dome. In front of Tom were two men. One sat on a stool behind a twin machine gun, mounted on a fixed tripod. The other peered out of a small view port, a radio mic in one hand, a pair of binoculars in the other. The man with the binoculars began to turn around.

"What the—"

Tom kicked out, catching the man by the view port in the back of the knee. He crumpled backwards to the floor, yelping in pain. Tom bent down, snatched the radio from his hand, and tossed it back down the ladder. The machine gunner looked around, scrambled to his feet, but Tom turned and smacked him across the face with his rifle butt. The man fell sideways, and his head hit on the wall. Blood trickled from his broken nose as he slid to the ground.

Tom looked behind him, saw the man with the binoculars trying to stand, reaching for a series of buttons set into a control pad on the wall. Tom pinned the man to the floor with his foot, then struck downward at him with his rifle butt, careful to not hit too hard. The man shuddered at the impact, then fell limp.

Tom looked down the ladder, saw Harold and Peter gazing up at him from below, their rifles shouldered and ready to fire. He gave them a thumbs-up, then turned to look out the view port. He could just make out the counterscarp bunker they'd entered through below and the forest beyond. In the distance, the area of the barracks complex was silent now. Pushing any remorse out of his mind, Tom turned to the small control pad set into the wall near the view port. Studying it for moment, he saw two buttons, shaped like arrows, set next to a joystick. He reached out, pushed the lower arrow button. He felt the floor sinking beneath him and heard a motor grumbling below, the metal flooring to vibrating under his feet. Then the motor stopped, the turret having fully retracted.

Tom clambered down the ladder as the speaker crackled again.

"Harry, why have you eclipsed? Harry?"

Tom motioned silently for Harold and Peter to follow, and they ran after him back down the corridor to the observation dome ladder.

"Harry? Are you there?" Bob's annoyance was obvious. The thunk of boots on metal sounded from above.

"You'd think they'd just replace the telephones," the voice was saying. "But no…" The man's feet appeared through the hole in the ceiling, climbing downward. Tom slammed the butt of his rifle into them. Bob yelped and fell straight downward, smacking his head on the ladder as he went. He crumpled into a heap at the foot of the ladder, and when he made a shaky attempt to stand up, Peter punched him, sending him back to the floor, out cold.

Tom stepped over Bob and hauled himself up the ladder. He reached the top — a cramped little steel room with a swiveling chair bolted into the floor. Three view ports offered 180-degree views around the dome. Tom reached into his pocket, pulled a bright white rag from it, his sooty hands leaving splotches on the cloth, then draped one end of it out the center view port. Assuming the others had done their job, the rest of the attack force waiting down in the woods would know they could approach safely.

Tom climbed down the ladder and led Peter and Harold back to the main corridor, where Oliver, Delphine, and Jennifer were walking back towards him. Jennifer was massaging what looked like a bruise over her left eye. They nodded at Tom, and together they went back to the rest of the group, who were still clustered at the bottom of the staircase that led toward the counterscarp bunker.

"Okay," Tom whispered. "We're moving into the fort. Be on your lookout for any signs pointing us toward a command area or control room. Our brothers and sisters are on their way up from the forest and will reinforce us, but we must cripple the fort as quickly as we can."

Tom led the way up the stairs, starting to relax. This wasn't going to be as hard as he thought. This fort was rotted and frail, like all the Alliance. Tom reached the top of the stairs, his troops crowding around him, and he was about to follow the sign pointing forward to the main level when movement caught his eye. He turned to his right, saw someone rounding the corner, a soldier with a rifle on his back. The soldier saw them, shouted, then reached for his weapon. Tom shouldered his gun, fired, and missed. The shots echoed and reverberated off the concrete walls, a hundred times louder in the enclosed space. Some of Tom's people covered their ears, cried out in surprise. The soldier backed away and down the corridor, firing as he went. Tom saw Harold clutch his chest and fall, blood spreading beneath his fingers.

Some of his people started running after the soldier.

"No!" Tom shouted. "Leave him and follow me!"

Tom dashed forward, rifle at the ready, the thunder of his people's footsteps behind him. The corridor turned to the right, then back to the left, opening onto a wide hallway. Doors dotted both sides of the hallway left and right, and four soldiers ran toward them from the opposite end.

"Shoot them!" Tom dropped to his knee, and fired, this time hitting his mark. The soldier fell onto his face while the others knelt and fired back. A grunt. A scream. Then an explosion of noise as Tom's people fired back. The three remaining soldiers scattered, one of them seeming to trip and then lying still where she fell. The other two ran for the nearest doorways, sending wild shots into the group bunched around Tom. Another scream. Tom aimed and cut down one of the soldiers. The other jerked and cried out as the fire from the rest of the group hit him.

Tom ran forward again, flinching when an alarm klaxon began to sound. They wouldn't have very long. As he moved down the hallway, Tom looked to either side, peering in the doorways as he ran. While signs above them declared they were barracks, their dark interiors, stacked with boxes, told Tom they were being used for storage. Tom's heart leapt. It seemed the garrison here really was incomplete, just like the Supervisor said. Ahead, one of the doors was opening, and a woman stepped out wearing olive green uniform pants and a white undershirt.

Tom closed the distance between him and the woman, who gaped at him in horror.

"Back in the room! Now!" Tom thumped the muzzle of his rifle into her chest, forcing her back. He stepped inside the room to see some twenty-five soldiers, standing between the two rows of bunk beds and all in the process of frantically dressing themselves, their blinking eyes and groggy movements telling Tom they'd been asleep.

"Hands up!" Tom fired a couple shots over their heads. One of them reached for a sidearm, but a shot blasted from behind Tom, and the soldier's head split open, showering his comrades with blood. The rest of them reached for the ceiling.

"You," Tom turned pointed at six of his people. "Stay here and guard them. Kill anyone who resists."

Tom left the room and ran back out into the hallway. He spotted a sign that said "COMMAND CENTER" and pointed toward a staircase at the end of the hall and to his left. To his right, a solid stream of his people — the rest of the attack force — was running to join him. Waving to them, he led the way down the hall.

CHAPTER 15

Captain Sam Holden threw open the gun locker in the command center, the emergency doors clanging shut. They wouldn't last forever, but they'd give him time.

Sam withdrew a rifle, slung it on his back, and then took the others out one at a time, passing them to the waiting hands of the others in the room, eleven in all, not counting Colonel Neville and Sergeant Gram, the radio operator, who were still at their stations.

Sam turned to face the gathered command center staff. "Sergeant, get a barricade in front of those doors. Use anything you've got."

"Yes, sir!" Sergeant Brécourt, a broad, bear of a man, dashed over to the set of heavy metal tables arranged in the center of the room. The rest of the group followed, helping him tip them over and haul them into place, papers flying everywhere, coffee cups shattering on the concrete flooring, the noise barely audible over the blaring alert klaxon.

"Corporal, help me with this." Sam motioned Corporal Cassas to join him.

She turned from where she was helping set up a barricade and ran over to Sam, her long black ponytail flying behind her. Beyond the sealed doors, a few more rifle shots rang out, their sound muffled by the heavy steel.

Sam took one end of a large crate filled with magazines and infantry helmets, waited for Cassas to grab the other.

He glanced to his right, toward the radio operator's station, set in the middle of the huge line of control consoles and computer screens running the length of the back wall, facing the door. The colonel was leaning over Gram, yelling into the handset.

"God damn you," he was saying. "We need support now! We've been attacked by an unknown number of enemy soldiers."

Sam tuned out Neville's voice, lifted the crate with Cassas, and lugged it to behind the barricade that the other soldiers had set up. Hands dug into it, pulling out stacks of magazines. Sam took out a helmet and pulled it onto his head. Something banged against the door, and sweat beaded on Sam's forehead.

They're trying to ram their way in.

"The Verdun is pulling out." Neville's voice sounded high, on the verge of panic. "They've been attacked as well."

Sam looked over at Neville, who was staring into space, his face ashen. "Sir, what about our ground forces?"

Neville looked up, his eyes distant. "They're still at the barracks."

Sam took a step toward Neville, trying to jar him out of his dazed state. "What are your orders, sir?"

"My orders?" Neville shook his head. "Evacuate. Alpha Blue."

Sam waited for Neville to address the group, but the colonel just stood there, looking dazed, silent. Sam wanted to smack the man across the face. He didn't have time for this. He turned around and faced the rest of the group.

"The fort is compromised. We need to make it unusable to them. Lock out main systems, break anything we can get our hands on, then we need to get out of here. As command staff, we know too much about the fort's systems, and we'd be a liability if captured. We either escape, or we die trying — take our own lives, if necessary. Is that clear?"

"Yes, sir!" The defiant reply came back as something banged against the door again. The soldiers tucked themselves in behind the barricade, slapping magazines into their rifles.

Sam turned to Cassas, who looked at him through bright brown eyes. She'd recently been assigned here, the newest member of the command center team, and every time Sam saw her, he felt for a moment like he'd slipped into a high school classroom. So damn young. *Too young to die.*

He would not let that happen.

"The silo launch keys, get them!" Sam handed his ID card to Cassas.

Cassas took the card in hand, nodded, and ran to a control console set into the wall on the right side of the room, sliding the card into a small terminal. Sam jogged to the silo launch controls, just to the left of the radio station, and faced the huge bank of buttons and switches. The chairs where they had all been sitting and working only minutes before were tipped over or pulled out and facing in odd directions. Out of the corner of his eye, Sam saw Neville sink into one.

Sam focused on punching in the buttons to bring up the silo launch interface. The computer screen in front of him flickered on, displaying the status of the missiles. There were more than twenty still available and ready to fire from the mountain silo. Air hissed through Sam's teeth. He'd been well acquainted with missiles like this when he'd done a tour near the Milipa border. A solid hit from one of them could knock a capital ship out of space. Sam accessed the security programming, typed in the code to access the lockdown protocols.

"Captain!" Cassas' voice called out from behind him.

Sam turned, saw Cassas tossing a ring of keys toward him. He caught it, then rifled through the keys to find the right one. He worked it off the key ring, inserted it into the port next to the control pad, and turned it to the right. The computer screen flashed blue, then went red, the words SYSTEM LOCK appearing on it.

"What else, sir?" Cassas was at Sam's side, holding out his ID card.

"I'll get the radio. Take Gram and open up that access panel," Sam pointed to a massive metal hatch set into the left side of the room.

Sam took the card and searched for another key. He found it, took it off the ring, and handed the key ring to Cassas. Sergeant Gram, a tall, skinny man with red hair, stood up and followed Cassas over to the access hatch.

Sam turned back to the control panel, pulled out the key, then walked past Neville to the radio station. Another bang came at the door, followed by muffled shouting. Sam picked up the handset, and flipped a switch to turn on the PA system.

"All remaining Army personnel, we are code Alpha blue, Alpha blue." He heard his own voice reverberating around the fort, put the handset on top of the radio booth. He hoped to God everyone still remembered what that meant. Under Neville, running drills had never been prioritized. Alpha blue meant the fort was hopelessly overrun. Any remaining personnel — at this point Sam guessed some of the turret crews and maintenance groups were probably still free — were to sabotage their stations and then secure the entrance to the fort on the bottom level, allowing the top members of the command crew with strategic knowledge to escape. If they were able, they were to then hold on to as much of the fort as possible until reinforcements could arrive.

Sam turned to the radio's computer terminal, brought up the files containing its decryption algorithms. The Alliance military used only certain encrypted radio channels. Without a computer and the proper algorithms, they were impossible to monitor without a skilled code breaker and specialized equipment. Sam typed in the command to purge the system, and then inserted the key into the hole beside the computer. The screen flashed, then went blank. Sam removed his key, stepped back, and pulled his rifle off his shoulder. He slammed the butt of the weapon down, smashing the computer, the radio station, the controls.

Satisfied, he ran over to Cassas and Gram, who were heaving open the back access hatch. He stopped in his tracks and listened to the sounds at the door. The bangs were gone, replaced by shouts and light taps.

They're placing charges!

Sam doubled his pace, reaching the small antechamber just as the two soldiers pulled the door fully open. He looked inside, his eyes running over the small hatch on the floor and the set of switches and keyholes built into the wall. He took the keys back from Cassas, found the right one, and inserted it into the seventh keyhole from the left. He turned it to the left, flicked down the switch controlling the power to the control console, then turned the key to the right twice, locking the system. He withdrew the key, and looked to his right. The screens were flickering off one by one, the glow of the controls and screens fading.

Good. Just about everything.

BOOM. The room shook and a thunderclap rent the air. Sam realized he was on the ground, pulled himself to his feet, taking his rifle off his back and pointing it at the door. The door was bent inward, warped, smoke billowing from cracks in the cement and steel around it. Sam lowered his rifle, realizing that the door had held. It couldn't handle another blast. It was a damn tough fort. Under better leadership...

Sam put his rifle on his back again and helped Cassas and Gram to their feet. He then turned to face the soldiers crouched behind the barricade.

"ID cards." Sam coughed as the smoke filled the air. "Give them to me!"

The soldiers dug in their pockets, pulled out their cards, and held them out. Sam ran from person to person, then looked for Neville. He spotted him, still sitting in the chair. Sam dashed over to Neville, who dug his card out of his front pocket and offered it to him.

"Cassas, grab me a trash can. Gram, get me one of the emergency flares."

Sam double-checked the ID cards, made sure he had them all, and added his own to the stack. Cassas appeared a second later with a metal trash can, Gram behind her with a red flare, normally used to mark hallways when power was out. Cassas set down the can, and dropped the cards in it. Sam turned to Gram, took the flare, and pulled the tab from its top. It spit and hissed as it ignited, washing out the room's pale fluorescent lighting with a red glow. Sam stuck the burning end of the flare into the can, coughed as the acrid smell of burning plastic wafted up at him. When the cards had been reduced to a pile of black slag, Sam dropped the flare into the can and turned to face everyone in the room.

"It's time to go—"

Another jarring explosion interrupted him. The lights flickered, and Sam heard someone scream. He looked toward the door, saw a gaping hole, the door hanging to one side. Bits of concrete covered the floor. Sam turned to Neville, who had pulled a pistol from somewhere. Neville pointed the weapon toward the door and fired a few shots into the smoke.

"Let's get you out of here, sir."

Sam grabbed Neville around the shoulder and hauled him to his feet, just as rifle fire exploded behind him. He turned, saw Sergeant Brécourt and the others mowing down several attackers as they rushed into the room, Cassas and Gram firing as well from near the back access hatch. Bullets thwacked into the dark command console, shattering one of the screens.

Sam pulled Neville low, then dashed across the room to join Cassas and Gram. He left Neville beside the two soldiers, then turned to the hatch set into the floor. He cranked the hatch open, revealing a dark, vertical tunnel, a ladder set into its side. The emergency escape to the cisterns.

"Take him! Sam shouted to the Cassas and Gram, pointing at the colonel. They slung their rifles on their backs and grabbed Neville, pushing him down onto the ladder. Neville started climbing down, and Cassas and Gram followed a second later. Sam looked over at the barricade. The bodies of enemy soldiers were piling up in the doorway. Bunched up as they tried to enter the room, they made easy targets.

Sam waved to catch the soldiers' attention. "Let's move out of here!"

Brécourt nodded, and Sam could see him turn to four of the soldiers, his mouth moving, the sound of his shout lost over the crack of rifles. Four of the soldiers — Fletcher, Gosse, Becker, and Maher — moved from the barricade and over to Sam, filing one by one down the escape hatch. A bullet struck into the wall nearby, and concrete fragments were blasted in all directions, grazing the back of Sam's hand and stinging his face.

"You too!" Sam called out, waving at Brécourt and the five remaining soldiers — Wang, Queen, Heysen, Banks, Schmidt. Brécourt met Sam's eyes, held them, and shook his head.

Sam winced as another bullet struck nearby, realization hitting him like a fist. Brécourt and the others were going to buy time for them to escape.

"You son of a bitch!" Sam shouted at the top of his lungs. He couldn't just leave them there. He had to leave them there.

Brécourt saluted, then turned back to his rifle, shooting down two more attackers as they crossed the threshold.

Sam looked at the soldiers at the barricade, and saluted back. Then he slipped into the tunnel, closed the hatch above him, and climbed downward in the darkness.

Sergeant Brécourt watched as Private Heysen crawled over to the back access hatch, locked it, then came back to the barricade. They'd need to hold out as long as they could, though at the rate ammunition was disappearing from the crate, their stand would be brief.

Brécourt aimed his rifle around the side of the table, dropping two enemies as they charged through the door. Every shot had to count. Bullets whistled through the doorway from outside, where Brécourt could make out the forms of enemy troops popping out from around the corner, firing, and then running back into cover.

There have to be hundreds of them.

Already the bodies of the attackers covered the floor, a couple feet thick in the doorway. As fast as new waves of enemy troops rushed in, Brécourt and his troops shot them in their tracks. It felt like hours dragged on as the firefight continued. Brécourt saw Private Schmidt pop up to fire to his left, then jerk and fall to the ground, a huge hole blasted out the back of his helmet. Brécourt ignored the tight feeling in his throat, reached over, and pulled the magazine out of Schmidt's rifle. The other soldiers were still firing, doing their best to not look at Schmidt. Before today, these men and women had been desk officers, requisitions personnel. But they were going to die like soldiers.

Brécourt fired again, shooting through one enemy and into the man behind him. He felt his bolt lock to the rear, dropped his magazine with a clatter, and slapped Schmidt's magazine into the gun. Releasing the bolt, he found more targets, shooting them each in turn.

"I'm out!" Queen shouted, ducking behind the barricade and looking over at Brécourt.

"Me too!" Heysen set his rifle on the ground.

Brécourt pointed into the crate. "Grab some grenades. Keep fighting!"

Queen and Heysen each grabbed one of the twenty or so round grenades, pulled their pins, and threw them out into the corridor. Brécourt ducked behind the barricade as they exploded outside. He heard screams from the corridor beyond.

They must be bunched up tight out there.

More enemies charged through the doorway, splattered with blood, their eyes white with fury. Almost mechanically, Brécourt, Wang, and Banks cut them down with rifle fire, before Queen and Heysen tossed grenades into the corridor beyond. All too quickly, the pile of grenades dwindled, until Brécourt saw Heysen and Queen reaching for the last three grenades.

"Leave those," Brécourt said. He saw comprehension dawning on the young soldiers' faces, the grim determination in their set mouths.

"Yes, Sergeant."

Banks fired over the barricade, then tucked back behind it, setting the rifle on the ground. A second later, Wang looked over at Brécourt, his voice calm despite the tears on his cheeks.

"I'm out, too."

Brécourt, turned, shot two attackers clambering over the mound of bodies into the room, felt his bolt lock back. Numbly, he met the eyes of the others.

"Fix your bayonets."

The soldiers reached into the crate, pulled out the bayonets, unsheathed them from their dented scabbards, and fit them onto their rifles. Brécourt reached in, took the last three grenades, and shoved them into a pouch on his belt.

Three enemies were rushing the barricade, firing wildly. With a scream, the soldiers stood and met them with cold steel. Brécourt saw Heysen fall, shot through the chest. He lunged forward, caught the attacker beneath the chin with his blade, felt the man's neck snap as he twisted the bayonet and withdrew it, then turned to see Queen and Wang showering the other attacker with strikes from their rifle butts. Banks was on the ground next to them, clutching a wound on his arm. There was a clinking noise, and Brécourt saw a small, round object land next to Queen.

"Grenade!" Brécourt dove back behind the barricade, but he was too late. The very air exploded, and a wave of heat and pain washed over him. Brécourt shook his head where he lay, gathering his senses. He looked around, tried to find Queen, Wang, and Banks, saw what was left of them draped over the barricade like broken rag dolls. He heard footsteps, and tried to crawl. Pain shot through his legs. He looked over his shoulder, saw shards of shrapnel sticking from his calves, and a dozen enemies creeping into the room. He turned onto his back, tearing the grenade pouch from his belt. Black spots danced against his vision, but he willed himself to stay conscious. He pulled one of the grenades from the pouch and held it and the pouch together in his hands.

The enemies spotted, him, moved toward him. One of them was saying something about taking him to a Supervisor.

You don't have me yet!

Brécourt smiled, and pulled the pin.

S am stepped onto the narrow walkway that ran around the edge of the enormous cistern, felt the ground vibrate gently, a distant boom carrying from above. He looked up the dark ladder, pushed aside the emotions in his chest. They still had a long way to go.

"What the hell is the plan?" Neville had regained his voice, which echoed off the damp concrete walls.

Sam ignored him, pointed at Private Fletcher. "Move us out."

Fletcher nodded and led the way, the others following behind him, Neville muttering under his breath. Sam took his rifle off his back, held it ready. Hopefully the bastards hadn't found their way down here yet, though by the sound of muffled gunfire coming from ahead, he doubted they were so lucky.

They skirted around the cistern, a huge dark pool with pipes leading out of it and into the low ceiling. Even Sam had to crouch. He stopped for a moment, dug the key ring and loose keys out of his pocket, and tossed them into the water.

Try finding them there, you bastards.

Sam caught up to the group as they passed through a doorway and into another cistern bay. They plodded along in silence, sticking to the narrow walkway that crossed the pool. The smell of rust and stale air filled Sam's nostrils. The sound of gunfire was growing louder as they went. They crossed another cistern, and another, finally reaching a heavy metal door flecked with rust. Fletcher cranked the handle, then paused, shifting to allow Cassas and Gosse to help him. The door crank squeaked and ground open.

The sounds of fighting exploded into the room. Screams. Gunshots. Shouted orders. Sam looked out and saw a short staircase leading down to the wide, main corridor that ran around the cisterns on the lower level. Beyond and to the left was the corridor that led to the vehicle bay and the main gate. Just in front of where they were, a barricade had been set up, and Sam could see a dozen or so soldiers clustered behind it, next to Lieutenant Lory.

Sam turned back to his troops. "Becker, Maher, we'll cover. The rest of you, break across for the barricade when we say go."

Becker and Maher worked into position near the doorway, as the others shifted to let Sam through. Sam walked partway down the stairs, took a deep breath, then aimed his rifle around the corner.

Bodies littered the hallway. Further along was another barricade, where enemy troops were hiding and firing in bursts. Sam waited for one to pop up, pulled the trigger, and watched as the woman staggered backward, clutching her chest.

"Go!" Sam shouted over his shoulder as he sprayed the enemy barricade with fire. He heard Becker and Maher shooting from over his shoulder, the din of their rifles filling his head. He saw Neville, Cassas, Gram, and Fletcher streak past him and run to the Alliance barricades, where the waiting soldiers pulled them into cover.

"You two, go!" Sam kept firing as Maher and Gosse slip past him. He took a deep breath and sprinted across the corridor. He dove behind the barricade, and the air left his lungs as he hit the ground.

"Glad you made it, sir!" Lory shouted over the cacophony of barking rifles.

Sam rolled, sat up to a low crouch. "We're getting out of here, Lieutenant. What's the status of the defense?"

Lory turned from his rifle, huddled close to Sam, his green eyes oddly bright. "There are hundreds of them pouring in through the northern counterscarp bunker. We've got a position on the second level defending the machine gun turret over the gate. If they've managed to hold, they'll cover your escape. If not…"

Sam nodded. "It'll be a short trip."

One of Lory's group crumpled to the ground, clutching his shoulder.

Sam clapped Lory on the shoulder. "Good luck, Lieutenant. With any luck, we'll be back."

Lory held out his hand. Sam took it, and they shook. "See you later, sir." Lory turned back to his soldiers. "Keep pouring it on!"

Sam made eye contact with Fletcher, who tapped the rest of the command center group, getting their attention. Sam ran, bent over, down the corridor toward the garage, his group following close behind him. They reached a staircase, ran down it, and emerged in the vehicle bay. The colonel's jeep was there, next to a larger truck.

Sam hopped into the driver's seat of the truck, stuffing his rifle in beside him, and started the electric motor. The vehicle grumbled as the rest of the group climbed inside the open back.

"Stay low!" Sam shouted over his shoulder as he backed the truck up and drove it down the wide corridor leading toward the front gate. Sam stopped the vehicle next to two dazed-looking soldiers standing by the guardhouse. One of them had a bandage on his arm.

"Give us cover as we move out," Sam shouted down to them.

"Yes, sir!" They disappeared into the guardhouse.

Sam could feel the fresh, clean air blowing over him, could barely make out the tree line and the road paralleling the rail line below. He took a deep breath, then gunned the motor. The truck shot out into the night and down the road, gravel spitting and tinkling off its undercarriage as they flew. To his right, running toward the gate, were a few dozen attackers, who aimed their rifles at the truck, shouting. Beyond them, near the edge of the woods to the fort's north side, hundreds of hostiles were running toward the fort and disappearing into the ditch near the north counterscarp bunker.

Bullets thwacked into the side of the truck, and Sam ducked his head, pushing the vehicle as fast as it would go. A wall of noise washed over him from behind. He looked in the rearview mirror to see the west machine gun turret, the one closest to the gate, firing toward the enemies. Sam almost wanted to cheer. At least something was going well.

Several of the enemy soldiers were knocked down in their tracks, while the rest dove for the ground. Sam looked ahead, saw the line of forest drawing nearer and nearer. They were almost to the main road now. Just a couple hundred yards more, and they'd be away.

A patch of ground in front and to the left exploded. Sam cursed, swerved around the smoking crater. He glanced over, saw some of the enemies standing and pointing what looked like rocket launchers toward the truck. The turret was gunning them down just about as fast as they could stand.

They aren't afraid of dying.

The realization terrified Sam. He bottomed out the accelerator just as he saw one of the attackers get to his feet. The man jerked as bullets hit him, and fell to his knees, his rocket launcher still tracking the truck. A jet of smoke lanced out. Sam tried to swerve, but the road in front of him disappeared in a fiery explosion.

A hard bump. A crunching sound. A scream.

Sam shook his head, trying to push the accelerator. A second later, he realized that the truck wasn't moving. He blinked, saw that the front of the vehicle had toppled into the crater left by the explosion. He found his rifle, pulled himself out of the driver's seat, and hopped down to the ground, careful to keep the truck's bulky form between him and his opponents. He reached the back of the truck just as Fletcher and Gosse hopped out and joined him. A second later, Becker, Maher, Gram, Cassas, and Neville followed them.

Bullets whined nearby, smacking the truck with a metallic clanging noise. Sam ducked and looked under the truck. All the enemies who had been running for the gate were lying still, but others were shooting from atop the superstructure itself, just outside the effective firing arc of the turret. He glanced at the dark line of the forest to the southwest, perhaps seventy yards away now.

"Who's a good shot here?" Sam yelled over the chatter of the machine gun turret.

Cassas raised her hand.

"You're with me," Sam said. "The rest of you, run for it as soon as we fire."

The others nodded. Neville looked more than ready to bolt.

Sam got onto his belly, wrapping his left arm in the rifle's sling and aiming the weapon under the truck. He saw Cassas do the same next to him. He picked a target, careful to control his breathing, and fired. A second later, the enemy stumbled and dropped to the ground, causing the others around him to dive to cover instinctively. As brave as they were, they clearly weren't well trained. Cassas' rifle barked beside Sam, dropping another enemy.

"Go!" Sam shouted as he found another target, fired. He heard footsteps padding away on the grass. Some of the attackers seemed to have spied the group emerging from behind the truck because they increased their rate of fire. Sam picked out another target, lying prone and aiming toward the fleeing soldiers. Sam fired, and the target fell limp, as if he had gone to sleep. And then another — someone trying to stand with a rocket launcher — but Cassas' bullet put the target down before he could pull the trigger. After they'd knocked down several more enemies with precisely aimed shots, Sam rolled to look behind him.

The others had made it to the trees and were set up to cover him. He waved, saw Fletcher return the signal.

"Cassas, move!" Sam stood, helped Cassas to her feet. They sprinted together toward the cover of the trees. Clods of dirt exploded around them as bullets hissed past. The group in the trees was firing past them, toward the enemies behind them. Sam didn't try to see if they were hitting anything, tried only to concentrate on pushing his body as fast as he could move it. Suddenly, Cassas screamed, grabbed her thigh, her step faltering. Without breaking his stride, Sam caught hold of her arm, helping her dash forward toward the trees. It was only a few yards now.

Blinding pain seared through Sam's back. He cried out, felt himself slowing down, felt Cassas starting to fall without his support. His vision swam in front of him. He saw Fletcher reaching out, the edge of the trees just ahead. He gritted his teeth, gathering all his strength into one last effort. He threw Cassas forward, launching her into Fletcher's arms. Another barb of pain tore through him. Unable to take another step, he fell to his knees, saw Cassas looking toward him, shouting something at him, her eyes wide in the darkness. She looked so young.

Too young to die.

Sam waved an arm weakly, trying to make the others run. He hit the ground, and then felt no more.

Neville ran, crashing through the woods after the forms of the other soldiers, two of them holding Corporal Cassas between them. He stumbled, cursed, and kept running. He ran until his feet ached, until his uniform was stained and torn from the branches that reached out of the darkness to grab him, until his lungs burned and he thought he would die, the sounds of gunfire fading away behind him.

CHAPTER 16

"Get us out of the water!" Kim winced as another vibration shook the *Verdun's* hull. "We can't wait here any longer."

"Aye, ma'am," Stetler shouted from the helm.

"Atmospheric escape course plotted," Urquhart added.

Kim leaned over Voth where he sat at Wilcox's station, looking at a camera view of the fight outside. Small attack ships, some of them standard cargo tenders, others a kind of light fighter Kim had never seen before, were swarming in all directions, firing toward the *Verdun* where she lay in the water, only their engines visible as tiny points of light in the night sky.

Where the hell had they come from?

They'd been on the radio with Wilcox, hearing his report on the attack at the barracks. Suddenly, Voth, who'd just happened to be standing near the operations console, had seen incoming contacts on the radar. Luckily, they'd been prepared, easily fending off their first few attacks with flak and machine cannon fire. But for every enemy craft they seemed to destroy, another would show up. The *Verdun* was vulnerable in the water. She couldn't deploy whatever was left of her magnetic ordnance deflector, and the fighters would have a harder time protecting a stationary ship in the water. The only option was to retreat to a position of strength.

"How far away are the ground forces?" Holsey's voice broke over the din as the lift thrusters began to fire.

"They're still cleaning up at the barracks, ma'am," Chief Baudouin said. "More than ten miles away."

"We can't consider leaving them." The anger in Holsey's voice mounted, called to Kim's own frustrations. "They'll be trapped until we can return."

"If we don't get out of here now, there won't be a 'we' for them to return to," Kim called back over her shoulder.

"We've got several larger contacts inbound," Voth shouted.

Kim turned, saw Voth punching the controls to change the camera view, switching it to infrared. Kim's insides dropped.

"Holy son of a bitch!" Voth's profanities were much politer than the ones in Kim's head.

On the screen were the flickering, grainy green shapes of six warships flying toward the *Verdun* from the north along the coastline. They looked a little smaller than destroyers, a configuration Kim hadn't seen before.

"We're out of the water," Stetler was saying. "Beginning ascent procedure."

"We're not here to win a maneuvering contest, Mr. Stetler. Get us into space." Kim tapped Voth's shoulder, breaking his continued stream of profanities. "Tyler, I need you down in fire control. I want timed, high-explosive shells right up their noses."

"Aye, ma'am." Voth stood and jogged to the door while Holsey relayed Kim's orders to fire control into her microphone headset.

"Baudouin!" Kim turned. "Get Ensign Fowler up here to take operations."

"Aye, ma'am."

Kim walked to Holsey, who had her arms folded across her chest.

"Without support, the ground forces will be destroyed. You know that, right?" Holsey arched an eyebrow and fixed Kim with an icy glare.

Kim shook her head. "They may make it, but we absolutely won't in the water."

Holsey nodded ever so slightly, but said nothing back.

The ship was moving steadily upward now, the vibrations in the deck plates becoming smoother as the ship picked up speed. Muffled booms broke through the air, and the room shook slightly.

Kim glanced at the door as Ensign Fowler bolted in, his hands working his jacket buttons, his flaming red hair ruffled.

"I was in the mess hall. I heard we're under—"

"Operations, Ensign." Holsey barked. "Move!"

Kim watched the young man run to Wilcox's station, not sure whether she was more annoyed or amused at his inexperience.

No sooner had Fowler sat down then he turned around, his eyes wide. "They're shelling us. They don't seem to be hitting much, though."

"Let's keep it that way. Mr. Stetler, don't spare the whip." Kim left Holsey and worked her way to her chair. "Chief, get the fort on the line, tell them we'll be needing their silos immediately."

Baudouin nodded, then frowned. "Ma'am, I'm already receiving a transmission from the fort." Her hands flew over the controls, changing to the appropriate channels.

From across the room, Kim saw her grow pale.

"The fort is under attack," Baudouin shouted, her voice oddly strained. "They're requesting immediate assistance."

Kim bit her lip. "Explain our situation, Chief. We're not in any position to help until we can engage these enemy ships in space."

"Without the fort to support them…" Holsey trailed off.

Kim didn't look behind her, but she knew she felt the same despair as her second-in-command. There was no other option, and they would all have to deal with it.

Another boom, louder this time. Then another.

"They're bracketing us!" Kim's patience was thinning. "Commander, where are those shells?"

"Firing now." Just as Holsey finished speaking, a pulse vibrated through the deck, followed by a thunderclap.

Kim stood, walked over to Fowler to look at the monitors again. Another bang. She reached the ensign just in time to see angry orange and black clouds blossoming around the enemy ships, which slowly spread their formation apart. They gradually fell behind as the repeated volleys of shells forced them to give the *Verdun* some distance. But the smaller fighter craft were still chasing the ship upward, shooting small rockets toward it.

The room rattled again. An alert klaxon sounded from the damage control monitor, and Fowler studied the screen. He rotated in his chair to look back at Kim. "They hit one of our lift thrusters, but it's still functioning at reduced capacity."

"We're breaking atmosphere," Stetler said. "We'll be in space in a couple seconds."

Kim looked toward Baudouin. "As soon as we're up, I want the interceptors launched."

Baudouin nodded, keyed her microphone, and called down to Lieutenant Blake.

"I think we may want to reconsider," Fowler said, something in his tone of voice making Kim's pulse quicken. She looked down at the screen, which was now showing the view from amidships, pointing forward along the *Verdun's* hull and toward the ship's bow. As the sky faded gradually from pale blue to the black of space, Kim saw them.

At least a dozen more warships were holding position above the planet. A second later, the area in front of the *Verdun* burst into a solid cloud of explosions.

"Activate the ordnance deflector." Kim gripped the back of Fowler's chair as the deck shook again.

"It's still only partially functional," Fowler called over his shoulder. "We were only just beginning the major repairs."

"I'll take it." Kim heard the faint hum of the ordnance deflector switching on.

"We won't be able to make it through them." Holsey was at Kim's elbow now, her voice quiet. "We'll have to stand and fight."

"And get sandwiched in the middle?" Fowler shook his head. "I—I don't think we can take it in our current condition, ma'am."

The deck shuddered, and the lights flickered.

Kim watched on the screen as another set of explosions erupted in front of the *Verdun*. A second later, the *Verdun's* front turrets fired back, though Kim couldn't see the result through the wave of shell bursts that always seemed to stay just in front of the ship as it pushed into space. Then an idea came to her.

"Mr. Stetler, keep heading straight at the blockade. Maintain maximum speed."

"They're not going to just step out of the way," Holsey said.

Kim turned to meet her eyes. "I think they will."

"Ma'am?" Fowler looked around, his facial expression clearly showing that he thought she was crazy.

"I don't think they want to damage us," Kim said, holding Holsey's gaze. "They've had plenty of opportunities to hit us, especially with our damaged ordnance deflector, but they're mostly shooting in front of us."

Holsey's eyes widened ever so slightly as the same thought hit her. "They want to board us. Get us tangled up in their blockade or force us back to the ground and then try to storm the ship."

Kim nodded. "Mr. Stetler, push right through them. Commander, have gun turrets with forward arcs concentrate fire directly ahead. High explosive shells, same as before."

"Aye, ma'am." Holsey dashed back to her controls.

The *Verdun* raced forward, its turrets throwing volley after volley toward the blockade. Kim turned back to Fowler's screen, saw one of the enemy ships list to the side, explosions sprouting from its superstructure. The other enemy ships started to move away from it, opening a gap in the middle of the fleet.

"Ten seconds," Stetler called.

The forms of the enemy ships were growing bigger and bigger every moment. One of them had seen the gap, was trying to turn around to block it, but ran into a wall of cannon fire. The *Verdun* flew through the gap and pushed into the open space beyond.

"They're still pursuing, but they're not as fast," Stetler said, the relief in his voice obvious. "They're falling behind. Their smaller attack craft are turning around."

Kim sighed, releasing some of the tension in her chest, then turned to walk back to her seat. "Ms. Urquhart, set a course out of the system and to the nearest fleet staging area."

"Aye, ma'am."

"Getting the cavalry?" Holsey's voice held a note of hope.

"And bringing them back to put down whoever these bastards are." Kim sat down in her chair. "We'll be back in a day, maybe two."

"That may not be fast enou—" Holsey was cut off by a tremendous crashing sound. The deck lurched, and damage alert sirens chirped.

Kim folded down her console as the ship shuddered again.

"Never mind the bumps, Lieutenant," she shouted to Urquhart. "Keep plotting that course." Kim set her monitor to mirror the damage control station, felt her stomach sink. The bastards were—

"They're targeting the main engines," Fowler said, finishing the sentence in Kim's head.

"I thought you said they wouldn't damage us." Stetler shouted over another explosion.

"They don't want us going translight," Kim snapped back. "Holsey, keep the rear turrets on them. Do whatever you can to break them up."

"Aye."

A second after Holsey's reply, Kim heard an up-tick in the rhythm of fire from the rear guns. They were pouring out everything they had.

Another impact rocked the ship, and Kim held on to the console in front of her to keep from getting thrown to the side. The turbulence subsided, and Kim reached over her shoulder and clicked her safety harness into place. She tapped the damage control readout twice to set it to its report function. It blinked red and displayed a cutaway of the *Verdun,* with several sections magnified in the center of the screen. An interrupted power cable on deck sixteen, cutting off lights in that area. The damaged lift thruster had been hit again — no loss there now that they were in space. A stray enemy shell had knocked out the ship's external communications array.

There would be no contacting the ground team until it was repaired.

If any of them — or us — survive.

Kim pushed her growing dread aside and kept reading the list of damaged systems. The enemy had also hit the—

"Dammit," Kim slammed her fist onto her armrest. "We've lost the Keahey drives. We can't go translight."

Kim turned, saw all eyes on her. She ran over the possibilities, trying to not display her own growing fear. Another boom, and the lights flickered slightly.

Kim raised her chin. "Mr. Stetler, maintain speed." She turned to look at Baudouin. "Tell Frost to launch the interceptors. They'll screen us until we're out of range."

"At this speed?" Baudouin arched an eyebrow.

"They've trained to do it. We don't have time for comfort." Kim looked at Urquhart, who was oddly pale. "Lieutenant, plot a course toward that gas giant we passed coming into the system."

"Aye, ma'am."

Kim met Holsey's piercing gaze. "We are not out of this fight."

Supervisor Brack drummed his fingers on his command console as he watched the screen in front of him. The *Verdun* appeared smaller and smaller every second, and now it was spitting out smaller shapes, no doubt its defensive fighters. He felt sweat break out on his forehead. Everything had gone perfectly for Supervisor Smith on the planet. From the sound of it, most of the fort was already in their hands. Brack was not going to be the weak link in the chain.

"Supervisor," the boy at the weapons station called over. "Their fighters are destroying all of our ordnance before it can reach them. At this distance, we can't make hits."

Brack sneered at the boy's dirty, thin face, his ragged clothing. "Keep shooting."

The boy nodded, repeating the commands to fire control. The crew wasn't much to brag about. It took more to make a sailor than a soldier, or at least that's what Brack had argued. Any idiot with a rifle can fight, but give that same idiot control of a warship, and you guarantee disaster.

Brack returned his attention to bridge's holoports, saw two shells from the *Verdun* streak past the ship to their right, bending around its ordnance deflector, then exploding between it and the ship to the other side of it. The explosions washed over both ships, and one of them started to slow down, atmosphere venting from holes peppered in its side. Brack cursed under his breath. The warships they had acquired had done adequately against the destroyer they'd taken, but against a battle cruiser? They weren't ready. The larger ships weren't built yet. Now the entire operation was going to go to hell, and Brack would take the blame for it.

A few more of the *Verdun's* shells landed near the damaged ship to the right, this time striking it head on. The ship swerved downward, fire flowing from view ports and cargo bays as it tore apart. The deck plating shook under Brack's feet.

"Supervisor, the Righteous has been hit, she's—"

"I damned well know!" Brack cut the boy off and stood. "Slow down. Let them move out of range."

"But we'll lose them." The boy sounded frustrated, eager for the kill.

"For the moment, maybe. Keep them on our tracking scanners as long as possible. They can't get far, we know that much. Not without translight."

At least one fucking thing had gone well.

He turned around, looking toward the radio operator, an old man that the ground forces hadn't wanted because of a bad back. Now Brack was saddled with him. "Radio Supervisor Smith." Brack turned back to the screen in front of him, watched the *Verdun*, now a distant blue-grey shape against the blackness of space.

"And tell him…" Brack trailed off, thinking of something that would not raise alarm. "Tell him our pursuit is in progress."

CHAPTER 17

Jack couldn't remember the last time he had hiked so far. He stopped, stepped off the trail, and looked up and down the line of marching troops, adjusting the straps of his pack. The mixed force of marines and rangers were plodding silently through the blue-black of pre-dawn, their heads bent low. It had been one hell of a long night.

After they'd secured the barracks, they'd started the process of finding and identifying the dead and wounded. Forty-one of the men and women under Jack's command had died in the attack, nineteen marines and twenty-two rangers. Sixteen others had been wounded, though thankfully none too severely. Jack supposed he should feel proud of that number. About ten percent casualties for a strategic objective and more than six hundred enemies killed. Still, he couldn't help but feel like he'd failed somehow. The ranger officers, Lieutenant Flores in particular, hadn't helped the matter much.

When Lieutenant Arnot had read the final casualty figures, Jack had said he was relieved it wasn't more.

"It would have been hardly any if you'd listened to us and swept the woods around the complex first," Flores had said, her eyes burning in the darkness.

The other ranger officers had nodded, though Jack had seen Squires place a hand on Flores' shoulder, clearly trying to help her remember her place.

"I'm sorry you feel that way, Lieutenant," Jack had responded. "We followed standard attack procedure."

A commanding officer couldn't make himself vulnerable, couldn't show regret, not when other soldiers were nearby, carrying bodies. He needed to be confident. And who was Flores to be so flippant with the chain of command?

There was a time and place for everything, even criticizing your commanding officer. But in front of others on the field of battle was neither the time nor the place.

Flores had all but snorted at Jack's response, then returned to her platoon. That was when the fort had called for help. Jack had crouched next to Private Dawson, one of Lieutenant Arnot's RTOs, as first the fort's radio operator and then Colonel Neville himself had begged them to come help. An overwhelming force had struck the fort, and there hadn't been a damn thing they could do about it. Even worse, the *Verdun* had been attacked at about the same time, and Jack had watched with horror as it had risen from the horizon miles away and thundered into the sky, chased by what had looked like enemy warships and fighter craft. Not long after, the fort had gone silent.

They were alone on Kensington, with no support and with nowhere to go. And what Jack couldn't understand is how the hell this had all happened. The enemy was supposed to have been destroyed at the complex, and it made Jack shudder to think how many more of them could be out there. True, they'd seen a few leaving the complex before they'd attacked, but Jack had figured they were stragglers, not an entire attack force.

And what of the *Verdun?* Had she managed to escape?

Jack's mind flashed to his shipmates, the image of them burning to death as the battlecruiser crashed from the sky jumping unbidden into his mind. His stomach turned. He sucked in the damp air, releasing it slowly through his mouth.

Regardless of how the *Verdun* was, he'd get his chance to strike back soon enough, and he'd make it count.

Lieutenant Squires was hiking past Jack, his face crinkled in an expression of concern.

"Are you okay, sir?" Squires stopped beside Jack, shifted his carbine on his back.

"I'm fine, Lieutenant, thank you." Jack forced a smile. He didn't want anyone to see how this mess was affecting him. "How is your platoon faring?"

"As well as you'd expect, considering…" Squires trailed off.

Jack knew exactly what he meant. As soon as the fort had gone silent, Jack had ordered the attack force to move out. According to what he'd read, the fort's artillery — more than likely in enemy hands now — was more than capable of reaching the barracks. They'd had to leave their dead unburied, their bodies moved into one of the barracks to protect them from animals. At least Lieutenant Flores hadn't objected this time. They'd packed their gear, put the wounded on stretchers, and hiked south, meeting Major Osterman's part of the attack force on the way out. They'd left the jeeps behind after every one of the rangers had insisted they'd only make noise, give away their position, and wouldn't make it through the forest trails. Instead, they'd unpacked the OTRs — ordnance transport robots — from the trucks, activated them, and loaded them down with the disassembled howitzers and their ammunition. Jack had been skeptical, but looking at the path they were walking now, he had to admit the rangers had been right.

"We'll get our shot to pay them back." Jack put every grain of confidence into his voice.

"I'm counting down the hours, sir." Squires grinned.

They shifted to allow a train of stretchers to pass by, followed by the OTRs. Looking at them, Jack could understand why all the rangers called them by their nickname, 'gun dogs,' though he thought 'gun mule' would probably describe them better, based on their size. The robots stood four feet high on four legs, and the body of each was six feet long. A large cargo pod was mounted to their backs, and their heads — really just a collection of optical sensing equipment at the machine's front — were panning back and forth, their various instruments glowing red as they scanned the path ahead of them. The whir of gears and motors was a faint whisper as they passed, their cargo sections filled with pieces of the pack howitzers and boxes of shells. The sun glinted off the worn spots and occasional scratches in their camouflage paint. The gun dogs' technician trudged behind them, a controller in his hand, his rifle slung on his back.

Jack looked from the machines to Squires. "Do you know how much longer until we arrive at our stopping point?"

Squires rubbed his chin, the sound of stubble on skin whispering in the half-light. "I'd say we have a mile-and-a-half more to Bunker Thirty-two. Getting tired, sir?"

Jack raised his chin. "Lead on, Lieutenant."

Jack's feet had started hurting an hour ago when they'd crossed the rail line under a bridge, but he wasn't about to say that, not to someone whose respect he required. He wanted to show these rangers just how much Navy men could handle.

Squires grinned, waited for a gap to appear in the line, and stepped onto the trail. Jack followed him, shifting his pack again. The trail was skirting a series of dry ravines, the slope dropping off sharply to the left. The trees were packed close together here, their foliage thick, their leathery grey bark reflecting the growing light. As they hiked, the ground sloped upward, becoming rockier as they climbed. They turned the corner of a ridge, then plunged down the ravine. Jack felt his feet skidding out from under him, caught his balance, and watched how Squires walked carefully down the slippery gravel, bending his knees and taking small steps. Jack did the same, working his way down the trail. At the bottom of the ravine, the trail became a muddy mess. The sound of heavy mud sucking on boots as the rangers and marines slogged their way through the muck seemed loud after the hours of silent walking.

The trail tilted up again, working its way up the other side of the ravine before leveling out and contouring the lip of a craggy ridge. Jack leaned forward as he tried to keep up with Squires, sweat dripping off his forehead. The challenge felt good, to be honest. Anything to keep his mind off the *Verdun.*

Just as the trail leveled off, a faint booming sound rolled over the trees. Everyone dropped to their knees. Jack saw four figures running back down the line, Lieutenants Garrett and Flores, followed by Lieutenant Arnot and Major Osterman. Jack frowned, noticing the pained look on the major's face. The stubborn marine would be the last to admit it, but all this heavy activity couldn't be helping his injuries from the Triangle much.

"We're taking a look up top," Flores said to Squires. "Keep everyone down here on their toes. No snoozing or grab-assing." It impressed Jack how much weight Flores' word seemed to carry. As the senior lieutenant in the company, she was the ranking ranger officer, but even so, he had to respect the woman for leading her fellow officers so naturally.

"Good idea." Jack stood. "I want to see as well."

Flores nodded, and she, Garrett, Arnot, and Osterman stepped off on a perpendicular angle to the trail and headed straight toward the ridge's summit. Jack followed them, keeping pace with Osterman, who lagged a few steps behind the others and refused to meet Jack's gaze. The trees thinned as they climbed higher, letting more of the morning pre-light filter through the blue-green clumps of foliage. The ground transitioned from fine rocks to small boulders, and Jack scrambled over the pale yellow talus, holding onto his rifle sling with one hand to keep the weapon from sliding off his shoulder. He saw the others work their way behind a large boulder, and he followed them, taking care to move as silently as they had. He dropped behind the boulder to find Flores pulling out a pair of binoculars.

The booming sound came again, and Jack peeked over the lip of the rock in time to see a flash mushroom over the treetops far to the northeast. A few seconds later, another boom carried over.

"The fort's shelling the barracks," Flores whispered.

Jack turned, saw her binoculars pointed directly east, and turned to look that direction as well. He could just make out a large, flat-topped hill. A flash sparkled from its summit, followed a few seconds later by more booms. Artillery guns firing in the distance.

"Glad we're here." Osterman squinted.

"They're not firing too fast, though." Garrett's voice sounded relieved.

"Yeah," Flores muttered. The shell hit the barracks with a burst of light and, a second later, a distant bang. "Whoever is shooting probably doesn't know much about the guns."

"Are we still in range?" Lieutenant Arnot's voice sounded just to Jack's right.

"Everything between there and the dockyards is under the fort's guns," Flores answered.

Jack looked over at her. Her brow knotted as she continued to look through the binoculars. Other than a fidgeting motion — she was tapping a finger on one hand against the barrel of the binoculars slightly — she seemed completely unperturbed.

The fort fired again, causing something at the barracks to explode, a fireball racing into the sky. But this time, the booms that followed a second later came with something else. A low thrumming noise, growing louder every second.

"Get down!" Osterman hissed. Jack tucked himself close to the rock, saw Flores and the others do the same. The sound grew until it filled the air and rattled Jack's teeth. Then two shapes rocketed past overhead. Jack waited a second, then followed Flores in peering over the top of the boulder. What looked like two fighter craft were flying close to the treetops, moving in a broad arc toward the bunkers. Their slow speed and low flight path could only mean one thing.

"They're trying to find us," Jack whispered.

"Let's not oblige them."

Jack turned, saw Flores stowing away her binoculars. They crept from behind the boulder and down the rocky slope while the two searching fighter craft moved farther away to the east. A minute later, they arrived back with the other troops, who had taken cover along the trail, the tension on their faces telling Jack that they'd realized the danger as well.

"Tell me that was my dehydration playing tricks on me." Squires greeted them as they reached the trail.

"Sorry, Nate, but your mind's working fine," Flores said.

"I wouldn't bet on it," Garrett hissed.

Osterman spoke up. "We need to pick the pace up here."

"I don't want us still moving when it's bright out," Jack added, taking a step forward.

Flores nodded. "Then I suggest we take this stuff off." Flores pointed to her body armor. "It slows you down."

Jack shifted a little on the spot. "And if we're caught in an ambush?"

"We won't be, so long as we follow *ranger* protocol." The challenge in Flores' voice was obvious.

Jack didn't want to give her a chance to disrespect the chain of command again, but she had a point. Moving in rough terrain in this armor was like trying to run a marathon in a straitjacket. "Agreed. But make it quick."

"Aye, sir." Flores ran off back toward the front of the line, Arnot and Garrett in tow. A collective sigh of relief passed among the troops, no doubt getting the word that they would be hiking without armor now.

Jack dropped to one knee, set his rifle down, and slipped his backpack off. He carefully unclasped the fasteners that held his cuirass together on either side of his body, and slipped it off. Beside him, Osterman was doing the same. Jack watched how Osterman strapped his armor and helmet to the outside of his backpack, then copied him.

"You seem to be quite comfortable in this kind of setting, Major." Jack gave the strap on his pack one last, firm tug, the armor clanking softly.

"My unit served with a ranger company when I was a lieutenant," Osterman said, standing up and wincing. "You learn a few tricks like that in the field."

Jack stood and slung his rifle back over his shoulder, flinching slightly as his pack pressed the freezing, sweat-soaked cloth of his uniform shirt, no longer insulated by the armor, against his skin. It *was* much more comfortable without the armor, cold sweat notwithstanding.

After a few minutes, they were hiking again, their increased pace more than making up for the time they'd taken to remove their armor. The trail stayed at a mellow grade before climbing slightly and curving around the shoulder of the ridge. It dropped down and through another ravine before gaining a steep hillside, the sounds of the fort's artillery fading behind them. This one was at least completely dry at the bottom. Jack could do without the mud, thank you. He peered above him, the dark form of what looked like a concrete bunker silhouetted against the brightening sky.

The rumble of fighters faded into hearing, and the troops scrambled for cover. Jack crouched under a tall, dense bush next to a ranger private he didn't know, watching the sky. The dark shapes cruised low over the treetops, the warm burst of air from their engines blowing through the foliage. Jack covered his eyes with his hand, blocking the spray of dirt and small twigs from the ground, the smell of leaves and rain-damp earth joining the scent of burnt fuel. Jack saw the soldier next to him fidgeting with the rocket launcher on his back, almost wished he could give the order to fire. But then the fighters moved off, the sound of their engines fading into the sky.

The troops picked themselves up and continued hiking toward the top. The trail curved around the hill in an undulating spiral, but Jack sent the order up the line to leave the designated path and hike straight up the hillside. Faster, more direct, but one hell of a climb. The steep rocky slope was strewn with some kind of plant that thrust its long barbs up from the ground in tufts.

"Ouch!" Jack bit back stronger words as one of the barbs went right through his right trouser leg, just above the gaiter.

"Those suck the big one," Squires whispered from Jack's left.

When they finally reached the edge of the trees just before the cleared area around the bunker, Jack breathed a sigh of relief. The bunker didn't look like much, its grey concrete spotted with greenish clumps of moss and washed with streaks of black from the rain. The steel observation dome at its top was colored red with the patina of age. Regardless of how the bunker might look, Jack knew from reading the schematics that it had enough facilities below ground to support and supply up to two hundred soldiers. With more than four hundred bodies under his command, it would be a tight fit, but at least there was probably something in there to sit on. Its gun ports were like dark eye sockets, the warm breeze whistling past them. The temperature was rising quickly as the sun peeked above the eastern horizon, the air heavy and damp.

Jack took a step forward into the clearing, but Squires put a hand out, stopping him.

"You're visible from any of the nearby bunkers, if someone's watching with a spotting scope. We have to wait until dark." Squires dropped his hand out of Jack's way, clearly feeling like the matter was settled.

Down the line, the rangers were setting up where they were, and the marines, looking slightly confused, were copying them. Jack saw a few of the stretchers being set down, the wounded men and women on them groaning softly as they came to rest on the ground.

"I'm sorry, but that's not good enough," Jack said, looking Squires dead in the eye. "I want the wounded moved inside the bunker with the medical personnel. I want them out of this heat."

Squires stared at Jack for a second. "Yes, sir," he finally said, turning to the nearby stretcher-bearers and issuing orders.

"Major," Jack turned to Osterman. "I'm placing you in charge of getting the bunker squared away. Lieutenants Flores and Arnot will be in command of placing fortifications here. We may be here for a while."

Osterman nodded. "Yes, sir." He walked off to find Flores and Arnot.

"We're ready, sir." Squires' voice caused Jack to look around.

The sixteen stretchers were in hand again.

Jack listened for a moment for any fighters. Hearing none, he nodded at Squires, who led the train of stretchers out into the clearing and up the hill, the marine and ranger field medics in tow. They were just about at the bunker when Jack heard the sound of brush cracking to his left.

"What the hell is going on?" Flores was striding toward him, her mouth pressed into a frown, Major Osterman a step behind her.

"We're moving the wounded into safer facilities." Jack said, squaring himself to Flores.

"You're exposing our position." Flores glared up at Jack, crossing her arms.

"Possibly. But my guess is that they're all over at the fort still. We need to take advantage of the time it takes them to reorganize to set up here." Jack kept his voice even, but he felt his temper beginning to rise.

"You don't know that for sure. You're making a mis—"

"Lieutenant!" Jack cut Flores off, stepping toward her. "To be frank, I've put up with a lot from you. You may not like my orders, but you will follow them."

Osterman shifted uncomfortably behind Flores, and Jack thought he saw him nudge her slightly with his elbow.

Flores raised her chin, keeping eye contact with Jack, her dark eyes glittering. "Yes, sir."

"Good. Prepare defensive positions around the area. Major Osterman," Jack looked up at Osterman, whose face was set in hard lines. "Please see to the bunker. And I want both of you to pass on the word. All officers will meet in one hour for a briefing. Dismissed."

Flores saluted stiffly, then turned on her heels, Jack and Osterman watching her go.

"I think you've got a problem you need to deal with," Osterman said finally, a slight grin tugging at the hard line of his mouth.

"I'm glad you agree." Jack turned and walked up toward the bunker, where the stretcher bearers were filing inside one by one with their burdens.

"I don't think you understand." Osterman's voice held a steel edge.

Jack felt a hand on his shoulder. He spun around, found Osterman's face a few inches from his. "Major, what are you—"

"You are the problem, and you are going to deal with it right now."

Jack grit his teeth to control the anger that filled him, flushed his face hot. "Back off."

Osterman let go of Jack's shoulder but stood his ground. "I don't know what your problem is or what you think you're doing, but you need to stop blowing off the advice of the ranger officers, and you need to stop now."

Jack stepped backward and pointed at Osterman's chest. "You're out of line, Gordon."

"We are in deep shit here." Gordon continued almost as if he hadn't heard Jack speak. "They know this terrain, they know this style of combat—"

"And I'm just a desk jockey, is that it? If you don't think I'm fit to command here, why don't you and Flores start a club?"

"There it is again," Osterman said, his brow furrowing. "What is this shit about whether you should be in charge or not? No one is saying—"

"Bullshit." Jack spat the words under his breath and ignored the furtive glances of a pair of marines walking by. "You've been critical of me since the docks."

"This situation is over your head. You're not an infantry officer, and you don't have experience with ground combat. These people do, and so do I." Osterman stuck his thumb over his shoulder, toward where the rangers were setting down equipment packs, unfolding entrenching tools.

"See!" Jack held his arms out to either side, didn't care who heard him anymore. "You don't want me in command."

Osterman opened his mouth, but Jack cut him off, his throat tightening.

"And I suppose you think Flores is right. I suppose you think I'm responsible for everyone we lost at the docks and at the barracks. Hell, just throw the Triangle in while we're at it. I wasn't there, I wasn't doing my job, so people died. Just blame me for all of it."

"Do I, or do you?"

Jack stammered, looked for words, couldn't find them. "I... I don't... I did the best ..." He trailed off and stared at the ground.

"I see," Osterman murmured.

For a while, neither of them spoke.

Osterman cleared his throat. "I think Flores is way out of line in how she's handling this. I don't know what her issue is, but she needs to shape up or spend some time in a brig."

Jack met Osterman's eyes, but said nothing.

"But she has a point," Osterman continued. "You need to stop acting like a man who has something to prove and start acting like a leader. We're going to need a damn good one to get off this rock alive."

"And you're going to help me with that, huh?" The words came out more sarcastic than Jack had intended them to.

Osterman sighed. "Yes. And I expect Flores can too, if you can reach her. You're a good officer, Jack. I've known you a long time. You made it through the war just fine, and I think you can get us out of this. But until we're back on the Verdun, this is going to be a different kind of fighting, stuff you haven't seen before. Learning about it from people who know will only help you make the right choice."

Jack shifted on the spot, not sure whether to be touched by what Osterman said or pissed off. "You think they'll work with me?" Jack looked down toward the trees, saw Flores attacking the ground with her entrenching tool, her back to him. Jack snorted. "I'd be surprised if they forgive me for breaking their protocol."

Osterman shook his head. "You've got it all wrong. There's only one person who needs to worry about forgiveness."

"And that is?"

"You," Osterman jabbed Jack in the middle of the chest. "For yourself. There's an officer named Jack Wilcox that you've been blaming for things that aren't his fault. Knock it off."

Jack shook his head, fought a sudden wave of emotion that stung his eyes, removed any trace of feeling from his voice. "If... if you say so, Major."

"I do." Osterman shifted the weight of his pack, winced, then smiled. "Good. Glad we worked this out. This shit is getting old. Now, let's get inside and find some water."

Osterman set off up the hill toward the bunker's entrance, and Jack followed a few steps behind, his friend's words still ringing through his mind.

CHAPTER 18

Christine paced back and forth by the machine gunner's nest, hands clasped behind her back, her thumb pressing tightly against her ring. She was not in the mood for some damn meeting, least of all with Lt. Commander Wilcox. The man just begged to have his ass handed to him, but, for reasons of rank, Christine wasn't allowed to do that. She could deal with Osterman. Sure, sometimes he supported Wilcox, but he was a fighter, a jarhead at least. Wilcox was another one of these damn officers who'd spent too much time with their ass off the ground. She'd dealt with the colonel long enough. She wasn't about to have some other idiot pull rank on her.

Guilt tugged at Christine, but she pushed it away. So what if Wilcox had a point? She'd guessed that the enemy was still down at the fort herself, that they wouldn't be observing the bunker just then. But when she'd seen those stretcher-bearers stepping into the open…

"That temper of yours is a work in progress, babe." Ryan's words came back to her. She could see him lying on his side in bed, his grey eyes seeing right through her, his sandy hair tousled, the intensity of his gaze making her heart pound. The bastard! He always knew exactly what to say, knew how to tread the line between pissing her off and wooing her. He might as well quit being a teacher and become a tightrope walker.

Under Ryan's imagined gaze, Christine's guilt intensified. Maybe she had reacted incorrectly. She'd seen Colonel Neville disregard her unit so many times, and to be fair, Wilcox's orders *had* got them in trouble at the barracks. Incompetence cost lives.

Christine thought of the troops she'd had to leave behind at the barracks, stacked in that building like fucking sacks of flour. She clenched her fists and tried to shake the image out of her mind — only for a worse one to replace it.

Smoke. A burning house.

Her breathing accelerated, her heart pounding, a bolt of panic searing through her. She paced left, then right, closed her eyes, shook her head again, and bent forward. She placed her hands on her knees, focused only on breathing.

Breathe in. Breathe out.

She stayed like that for a few minutes, then stood again, her mind clear. She wiped her eyes and hoped no one had seen her. No one but Néri and Squires would understand. Her thoughts returned to Wilcox. If the man was another Neville, she'd make damn sure she'd keep him in line.

"But what if he isn't?" Ryan's voice played through her head again.

She felt the press of her ring in her palm, took a deep breath. No, she didn't trust Wilcox. He hadn't earned that yet, and he'd set himself back in her eyes at the barracks. Did he even give a damn about Kensington? About any of the troops his error had cost them?

She saw Wilcox standing next to Squires in her mind, pointing at the wounded soldiers sweating and groaning in the thick, humid air.

"I want the wounded moved inside the bunker with the medical personnel. I want them out of this heat."

Guilt pried itself into Christine's chest. When had Neville ever showed concern for his troops like that?

She didn't like how the answer made her feel.

Wilcox may have given orders he wasn't qualified to give, ignored the advice of people who knew how to fight on the ground. He may have been one of these arrogant desk officers who couldn't see past his own fleur-de-lis. But another Neville?

"Christine, you can't blame everyone forever for what a few people did." Ryan's voice returned, and she saw him staring at her, an eyebrow raised.

No, Wilcox was not Neville. Or at least she'd wait a bit to find out for sure. If she just shot off her mouth without thinking, *she'd* be the same as Neville, and she wouldn't let that happen.

"Thanks, Ryan," she whispered.

Christine shook the growing sense of guilt out of her mind and turned to survey the defenses the combined force had set up. They'd gathered downed branches and laid them in a deep pile circling the hill a hundred yards or so below their position. Anyone trying to assault their position would get tangled in it, though it was far too wispy to provide an enemy any cover if they tried to hide in it. Then they'd dug shallow scrapes, piled stones in front of them, and covered those with dirt to prevent bullets from blasting rock fragments at them. It was hard work, especially after a battle and an overnight hike, but the troops had got through it just fine, even faster than she expected. They'd spaced the heavy machine gunners out around the perimeter and on the flanks, then concentrated the mortars so they could fire toward the most likely avenue of attack, the ravine and the trail to the east. The pack howitzers had been left partially assembled. Should the Alliance troops need them, they could simply drag the carriages up into the empty gun pits next to the bunker and lock the barrel and recoil assembly into them.

Now that the work was done, half the company was manning the line while others were laid out behind them, napping. They needed everyone at their best. If the enemy had managed to take the fort, they likely had a very large force at their disposal. Perhaps not the best trained, based on what she'd seen at the barracks, but strength of numbers was sometimes enough. Only by putting every factor they could control in their favor could the Alliance force hope for a victory. And that certainly wasn't going to happen if everyone nodded off, like the private next to Christine was doing.

Christine nudged the woman in the side with her boot. "No time for that, now."

The private — Lloyd — shook her head and sat up straight, taking hold of the spade grips of her machine gun.

"Sorry, ma'am." Lloyd looked up at Christine, then over at her assistant gunner, who was also snoozing. "Wake up, Dale!" She slapped his helmet.

Dale gasped and looked around wide-eyed. "Ammo's coming, ammo's coming!" He blinked, seemed to realize he wasn't under attack, then flushed red.

"Sorry, ma'am." He looked at the ground.

Christine fought the urge to laugh, keeping her face serious. "I suggest you two find a way to stay alert. Tic-tac-toe or something."

The two soldiers nodded, blinking hard. At least they wouldn't have to wait long until they could trade places with the napping soldiers and have a break. As a matter of fact, she wouldn't mind one herself. Christine suppressed a yawn, squinting through the foliage toward the sky. The sun was beating down again, its heat made all the worse by all the moisture in the air. The smell of warm, wet wood filled Christine's nose as she took a deep breath, trying to keep herself alert.

"Lieutenant, they're waving for you." Lloyd's voice shook Christine out of her stupor. She turned, saw Major Osterman motioning for her from just outside the hatch to the bunker. She listened carefully for the sound of the fighters — they'd passed by again a half hour ago — before stepping out into the clearing. It was a walk of about one hundred yards to the bunker over cleared ground. Before this mess, the rangers had carefully kept the summit around each bunker clear. At last the damn thing was being used now and that work was paying off.

As she neared the bunker, her sight line cleared the top of the trees. She could see other bunkers dotting the nearby hills. If only they were garrisoned! Designed to support each other with gunfire, they'd form a formidable boundary to whatever force was attacking them. Then again, if Kensington were fully garrisoned, Christine doubted that the enemy would have even been able to reach the fort, let alone attack it.

Christine looked ahead to the bunker door, set into an alcove on the side of the structure and covered by a machine gun port.

"We're about to get started." Osterman gestured for Christine to enter.

Christine stepped inside, blinking at the sudden lack of light. The interior of the bunker was the same as when her platoon had last serviced it a few months ago. A polygonal concrete room with a steep spiral staircase in its center that lead to the observation dome. Eight gunnery alcoves were spaced evenly around the room, each with a pair of marines standing guard next to their squad support light machine guns. Not as good as the heavy machine guns that would have been installed there during Kensington's prime, but they'd do. In the floor was an open metal hatch, a concrete staircase leading to the lower levels, which Christine knew housed a few barracks rooms, supply vaults with food and ammunition, a lavatory, a kitchen, a water cistern, a compact generator, a radio and basic computer workstation, as well as a small infirmary. The air smelled stale, heavy with the odor of moist, crumbling concrete and moss. At least it was cooler inside.

Christine walked to the hatch to the lower level, Osterman a pace or two behind her. She stepped down the long, narrow staircase, her footsteps echoing slightly, then turned right when she reached a narrow landing. She flattened herself against the wall to let a marine private walk by, the corridor too narrow to let two walk abreast. At the end of the corridor were a few supply vaults and an open door leading into the radio room. She walked to the doorway and stopped, looking inside. Wilcox stood next to a small steel table, the other officers clustered around him. Squires, Garrett, Rankin, Mahoney, and Ames were there, next to the three marine lieutenants, Arnot, Colion, and Perez. Flores raised her chin and walked inside, meeting Wilcox's eyes.

"Let's get started." Wilcox held Flores' gaze for a moment before he looked toward the others. "How are your units coming along? Do you have everything you need?"

"Our MGs expended a lot of ammo during the fight." Mahoney, a petite, green-eyed woman with blond hair drawn into a bun behind her head, spoke up. "We'll need to re-stock."

"We'll open up the ammo lockers and see what we've got." Wilcox looked past Christine's shoulder. "Major, that's your responsibility."

"Aye, sir." Osterman's voice sounded from behind Christine.

"Anyone else?" Wilcox's eyebrows raised slightly as he looked from face to face. Other than Squires coughing in the moldy air, no one spoke. Christine shook her head, fighting the jagged edges of her fatigue.

"We've got a big problem in front of us," Wilcox said.

No shit.

Christine could guess that.

"The fort has remained off the radio. If we had any doubt about whether it's been taken, I think we can lay that to rest. The Verdun is gone. We've tried sending encoded radio pulses, but we've received no response. The range of this bunker's communications set is limited, and probably doesn't extend outside a low orbit. Either the Verdun is outside our range or… unable to respond." Wilcox's jaw tightened when he spoke of his ship.

Christine couldn't blame him. If her platoon were somewhere she didn't know about and possibly in danger, it would affect her, too.

"From my point of view, we have two objectives," Wilcox continued. "First, we need to determine the size and disposition of the enemy's force, and second, we need to re-take the fort as quickly as possible, while the enemy is off balance."

Christine's pulse kicked up a notch, all fatigue fleeing her body. She knew what the fort's defenses were. If the enemy garrisoned it even halfway properly, it would be one hell of a tough nut to crack.

Garrett stepped forward. "Sir, hadn't we better stay and hold out here and wait until the next ship comes for maintenance?"

Wilcox shook his head. "That could be weeks."

"Three weeks," Flores added, picturing the docking schedule in her mind. She'd always kept it memorized so she could plan her platoon's patrols accordingly. After the *Barracuda,* there wasn't another ship due until the

Leclerc, a cruiser that passed by every three months to replenish its air reserves and take on supplies.

"Three weeks." Wilcox nodded. "In that time, there's no telling how many more warships the enemy could bring here, each with additional reinforcements. Based on the numbers we saw at the barracks, it's clear that they've been amassing forces for some time. They wouldn't leave the majority of their people to deal with us and then send a handful to take the fort, so we have to assume that most of their force is still intact. The force at the barracks was just a rearguard to tie us down while the main body attacked the fort."

A mutter passed around the room.

Most of the force still intact?

That could be thousands, if the six hundred at the barracks had really just been a distraction.

"How do you suggest we attack the fort, sir?" Lieutenant Arnot's face showed more than a little apprehension.

"The usual way, Lieutenant. Frontal assault, but with a twist."

What the hell does that mean?

Christine could not believe what she was hearing. A frontal assault against that fort could only end one way — a massacre. She was about to shoot a reply at Wilcox when he pulled a small data pad from his breast pocket.

"I've...." Wilcox seemed to struggle for a second. "After our last engagement, I've taken some inspiration from the official ranger field manual." Wilcox placed the pad down on the table.

Christine bit her lip, grateful she hadn't said anything. He'd stopped short of admitting a mistake — and how could he, if he wanted to maintain the respect of the other officers? — but the gesture surprised her anyway. No, she decided, he was no Neville.

"I've studied the topographical maps of the area." Wilcox pointed at rolls of maps on the table. "There is a ravine that runs on the fort's south side. If we stick to it, we can get within two hundred yards of the fort undetected. If we use the cover of night to our advantage, we may be able to get under the fort's machine guns undetected. I think it's safe to assume these people are not yet completely familiar with the fort, and we won't be able to expect the best defense from them."

Christine shook her head. Wilcox had a point, but she didn't like the plan all the same. It meant exposing themselves, and they just didn't have the numbers to pull it off. If the machine guns saw them… She'd be surprised if any of them made it to the ditch, and then there were the counterscarp bunkers to contend with. But the plan *was* better than she'd expected. Clearly Wilcox had taken his reading seriously. Using the ravine was straight-up ranger.

She'd watched Ryan give critical feedback to his students once, and Christine tried to remember just how he'd expressed himself, the mix of praise and criticism, delivered with a warm smile.

"Sir?" Christine cleared her throat.

Wilcox looked at her, frowning slightly, clearly expecting a fight. "Yes, Lieutenant?"

"I think this is a decent plan." Christine spoke slowly, trying to copy Ryan's upbeat intonation. "But I think there are ways we could improve it also."

Wilcox blinked, taken aback. He glanced over Christine's shoulder at Osterman, then back to Christine, his face relaxing. "Let's hear it."

Jack studied Lieutenant Flores' face as she leaned over the map, explaining her strategy. It wasn't what he would have thought of, but he liked it anyway. At least Flores seemed to have stopped seeing him as the enemy. She wore a slightly scrunched expression, as if what she was doing was very difficult for her. Politeness had not been her forte, but he appreciated the effort nonetheless.

"I think if we try to attack the fort right off, we'll get cut up pretty bad," Flores was saying, looking Jack in the eye.

The other ranger officers around the room nodded.

"Even if we can slip in under the turrets?" Lieutenant Colion raised his eyebrows, clearly skeptical.

"That's a big if." Squires stepped beside Flores, pointing at the block shape on the map representing the fort. "And we'd have the counterscarp bunkers to deal with. If we got past those, we'd be fighting a huge garrison in the corridors of the fort. Anyone here ever deal with a fort of this design?"

Lieutenant Arnot raised his hand, as did Major Osterman, who nodded. "A big 'if,' to be sure, Lieutenant. But how you can assume they will be manning the fort properly?"

Flores straightened up, turning her head to the side to direct her voice toward Osterman, who was standing behind her. "I think if they managed to take the fort, it's 'cause the garrison were sitting on their thumbs. Even with a small garrison, if the fort was properly manned, they'd be able to cut up any attackers, especially untrained ones. They won't make the same mistake that let them get the fort."

Jack shook his head. "Just because the fort was taken does not mean the garrison acted incompetently. There could have been other factors at play. They may have been overwhelmed."

"I know the defenses there. And the fort hasn't been run well in a while, sir." Flores crossed her arms. "Under Nev—"

"I see your point." Jack interrupted.

He hadn't much liked Neville either, but he wasn't going to allow any officer to be insulted at the meeting, even a foolish one. A low snicker ran throughout the room. Apparently, Neville's command was unpopular with more than just Flores.

"What is your plan, then?" Lieutenant Arnot looked at Flores.

"I think we should attempt to draw them out a bit at a time instead of striking where they live. We can weaken their garrison enough that when we do attack the fort eventually, we'll have a better chance of taking it. At least we may not be as badly outnumbered anymore."

Jack frowned, thinking back to what he'd read about the fort, a glaring problem presenting itself in his head. "There's one thing you're forgetting, Lieutenant. The silos. So long as they have them, they can control the skies and repel whatever task force eventually comes here. Getting those silos is our number one priority—"

"Before the next Alliance ship arrives, yes, sir." Flores finished Jack's sentence. "But we already agreed that could be weeks."

"It's possible the garrison managed to lock the silos." Lieutenant Rankin spoke up from Jack's left.

"We're betting the garrison dropped the ball, remember?" Squires grinned in spite of the grim topic.

"But what about the Verdun?" Lieutenant Perez's voice cracked slightly as he pronounced the ship's name. No doubt he was as worried as Jack was. "They could still be out there."

"If they're as smart as your Captain Morden seemed, they've high-tailed it to get reinforcements. If they couldn't make it out of the system, well..." Flores trailed off, looking at the floor.

Jack wouldn't accept that possibility, couldn't accept it. The *Verdun* would come. They just needed to give her time.

"We have the advantage in the wilderness," Flores continued. "We draw them out and take them down. In a few days or weeks when we've softened up the garrison sufficiently, we can strike the fort with a greater chance of actually taking the damn thing."

Jack realized that all eyes were on him. He cleared his throat. "It's taking some risks. We could end up wasting enough of our strength that an attack on the fort is not possible, and there's no guarantee that the enemy won't continually reinforce their numbers. However..." Jack met Osterman's eyes. Osterman nodded ever so slightly. "I think it's less of a risk than attacking that fort straight off," Jack finished.

"I'd say we have a plan." Osterman smiled. "How will we break up our force to pull this off?"

Jack pondered for a second, thinking back to the ranger manual. "I think we'll devote our four ranger rifle platoons to staging the ambushes. Marines will stay here with the ranger artillery and heavy weapons sections and keep the home fires burning."

Rangers were better suited to the wilderness fighting anyway, while the marines would do as well as any at defending a fixed position.

Jack met Flores' eyes again. "Lieutenant, please prepare your plan and submit it to me in an hour. As the senior ranger officer, I'm counting on you."

"Yes, sir." Flores' mouth tugged slightly at the corners. Was there a smile in there?

"Anything else?" Jack looked at the other officers, who shook their heads or stared into space. "Very well. Dismissed!"

As the rest of the officers filed from the room, Jack met Osterman's eyes.

Osterman broke into that damn disarming grin of his. "See? What did I—"

"That's enough from you." Jack fought back a grin. "Get to work on re-supplying those units."

"Yes, sir!" Osterman turned and walked from the room, Jack staring after him.

Maybe this situation wasn't going to be so bad after all. So long as the *Verdun* could return soon… Jack's mind leapt to the faces of everyone he knew on his ship. He looked out into the corridor, making sure he was alone, then sat down, putting his head in his hands.

No, this was as bad as it could get.

CHAPTER 19

"Why the hell are you smiling?" Tom wanted to pick up his rifle and throw it into the Supervisor's face. He'd just spent ten minutes explaining the situation, but the man seemed completely uninterested, his legs propped up on the desk of the fort's previous commander — a name plaque said *COL. R. NEVILLE* — an infuriating smile on his face.

"My dear Tom!" The Supervisor shook his head. "When will you learn to not concern yourself with the little things?"

Little things?

Tom couldn't believe what he was hearing. Even with the fort's meager garrison caught off guard, they'd still lost more than two hundred warriors before all the defenders' barricades had been overrun. Supervisor Brack had failed to seize the battlecruiser. The forces at the northern sea, where they had staged their warships, weren't any closer to cracking the AI on the *Barracuda,* despite having tortured a handful of the ship's crew. Worse still, the Alliance force that had attacked the barracks had slipped into the woods and disappeared. Even patrolling fighters were unable to spot troop movements through the dense forest canopy, though it didn't matter now that the Supervisor had ordered them to join the fleet in orbit.

The fort's radio set was damaged, and its decryption computer destroyed, forcing them to use one of their own weaker, mobile radios. Even once the fort's communications equipment was back in order, they wouldn't be able listen in on the Alliance's encrypted channels. The silos had been completely locked out, and their attempts to crack the code had failed. Even torture wouldn't help — which relieved Tom, to be honest — since none of the surviving soldiers had had access to the system or sufficient clearance to open it up. Half the fort's command staff had managed to escape during the battle, while the other half had severely damaged the command center by blowing themselves up. To add insult to injury, the reinforcements they'd been expecting were late. While Tom had made some of his people who came from construction trades draw up plans for a series of special barricades to defend the fort's corridors, he feared they wouldn't be of much use if the Alliance arrived in force.

Tom took a deep breath, tried to remember that the man in front of him was a servant of the movement and thus a brother, no matter how foolish he seemed.

"Supervisor," Tom began, keeping his voice even, "there could be a military expedition on their way here. If the battlecruiser escaped—"

"Uh-uh!" The Supervisor wagged his finger, interrupting Tom. "Brack said they damaged the ship's engines. At sub-light, it would take them years to get anywhere."

"Until they repair their engines." Tom crossed his arms, giving his hands something to do other than slapping the Supervisor, which is what he wanted to do.

"And before they get a chance, our ships will find them and either destroy them or seize their vessel." The Supervisor put a simpering, pitying expression on his face. "You work yourself up over nothing. Relax. It's all going well."

"If you say so, Supervisor." Tom wasn't convinced, but he could see that the Supervisor was in one of those moods that couldn't be argued with.

"Smith, Tom. Smith. I have a name!"

Tom ignored him. "And what about our reinforcements? Why aren't they here?"

Smith shrugged. "Probably a delay. No need to worry yet. We do have more than two thousand troops at our disposal already."

Tom changed the subject. "I'd like to organize patrols to begin searching out wherever the remaining Alliance forces are. It would be easier had you not ordered our fighters to return to the fleet. We had air superiority and—"

The Supervisor clapped his hands, cutting Tom off. "And now they will help our armada find the enemy ship. They are much more useful up there."

Tom pretended to agree, nodded his head. "I will return to the command center and help with the efforts there. I want to begin work on the barricades."

"Good man." The Supervisor stood. "How long do you think it'll take to get the silos operational?"

"Our best computer technicians say at least a month." The Legion was a movement of simple people, but many of his warriors had been skilled with technology because of their work for the companies. However, the system of mechanical locks and computer codes protecting the silo controls was formidable.

"Plenty soon!" The Supervisor beamed.

"If you'll excuse me." Tom didn't want to see the man's smile anymore. He turned to walk away.

"Tom?" The Supervisor's voice made Tom turn around again.

"Yes, Supervisor?"

"Don't forget to have my transport brought over."

The Supervisor had claimed one of the cargo tenders as his personal transport. It grated against Tom's sensibilities. The movement was not about personal gain. But whatever the Supervisor wanted, he got.

"I'll send someone north immediately." Tom gave Smith a nod, then stalked out of the room.

As he walked through the concrete corridors from the Supervisor's office to the command center, he mulled over a mental list of dangers facing him and his people in his mind. The Supervisor didn't understand the peril, or else he didn't care. That fact bothered him, because the threat was real, and all of it seemed to revolve around that battlecruiser. Would it repair its engines and bring a fleet before the Legion could solidify its position here, or would it be caught and transformed into the movement's greatest warship?

Damn that ship!

Everything had gone perfectly until it had arrived, unscheduled and unexpected. Now it jeopardized any chance of holding Kensington.

Not for the first time that day, Tom found himself pleading with the universe to let the battlecruiser fall into their hands. Or, if that was not possible, to reduce it to burning waste. Everything depended on it. Either the battlecruiser would be seized or destroyed, or it would lead to their end. They were in too far now for any other outcome.

"Steady, Mr. Stetler." Kim felt the *Verdun* tilt to starboard slightly as it pulled out of the gas giant, the holoports clearing of the green gases and showing the distant forms of three enemy ships. They were making way toward the inner part of the solar system, no doubt sent to reinforce the enemy contingent on Kensington. But, like the group that had tried to pass through yesterday morning, Kim had other plans for them.

"All batteries report ready." Isabelle's voice chimed over the loudspeakers. "Shells loaded and ready to fire."

"Good." Kim looked over her shoulder at Holsey, who was bent over her console. "Pass this on to fire control: I want our fire divided between all three ships. I want them all gone in one, smooth pass." They couldn't risk spending much time in the open. Kim was certain the armada around Kensington would still be looking for them, and they couldn't afford to give away their hiding place.

"Aye, ma'am." Holsey keyed her headset and relayed Kim's orders.

"I've got our return course to the gas giant plotted." Urquhart called out, her chipper voice somehow soothing.

Count on Callista to lighten the mood.

"Ten seconds to optimal range," Fowler called out. "They still haven't seen us."

Kim heard the light tinkling noise of small rocks and ice bouncing harmlessly off the *Verdun*. The gas giant's orbiting cloud of debris was doing its job, saturating the enemy ships' sensors with white noise, hiding the massive warship bearing down on their positions. The *Verdun* was almost on top of them, and they didn't even know it. With the element of surprise behind them, they would strike before the hostiles had a chance to charge their magnetic ordnance deflectors or even bring their defensive emplacements to bear. As long as the *Verdun's* turret gunners did their job and scored good hits, this should be easy. But Kim knew better than to expect best-case scenarios.

"All guns are clear to fire at will when in range." Kim took a deep breath.

This had to go perfectly.

"Shells on the way!" Holsey shouted over the dull boom and vibrations that always came when the fifteen-inch turrets fired.

Kim concentrated on her screen, watching as the shells streaked toward their targets, willing each of them to hit their mark. The enemy ships blossomed into a series of explosions as the shells breached their hulls and detonated inside. Kim's screen fizzled as a series of white flashes obscured the ships. She blinked, and when she looked back, the three vessels were listing, fire spouting from their sides. Two of them converged together and crashed into each other. Another flash, this one larger than before, and the ships were completely torn apart as their reactors went critical.

The crew on the bridge cheered.

"Turrets report all salvos fired." Holsey's delight was obvious.

Kim had to admit, that had been an impressive display of firepower. Even damaged, the *Verdun* had plenty of teeth.

"Tell them to reload and return to ready status." Kim looked up from her screen and at the back of Stetler's head. "Mr. Stetler, bring us about. Best safe speed back to the giant."

"Aye, ma'am." Stetler bent over his console slightly as he manipulated the thruster controls. "Home again, home again, jiggity jig."

The seconds dragged on as the *Verdun* banked about, then powered toward the gas giant, the tension inside Kim's chest a stark contrast to the happy chatter of her bridge crew. Until they were back in cover, the game wasn't over.

"I almost feel bad for them." Urquhart turned to look over at Voth. "They didn't even have a chance."

"They had a chance." Fowler grinned, stowing his headset back in its holder. "They threw it away when they chose to take on the Navy."

Stetler chuckled. "The Navy: Every day an adventure—"

"Every day a victory!" Urquhart and Fowler joined in, completing the phrase from the familiar recruiting poster.

"Cut the chatter and pay attention down there." Holsey's voice silenced the others, who looked back at their stations.

Morden made a note to thank Holsey when she got the chance. At least someone else seemed to realize that the threat wasn't gone. Then again, with so much tension and concern on board for the ground team, who could blame the crew for celebrating the lighter moments when they came?

"Entering the outer atmosphere in ten." Stetler's hands made micro-adjustments to the controls, and the slight creaking of the hull told Kim that they were pulling into the planet's turbulent gases.

Kim turned back to her view screen, clicked to change the view to the aft camera, and watched as the stars were swallowed up by green vapor. It didn't look like anyone had been behind them. She exhaled, finally releasing the anxiety inside her. So far, so good.

She folded up her computer and stood from her chair. "Ms. Urquhart, continue to monitor readings from the sensor drones in the debris cloud."

Urquhart looked back over her shoulder. "Yes, Captain."

Morden turned toward the communications station. "Chief, if another group passes by, call me to the bridge. And inform Lieutenant Geonor to prioritize the engine repairs. I want translight capabilities sometime before I retire."

"Yes, ma'am," Baudouin nodded and keyed her mic.

"And don't forget to bug him about fixing the external communications array. If the landing party is still alive on Kensington, I want to be able to get a message through to them. Not next week, not tomorrow, now. I'll be in my quarters."

"Yes ma'am."

It had been a long couple of days, and Kim hadn't slept well. They'd hidden in the gas giant while the enemy armada had searched for them. Their efforts frustrated, the hostiles had returned toward Kensington. Repairs onboard the *Verdun* had begun immediately, interrupted only by these occasional sorties. They couldn't allow any more enemy ships into the system, not if they wanted to take on the armada later. They were already outnumbered, so why let the odds get worse? Besides, it kept the crew motivated. So many of them had friends among the ground contingent that had been left behind, and Lt. Commander Wilcox's presence was keenly missed. Without a working external radio, it was impossible to contact Kensington for the moment, so it was anyone's guess what was going on there. There was nothing more frightening than not knowing, and anything Kim could do to keep her crew in better spirits was worth it.

Kim stood and rounded her chair, walking toward the door, but stopped when she found Holsey standing in front of her.

"Mind if I join you?" Holsey's mouth was set in a firm line.

"By all means." Kim looked over her shoulder. "Commander Wilcox, you…" Kim stopped herself. She was so used to him being there that she'd spoken out of habit. "Mr. Stetler, the bridge is yours."

"Yes, ma'am." Stetler replied, the slightest hint of emotion in his voice.

Isabelle announced the change of bridge command as Kim and Holsey exited the room. They walked for a while in silence down the corridor, stepping into the stairway leading down to the next deck.

"We can't keep this up forever," Holsey said, finally.

Morden shook her head. "I don't think so, either." Their footsteps clanged against the metal grating of the stairway.

"What's your plan, then? You're not considering leaving the system without our ground party." The certainty in Holsey's voice caused a brief prickle of irritation to work its way into Kim's jaw.

"I consider all options, Commander."

They paused to return the salute of a shipman heading up the stairs, then reached the bottom landing, heading out into the corridor and taking a right toward the captain's suite.

"My decision will depend on how repairs go." Morden chose her words carefully. "If our engines can be brought back online quickly, we'll break our orbit here and leave the system, find reinforcements, and come back with a task force."

"In a few weeks." Holsey frowned. "By which time, our people will be dead."

Kim stopped in her tracks and looked Holsey in the eye. "The communication relays in this sector are out, probably taken down by these bastards before they attacked. The only way to alert the rest of the fleet is to play messenger and go to them ourselves. We have no idea what else is going on. There could be a fleet on its way to attack some other part of the Alliance right now. Given the scale of the incursion here, I think it's a safe bet that these guys are part of a larger force."

"Agreed there." Holsey put her hands on her hips.

"If we don't tell the rest of the fleet soon, a lot of people could die, a hell of lot more than are in our shore party, or even this entire ship. If we went off and tried to re-take Kensington against that many enemy vessels, there's a chance we'd be destroyed in the attempt, and no one would learn what has happened here."

Kim paused, putting to words the fear she'd been harboring ever since she'd discovered their enemy was human. "We could be looking at a full-scale civil war here, and what this ship does next will impact the outcome of the first battles, wherever they may be. For all we know, they've already happened."

Holsey's eyes had widened almost imperceptibly. Clearly the idea of conflict within the Alliance was as disturbing to her as it was to Kim. They started walking again in silence.

"Civil war?" Holsey's voice held the slightest twinge of fear, something Kim rarely heard from her.

"Think about it." Kim rounded the corner and stopped at her door, punching in her key code. "Our enemy is human. You saw their small arms. They're using Alliance technology, and there's no sign of outside influence. This sector doesn't hold strategic value to anyone anymore—"

"Unless it were someone trying to disrupt lines of supply and communication internally." Holsey finished Kim's sentence as they both stepped into Kim's darkened quarters.

Kim touched the light pad, then turned to face Holsey again. "I don't like it any more than you do, but if it means preventing our forces from being hit in a surprise attack, our landing party is to be considered expendable." Kim hated the taste those words left in her mouth, but she'd learned from years as second-in-command that being the captain sometimes meant voicing the most terrible truths, making the most inhuman decisions.

Holsey nodded. "And if they don't work?"

Kim blinked. She'd expected Holsey to fire back at her. Apparently, her rapport with the woman had improved more than she thought. "Pardon?"

"The engines? If they don't work?"

Kim smiled despite the situation. "Then we ram this ship down the bastards' throats. We're not letting them get a foothold on Kensington, and if we're the only ship that can respond, we'll have to do the job ourselves or die trying."

Holsey returned Kim's smile. "I think this is the first time I've ever *wanted* a system to be broken."

"Don't let Isabelle hear you." Kim reached her desk and sat down, fatigue suddenly weighing her down. "Regardless, our focus now is on repairing whatever we can and finding some way to get a message to our shore party."

If they're still alive.

Kim kept those words to herself, preferring to not express her fears, to not make them any more real.

Holsey nodded, seemed to look around for somewhere to sit. Kim suddenly felt very conscious of the lack of furniture in the room. She glanced at her refrigerator, wondering if there was anything in there she could offer Holsey, but the moment had passed, and the commander was already moving toward the door.

Holsey stopped when she reached the doorway, turned to face Kim again. "I'll light a fire under Geonor's behind and make sure he stays on task."

"And I'll tell him to keep an eye on you if you're near the engines. No sabotage on my ship." Kim smiled again.

Holsey's face remained impassive, except for a small twitch at the sides of her mouth. "No promises."

Kim watched Holsey exit the room and waited for her to close the door before walking into her bedroom and dropping into bed. But somehow, even though she could barely keep her eyes open, sleep didn't come, her thoughts lost among thousands of acres of forest.

CHAPTER 20

Lying on his stomach, Jack peered through the trees at the man trailing the enemy patrol, the one who'd been shouting at the others, encouraging them to keep up their pace. There were no markings on his uniform — if you could call the pale, stained rags that these people wore uniforms — but Jack would bet his fleur-de-lis that the man was some kind of officer.

"Everyone's in position." Lieutenant Flores' voice murmured from near Jack's elbow.

He glanced past Flores and down the line, impressed that the platoon was all but hidden from sight, not even the occasional bayonet or helmet peeking out from cover. No matter that he'd lost count of the number of ambushes they'd staged in the past four days. When push came to shove, these rangers knew how to do their jobs.

Patrols from the fort had started scouring the woods the day after the command briefing. The four ranger rifle platoons had been ready, dispersing into the woods and eradicating enemy patrols where they found them. It wasn't hard — whoever these opponents were, they weren't good soldiers, and even Jack could tell that they didn't know much about wilderness combat. They stuck to the roads, made too much noise, always clumped together, and never thought to use scouts to check for ambushes. He almost felt bad for them, but remembering the faces of men and women he'd already lost to them wiped away any trace of sympathy. More than that, he was too tired to care. They'd hiked many miles during the past few days, changing their position after each ambush. As Flores had explained, they couldn't risk staying in the same place, and they had to keep the enemy guessing about the location of their headquarters at the bunker. Jack couldn't argue with that logic, even if putting it into practice had pointed out certain deficiencies in his physical fitness. They had tracked this particular group for a couple hours, using the shouts and conversations of the enemies to locate them. They'd covered about a mile of tough ground almost as fast as Jack could jog it and then prepared their position on a hillside overlooking the old jeep road. Jack had only just caught his breath. He'd always thought of himself as a sporty individual, but it had taken all his willpower to keep up with the rangers — and not let them see his fatigue.

"We'll open fire on my signal." Jack turned his attention to his carbine, opening the bolt slightly to make sure it was loaded. He'd pulled the trigger on an empty chamber during their first ambush, and he wasn't about to repeat the mistake. He saw the silver glint of the bullet's base, then eased the bolt forward again. Since they'd begun staging ambushes, they'd burned through ammunition at a surprising rate, even despite the rangers' careful, accurate fire. The bunker had less than half of its reserves left, and the enemy patrols had curtailed the rangers' supply runs on the other bunkers and warehouses, making them extremely dangerous. It was impossible for them to carry off more than would fit in their packs or encumber them if they didn't want to risk being found. If the Alliance troops were to deplete their supplies before the *Verdun* returned…

Jack shook his head and focused his attention on the task at hand. The first parts of the enemy column were passing by on the road below, lit by the spots of sunlight that filtered through gaps in the canopy. He looked over at Flores and saw her squinting at the approaching enemy patrol from under her helmet.

"We're running low on ammunition, so make every shot count." Jack kept his voice as low as possible.

"If you need me to go through the fundamentals of marksmanship with you, just let me know." Flores turned to meet Jack's eyes.

"Excuse me?" Jack raised his chin. Everything had gone so well with Flores for the last few days. Was she really starting a fight again?

Flores stared back at Jack for a few seconds before a smile spread across her face, the white of her teeth standing out against her dark skin. "No sense of humor, sir?"

Jack relaxed. "The Navy forgot to issue me one."

Flores chuckled softly and returned to her weapon, a smile still on her face. "Copy that."

Jack felt himself grin. His working relationship with Flores had improved in leaps and bounds since the briefing. She was a little rough around the edges — forceful, stubborn, proud of her own and her rangers' abilities, definitely a field officer more than an administrator — but she was a damn fine lieutenant, and he'd been glad for her expertise on more than one occasion. Hell, he could almost say he'd come to like her.

The small, light bubble in Jack's chest deflated as he looked back down at the enemy troops. He shouldered his rifle, digging his elbows into the moist earth, its rich, soggy smell drifting up to him. Movement in the corner of his eye told him Flores and the rest of the platoon had done the same. He aligned his sights on the enemy officer's torso, finding center mass. He exhaled, taking up the slack in the trigger. He felt his heartbeat pulsing in his temples. The officer shouted something at the men ahead of him.

CRACK.

Jack felt the rifle recoil into his shoulder, and when the sights came down again, he could see the officer dropping forward, clutching an expanding red spot on his chest. A chorus of shots erupted around him as the rangers opened fire, and he trained his sights around for another target.

An enemy running almost straight toward him for the cover of a tree.

CRACK.

Another one fumbling with a grenade on a bandolier.

CRACK.

Jack had learned fast during the last couple days, and the rangers had been good teachers. Showing him how to use a rifle effectively, how to screen out any recognition of the target as a person, to treat each one as an object to be brought down. It made this easier to stomach. Jack methodically worked his way from target to target, dropping each of them with precise hits — and the occasional miss. The enemy patrol was coming apart, some of them trying to run back down the trail, while others, lacking orders, fired blindly into the woods. Little bits of branches and pieces of leaves sprinkled down around Jack as the enemy bullets shredded the foliage but missed their marks.

Jack raised his head from his rifle and shouted over the din to Flores. "Remember, I want a prisoner this time."

Throughout all their engagements so far, going all the way back to that first ambush on the docks, they had not yet managed to catch one of the enemy troops alive. The ferocity of the fighting had been such that none had surrendered, and Jack had noted that taking prisoners was not the rangers' first nature.

"Aye sir!" Flores' response was barely audible as one of the rangers peppered the enemies below with a machine gun.

There were only a few enemies left now, trying to return fire from behind trees or among the toppled bodies of their comrades. One by one, they fell under the precise fire of Flores' platoon.

"Cease fire!" Flores turned on her side, waving her open hand in front of her face. The ranger's guns fell silent, the boom of one last shot knocking down another enemy soldier. Jack scanned the trail for survivors, didn't see any.

"Damn!" Jack shook his head. "We can't keep screwing this up." He started standing up, but felt Flores' hand push him back down.

"There." She pointed her bayonet in the direction of a fat tree with a large knot near its base.

Jack caught sight of what looked like an elbow protruding from behind the trunk, felt a brief wave of embarrassment wash through him for having not seen it.

Jack cleared his throat. "Surrender!" He set his rifle down and cupped his hands over his mouth. "If you come out now and throw down your weapon, you will not be harmed."

The person answered by firing in Jack's direction, the bullet striking a tree a few feet to Jack's left and blasting a chunk out of its side.

Jack flinched and watched as the man below ducked back into cover. "There's no reason for you to die. Come out now and surrender."

Silence. Jack glanced over at Flores, who shrugged her shoulders.

"We know you're tired, son."

Jack looked around to see where the voice had come from, and turned to see Sergeant Néri crawling up next to him from the left.

"It's hot. Your friends are dead. Let us help." Néri continued, his deep, gravelly voice filling the woods and carrying with it a clear sense of the size and strength of the man who produced it.

Jack gaped at the sergeant. Since when had the gruff NCO become a psychologist?

"Fuck you!" The panic in the enemy's voice was obvious. "You killed them! You bastards! Don't you know we're trying to save you? We're trying to save you all! And you serve the monster. You're just like them." The man fired several shots toward the rangers, stopped. Jack could hear him muttering curses under the metallic clacking of the man dropping an empty magazine.

Jack saw Flores raise her carbine out of the corner of his eye.

"We don't have time for this," she hissed between her teeth.

Jack couldn't argue with that. The noise of the ambush would no doubt attract any nearby enemy patrols, and the Alliance troops would need to move quickly to avoid being caught. With their ammunition almost gone, they needed to return to the bunker to re-supply, but only after a circuitous, confusing, exhausting route that would throw off their pursuers. They couldn't risk doing that if another patrol was following them too closely.

"Be careful," Jack said. He watched as Flores took careful aim, then fired.

The bullet struck the edge of the trunk near where the man was hiding. He screamed, no doubt stung by the shards of wood from the round's impact. Suddenly the man darted from behind cover, one arm over his face, a rifle held in his free hand. He was running back along the road, his ragged clothing flying behind him. Jack gasped as Flores fired again. The enemy screamed and fell onto his face.

Anger built at Jack's temples. This had been the best chance in a long time to finally get some information about this damned mess, and they'd ruined it.

"I said be careful, Lieutenant!" Jack turned to Flores, but found himself looking at her boot.

"I was." Flores ran down the hill toward the man. Jack stood up and followed, seeing with a rush of relief that the man was squirming where he lay, clutching one hand to his calf.

Flores was nearly to him, and the man was reaching for something at his side. Adrenaline surged up into Jack's throat as he saw what it was.

A grenade!

"Lieutenant, get ba—"

"Knock it the fuck off!" Flores interrupted Jack's shout as she knocked the man's hands away from the grenade with the flat side of her bayonet. She pushed the blade point up to the man's throat. "Unless you want to be shish-kebab, you stop moving, okay? My troops are real hungry after tracking your ass."

"Bitch!" The man spat up at Flores, but Jack saw the lieutenant merely put her foot on the enemy's wounded leg and press down. The man yelped and whimpered.

"That's cute, buddy. Real cute."

Jack reached Flores' side, felt Néri, Corporal Lazaar, and one of the other rangers — a rifleman named Aziz — beside him.

"Get him up, and see to that injury." Jack turned to Néri. "I don't want him bleeding out."

"Sir." Néri nodded, gestured to Aziz, and the two of them hauled the prisoner to his feet. He shrieked when his weight came onto his wounded leg.

"Strap him to something." Flores stepped out of the way, tearing the man's grenade belt off of him as Aziz and Néri dragged him away. "And gag him. We need to move out of here now."

They spent a few more minutes picking the fallen enemies clean of ammunition and grenades while the platoon medic clotted and bandaged the prisoner's wound. They then struck out south, climbing high into the wooded ridge.

Jack breathed hard, sweat dripping down his nose from under his helmet in the thick, humid air. It would be a few more hours before they got back to the bunker, and it would be one hell of a hike. Jack was beginning to get a solid sense of the topography, and he knew Flores would take a hard route there, something that would throw off or slow down pursuers.

He turned his thoughts from his screaming calf muscles and almost moaned at the thought of the coolness of the bunker's concrete interior and the cold cistern water that would be waiting there.

"You did good." Flores' voice interrupted Jack's reverie.

Jack turned to see Flores walking next to him and felt a stab of annoyance at the fact that she wasn't even breathing hard. He brushed it aside and grinned. "Thanks. You too, Lieutenant. That was a good shot. I thought you'd killed him for a second."

"Thank you, sir." Then all humor left Flores' face, and she looked at him with exaggerated seriousness, her eyes wide. "I can always arrange that marksmanship course for you, sir."

Jack shook his head and laughed in spite of himself. "As long as I can give you a course in military decorum."

Flores frowned slightly, then did something Jack didn't expect and laughed, throwing her head back slightly and then shaking it from side to side. "Aye sir. But you be careful now. The Navy didn't issue you a sense of humor, remember?"

"I won't tell if you don't."

Flores laughed again, then accelerated her pace. Jack smiled, watching her dodge between trees as she jogged up the slope toward the head of the column.

N eville stopped walking and leaned against a thick tree to catch his breath. He squinted up at the bright sunlight breaking here and there through the blue-green canopy of leaves, wishing that a breeze would rustle through them. The damp heat was growing every hour, and Neville felt like he was burning up. He wiped the sweat off of his forehead, flapped his arms slightly to fan the sweat-soaked fabric of his uniform shirt. Doing this alone was even harder than he'd thought, and the reality of his decision was sinking in. He peered along the forest trail in the direction he'd come from, doubt working its way into his throat.

Should he go back?

They'd been woken up this morning by a sudden explosion of gunfire. Fletcher, Maher, and Gram had left the group to check on what it was, leaving Gosse and Becker to guard their camp. Neville had stayed seated on the ground next to Corporal Cassas, who had moaned and shifted about, her face ashen, while Gosse and Becker had picked up their rifles and strolled to the edge of the trees around the clearing. Neville had watched as they'd hidden themselves behind large trees and peered out into the woods. He'd almost wanted to laugh. Why even bother? They were all doomed. They'd wandered for days through the woods, tired, hungry, and thirsty. It was only a matter of time before they were captured or killed. Their only hope was to get the hell off of Kensington as fast as possible.

He'd looked down at the red-stained bandages around the Corporal's leg as he'd listened to the sustained roar of gunfire in the distance. Cassas had been growing weaker every day since they'd escaped from the fort, the loss of blood and the pain wearing her down. They'd been able to keep infection away with a small first aid kit Fletcher had worn on his belt, but she wouldn't last forever. Neville shuddered. That — or worse — would happen to all of them if they didn't get out of here, if they didn't find a way off this planet.

Fletcher, Maher, and Gram had returned as the noise had begun to die down.

"One of the enemy patrols is getting torn to pieces," Gram had panted. "It looks like one of our ranger platoons is over there."

There had been an audible sigh of relief among the soldiers, broken only by the sound of distant shouting, followed by two gunshots. Then silence had engulfed the forest once more.

"What are your orders, sir?" Fletcher had crouched in front of Neville, his dirt-smudged face softened with what could only be hope.

"I… I say we continue toward the dockyards," Neville had said. "Find transport off the planet."

"Sir, if there are still other Alliance units on the planet, that puts you in command." Fletcher's lips had pursed together. *Condescending bastard.* Neville knew his own rank.

He had raised his chin, doing his best to hold Fletcher's gaze. "It's up to us to get off this planet." Seeing the confusion in the other's faces, he'd added, "We have to get help. Warn the Alliance."

"If we could get off," Becker had said, crossing his arms. "There's no guarantee we'd make it to space. Those air patrols could come back at any minute. They'd catch us as soon as we lifted off."

"And the rangers…We can't just leave them." Gram's voice had held a note of finality, and when Neville had looked at him, seen the set expression in his eyes and the eyes of the other soldiers, he'd realized that the choice was no longer his. He'd known then what he had to do.

"You're right," Neville had said, standing up. "We'll meet up with the ranger unit."

They'd packed their supplies in a few minutes and shifted Cassas onto the makeshift stretcher they'd put together out of a few uniform jackets and some branches. Neville had stayed at the rear of the group as Maher and Becker had lifted the stretcher and followed Fletcher, Gosse, and Gram into the woods toward where the sounds had come from. He'd waited a minute or two, allowing himself to fall farther and farther behind, then turned off into the woods, heading back toward the trail they'd been following before, the one that was supposed to go to the harbor.

That had been hours ago. He wished he'd thought to snatch one of the water bottles or one of the rifles, but that wouldn't have been subtle. The important thing was to get away. He had no illusion about who his superiors would blame for losing the fort, and he wasn't about to suffer for the incompetence of his garrison. He had to be the first one to reach the authorities, the first one to share what had really happened, shape the story.

His breathing even once again, and feeling a little cooler, Neville continued along the trail, which curved around the shoulder of a hill as it climbed higher. His legs hurt with every step, his muscles unaccustomed to the activity.

Office legs. That's what Lieutenant Flores had called them once when talking about him to the other officers.

"Leave it to candy asses with office legs to not go where they can't drive."

No doubt she'd thought he hadn't heard. At least she was probably dead now. Good riddance.

The trail rounded the edge of the hill and emerged onto a high overlook. Neville sighed with pleasure as a cool breeze swept over him, carrying some of the heat of the day away. He peered over the tree tops in front of him, could make out the long, dark line of buildings along the dockland, the brilliant blue of the water. It couldn't be more than a day's walk away now, maybe ten miles. Below him and to the right, the slope dropped away sharply, marching down toward the main road and the rail line. He studied the road carefully, looked for anyone moving along its length. Completely abandoned. He knew enough not to strut in the open down the trail, not when he was alone, but if he kept just inside the cover of the trees... The ground on either side of the road was so much flatter than these damn forest trails. He didn't have time to waste.

He turned off the trail and descended the slope, heading in the direction of the road. His boots crunched through branches and twigs as he moved downward, the occasional loose rock rolling ahead of him, clacking as it struck other rocks or tree trunks. His feet suddenly skidded out from under him, and he caught himself from falling onto his back. His hands stung as pebbles scraped them. He was about to curse, when he stopped, a bolt of terror moving up his spine.

Voices! He tilted his chin up slightly as he tried to pick out the sound, his eyes darting down the slope and among the trees, looking for the source of the noise. A breeze sighed through the woods, carrying with it the scent of trees and seawater. The forest stared back at him, unmoving.

Neville let out a breath. His imagination was getting the best of him.

He pressed on, stumbling and scrambling on the rock. He reached the bottom of the slope and trudged in the direction of the road. He came to the edge of the trees, took a moment to reassess his bearings, then turned left and continued walking, keeping just inside the forest.

He tried to think of something to keep his mind occupied. He looked down at his feet as he moved, his thoughts drafting exactly what he was going to say when he made it to the next Alliance post, how his garrison had lain down in front of the enemy, how the ranger officers had rebelled against his command, how even the crew of the *Verdun* had proved useless when the enemy attack had begun. He looked up, blinked.

Some twenty yards away, there was a man, dressed in tan rags and what looked like work coveralls, standing next to a tree. He had his back to Neville, and from the position of his arms, looked to be relieving himself against a tree. Another fifty yards beyond the man was a group of people, also dressed in dirty, torn work clothes, who seemed to be resting. Neville's heart knocked in his chest as stared at the rifle hanging over the peeing man's shoulder.

Neville took careful steps backward, afraid to turn away and make noise. He would find his way back to the trail, flat ground be damned! His heel lowered over a branch, which snapped loudly as he put his weight on it.

The peeing man looked over his shoulder, did a double take. He shouted, turning around as he zipped up the front of his coveralls. Neville didn't think twice, but ran as hard as he could back the way he had come. Gunshots broke the air, and he heard shouts and footsteps following him. He glanced to his left, saw another group of enemies running toward him from across the road, rifles in hand.

Neville paused, not sure what to do. His pistol? He'd emptied it in the fort. A chunk of bark exploded off the side of a nearby tree as more shots reverberated off the rocky slopes above. He bolted up the hillside, fighting against the stitch in his side to climb the steep slope. He slipped, fell onto his face, but was back on his feet in a second.

"Grab him!" A voice shouted from behind him.

Neville glanced over his shoulder, saw the peeing man running up the hill at him on skinny, wiry legs. Neville fought with everything he had to go faster, to push his legs as fast as they could go, but lead weights seemed to be attached to his waist, and he felt his pace slowing.

Then something struck him hard in the side and he hit the ground, struggling against the peeing man, who had tackled him. Neville rolled, kicked blindly at the man, connected with something. But then others were around him. Neville felt himself being dragged upward by his collar, saw a tall, thickly built woman raising her fist, and then stars burst across his vision. He tried to raise his hands to protect his head, but then another impact jarred him, and everything went black.

CHAPTER 21

Kim raced up the stairwell, savoring the burn in her legs, the feeling of motion. The metal grating of the stairs clanged beneath her athletic shoes as she reached the landing for deck four, turned, and continued up, her pulse pounding in her ears. A small group of men saluted briskly as they clattered past her in the other direction, their white PT shirts stained with sweat. Kim had just enough time to recognize them as she returned the salute without breaking her stride. Lieutenant Hillman in front, trailed by Trusso and Hardin — both of them marines — and Sergeant Kilwalski. It was good to see Hillman and the others keeping busy, and it was even better that Kilwalski was active again. The tough marine sergeant had nearly died facing the Frontin leader at Kim's side. By the looks of him, he had recovered well.

The stairwells were always popular in the mornings and at night with the more fitness-conscious members of the crew. While the *Verdun* had a small weight room and fitness center, it was necessary to take to the corridors and stairways when they were deserted in order to get a good run. In the years since Kim had come aboard the *Verdun,* she had come to look forward to seeing the familiar faces of her fellow morning runners, the brotherhood of the corridors. Now that Lieutenant Urquhart and Commander Holsey had joined the fitness crowd, she anticipated running into them both at least once every morning.

Kim reached the landing for deck three, took a left, and ran out into the corridor, the flat flooring feeling strange beneath her feet after the grueling staircase. She tried to clear her thoughts of the past few days, focus only on her breathing, but found herself running through the same scenarios again and again.

The engines are repaired. The *Verdun* leaves to get help, returns with an armada, and finds the shore party dead. The engines are ruined and the

Verdun tries to attack the armada at Kensington, but goes down in flames. None of her scenarios seemed to end well, and the past couple days since her conversation with Holsey had given her lots of time to mull them over.

The enemy convoys into the solar system had stopped more than twenty-four hours ago, no doubt meaning that whoever was sending the ships was aware that their reinforcements weren't getting through. Without the distraction of easy prey, the crew had become measurably more apprehensive. Kim had hoped that the bustle of the ongoing repairs would keep them occupied, but she could sense their mounting tension, their growing desire to know.

What next?

Kim rounded a corner, saw the slender shape of Lieutenant Urquhart up ahead. If running weren't going to clear her head, maybe Callista's bubbly optimism would do the trick. Kim accelerated to join the younger woman, her calf muscles burning in protest.

"Good morning, Lieutenant."

Urquhart looked over at Kim, jumped slightly, and yanked her headphones off her ears. "Good morning, Captain. Sorry I didn't hear you. I was..."

"No need to apologize." Kim did her best to control her breathing, to keep up with Urquhart's pace.

"You don't, uh..." Urquhart pointed to her headphones as they reached a straight stretch of corridor.

Kim felt her brow furrow, then realized Urquhart was referring to music. "No, they just fall out of my ears."

"Oh." They rounded another corner. "I couldn't run without music. You should try different headphones maybe."

"Maybe." Kim bit her lip as they reached another staircase, entered the landing, and then ran down the stairs.

Talking about running tunes wasn't exactly chasing her demons away. Kim looked sideways at Urquhart, taking in how young she looked, wishing for just a moment she could be a decade younger and have half the responsibility, to be like Urquhart, a member of the crew and not its leader. In times like this, when a tough decision lay ahead of her, Kim always felt so separated from the men and women under her. She secretly wished she could stand in front of them all and simply talk to them, ask them for their ideas, explain herself, seek their absolution.

It was a stupid idea. She was here to lead, not run a democracy or a therapy session. Still… She looked over at Urquhart again, an idea coming into her head.

"Lieutenant," Kim began, raising her voice over the clatter of their shoes on the stairs. "You spend a fair amount of time with the other junior officers?"

"Yes, ma'am."

"With the enlisted ranks?"

"Yes, ma'am." Urquhart looked over at Kim, curiosity written on her face.

They reached Deck Five, turned left and out into another corridor. Kim suppressed her sigh of relief to be off the stairs again.

"What…" Kim found it hard to form words, feeling suddenly exposed. She swallowed, started again, speaking between breaths. "What is the feeling… among the crew? What is everyone… hoping our next move will be?"

"I…" Urquhart was clearly caught off guard by the question. "I think we trust you, ma'am."

"Lieutenant, you can be frank with me."

Urquhart slowed her pace, and Kim followed suit. "Well, I think we'd all like the shore party back. We wonder when we'll hear from our friends." Urquhart was looking down at her feet as they kept jogging.

"Are you afraid?" Kim blurted out the question before she could think twice about it.

"No." Urquhart looked up, smiled.

"No." Kim shook her head, repeating Urquhart's single word as if she had never heard it before. She had expected Urquhart to say yes, to share with her the common experience of fear, of worry, and find relief from the sharing.

"No," Urquhart repeated.

They kept jogging in silence, their pace slowing gradually as they started to cool down their run. The main shift would start soon. Kim drifted back to her own thoughts, her lists of things to do, her plans to keep harassing Geonor about repairs, the meetings she'd planned with Lieutenant Voth about—

"My stepfather used to say something." Urquhart's voice cut through Kim's thoughts.

Kim looked over at Urquhart, could see her smiling, though there was some other, sharper emotion in her eyes as well.

"He said that, when we serve, our lives don't belong to us, so we have no business worrying about them." Urquhart met Kim's eyes. "I've always found that very comforting."

Kim considered the stark simplicity of the statement, felt a sort of calm enter her, save for one nagging worry. "If your lives don't belong to you, who do they belong to?"

Urquhart was opening her mouth to answer when a chime played over the loudspeakers, followed by the voice of the night shift radio operator.

"Captain Morden, Captain Morden. Lieutenant Geonor and Commander Holsey are calling you to the staff lounge immediately."

A surge of worry filled the space behind Kim's breastbone. Lieutenant Geonor wanting to see her in person meant a repair report, and a bad one at that. She'd been in the Navy long enough to know that a good report was usually forwarded via computer. Only bad reports caused engineers to set up meetings, no doubt so they could explain themselves.

Kim slowed to a halt. "I'll catch you later, Lieutenant."

"See you in a bit." Obviously too young to know the dire omen of meetings with engineers, Urquhart continued off down the hallway, pushing her headphones back into her ears.

Kim turned and jogged back up the stairs, then expended herself in one sustained burn to Deck Two. A minute later, she walked, breathless, into the staff meeting room. Holsey stood beside Lieutenant Geonor on the opposite side of the big rectangular table.

"Good morning," Kim said, sensing the tension hanging in the room and mingling with the odors of grease, oil, and metal.

"Good morning," Geonor wiped his grime-covered hands on the front of his dark blue work coveralls.

"We've uploaded the latest repair report, Captain. We think you should see." Holsey's hands were crossed in front of her chest, dark circles under her eyes. She'd made it her personal mission to keep the repairs on task during the past few days, and Kim doubted if she'd slept much.

That makes two of us.

Kim stepped forward and sat down at the closest computer terminal, opening its screen and waiting while it started up.

Geonor stepped to the large display panel on the wall, his hands leaving black smudges on the white buttons as he punched in a series of commands. "I'm sending the report to your terminal now."

Kim drummed her fingers on her desk, keeping her posture straight, her breathing even. Whatever the news was, she wouldn't let anyone see her react.

The screen flickered white, then blue, then faded into the familiar layout of an engineering report, with columns of text separated by diagrams of ship systems with red arrows on them, explaining the problem. Her eyes rested on the words "irreparable damage."

She looked up, met Geonor's gaze. "The summary, please."

"Our engines were already in a bad way after our encounter with the Frontin." Geonor wiped sweat off his forehead, leaving a black streak to join the splotches on his cheeks and chin. "This latest damage is beyond what I can repair without landing again. Even then, I think I could only get it to half our normal cruising speed. We'll need a dry dock overhaul to be back to normal. Three weeks at best. Six is more likely, given the number of repairs to other systems I've got to make."

Kim looked down at her screen, avoiding making eye contact with Holsey, putting off the decision for just a moment longer. "And the communications system?"

Geonor's facial expression morphed from pained worry to glowing pride in an instant. "I have good news for you there, ma'am."

"You fixed it?" Kim looked up at Geonor again, her eyebrow raising.

"Aye. We've managed to rig an antenna using some spare parts. We had to get a little creative with the wrecked circuitry. The signal will be fuzzy, but the system will be operational in a few hours or so."

"Good work."

"Thank you, ma'am. I got a fair experience with long-range radio equipment in the last war. Our ship got hit right smack in the communications array. We were adrift, and we had to get a signal out, or run out of supplies and die. Our engineer put some odds and ends together and — presto! — we got the radio working and were picked up."

Kim tuned out Geonor's anecdote, meeting Holsey's eye.

"What are your orders?" Holsey uncrossed her arms.

There was only one choice.

"Mr. Geonor, finish the communications system and then turn your priorities to any remaining repairs of the defensive and offensive systems. I want this ship ready for combat immediately."

"Yes, ma'am." Geonor saluted, pressed a few buttons on the computer panel again to close the report, and walked from the room.

"Commander." Kim looked at Holsey again. "Begin drawing up a plan to attack Kensington. I want all factors accounted for. Use whichever officers you need."

"Aye, Captain." Holsey held Kim's gaze for a moment before following Geonor out to the corridor.

Kim sank down into her chair, turning to the now blank computer screen in front of her. How long had she sat in her room, in front of a computer just like this, writing reports after their last battle? Kim sighed, fighting the sinking dread in her chest.

She'd already had to write five more condolence letters on this mission and another action report for the ambush at the docks. Now they were headed toward another battle. Somehow, a captain could never know if she was making the right choice before it had been paid for with blood. She wished she could reach into the future and grab the answers to her questions. How many crewmembers would she lose? Had she considered all the options? Was she leading her ship into another massacre?

"If your lives don't belong to you, who do they belong to?"

No one answered, but Kim saw her own reflection on the computer's polished glass screen. She stared back at herself for a second.

Then she reached out and eased the screen shut.

CHAPTER 22

Jack leaned against one of the empty, steel-framed medical beds, just outside the light thrown by the wire-caged bulbs on the infirmary's ceiling, watching as Sergeant Curry, one of the marine medics, finished bandaging the prisoner's wounded leg. The young man's face scrunched together with each layer of gauze being wrapped around his calf, his limbs pulling tightly against the restraints. Jack pushed aside any sense of pity, concentrating instead on the questions he was going to ask, his mental strategy for the interrogation.

Jack had never questioned a captive before. Normally, that job fell to trained intelligence personnel, not line officers. But the situation on Kensington was anything but normal, and Jack was tired of fighting an enemy he knew nothing about. Why would humans attack other humans? Why had they attacked Kensington, of all places? Why were people under Jack's command dying on this backwater dump?

"He's ready for you, sir." Curry turned around and faced Jack as he tucked his medical kit back into his khaki musette bag, his thin face thrown into relief by the play of deep shadows and harsh light from the light bulb above him. "I've held off giving him any pain suppressors for the moment like you asked."

"It was an order, Sergeant, not a request."

"Regardless, that wound is going to hurt terribly without medication."

Jack ignored the note of disapproval in Curry's voice. They weren't going to waste any more of their dwindling medical supplies than they needed to, not when they may be waiting weeks before a rescue. Besides, while Jack wasn't about to violate the Alliance's ban on the torture of advanced, humanoid species, he wasn't going to fall over himself making the prisoner comfortable.

"Thank you, Mr. Curry. Dismissed, and shut the door behind you."

Curry padded past Jack toward the door. Jack took a step toward the prisoner, but stopped when he heard Major Osterman's voice behind him.

"Hold the door. Thank you, Sergeant."

The tension in Jack's shoulders eased a bit. At least he wouldn't have to do this alone. He turned to face Osterman, who looked strangely small without his helmet or body armor. "What's the latest?"

"Everyone's bedded down, and ammunition is being distributed." Osterman ran a hand through his short, blonde hair, the drops of sweat on his forehead gleaming slightly in the yellow light. "We're getting down to the end of our supplies, but each platoon should have enough ammo for another patrol cycle. Two if they can scavenge a lot off the enemy."

"Good work, thank you." Jack knew Osterman was a professional, but the major's efficient operation of the bunker over the past week — keeping its defenses ready, re-supplying ranger platoons as they came in from their ambushes — had been truly impressive. If it weren't for the lack of ammunition and ordnance, Jack had no doubt the major could keep them running indefinitely.

Jack saw Osterman's eyes look past him, reminding him of the task at hand.

"Have a seat, Major." Jack turned around and looked over at the man tied to the medical bed, who had given up pulling on his restraints and was looking around him with wide eyes. He couldn't be much past his early twenties, though the grey color of his skin and the hollows of his cheeks made him look much older. Judging by the worn coveralls he wore and his slight, wiry frame, he had been some kind of worker, though not a well-fed one.

"I'm Lt. Commander Jack Wilcox of the Alliance ship Verdun," Jack moved to stand beside the medical bed. "What is your name?"

"Are you going to kill me?" The fear in the man's voice was palpable.

Jack ignored the question and his conscience. The man's fear would be a useful tool.

"What's your name?" Jack repeated.

The man looked up at him, anger and terror mixing in his green eyes.

"I don't think you're giving away any military secrets if you tell us your name, kid." Osterman's voice sounded from somewhere behind Jack.

"Steven." His voice was almost a whisper.

"Okay… Steven. Why don't you tell us a bit more about yourself? How old you are, what you do for a living, where you're from, and most importantly, why you have attacked us." Jack walked around the medical bed as he spoke, coming to stand on the other side.

"You want to know where I'm from, huh?" Steven's facial expression hardened, and his face turned red. "You must think I'm some kind of idiot. You think I'd tell you where my folks are? You think I'd let you send the company goons after them?" Steven's shouts reverberated off the concrete walls, and Jack heard the metal frame of the bed squeak as the young man pulled against his restraints. Then Steven's face crumpled with pain, his movements no doubt reminding him of the bullet hole in his leg.

"What are you talking about?" Jack's brow knotted. "What company goons are you talking about?"

"You know who they are!" Steven shouted back. "You're working with them. Why else would you fight us? We're trying to save you!"

Jack looked up from Steven and over at Osterman, who was sitting on an empty medical bed against the wall near the door, his chin in his hand, his eyes fixed on Steven, his expression unreadable in the dim light.

"Okay…" Jack began, gathering his thoughts, wondering if the kid was insane. "Just tell me what you do for a living."

Steven glared at him suspiciously, he nostrils flaring.

"I don't think the goons will find your family just based on your job." Jack crossed his arms behind his back, did his best to make his voice unthreatening.

Steven swallowed hard, winced again. "I'm a machinist."

Jack nodded. An industrial worker. That made sense, and it explained the work clothes, though not his thin, undernourished appearance. What it didn't explain was why these people had attacked Kensington, a week away from any industrial planets.

"And what did you machine? What sort of product?"

"I milled small parts."

"For which company or organization?"

Steven shook his head, sweat rolling down his face, his jaw clenched against the pain. "No. You're trying to figure out where my family is. I told you… I won't let you get them."

"Listen," Jack said, kneeling near Steven's head, an idea coming to him. "We're with the military, do you understand me? We are not trying to kill your family. Whoever you're afraid of, we can protect you from them if you just tell us who sent you to attack us."

Steven shook his head again, more frantically this time. "You're working with the enemy. You're serving the monster!"

Jack sighed, massaged his temples again. This was going nowhere. Jack had never heard any human in the Alliance react this way to a member of the armed forces. Every child in primary school grew up learning that the military was all that stood between the Alliance and its destruction. The Frontin, the Milipa — they all demanded a constant show of strength to keep them at bay. Facing so much fear and conflict, so many people were in uniform, and it seemed to Jack that the news was always showing servicemembers as heroes. To be treated like an enemy was something Jack had never expected. There could only be one answer.

"Have the Milipa trained you to think we're the enemy?"

"The Milipa?" Steven's eyebrows rose with surprise. "Don't you see what they've done to you? They've convinced you we're working with murderers! We just want to save ourselves, save you!"

"From who? Who do you think we are working for?" Jack's voice rose as his temper flared, causing Steven to flinch. Jack stepped back from the bed, breathing deeply, trying to reclaim his calm. None of this made any damned sense.

"You talked about the monster. Who is the monster?" Osterman had stood up, and had walked to stand next to Steven on the opposite side of the bed from Jack. "If I've been tricked into serving someone, I want to know who it is."

Steven looked from Jack to Osterman, his complexion pale.

"You work for the companies." Steven whimpered in pain.

"The companies." Jack repeated, his mind blank.

"Yes. Our… Our bosses." Steven's eyes closed. "And you've killed all of us. And now you're going to kill me. Oh God. Just let me go home! Let me go home!" Steven babbled on, his voice becoming ragged, the pain of his wound and the weight of his fear no doubt wearing him down.

Jack looked over at Osterman, and saw the same comprehension he felt dawning in the major's eyes.

"Steven. Steven!" Jack reached out, put a hand on the prisoner's shoulder. "You're trying to fight your bosses? You're trying to fight the companies you work for, is that it?"

Steven nodded, his eyes meeting Jack. "We won't let them keep us down anymore. We… We need to fight back. You killed them! You broke in at night, we were late on the bills, you knew I was going to the meetings… and Mom tried to stop you. You killed her. You killed her!" Steven was writhing in the bed, becoming more hysterical with every moment. Jack could tell that whatever window he had to talk to Steven was closing.

"Steven, who is we?"

Steven glared up at him. "We… We are the United Worker's Legion. We… We'll destroy the capital class." Steven's eyes bulged from his thin, ashen face as he spat the words up at Jack. "We will bring justice to the Alliance!"

"This barrel has a thousand shots in it before your accuracy will start to degrade. Maybe two. If you can avoid rapid fire, that'll make it last longer." Sergeant Collins, the company armorer, pulled the muzzle gauge out of the barrel of Christine's carbine and handed the weapon back to her, its smooth metallic surfaces glinting in the moonlight.

"I'll arrange it with the enemy so I can shoot more slowly." Christine slung the carbine over her shoulder and stood up from the overturned crate that Collins had been using as a chair for rangers and marines visiting his makeshift foxhole workstation.

"Anything else I can do for you, Lieutenant?" Collins looked up at Christine through blue eyes ringed with dark circles and wiped his forehead with hands mummified by athletic tape.

Given the heavy, sustained use that all the weapons in the company were getting, Christine had no doubt the armorer had been working his fingers raw. Stacks of rifles and carbines leaned against the foxhole's earthen wall next to a bucket of assorted parts. The small worktable in front of Collins — another upturned crate — was scattered with tools, broken rifle parts, and grease stains.

Movement drew Christine's attention, and she looked to see the shadowy outlines of Commander Wilcox and Major Osterman returning to the bunker, no doubt finished with their tour of the defenses. They'd been spending a lot of time walking the lines after they'd broken the news about their enemy's identity, no doubt trying to gauge the effect of the information on everyone's morale. Christine could only guess how successful they'd been. She herself was still trying to make sense of it all.

"No, that covers it. Thanks, Sergeant." Christine clambered out of the foxhole and took a moment to re-orient herself in the darkness. She then strode off just along the edge of the clearing that surrounded the bunker, behind the network of foxholes that the rangers and marines were settling down into for the night. She took in the sandbagged machine gun pits, the teepee stacks of rifles, the men and women cutting open ration packs with bayonets and nodding at her as she passed. She returned their acknowledgement, but her thoughts had fallen back to the officer's meeting that Wilcox had called an hour ago.

"We believe we now know exactly whom we are fighting," Wilcox had begun, leaning forward onto the metal briefing table in the radio room, his face grim. "These people are workers from industrial centers — we don't know which — who have initiated a full-scale revolt. Their objective appears to be the destruction of something our prisoner called the capital class. We can only assume that means the wealthy — bankers, industrialists, company owners."

The officers had been silent for a moment, none of them knowing how to respond. Christine had shaken her head slightly, not wanting to believe what she was hearing. She had almost expected Wilcox to grin and say that it was all a joke.

Finally, Lieutenant Arnot had spoken up. "And what about the Milipa, or the Frontin? Do they seem to be involved at all?"

"Negative, Lieutenant. There seems to be no outside influence here at all."

"How big is this revolt?" Squires had looked oddly pale in the lamplight, his uniform sleeves rolled up to his elbows, his bare arms crossed in front of his chest.

"We can't say for certain," Major Osterman had said, stepping forward. "But based on what we got out of the prisoner before we had to sedate him, it sounds like there may be millions of workers involved."

"We don't know what their leadership looks like yet." Wilcox had stood up straight, meeting the gazes of the officers in the room one by one. "But it sounds like they have some kind of organizational structure. They call themselves the United Worker's Legion."

Worker's Legion?

Ever since they had discovered that their enemies were human, the rangers and marines had been debating non-stop who was behind the attack on Kensington. Christine had overheard some entertaining theories. The marines, who had apparently had a confrontation recently in Derek's Triangle with a group of humans in league with the Frontin, had thought that maybe their opponents on Kensington were part of the same plot. The rangers had favored the Milipa or even troops from the old Black Star Empire as the culprits. One had suggested mass mind control. Corporal Lazaar, looking up from the comic section of *Alliance Servicemember's Magazine*, had suggested that maybe their enemies were some kind of zombie, stricken by a disease. Christine would almost prefer that to the truth.

After all the wild theories, their enemies were just angry workers, part of some kind of revolution like the ones back on Earth in ancient Russia.

Some of her rangers had reacted with anger when they'd learned.

"You're telling me they want to kill us because they don't like their bosses?" Private Clos had stood up, her voice rising high enough that her squadmates had shushed her and pulled her back to where they were all seated on the ground.

"Don't shush me." Emotion had made her voice crack. "We've been burying our friends because of these assholes, and you're telling me they don't have the Milipa bending their arm? How could they do this? They're animals!"

"None of this means they can't still be zombies," Lazaar had added, the slight grin on his face collapsing into a scowl when Private Miller punched him in the arm.

But then Henrikson had expressed the dark, slimy feeling that had been growing in Christine's chest. "They're not animals. They're just like us."

For what felt like the hundredth time since the officer's meeting, she could see again the dim, cramped house of her parents, the bowls laid out to catch the rain, her father's haggard face as he came home late from the factory.

"They're cutting wages until we get productivity up." Her father had said, hanging his helmet by the door.

Her mother had put her hands on her hips, her schoolteacher's uniform faded and worn, her face filling with anger. "But they can't do that! You need to tell—"

"Who? Who are we going to tell? The magistrate's campaign was funded by the company!"

Christine had watched the argument from where she was playing on the worn linoleum floor, not really understanding, but learning to hate the phrase, "the company." As the years passed and she'd seen her father gradually crushed beneath his job, she'd wanted desperately to get out, to run away, to leave the factories of her home world behind.

"I've enlisted in the Army," she'd told her parents, tilting her chin up, expecting them to shout her down. "I'm going to be a ranger. They're the hardest to get into. The pay's better. I'm leaving next week."

She'd figured waiting to the last minute would make the parting easier. She'd been eighteen, and she wasn't going to let anybody tell her what to do.

Her mother's eyes had run with tears, her lips pursed. But her father had broken into loud sobs and moved toward her so quickly that she had stepped back. He'd raised his arms, and she'd thought he was going to strike her, but then he'd taken her face and held it gently in both his hands.

"You made it, girl. You've made it away from here." He'd pulled her against him, and held her so tight that she almost couldn't breathe. Her mother had come over a second later, holding them both in her willowy brown arms. Nine years later, after the accident, it was that hug that she remembered the most.

Were the people they were fighting animals? No. They'd killed people under her command, murdered countless other servicemembers, her brothers and sisters in arms. She hated them. But some small part of her understood them, and that frightened her. She'd much prefer monsters or zombies to fight. It would make pulling the trigger easier.

Christine cleared her thoughts as she continued walking along the foxholes and machine gun nests, pressing against her ring with her thumb, concentrating on the warm, smooth feeling of the gold band. If only Ryan were here. He was the professor, the scholar. He'd have some philosophical conclusion to offer her.

She finally reached her own foxhole, took a deep breath, and stepped down into it. Sergeant Néri, Corporal Lazaar, and Private Henrikson looked up at her in the dark.

"Got it working again?" Henrikson pointed over Christine's shoulder at her carbine.

"Yeah." She pulled the weapon off her shoulder. She leaned the carbine against the side of the foxhole, and looked about in the dark for her pack. She needed something to keep her hands busy, to stay occupied. That, and they'd be heading out on patrol again tomorrow. She wanted to make sure her weapon was clean when she needed to use it again.

"Are the troops handling it okay?" Néri held out Christine's pack with one arm, meeting her gaze, his face unreadable in the dark.

Christine took the pack, put confidence in her voice. "Yes. They're doing fine."

"I see." Néri leaned back against the foxhole. Nothing ever got past Néri, and from the pensive look on his face, she doubted he'd believed her.

Christine sat down, looking through her pack. She found the small bag that held her cleaning kit and set it down beside her. She unzipped the kit, pulling a rolled-up cleaning mat, a collapsed rod, a couple small brushes, and little bottles of oil and solvent out of it.

"You're doing that now?" Lazaar shifted where he sat next to his radio unit, which was set to scan. "How are you going to see?"

"I paid attention in basic." Christine checked her carbine to double-check that it was unloaded, then laid it out on the cleaning pad and began breaking it down into its component parts.

"They must have punished you with a lot of disassembly drill." Lazaar's voice intruded on Christine's concentration.

"Or maybe she's not an idiot like you, Ali."

Christine smiled at Henrikson's response, returned her attention to her weapon. In truth, she always enjoyed cleaning and disassembly. Something about the routine predictability of the procedure was soothing for her.

"You made it girl. You made it away from here."

She organized the major part groups of the rifle in front of her — trigger assembly and fire control circuitry, barrel and receiver group, and the various handguards — stopping only to check the battery on the weapon's light. She knew from experience that it was best to not disassemble those pieces any further in the field.

"I'm so sorry to give you this news, Corporal Flores. There were no survivors."

Christine tried to shake the memories out of her head and set to work cleaning the bolt and barrel raceways, wiping away the gooey mixture of dirt and old grease that had built up on them. All the hiking and fighting in the muck and dust had got the weapon dirtier than it had been since, well, ever. Once every moving part had been cleaned, Christine lubricated them with generous blobs from her grease bottle, then started reassembling the jumble of parts in front of her.

"I've enlisted in the Army. I'm going to be a ranger."

"This is the RAS Verdun to any remaining Alliance forces on Kensington. Please stand by to receive an encoded message."

Christine glared at the rifle components in her hand, chasing away the memories, the image of the burning house in her head, but her thoughts kept racing.

"Congratulations, Lieutenant. I know how much this commission must mean to you, given the circumstances."

"I say again, this is the RAS Verdun to any remaining Alliance forces on Kensington. Please stand by to receive an encoded message."

Christine blinked, the partially assembled carbine in her hands. That last voice, the one tinged with radio static. That wasn't a memory. That was happening now. Christine cursed herself for not paying attention, met the wide eyes of Sergeant Néri and the gaping expression of Lazaar, who was looking at his radio as if it had sprouted legs.

"What the hell—?"

Christine didn't hear Henrikson finish his sentence, but set down her carbine and sprang out of the foxhole, running for the bunker.

"RAS Verdun, please confirm identity." Jack's hands shook as he held the radio handset to his mouth. A bright, almost painful relief was expanding in his chest, but he held it down. If the fort had somehow managed to hack into the secured radio channels, they could be trying to trick him to give away his position. Then again, despite the heavy static that crackled on the signal, that voice sounded a lot like Chief Baudouin.

Jack waited for a response, sliding into a chair at the radio console, each second seeming to last four times as long. They'd been about to pitch their sleeping rolls on the floor of the radio room when they'd heard the voice, grated with static. The transmission quality had been so bad that they'd almost ignored it, thinking that the radio was picking up environmental noise from a storm somewhere. But then the call had come again, and Jack had almost fallen over himself to get to the radio.

Please. Please let this be them. Please let them be alive.

"Are they in orbit?" Major Osterman was standing behind him, his arms crossed over his chest.

"Shhhh!" Jack listened as the handset fizzled again and the same transmission played for third time.

"I say again, this is the RAS Verdun to any remaining Alliance forces on Kensington. Please stand by to receive an encoded message."

Jack laid down his handset. "It's a recorded message. They must be transmitting from extreme long range." The bunker's radio would be far too weak to respond.

"This is the RAS Verdun. Transmitting coded message now."

A series of high-pitched sounds played over the speakers, and Jack swiveled his chair to face the radio's computer interface, which was processing the tones through its decryption algorithms.

Jack heard the thump of boots on concrete and turned to see Lieutenant Flores run into the room, her face alight with excitement, her black hair done into a bun behind her head. Without any equipment belt, helmet, or backpack, she looked oddly vulnerable.

"I heard… On the radio!" Flores pointed past Wilcox at the radio station, her words coming between breaths.

"We're decrypting the message now," Osterman replied.

Jack turned back to the screen, saw it flash green and display a typed message. Jack looked at Morden's name at the bottom of the message and fought down the lump in his throat, letting his relief move through him. Wherever they were, they were alive — or at least they had been when they'd sent this message. Depending on their distance, that could have been hours ago.

"What does it say?" Jack heard Flores' footsteps as she came to stand next to Osterman.

Jack cleared his throat and read the message slowly, trying to imagine the words in Morden's voice.

"To any remaining Alliance personnel in or around Kensington Station: the RAS Verdun will be attacking the enemy warships in orbit of the planet in seventy-two hours. Upon destroying this force, we will commence bombardment of the fort unless we are able to confirm that it remains under Alliance control."

Jack met Osterman's eyes, saw the same mix of apprehension and excitement that he felt. The *Verdun* was coming. It was going to face battle, but, by God, it was coming. Jack returned his gaze to the message and continued reading.

"Any Alliance forces on the planet are to disengage from offensive operations, distance themselves from enemy positions, and take shelter where appropriate until the Verdun arrives. Further orders will be issued at that point. Signed Captain Kim E. Morden, commanding officer, RAS Verdun."

Jack sat back in his chair, processing what he had just read. No more hikes. No more patrols. No more ambushes. It was all over. This mess was over. He wanted to smile, to laugh, to shout his relief.

"Well, I for one don't mind if the Verdun cleans house for us." Jack could hear the smile in Osterman's voice.

"You lazy ass," Flores scoffed, though Jack could tell that she was grinning, too. "You're not the one who's been hiking all over creation."

As Osterman and Flores bantered with each other, Jack's feeling of levity faded. There was no doubt that the fight ahead of the *Verdun* would be tough. Maybe impossible if the enemy controlled the fort's missile defenses. Jack tried to ignore the image of the ship he knew so well falling from the sky in flames. Suddenly, he found himself wishing the *Verdun* wasn't coming, even if it meant hiking up a hill with a full combat load for the next year.

He sighed, looked over at the radio handset on the table, and whispered the words he wished he could say to his friends. "Good hunting. Godspeed."

But no one, not even Flores and Osterman, heard a word he said.

CHAPTER 23

"You know what happens when you aren't honest, Colonel."

Tom watched as the Supervisor fluttered his hand dramatically over the activation switch of the truth device — that's what the Supervisor was calling it, at least, a tangle of wires, electrodes, and vehicle batteries that one of the men had rigged up for him.

"I don't remember, I don't remember!" The colonel, his skin ashen, his face dripping with sweat, shook his head frantically, the electrodes attached to his head, chest, arms, and legs moving like odd, tentacle outgrowths of his body.

The Supervisor made a clucking noise. "This happens."

He flipped the switch, and a low electric hum sounded. The officer, Neville, jerked against his restraints, his eyes bulging out of his head, all the muscles in his body tensing with the electricity, a long, low, animal groan escaping his mouth. Tom closed his eyes, pressed his arms around himself against the cold of the fort's concrete interior, the painfully hard press of the pistol in the waistband of his trousers a distraction from the despicable scene.

Tom would do what he needed to do for the Legion, whatever would free his brothers and sisters, even if it meant doing something he hated. He'd seen the companies cheat, rob, intimidate, and even murder whoever got in their way for far too long to shy away from violence. But if there were any way to get the information without torture, he'd take it. He was a warrior, not a monster. The Supervisor, on the other hand, enjoyed this bullshit.

One of their patrols had pulled Neville in the day before, his uniform caked with dirt, his mouth spewing curses and threats. The Supervisor had fed him and let him clean up and get a good night's sleep — then hauled him up to the infirmary early in the morning to start the questioning process, if you could call it that. For the first quarter hour, the Supervisor had contented himself with shocking Neville on and off without asking a single question. Tom found himself wondering again why Smith was part of the Legion. Did he really want to create a more just Alliance, or was he just the kind of man who jumped at the chance to be involved with violence?

The buzzing sound stopped, and Tom heard Neville's sobs. He heard the scrape of wood on cement and opened his eyes to see the Supervisor pulling a chair across the floor. He sat down, put his hand on Neville's knee.

"I know you're tired of this, Colonel. I am, too."

Somehow, Tom didn't believe that.

"Let me help you. Help both of us. Give me your computer access codes, and this will all be over." The Supervisor's voice was soft, gentle, almost as if he were speaking to a child.

Neville didn't respond, but kept sobbing softly. From the bits and pieces Tom had overheard from the rest of the captured fort garrison, Neville was considered an inept officer, a coward. The men who'd captured him said he'd been alone, was maybe trying to desert the other Alliance forces. Tom hadn't expected him to last this long.

"You need to think about yourself." The Supervisor sat back in his chair, brushing his hand near the switch. Neville watched the Supervisor's movements through bloodshot eyes, his face the very image of terror.

"I a-am thinking of myself." Neville's voice was a hoarse, faltering whisper. "I... I know h-how this works. As soon as you don't need me, I'm dead."

"We're not murderers." The words came from Tom's mouth before he could stop them. The Supervisor looked around at him, the pleasant mask on his face touched with a hint of annoyance. "Yes, you see? You have a friend here." The Supervisor turned back to Neville. "We won't kill you *if* you give us what we want."

Neville said nothing, but his face told Tom he hadn't believed a word they'd said.

"Fine." The Supervisor flicked the switch. Neville jerked against the restraints, then relaxed as the Supervisor turned the device off again.

"I don't understand you, Robert. Can I call you that?" The Supervisor reached into his pocket, pulled out what looked to be a small knife. "We've told you we won't kill you. We've been nice enough to not do any lasting—" The Supervisor made a quick motion and cut a small gash along the top of Neville's thigh. "—harm to your body."

Neville made a small, terrified noise, looking at the blood seeping from the fresh cut on his leg.

"Maybe you have a hearing problem. Let me look at that for you." The Supervisor leaned forward and slid the knife behind Neville's right ear.

"No! No!" Neville's hoarse cries echoed off of the low ceiling as he tried to squirm away. This had gone too far. Tom stepped forward to intervene, one hand going to his sidearm.

"No! Don't! I'll tell you, I'll tell you."

The Supervisor hesitated, sat back down, the knife still in his hand, Neville's ear unharmed and still attached. Tom pulled a small scrap of paper and a pencil from his pocket and wrote down the number that Neville rattled off.

"Very good, my friend. Now, on to the next question. Where are the enemy forces that keep attacking our patrols hiding?"

Neville blinked. "I-I don't know. I left the others before we could reach them."

"That is consistent with the way we found him" Tom was finished with this cramped room and the Supervisor's love of pain. They had more important work to do anyway. Even with the code, it would take time to unlock the system, since they hadn't been able to find the ID cards or the keys that initiated the system.

"But it's not the right answer." The Supervisor sighed, and flicked the switch, this time for much longer, Neville's eyes rolled up into his head, and Tom could tell that he was losing consciousness. Tom felt his stomach turn. Without thinking flicked the switch off with one hand, pulled his pistol with the other, and then smashed the contraption's control box with the sidearm's butt.

"What the fuck do you think you're doing!" The Supervisor was on his feet in a second, his eyes almost popping out of his head, knife in hand. Tom took a step back. He had never seen the man react this way. Was this the real Smith, under all the smiles and false laughter?

"You forget yourself, Supervisor." Tom pointed the muzzle of the pistol toward Smith. "We will not be a movement for evil."

"Oh, please!" The Supervisor threw his hands up. "You weak little fool! Without people like me, you'd all still be hoisting protest signs, forming little committees, doing nothing! You want to see how you accomplish your goals?" The Supervisor stepped toward Neville's unconscious body.

Tom raised the pistol, gripped it with both hands. "I think I know how."

The Supervisor stopped in his tracks. A smile spread over his face, and he closed his knife, slid it back in his pocket. "Tom. Tom! Let's not fight each other. We're the glue that holds this place together."

Tom kept his pistol on target. "Yes, we are. But don't forget: I command our forces here, and I won't let us stray from our ideals."

The Supervisor nodded, though Tom could see rage burning in his eyes.

Tom turned to the door. "Mackenzie!"

The door opened, and Mackenzie and a couple other warriors came into the room, their rifles slung over their shoulders.

"Take the colonel down to the other prisoners. See to it he's looked after."

"Yes, Tom."

He watched as they freed Neville from the smashed 'truth device' and hauled him out of the room.

"I'll see you at the command center." The Supervisor's artificially cheerful voice had returned, and he strolled into the corridor with a smile on his face.

Tom took a deep breath, looked down at the detached electrodes. He supposed he ought to feel elated. They had the codes. They would be able to break the silo lockout in days, not weeks. Within a short time, Kensington would be as good as theirs.

His problems were solved, weren't they?

Tom shook his head, listening to the Supervisor's cheerful whistling, growing quieter as the man walked away down the hall.

"Steady as she goes, Mr. Stetler." Kim watched as the green mask of the gas giant cleared from the holoports, fading into the diffuse, yellowish-brown cloud of the planet's debris field.

"Course is plotted to Kensington, ma'am." Lt. Urquhart was the only one who didn't sound or look tense, as usual.

"Very good." Kim looked over toward Chief Baudouin. "Chief, call all hands to general quarters." It was a three-day journey to the planet at sublight, but Kim wasn't going to risk running into any enemy reinforcements or patrol squadrons without being prepared.

"Aye, ma'am."

Kim took a deep breath, listening to Baudouin's voice call over the ship intercom.

"General quarters. General quarters. All hands, man your battle stations."

The pulsing electronic klaxon sounded, broken occasionally as Isabelle's voice repeated the command, her soft, feminine voice in contrast to the harsh alarm.

"General quarters, general quarters. Go up and forward on your starboard side, down and aft on your port side."

Kim pulled her safety harness over herself, clicked it into place. She could hear the distant sound of hundreds of feet pounding along the corridors, fireproof, air-tight doors slamming shut, and she imagined the crew climbing into gun turrets, slipping into damage control suits, emptying weapon lockers.

There was something comforting about this, the certainty of thousands of people acting together, moving through a fixed sequence of events.

She heard a set of heavy footfalls behind her, glanced over her shoulder to see a pair of marines in full body armor taking station in the guardroom just beyond the bridge entryway.

"Fire control reports ready. All turrets armed and loaded." Holsey's voice was still raised as the klaxons fell silent.

"General quarters confirmed, all decks, all stations," Baudouin added.

"What of the defensive systems?" Kim looked over at Holsey, whose face was under-lit by the glow from her control panel. Lieutenant Geonor had been working right up to the end on the magnetic ordnance deflector. With any luck, the last few hours had been productive.

"Ordnance deflectors show ready." Holsey's brow knotted. "We'll have about eighty percent coverage. Some of the gaps were impossible to fix without time at dry dock."

Kim nodded. Much better than she'd feared. "Chief Baudouin, pass along fighter launch confirmation."

"Yes, ma'am."

Kim faced forward, listening to Baudouin repeating her orders to Commander Frost and Lieutenant Blake over the intercom, and ran once again through the plan Holsey had worked out. The *Verdun* was to smash through the enemy armada, a task that was to be much easier now that the ship was approaching from space and was prepared for a fight. Once they'd disposed of the enemy fleet, they would bombard the fort from orbit, pounding it into submission, unless it was still in Alliance hands. With the fort reduced, the *Verdun,* which would stay in space this time for safety's sake, would launch landing craft with marine reinforcements, and, if they were able to contact the shore party, the combined ground forces would proceed on foot with air cover to capture or dispatch any remaining enemy troops in the area.

According to Holsey's calculations, a siege of the fort could take days, given the structure's impressive defenses. But somehow, based on what they'd seen of the enemy force's lackluster training during the fighting around the dockyards, Kim hoped that this would be over long before then. An unskilled garrison would not hold out for long under the crushing firepower of the *Verdun's* main guns, and the enemy would be powerless to strike back. That was, of course, only if that the fort's garrison had done what Holsey had assumed based on her studies of the fort's schematics and operating procedures and locked out Kensington's missile system.

If they hadn't...

"Well," Holsey had said, looking uncomfortable. "I have some ideas about how to deal with that, but it won't be pretty."

Kim craned her neck to look over at the portside holoports, saw the small dots of fighter craft flying away from the *Verdun* and taking up formation. Her mind was blank for a moment as she appreciated the obvious skill of the pilots, the grace of the crafts' weightless movements. Each craft with a pilot, each pilot a member of her crew, each crewmember — all two thousand of them — living people with family, friends who had no idea their loved ones were in such danger. Her shoulders tightened, a knot forming in her stomach.

She exhaled, trying to diffuse the growing tension in her body. She'd be writing many more condolence letters thanks to the people who had attacked them. Kim would see them brought to justice, whoever they were.

Yes, she told herself. This would be satisfying. This would be vengeance for everyone she'd lost already to this new enemy, for everyone she was about to lose. And if everything went as it should, she would have her satisfaction very soon. She should feel relieved.

Kim gazed ahead as the debris cloud cleared the holoports and the empty, studded blackness of space stared back at her, brushing aside the confident words she tried to tell herself with its blank, stark emptiness.

CHAPTER 24

"Welcome back, you lard-asses!"

Christine rolled her eyes as Corporal Lazaar stood and called over to the line of rangers filing toward them up the hill. She could see Lieutenant Squires at the head of the group, looking tired but cheerful as always in the morning light. Ignoring her relief at seeing Third Platoon return without casualties, she reached out and smacked Lazaar hard across the shoulder.

"Ouch! What's that for?" Lazaar turned and looked at her, incredulous.

"Has the fort been neutralized?" Christine stood out of the foxhole, placing her hands on her hips.

"No."

"No, *Lieutenant*." Christine repeated. Sometimes she had to remind people that she was an officer, not just another battle buddy. This was one of those times.

"No, Lieutenant." Lazaar looked at the ground.

"Have the woods been completely cleared of enemy forces?"

"No, ma'am."

"Have we magically been transported off Kensington to some kind of campground for people with guns?"

"No, Lieutenant."

"Then noise and light discipline still applies. This ain't over 'til it's over."

"Yes, ma'am."

Christine kept Lazaar under what she hoped was a withering stare for a moment longer before she walked down the hill to meet Squires. Third Platoon was the last group to return from patrols after Captain Morden's new orders had come through, and by the looks of them, they'd had a long haul. The sun had barely been up an hour, and it was already unbearably hot.

Squires, his uniform stained with sweat, grinned faintly when he saw Christine moving toward him and stepped aside from the others, who continued marching past him toward the waiting foxholes of the other rangers and marines.

"Keep the home fires burning?" Squires shifted under the weight of his backpack, the armor and helmet strapped to it clanking softly.

"We got a nice, warm box of emergency rations ready for you."

"Perfect." Squires closed his eyes, looking as if olive-green bags of freeze-dried meals were the best thing he'd ever heard of.

"How's it looking out there?" Christine had been feeling anxious the entire day. As much as she was relieved to not be attacking the fort, she didn't like the idea of just waiting around.

"Hot. Full of trees." Squires' grin faded. "We ran into two groups, eradicated them both. Still no sign of their air patrols. Their ground units still seem to have no idea where we're coming from."

"Good." Christine exhaled. The last thing she wanted was to be caught sitting on her ass while waiting for someone else to take care of business.

"Now, if you'll excuse me, those hot, tasty rations are calling." Squires started to move, but Christine held out a hand to block him.

"Make sure you see Wilcox right away." She met his gaze. "He's got some important things to tell you."

Christine doubted that Squires had been given the full story about the Legion, and she imagined Wilcox wanted to be the one to brief him on it.

"No need to rush things, Lieutenant."

Christine turned around to see Wilcox striding down the hill toward them, his sidearm and its holster bouncing slightly against his hip as he walked.

"Third Platoon reporting back from patrol, sir." Squires squared himself with Wilcox. "Three of our own wounded, one hundred twelve enemies neutralized."

"Very good, Mr. Squires." Wilcox thrust a thumb over his shoulder. "Go ahead, get your group settled in, and have some chow. I'll be expecting you in the radio room in thirty minutes for a briefing."

"Yes, sir." Squires started up the hill.

Christine made to follow him, but Wilcox held up a hand.

"I'd like to have a word with you, Lieutenant Flores. Walk with me."

Christine blinked, taken aback. "Yes, sir."

They turned right and strolled together for a distance, paralleling the defensive lines as they circled the hill. They passed one of the trios of marines patrolling the perimeter, returned their silent nods, and continued walking. Neither of them spoke for a while.

"To be honest," Wilcox said at last, "when we started this mission, I was sure I was going to report you for insubordination."

Christine swallowed hard, remembering the harsh words she'd said to Wilcox, the times she'd questioned his orders, all but called him a fool.

Wilcox stopped and turned to face her, his face all hard lines. "I think you have a fast mouth, Lieutenant. I think that'll get you in trouble if you don't watch it."

Christine felt her temper begin to rise, but heard Ryan's voice.

"Your temper is a work in progress, babe."

"Yes, sir."

"But I also think we know that—" he took a breath "—part of it was my fault too. I didn't follow protocol, and when you and the others tried to help, I ignored your advice. I let down my command."

Christine had to remember to keep her mouth closed to avoid gaping. She'd never heard a superior officer go this far to admit a mistake, to humble himself like this. What was he after? She realized he was waiting for a response from her.

"Y-yes, sir."

Wilcox relaxed, and a grin crept onto his face. "Lieutenant, during this… campaign, if we can call it that, I've seen an incredible improvement in your attitude as a subordinate officer and as an example for your rangers."

Where was he going with this?

"Thank you, sir."

"I'm giving you a field promotion to the rank of captain. I'll be placing an official request as soon as this is all over, but I have no doubt they'll approve it after my report."

Christine actually did gape now. She took a small step backward. "Sir?"

Wilcox was grinning broadly. "You've been a major source of expertise and advice during this entire mess. And it's obvious to me that the other officers in your company look up to you. Giving you this rank will simply be making that fact official."

A captain? Christine didn't know what to say, but found herself returning Wilcox's smile like a damned idiot schoolgirl. She saw her father's beaming smile, her mother nodding her head with pride, Ryan's sparkling eyes.

She really *was* making it.

"Thank you, sir. I-I can't believe this." It sounded stupid to say, but it was the truth. She never would have imagined Wilcox pinning a captain's coronet on her after all the shit she'd given him.

"You have only yourself to blame." Wilcox chuckled, then a frown replaced his smile. "This area could be the frontline in a long fight against the UWL. After this is all over, there's going to be a need for strong leadership on this planet, someone to help get this station back together until a proper command platoon arrives for the company. I want to do what I can to put the best officers in place."

Christine nodded, her thoughts returning sharply to the prospect of a mass revolt, of civil war. Even if the *Verdun* did come and save them, this was only the beginning.

"Thank you, sir."

"Congratulations, Captain." Wilcox held out his hand. "Though I do expect you to work on that attitude if you don't want your next superior officer to knock your ass down to private."

"I'll work on it, sir." Christine took his hand, shook it. As she released it, she found herself looking up at Wilcox, wanting to find words for something she'd hardly ever expressed to anyone, except for Ryan and a couple close friends.

"Is something bothering you?"

"Sir, I…" Christine shifted on the spot. Facing enemy fire, she could do. Hiking ten miles over rough terrain in three hours, she could do. Talk about this, on the other hand…

"I wanted to let you know. It wasn't personal, anything I said before. It wasn't about you." Christine cursed herself for the vulnerability, the emotion in her voice.

Wilcox nodded, seeming put off. "You don't need to explain. You've been stationed here with an inept commander for a long time. I'm sure I just reminded you of—"

"No, sir. It's not that." Christine fought for the words, found her ring, and pressed hard on it. "Or at least it's not just that. I grew up on Artemis, an industrial planet."

"Oh." Wilcox clearly was not sure what this had to do with anything.

"Things were pretty nasty there, and Dad... he worked for a manufacturing plant. Mom was a teacher, but she knew that all the kids stayed on the planet and worked in the factories eventually."

Christine paused to gauge Wilcox's reaction. He said nothing, so Christine continued.

"I left when I turned eighteen. I joined the Army, got into the Ranger Corps, served a couple years in the ranks. Anything to get off that damned planet. The Rangers were—are—everything to me. They saved me from that dump." Christine closed her eyes, seeing the dark clouds rising from smoke stacks, the lines of workers walking into the factory gates in the morning, the taut exhaustion written on her father's face each night when he came home. She didn't want to talk about this. She had to talk about this.

"One day, a foreman had a truckload of explosive chemicals he was going to deliver to the factory, but... he broke protocol. He was irresponsible and parked the vehicle on the street while getting food from the dispensary." Christine almost wanted to laugh. It seemed so stupid.

"There was... an accident. An explosion. My house was across the street. It was destroyed, and my parents..." She couldn't say the words, but she saw instead the data pad she'd received one day in her barracks, the cold, hard facts on an emotionless screen.

John and Charlotte Flores were both killed instantly in the blast. The house burned and couldn't be saved. Our deepest regrets, Corporal.

"Flores, I... I'm so sorry. I..." Wilcox struggled for words.

Christine opened her eyes, saw Wilcox's face through tears. "I decided that I needed to be a leader, to be the one to make sure things turned out right. I applied for OCS. I got in."

She saw again the sympathetic look of the officer who had pinned the silver shield on her collar.

"Congratulations, Lieutenant. I know how much this commission must mean to you, given the circumstances."

"When you're in charge, you've got the lives of people in your hands." Christine wiped away the tear rolling down her cheek, suddenly feeling very childish. "It's not about spit and polish or treating a rulebook like it's the Bible or something. It's just about doing it right for the situation. Every time. All the time. When you don't, when you fuck up…" Christine trailed off, looked away, at anything besides the sympathy she saw in Wilcox's eyes. It made her feel too vulnerable, too much like she had that day, like she had every time the other officers in OCS had looked at her. She didn't want that, not from anyone. Except Ryan.

Wilcox nodded, and neither of them spoke for a moment.

"I'm glad you don't think I'll fuck up anymore," Wilcox said, finally.

Christine looked back up at him, smiled. "I've just about got you broken in."

Wilcox grinned, turned to head up the hill. "Come on. I need to brief Lieutenant Squires and tell him I'll be promoting you over him."

"Oh, he'll love th—"

A rustling sound somewhere to Christine's left and down the hill cut her off mid-sentence. She reached out and grabbed hold of Wilcox, pulling him into a crouching position behind a scraggly mound of bushes.

"What's going on?" Wilcox whispered.

Christine put her finger in front of her mouth, then turned to face up the hill and made a low, whistling sound. A second later, the sound came back to her, repeated by someone on the line. She turned, peering down toward where she'd heard the noise. She could just make out the shapes of several people moving toward them through the trees. She reached into her holster, drew her sidearm, and clicked off the thumb safety, saw Wilcox do the same.

The whistling sound came again, this time from close by, and Christine looked to see the marines on perimeter security that they had passed earlier taking position by a clump of trees a dozen yards to her left. She caught their gaze, made a hand gesture for them hold their fire. Something was different about these people walking toward them. Yes, something was definitely different.

They were one hundred yards away now, and Christine could see they were in olive green Army uniforms, their rifles slung over their backs. Two of them seemed to be carrying something, a stretcher. Their movements were slow, clumsy, fatigued. But there was something about them, something familiar, though she couldn't make out their faces in the broken patches of light that filtered through the trees.

"Do we have any groups still out on patrol?" Christine breathed the words as quietly as she could.

"No. They're all in," Wilcox replied, his voice barely a whisper.

Christine scanned the woods behind the approaching group, looking for anyone, anything that might suggest an ambush. Seeing nothing, she made eye contact again with the marines, then cupped her hand over her mouth.

"Halt!"

The people stopped dead in their tracks, and two of them reached for their rifles.

"Don't touch your weapons, or we'll shoot!" Christine saw the marines to her left taking aim.

The people below stood still, awkwardly looking around to find where Christine was calling from.

"Raise your hands in the air and walk forward slowly. Set whatever you have there down."

Three of the people raised their hands, but the two holding the stretcher hesitated.

"Set it down, or we shoot." Christine peered through the mixed light, her body relaxed and ready to move.

"Please!" One of the people below shouted. "She's wounded! She'll die if we leave her!"

Christine's brow furrowed. There was something about that voice. She knew it from somewhere. Christine closed her eyes, searching back in her mind for the face that went with it.

"If you're going to let her die, you'll have to shoot the rest of us, too." The desperation in the man's voice was palpable.

Then, it came to her. "Private Fletcher?" In her mind, she could see his tall frame, his red hair. She could hear him complaining about Colonel Neville in the mess hall.

The man jumped at Christine's shout. "Y-yes?"

Christine turned to Wilcox. "He's one of the soldiers from the command center in the fort."

"He could just be pretending." Wilcox's murmured voice expressed the doubt that still slithered in Christine's belly. She wouldn't put it beyond any enemy to pull a trick.

"Agreed." Christine nodded, turned back to face the people downhill. "Go ahead and keep hold of the stretcher. But the rest of you keep your hands up. Come forward. Slowly now."

The group walked forward, and it seemed to Christine that they took an eternity to cross the distance. When they were twenty-five yards away, they passed through a patch of sunlight and Christine let out a long sigh.

"It's Fletcher all right." And that wasn't the only person she recognized.

There were five of them in all, not including the one on the stretcher, whom she couldn't see, and she knew all of them from the fort garrison — Becker on the other end of the stretcher from Fletcher, Gosse in front, Maher and Gram tagging behind.

Christine motioned the marines to lower their rifles, then stood slowly up.

They flinched when they saw her, clearly not expecting anyone to pop out of the bushes in front of them.

"Lieuten—uh, Captain Flores, Fifth Platoon, Third Rangers."

They gaped at her, recognition crossing their faces. Then Gosse fell to his knees and started crying softly.

"You're the damned most beautiful thing I've ever seen," Fletcher said, shaking his head, his voice cracking with emotion.

Then you've hit rock bottom, bud.

Christine held back her reply, seeing her own dirty, stained appearance in her head.

"We've been lost out here for days, trying to find you," Private Gram said.

Christine felt an unexpected relief move through her. She'd assumed everyone from the fort was dead or captured.

"We're glad you made it." Wilcox was by Christine's side now. He gestured over to the marines, who stepped out of the trees, slung their rifles, and walked toward the group. By the surprised look on Fletcher's face, he hadn't seen them either.

"What's your condition?" Christine's eyes flew over the tattered group, taking in their stained, filthy uniforms, their haggard faces, their cracked and dried lips. She re-engaged the thumb safety on her pistol, holstered the weapon, stepped forward, and unclipped her water bottle. She held it out to Private Maher, who snatched it immediately.

"Corporal Cassas is wounded. A bullet to her leg. The rest of us are…okay." Maher passed the water bottle to Gram, who gulped greedily from it.

"Get her up to the infirmary immediately." Wilcox motioned at the marines, who took the stretcher from Fletcher and Private Becker. Christine could almost hear the creaking soreness in Fletcher and Becker's muscles as they stretched their arms.

"I want to hear about what happened at the fort," Wilcox said. "But let's take care of you first." He gestured up the hill.

They started walking slowly, as if their bodies refused to work now that they knew they were out of immediate danger. Christine strode over to Gosse, who was still on his knees, and helped him gently to his feet.

"Come on, soldier. I've got you. That's it." She kept her arm around his back as they shuffled up the hill, a few steps behind the others. She could hear Fletcher describing the attack on the fort, his voice hollow and flat, as if he were recounting a story from someone else's life.

"They came in through an open counterscarp bunker. They were on top of us before we could respond." Fletcher took Christine's water canteen from Gram's outstretched arm and tipped it up, draining the last drop.

"We locked out the missile controls and escaped through the water cisterns," Fletcher continued. "We left Sergeant Brécourt with some others. I… I don't think they made it. We got to the forest, but Captain Holden…" Fletcher trailed off.

Christine swallowed, tightened her grip on Gosse. She had avoided thinking about all the people she'd known at the fort, how they'd met their end. She'd had her own platoon to worry about, and she wasn't going to get torn up and let her rangers down over something she couldn't change. But now she could see Holden and Brécourt in front of her, gasping, falling, screaming in pain. She hadn't known them all that well, just the occasional conversation when her platoon had passed through the fort from time to time to re-supply, but she'd heard enough to know they were good soldiers, better than Neville deserved.

Neville.

Christine looked around, almost expecting the colonel to saunter out of the woods and start insulting her. If these people had made it out of the command center, what had happened to him?

"You soldiers can rest easy," Wilcox was saying, his hand on Fletcher's shoulder. "In just a couple days, the Verdun is going to take out the enemy fleet and start bombarding the fort from orbit. It's all over."

Fletcher stopped in his tracks, causing Christine to almost bump into him.

"From orbit?" Fletcher looked sharply over at Wilcox, then met the faces of the other soldiers from the fort.

"That's right," Wilcox said, his concern at this change of demeanor mirroring Christine's own. "And thanks to you soldiers locking the enemy out, there's nothing the fort can do about it."

Fletcher shook his head. "Sir, the Verdun can't attack. She'll be destroyed."

Wilcox shifted uncomfortably. "The captain's confident she can handle the ships in orbit. And as for the fort, like I already said—"

"No," Fletcher shook his head emphatically. "You don't understand."

Dread washed through Christine as it came to her. "Private," she said, pulling Gosse with her as she stepped to face Fletcher. "Where is the colonel?"

CHAPTER 25

Tom paced back and forth across the command center's pitted floor, his hands clasped tightly behind his back. Something about this wasn't right. He stopped in his tracks, his eyes moving over the small holes gouged out of the room's walls by bullets and grenade shrapnel, past the blood spatters still visible on the concrete walls, the barricade that his warriors had installed at the blasted-out doorway. He'd seen these battle scars every day since the fort had fallen to his forces, and yet they'd never bothered him before. Now they seemed to press in on him from all sides, whispering of desperate fighting and fierce violence.

Something was definitely not right.

"Has the most recent patrol come back yet?" Tom turned on his heel to look at Eugene, who was sitting at the radio operator's console, fiddling his thumbs.

The fort's radio had finally been repaired along with its computer, though the set's decryption functions were gone for good.

The young man looked up, clearly bored with his job. "Yes, about ten minutes ago."

"And they didn't encounter anything?"

"Not a thing." Eugene grinned. "I think maybe our enemies have found a hole to hide in."

Tom wanted to roll his eyes at the young man's bravado, but chose instead to look over at the technicians hunched over the silo command console. They were down to the last mechanical components of the silo lockout now. Just a few more hours, and they'd be in business — none too soon for Tom's tastes.

Ever since the fort had fallen, fully half of the patrols he'd sent to locate the remaining military forces in the area had been systematically wiped out, their attackers vanishing into thick woods and leaving no survivors. Tom had watched helplessly as patrol after patrol had failed to return, steadily whittling down his garrison. The certainty of death for any man or woman who went on patrol had seemed so great that Tom had feared his people would start refusing to leave the fort.

Then suddenly the ambushes had stopped. Not a single patrol had been attacked the entire day. Not that Tom minded that. He was glad to not lose any more of his people. Still, something about it bothered him. It made no sense for the enemy to abandon tactics that had been working for him.

They were up to something. The situation had changed somehow, and their enemy was choosing a new way to fight.

"Don't let this lack of fighting trick you," Tom said, crossing his arms. "Until every Alliance soldier on the planet is killed or captured, they're still dangerous."

Eugene looked back down at the radio console, his expression that of a scolded child.

Tom thought for a moment, then took a step closer to Eugene, his mind made up. "Call all remaining patrols into the fort. Cancel any further searches."

"What?" Eugene spun back around.

Tom felt the eyes of everyone in the command center turn toward him.

"Shouldn't we continue searching for the Alliance forces?" The Supervisor's voice carried over from near the door. "Surely you aren't giving up on finding them. That would hardly serve *our* movement."

Tom turned, saw the Supervisor standing with his arms crossed, his face a smiling mask. Ever since their confrontation, the man had been polite and submissive, though the veiled aggression in his words told Tom that Smith was, as usual, not displaying his true self.

"I think they are coming for us." Tom lifted his chin. "The only reasons they could have ceased their ambushes are to either run away or to launch some other kind of attack. They have nowhere to run, so they must be planning an assault. I won't make the same mistake as the previous occupants of this fort and leave it undefended."

"Speculation." The Supervisor's smile broadened, his eyes glittering in the dim light.

"Perhaps. But I won't take the risk." For about the hundredth time, Tom wished that he and his people had been able to seize the command center before the enemy had managed to destroy the fort radio's decryption computer. It would be so much easier to know what was going on if they could listen in on the Alliance channels and hear the enemy's radio chatter. But radio or no, Tom trusted his instincts.

"As you wish." The Supervisor's smile became even wider, if that was possible.

Tom held the Supervisor's gaze for a second before turning back to Eugene. "Call the patrols in."

Eugene nodded, raised the handset to his mouth, and began to relay Tom's orders. Tom ignored the prickling on the back of his neck that told him the Supervisor was still watching him.

He walked about the room, checking on the other consoles and the men and women behind them, making a show of not caring about the Supervisor's gaze.

Let Smith glare if he wanted. The Alliance forces were coming — Tom was sure of it. And when they did, he would be ready for them, regardless of whether the Supervisor agreed or not.

"The Verdun is going to be destroyed. There's no way around that if we stay here." Wilcox leaned forward onto the table in the center of the bunker's radio room, searching out the eyes of the gathered ranger and marine officers one by one.

Gordon met his gaze, saw the same veiled fear, the same desperation.

Their ship, their friends, were headed toward certain death.

They had spent the better part of the day caring for and debriefing the survivors from the fort's command staff. They'd been in bad shape — hungry, dehydrated, and terrified. The wounded woman, a Corporal Cassas, probably wouldn't have lasted much longer without treatment, according to Sergeant Curry, who'd rushed her to the infirmary immediately.

Wilcox had insisted on debriefing the survivors at once, and they'd finally learned the full, terrible truth about their situation.

"Yesterday, we heard fighting, and we saw one of the ranger units taking down a group of enemies," Fletcher had explained, stopping frequently to gulp from a fresh water canteen.

"We figured we'd follow the unit — that's how we found you."

"That was good thinking." Wilcox had put a hand on Fletcher's shoulder. "But what about the colonel?"

Fletcher had almost turned red from anger, and the other gathered survivors had muttered insults under their breath that even Gordon, with all his years in the marines, had never heard.

"He wanted to head for the docks, to get off Kensington. We knew our duty and insisted we find you. He was behind us, and then…" Fletcher had taken another drink, then shook his head.

"He slipped away," Private Gram had said, wincing as Captain Flores applied antiseptic to a cut on his arm, her new cornet rank pin on her collar. "We doubled back to find him and saw him being carried away by a group of enemies. The bastard couldn't even desert without being captured."

"Are you absolutely sure he'd give away the silo codes?" The urgency in Wilcox's voice had matched Gordon's rising fears.

"Are you kidding?" Flores had looked up from Gram's arm, her face drawn into a grim frown. "If they do more than tickle him and insult his mama, he'll cave."

Flores and Wilcox had held each other's gaze for a minute before Wilcox had nodded. Gordon had almost wanted to laugh. Considering how adversarial they had been at the start of this mess, they had become one hell of a team, relying closely on each other's thoughts and opinions.

"Major?" Wilcox had turned to look at Gordon, who had understood his question without asking.

"I agree," Gordon had said, raising his chin. "We have no other choice."

Wilcox had nodded, then ordered Flores to gather the officers in the radio room for a briefing.

"Sir, you can't give up on the Verdun." Lieutenant Arnot's voice brought Gordon back to the present. The young lieutenant shot up from his chair and leaned forward over the map on the table, which was now covered with red x-marks that showed where various enemy groups had been caught and destroyed. "She may still be able to fight through it. She's a ship of the line and she—"

"Is outnumbered, outgunned, and still not back in one piece after our last engagement." Gordon interrupted Arnot, shaking his head. As much as he wished the younger man were correct, there was just no way. "Even partially dismantled and without all its silos, the fort's missiles pose a major risk."

Arnot glared, despair turning into anger. Gordon could understand that. How he wished that he could physically rip apart every damn hostile on the planet with his bare hands rather than let them take a shot at the *Verdun*.

"If it were just the enemy fleet, that would be one thing." Wilcox's calm, collected voice filled the room. "But it will be facing a fleet and a planetary defense system. Either one of those would be a challenge for a fully operational ship. But together..."

"There has to be a way to warn them." It was Lieutenant Perez who stood up now, squaring his shoulders with Wilcox.

Flores shook her head, looking across the table at Perez. "This bunker's radio won't reach much past orbit. By then it would be too late."

"But we can't just give up." Lieutenant Squires held out his hands in exasperation, looking around at the other officers. "I think I can vouch for all of us, rangers included, that we aren't going to let the bastards get your ship."

Gordon smiled, saw Wilcox do the same. "We're glad to hear it, Mr. Squires, because you're going to get your chance."

Wilcox took a long, steady breath. "We're assaulting the fort."

Murmurs rippled around the room as the officers looked at one another, their faces expressing fear, disbelief.

"Me and my big mouth," Squires muttered.

Wilcox met Gordon's eyes again. "Major."

Gordon stepped to the map table and drew his bayonet from his belt, remembering the plan that he and Wilcox had hammered out. "We're going to split our force into two sections. The first will consist of Lieutenant Ames' pack howitzers and Mahoney's heavy weapons platoon, plus two ranger rifle platoons. This group, under my command, will feint a frontal attack from the ravine to the north of the fort, then retire three miles to the rear, letting the enemy stay close enough behind them to keep them interested." Gordon traced the bayonet tip from the greenish splotch that represented the wooded ravine toward a set of hills above a clearing. "Our goal is to draw the fort garrison out and keep them tied up in this rough terrain to the northwest, where our howitzers and heavy weapons will be in a prepared position waiting to tear them up. As soon as they enter this clearing, we light them up."

Gordon drew the bayonet over to the southwest, then tapped lightly against another green splotch of forest. "The other group — that's two ranger rifle platoons and our three marine platoons — will attack from here, forcing the front gate. We figure they'll expect us to try the counterscarp bunkers, since we know that's how they got in."

Gordon looked up, saw the skeptical stares of the officers in front of him. He didn't blame them. It was a risky plan, and there were a hundred reasons it could fail. But what choice did they have?

"Those machine gun turrets on the fort's superstructure can put out a shit ton of fire." Flores put her pointer finger on the grey block that represented the fort. "We'd be mowed down before we could make it across."

Lieutenant Arnot massaged his temple, clearly trying to control his temper. "Why not attack the silos directly?"

Flores straightened up. "They're built directly into the sheer wall of the mountainside, and well under the fort's guns. You can't hit those silos with the fort intact."

Wilcox shifted uncomfortably. "I don't like it any more than you do, but we have no other choice. If the Verdun is destroyed, we're stranded here indefinitely and the enemy will be able to consolidate their position here before any Alliance reinforcements arrive. We can't hide forever. The way I see it, we only have one choice. Be hunted down eventually or—"

"Or go down in a blaze of glory." Flores grinned ruefully. "I suppose I know which one we'd all prefer."

"We're not going down, Captain." Gordon fiddled with the bayonet in his hands. "Our hope is that the distracting force will draw enough fire to allow the main attack to cross much of the distance to the main gate without receiving fire. When they send out their garrison and start seeing their friends shelled, I think their attention will be divided. Their training and discipline is poor." Gordon tried to put all the confidence he had into his voice, tried to conceal his own doubts about the plan.

There was silence for a minute as the other officers considered Gordon's words and rejected them, though they did a good job of pretending to agree.

Flores pursed her lips. "All right then. We'll give it the best damn try we can."

"Shells," Wilcox said.

Everyone looked at him.

"Sir?" Flores raised an eyebrow.

"Shells," Wilcox said again, a grin spreading over his face. "You said the fort's turrets would be seeing their friends get shelled."

Gordon stared back at Wilcox, perplexed. "Uh, yes, sir."

"Why not shell the turrets themselves?" Wilcox looked at Flores. "Captain, what do those turrets do under fire?"

Flores' eyebrows went higher. "You know this already. They're designed to eclipse into the superstructure to protect them from enemy fire. The crew can raise them to fire, then drop them again to reload."

Gordon had seen the process once when he'd been in field training near one of these old outpost forts. The garrison had been able to raise their artillery turret, fire, and lower it again within a span of six seconds.

"Exactly." Wilcox straightened up, paced around, came back to the same place, seemingly oblivious to the looks he was getting from everyone around him. "And if they're under sustained fire?"

"Then they'd leave them retracted. That's what you do under orbital bombardment, anyway."

"And they can't shoot if they're retracted."

Gordon met Wilcox's eyes as comprehension dawned in him. It was so damn simple! He felt a grin spread over his face.

"There's a problem," Flores continued, looking between Gordon and Wilcox. "Our pack howitzers throw a 75mm shell, and we only have three of them. They won't dent one of those turrets, even in the raised position."

"They don't know that," Wilcox said.

There was a pause, and then Flores was grinning as well.

"Okay, somebody explain what the hell is going on." Squires snapped his fingers in front of Flores' face.

Gordon pointed his bayonet back at the fort. "The garrison probably has little experience or education about these kinds of forts. They'll have figured out by now that the turrets retract, but they won't know the kind of fire they can take."

"A seventy-five won't punch through those turrets, but it makes a ton of noise," Flores said, finishing Gordon's thoughts.

"And we use this to our advantage how?" Squires turned to face Wilcox.

"When we make our distracting attack, we hit the fort directly with artillery fire." Wilcox tapped his finger on the fort. While their turrets are down, the main attack force rushes the gate unscathed. We can have the artillery take out their radio antenna as well, cut the garrison off from the fort, and keep them confused."

The rest of the officers nodded, and the mood in the room lightened. This was not as impossible as it seemed.

"Timing and precision will be everything. This will be way closer than danger-close." Wilcox looked over at Ames, who was staring at the map from where he was seated between Colion and Rankin. "You know your artillery crews best, Lieutenant. Can they do it?"

All eyes were on Ames as he examined the map in silence, his blue eyes slightly squinted. He looked up at Flores, then over to Wilcox. "Yes sir, they can."

"Hell, yes, they can," Flores said, a lopsided grin on her face.

"That's what I like to hear." Wilcox straightened up, the pride on his face obvious. Gordon had to admit that, despite everything that happened, this group of rangers and marines was one hell of a fighting force. As Wilcox continued speaking, he silently wished that they'd all survive to be rewarded for it.

"Captain Flores and Lieutenant Squires' platoons will be with the marines," Wilcox was saying. "We'll need your knowledge of the fort when we're inside. That leaves Lieutenants Rankin and Garrett and their platoons with Major Osterman."

There was a chorus of "Yes sirs."

Gordon couldn't help but frown. He hated the idea of being separated from his marines, but given the need for strong leadership with the distracting force, it had made sense to put a command officer in charge.

"I don't think I need to remind you that if there is fighting in the fort, it'll be tight quarters, urban-style warfare." Wilcox looked between the ranger officers, his brow slightly furrowed. "The marines will have more experience with that kind of fighting. Look to them if you need help."

"You can count on us, sir," Flores said.

Wilcox took a deep breath, let silence hang in the air for a second. "Alright then. Get your troops and equipment ready. The Verdun gets here tomorrow night, and we won't take that fort on our asses."

The seated officers rose, and they all saluted Wilcox before filing out of the room. Gordon stayed where he was, watching them leave. Wilcox sighed again and sat down, and Gordon saw his friend's confidence deflate.

"There are still a lot of ifs here," Gordon walked toward the door, wincing as his wounds protested the motion. They'd been hurting more with each day's effort, but what could he do? He needed to start helping with preparations, especially with the artillery crews. They couldn't afford a single error or hesitation with this kind of plan.

Wilcox leaned back, rubbed his chin with his hand, the rasp of stubble filling the silence in the room. When he spoke at last, his voice was quiet.

"But it's a damn good if, don't you think?"

They held each other's gaze for a second, then Gordon walked out of the room, leaving Wilcox alone.

CHAPTER 26

"Enemy ships becoming visible on long-range scopes, Captain."

"Transfer the data to my station." Kim flipped her screen open, removed the stylus from its groove beside the display. She waited, tapped the screen's metal frame, impatient for the image to appear. "Mr. Fowler?"

"It's coming through now, Ma'am."

Kim looked at Ensign Fowler, who was hunched over Wilcox's station. The young man was obviously still adjusting to Jack's job.

The faint flash of the activated screen brought Kim's attention back to her display. A wire frame image of Kensington appeared, as well as about twenty small, white dots clustered together in orbit over a landmass on the planet's northern hemisphere.

The armada.

She bit the back of her stylus, heard the sound of boots on steel, and felt Holsey's gaze over her shoulder.

"Amateurs." Holsey scoffed. "They're so low in orbit."

Kim didn't respond, but watched as the computer outlined concentric spheres around the ship, with percentage probabilities written on them, followed by arrows showing course and speed of the ships.

Kim closed her eyes for a second, and she could almost hear Captain Danner's lecture at the academy her freshman year.

"At distance, any information gathered by the scopes can be minutes or hours old. Therefore, planning an attack vector is a game of probabilities, not facts—"

"A crapshoot," Holsey said, unknowingly completing the sentence in Kim's head.

Kim nodded. She traced a line with her stylus, then tapped on the keyboard to send the course to helm and fire control. If Kim's guess proved correct, her course would keep the planet between the *Verdun* and the enemy ships until the last minute, and it would keep them uphill of the enemy ships, at a higher orbit.

"If they're consistent with what we've seen, that should be a pretty good bet." Holsey sounded confident, though Kim could detect the note of doubt in her voice.

Kim slipped her stylus back in its groove, looked over her shoulder at Holsey. "They don't seem to know much about maneuvering ships in space, or gravitational advantages. They're inexperienced, whoever they are."

Holsey scratched the back of her neck. "And superior numbers can't fix stupid."

"Most of the time, Commander." Kim held Holsey's gaze for a second longer before facing forward again. "Mr. Stetler, begin approach for attack maneuvers."

Christine lay down onto the moist, warm ground, arranging herself so that she could peek out at the fort's massive form from behind a thick, thorny bush.

"Victor Five, Victor Six. We're in position." Wilcox's whisper was barely louder than the distant mechanical hum of the fort's gun turrets, which were traversing back and forth, searching, their shapes backlit by the sun setting over the mountains.

Christine listened to Osterman's reply over her headset, watched Lazaar fiddle with the gain controls on his radio pack, sweat running down his temples.

The past day had been a rush of preparing equipment, gathering and distributing ammunition, briefing and re-briefing her platoon on the plan, and then hauling themselves as fast as they could — with a full combat load and in armor — across the miles of rough terrain between their bunker and the fort. They'd split from Major Osterman and his group some miles ago and veered to the south, keeping to cover as they'd made their way down to the edge of the forest across from the fort's main gate, the humid, hot air of monsoon season roasting them in their turtle shells.

"Doesn't look all that different." Squires whispered from Christine's other side. "Just looks like the grounds crew has some work to do."

Christine peered out at the fort again, wishing for a moment that she had x-ray vision to see what the enemy garrison was doing. Her eyes traveled over the disturbed clods of dirt in the grassy, flat plain surrounding the fort, the tell-tale sign of weapons fire and projectiles digging up the earth. There was a wrecked supply truck not far from the edge of the woods, but no cover otherwise. Christine bit her lip, tapped her ring gently against the stock of her carbine. There was a lot of open ground to cover. If this didn't work…

You won't be around to worry about it.

"We'll begin firing in approximately one minute," Osterman finished, breaking Christine's train of thought.

"Copy," Wilcox said. "Captain, Lieutenant?"

"Sir." Christine turned to face Wilcox, seeing something steady and fixed about his expression that pushed away her doubts. There were no more uncertainties, no more questions about plausibility or whether or not this was a good idea. There was only the task at hand.

"Get your platoons in order."

"Yes, sir."

Christine followed Squires through the brush back to where the rest of the attack force was waiting, her heart beating against the rigid plate of her armor, her body tensed for action. She had always wished that she fell naturally into a state of calm before a battle, like a hero in a movie or one of the medal recipients they bragged about in *Alliance Servicemember's Magazine*. But calm was something she'd learned, something she imposed on herself each time.

She concentrated on the press of her ring against the carbine's stock, nodded to Squires as he slipped into the trees to the right toward his platoon. Christine continued for a dozen more yards or so, until she was just in front of the thicket where she'd left Sergeant Néri. She knelt down on the ground, and her rangers slipped out of cover and gathered around her.

She took a moment to look around at all of them, taking note of each of their faces. Néri, his dark eyes impassive as always. Clos, Miller, Henrikson, Harris, Watts… Some of them were obviously frightened, breathing in controlled in-and-out cycles, as if they were trying to catch their breath or fight back nausea. Others seemed relaxed, almost bored, though small details — tightened jaw muscles, lips drawn just a little too tight, eyes that seemed to look out from behind transparent walls — told Christine what they were really feeling. But all of them, all thirty-seven of them, were looking at her with something Christine almost didn't want to name. Trust? Faith? Love? Christine fought back the rush of emotion she felt for this group of dirty, sweat-stained rangers — and the weight of the responsibility she carried for them. They would do this right. She would get them through this.

Christine took a breath. "We'll be moving in a few minutes, after the diversionary attack is complete. Morrisseau, Wu," Christine turned to the two engineers. "We'll be counting on you to get those doors open fast. Anyone have any questions?"

She looked between the faces of her troops, saw a few of them shake their heads.

"Good." Christine paused, took a breath. "Move as fast as possible. If you see anyone go down, leave him where he falls. We're all better off if we hurry up and get this job done."

There was a general chorus of "Yes ma'am" and a flurry of nodding heads.

Christine forced a smile onto her face, projecting confidence. "Good. I'll see you all in the command center, drinking some of Neville's brandy."

A chuckle. Some grins. A moment of normal life.

"Now," Christine's smile vanished as she reached for the scabbard on her belt. "Fix bayonets."

"Foxtrot, Victor Five. Commence firing on my mark, target Alpha-Alpha-one-seven-four-five, over." Gordon tilted his headset mic toward his mouth, trying to keep his voice low as he called in the coordinates for the fort's communications stack. The outer glacis of the fort was a good two hundred yards away from the edge of the tree line where he and the forward observation team were stationed, but somehow it didn't feel right to speak in a normal voice.

The reply came a second later. "Victor Five, Foxtrot, will fire on your mark, out."

Gordon turned to Lieutenant Garrett, who was crouched to his left with his platoon. He didn't envy them their job.

Lieutenant Garrett nodded wordlessly back at him, and Gordon could see the light catching the eyes of his troops, shining in the growing darkness. Their faces were all drawn into hard angles and tight lines.

Gordon turned to his other side, looked down the tree line to the right, over in the direction of where he knew Wilcox, Flores, and the others were waiting. Everyone was in position. An image from his childhood of a line of dominoes on the floor popped into his mind. He remembered sitting there, finger cocked and ready. They could still turn back at this point. Find some other way. Once the word was given, there was no choice but to see the attack through.

Gordon looked forward at the fort again, raised the handset to his mouth.

"Foxtrot, Victor Five, mark, over."

"Victor Five, Foxtrot, copy, out."

The twilight air split into thunder that had nothing to do with the gathering clouds.

Tom raced down the concrete passageway, ignoring the wide eyes and questioning glances of his people as he passed them. He slowed down to zig-zag between the barricades, the strange, muffled booming sound echoing along the corridor.

Tom took the scarred steps into the command center two at a time.

"What the hell was that?" He looked around at the handful of people manning the various stations in the command center, but they all stared blankly back at him.

Eugene had his headset around his neck, the internal fort's internal telephone pressed to his ear. He looked up, saw Tom.

"They're shooting at us!"

"From where?" Tom walked over to Eugene, placed his hand on the seatback.

"We... we don't know. Observation domes can't see anyone."

Another series of deep, rumbling booms. Tom felt a slight tremble in the concrete flooring, and he realized with a chill what was happening.

"They're shelling us. The Alliance attack is here. Can we fire back?"

Eugene shook his head. "We don't know where they're coming from."

Tom took a deep breath, felt the eyes of everyone on him. "Then we wait for the attack to begin. We should be safe in here."

Another explosion, this one louder than before, drummed through the air. Tom heard an electronic buzzing noise gush from the radio headset.

"Dammit!" Eugene raised one headphone to his ear, tapped on the keyboard of the computer, which was displaying a black screen with the word 'error' blinking across it in red.

"They're hitting near the radio stack," Eugene said, cursing again. "We're losing signal strength."

The report of the shells grew closer together, blended into a rapid string of blasts. Eugene stood up, dropping the telephone and throwing off his headphones. "We need to get out of here!"

"Easy," Tom said, gently pushing the kid back into his chair. He couldn't have Eugene spreading panic, not when the assault had just begun. "Easy."

"We should order the turrets to retract."

Tom turned to see the Supervisor standing at the doorway, arms crossed over his chest, a look of concern painted onto his face.

"We want the fort's defensive capabilities to remain intact," the Supervisor continued. "Send an attack force to meet the enemy infantry when they—"

"Tom!" Eugene's terrified voice interrupted Smith. "We're being attacked—soldiers from the woods to the northeast. A—And I'm getting a signal from the fleet."

Tom watched Eugene's features screw up in concentration. If the fleet was signaling, it could only mean one thing.

"Well, out with it!" Tom waved his hands impatiently.

"Sorry," Eugene murmured, closing his eyes. "It's hard to hear with the damage to the radio." Then his eyes flew open.

"The Alliance ship has returned—and it's firing on them!"

The room trembled again, and Eugene shook his head. "That's it. They've hit the antenna again. We've lost all of it."

Tom put his hand on Eugene's shoulder again, trying to think. The Alliance forces had chosen their moment well. A massive fist was closing around him, suffocating him. Some sort of trap had been sprung, and he and his followers were in the middle of it. If there was even a chance of escaping the snare, the next moments would be critical.

It was so damn surreal.

A year ago, he'd never have imagined himself in the middle of a battle, in charge of the thing. Tom had to keep himself from laughing. And yet, outside the fort and above them in orbit, a battle was starting. In the command center, it was so calm, so quiet all of a sudden. Even the sound of the artillery had—

The shells have stopped!

Tom grinned as he realized that the thunder of artillery was over.

"The barrage has lifted. They won't risk hitting their own people. Keep the turrets up to repel the enemy. And prepare our troops to counterattack." Tom turned to the Supervisor, and could, for once, match his smile. "We'll finish off the Alliance forces here and now."

"And what about the warship?" Eugene's voice was barely more than a whisper.

Tom turned around again and meet the eyes of everyone in the room in turn. He took a breath, and he knew what they had to do.

Tom turned on his heel and walked over to the missile control console, snapping his fingers in front of the stunned face of the man sitting at it.

"Jordan. Jordan!" Tom grabbed the man's chair by the armrests and looked into his terrified eyes. "Activate the targeting computer, and bring the launch systems online."

The bridge turned bright white for an instant as an explosion flashed across the holoports. Kim squinted her eyes and looked back at the image of the enemy ship engulfed in the fire of its own destruction, breaking into pieces.

"Enemy vessel destroyed." Isabelle's voice played over the intercom, and the bridge crew erupted into cheers.

"Keep focused." The knot in Kim's chest unwound slightly. "There are still plenty more where that came from. Direct fire control to concentrate lee-side guns on the ships breaking formation. Don't let them get around us."

"Aye, ma'am."

The attack was going as well as Kim could ask for. The enemy ships had been close to where Kim had predicted they'd be, and they'd been unaware of the *Verdun's* approach until the last minute. Stetler had been able to maneuver the ship into a broadside position and open fire before the target vessels had even been able to move. Clustered together in tight formation, the ships had sustained plenty of damage from the *Verdun's* main guns in the first volley. When the enemy fleet had sent a wing of fighters forward — cargo tenders mixed with the same light craft that had chased the *Verdun* off of Kensington — the skilled Alliance pilots had ripped them to pieces within minutes. The enemy ships were far more maneuverable than the massive *Verdun,* and Kim knew the key to beating them was to keep them at bay with superior firepower. Based on how their opponents kept trying to spread out and flank the *Verdun,* it was clear the enemy understood that fact, too.

Kim looked down at her display, felt the deck tremble under her as the *Verdun* fired again. She changed the camera view, saw the enemy fleet slowly dispersing, trying to close the distance with the Alliance ship. A pair of vessels was breaking to the left, no doubt attempting to move out of the planet's gravity well and encircle the *Verdun.* A cluster of shells, small points of ignited plasma against the black of space, shot toward the main group of enemy ships, then disappeared for a moment against the brightness of the planet beyond. A second later, a series of explosions sparkled between the enemy ships as the shells' time fuses ignited.

The deck trembled again, and Kim saw another swarm of shells, fired from the guns on the side of the ship facing away from the enemy fleet, fly straight forward, their course putting them at right angles to their target. Kim bit her lip, watched as the path of the shells curved slowly, the planet's gravity bending their trajectory. The shells traced a graceful parabola through the darkness until they were heading directly for the two ships breaking from the rest of the fleet. Then—

"Boom!" Stetler rubbed his hands together. "There's another one."

"Enemy vessel destroyed." Isabelle's voice calmly confirmed Stetler's observation a second later.

"Nice shooting!" Urquhart said.

"See to your stations, people." Holsey barked down from behind Kim. "This is not close to being over."

Kim looked over at Fowler, then across the room at Baudouin. "What is the status of the fighters? Any damage?"

"No, ma'am." Fowler leaned back from his station and met Kim's eyes. "Enemy ordnance is at the limit of its range."

"The interceptors are mopping up most of it," Baudouin said, holding a hand over her headset. "Ordnance deflectors are throwing off the rest."

Kim drummed her fingers on her armrest. Maybe this was going to turn out fine after all.

Yeah, right.

It was never that simple.

"There are a few more breaking from the group," Kim said, inclining her head. "Instruct fire control to maintain rate of fire. We don't let up until that fleet is ashes."

"That's good enough, damn it!" Gordon cursed as he watched another of the rangers fall under the withering fire of the fort's machine gun turrets.

Lieutenant Garrett's platoon had made it to within one hundred yards of the glacis and were crouched or kneeling in place, returning fire at the closest turrets. Gordon watched as a rifle grenade from one of the rangers struck a turret dead-on, exploding harmlessly against the thick steel. A second later, that ranger fell over on his side.

"They're losing too many," Ward hissed. "For fuck's sake."

"This is part of the plan," Gordon replied. He wished that made this easier to watch.

Suddenly, one of the rangers — Lieutenant Garrett, though it was hard to tell in the dark — stood up, waved his hand, and started running back to the woods. The others leapt to their feet and followed a second later.

Gordon shook his head, each second grinding past as Garrett and the rest of his troops sprinted toward him. Another one fell, and another, caught in the back by the hail of bullets from the fort's machine guns. Explosions burst behind them as one of the fort's artillery turrets joined in. "Come on. Come on."

Two more rangers vanished in an explosion. Another fell face forward like a rag doll.

But then Garrett was leaping into the woods, turning, and hustling the remainder of his troops into the tree line, shouting encouragement at them as they passed.

"Good job! Come on! Back to the rendezvous point! You can make it!"

Gordon waited until the last ranger had run past him and into the woods before hitting his shoulder mic. "Foxtrot, this is Victor Five. Repeat, target Alpha-Alpha-one-seven-four-five, over."

Gordon got to his feet, keeping his head down as bullets began to thwack into trees around him. "Let's move."

He pulled Corporal Ward to his feet, flinched as shells whistled overhead. He looked over, saw balls of fire appear on the top of the fort. He knew they weren't doing much, but it felt good to punch back.

"Raven Two-Six, this is Victor Five. The rest of the platoon is falling back. We'll be on station." Gordon called into the radio as a tree exploded nearby, shooting fragments of wood in all directions. The fort wasn't letting them run away without trouble.

"Copy." Lieutenant Rankin's voice crackled over the radio.

Another shell exploded fifty yards to the right. Dirt and small pieces of wood rained down on Gordon's helmet and body armor. If this didn't work, they'd be in real trouble in a second or two.

"Lieutenant!" Gordon shouted over the crash of more shells slamming into the fort. "Prepare our exit!"

Garrett nodded, pulled a rifle grenade from his belt and began fitting it to the muzzle.

"Sir, look!"

Gordon followed Ward's pointed finger toward the fort, could barely see the outline of the turrets vanishing into the fort in the dimness.

"Hide in your hole, you bastards!" Ward's shout was all but lost as another set of shells struck the glacis, spitting fire into the night.

Gordon couldn't blame him for his rage, not after what they'd seen happen to Garrett's platoon.

"Don't celebrate yet, Corporal." Gordon glanced over, saw Garrett kneeling down and angling his carbine with its butt in the dirt, the rifle grenade pointed into the air. He turned back toward the fort, straining his eyes to make out the main gate. Shut tight.

They waited, listening to the whine of the shells. *Where were they?*

"We… We could make another go of it, sir." Garrett looked up at Gordon, wiped sweat and dirt from his face. "They may not come out if we—"

"There!" Ward interrupted.

Gordon's heart surged into his throat. A sliver of light appeared, growing into a rectangle. The main gate was sliding open. And from inside came pouring the shapes of people, weapons catching the light from the fort's interior as they rushed outside and into the dark. For a moment, he fought the urge to laugh, thinking of clown cars from ancient silent films. There were so damn many of them.

Gordon saw Ward step back slightly.

"We hold our position," Gordon said. "Stand fast."

The scream of the charging people became audible over the shellfire. Sweat trickle down Gordon's forehead.

"Hold on…. Hold on." He raised his arm.

The wave of enemies was closing the distance. Only a few hundred feet now. Then the rectangle of light began to narrow into a slit and, after a second, vanished completely.

"Now!" Gordon moved his arm down in a slashing motion, and he heard the muffled boom of Garrett's rifle grenade. A second later, it detonated, and Gordon heard agonized screams as the explosion cast the attacking crowd into light for a second.

"That pissed them off." Ward shouted over the shellfire.

Gordon didn't respond, but he shouldered his rifle and fired a few times, knowing he'd hit his mark. There was no missing with a dense group like that.

Flashes and the crack of weapons fire told Gordon that Ward and Garrett were doing the same. Bits of wood flew off of trees, clods of dirt spat into the air. The air hissed as bullets from the oncoming group knifed into the tree line.

Gordon fought every urge to run. They had to wait, had to keep harassing the enemy, keep them interested, committed to the chase. If the enemy gave up on following them and returned to the fort, the plan was shot.

They were so close now. One hundred yards. Fifty. Gordon fired three more shots, turned, and shouted over the din. "Let's move!"

Ward nodded and plunged into the trees in the direction the rest of Garrett's platoon had vanished. Garrett stood from where he was kneeling behind a tree, took a hard look toward the fort, and Gordon knew that he wasn't looking at the enemy, but at the third of his platoon that was still lying out there.

"Lieutenant, after you!" Gordon put his hand on the man's shoulder, gave him a slight push.

Garrett sprinted into the woods, and Gordon followed, stopping and firing behind him every few dozen yards. The enemies seemed to have taken the bait, were still chasing after them.

This might actually work.

They were only twenty yards behind, crashing into the forest, firing wildly after the Alliance troops.

Gordon fired his rifle, then reloaded on the run, following the dim form of Lieutenant Garrett into the night. The scream of charging thousands followed him.

CHAPTER 27

"**H**old your positions... Wait until my order."

Jack squinted out as the flood of enemy troops moved off into the trees a few hundred yards to their left. He'd heard the radio traffic — Osterman and his team were pulling back. Now they only had to wait for the enemy to pass out of sight. Easier said than done.

"Christ, they're like ants," Henrikson whispered from nearby.

"Keep your head out of your ass, Private," Flores responded.

Jack couldn't blame them for their agitation. Watching Garrett's platoon get cut to pieces had been hard enough. Standing by while an entire army chased after Osterman's team just rubbed salt in the wound. Jack bit his lip.

He wouldn't go there, wouldn't let fear for his friend, for the other rangers, slip into his thoughts. He had his own team to worry about.

Jack watched the shells explode on the outside of the fort, let the noise empty his mind of worry. He had to admire the artillery crew's work. The rounds were consistently striking right on the fort's superstructure. Not one had fallen short onto the surrounding plain. That was something of a relief considering he and his group were about to run across that area. Danger close? Safety distance? All of that was out the window.

"They're all in the woods." Flores interrupted Jack's thoughts.

Jack nodded, more to himself than anyone else. *Just a minute longer.*

He waited just long enough for the yells and battle cries of the enemy force to start fading in the distance, then stood up, turned to face the blackness of the woods behind him, and waved. The marines and rangers slipped out of cover, their footsteps silent as they moved toward him.

Jack gripped his rifle tightly, turned around, and started running. The trees disappeared from around him, the comforting closeness of the vegetation giving way to the naked openness of the plain. Jack felt the soft, spongy grass under his boots as he ran toward the fort, the acrid smell of explosives burning his nose. Shells whistled overhead and detonated on the fort, drowning out the sound of the others running beside and behind him, washing him with noise. He fixed his eyes on the dark shape of the fort, watching the low silhouettes of its retracted turrets. One of the turrets disappeared for a moment in a direct shell hit, then reappeared as the smoke dissipated, completely undamaged. If the garrison realized that the small shells weren't capable of penetrating the fort's defenses while Jack and the others were still in the open...

But they were getting close to the gate now. Just a bit farther. Just a bit farther.

The air crackled as more shells sailed overhead, exploded. Jack flattened himself against the cold, hard retaining wall of the entrance tunnel, breathing hard and looking behind him at the rest of the group, shadows streaking across the open ground. He scooted along the wall and peered into one of the exterior guardhouse's gun ports. It was empty and dark inside, and Jack could see the door to the interior guardhouse shut tight. No doubt the artillery had scared whoever was manning the fort's gate, and they'd retreated inside.

Flores came to a halt beside Jack. "Are we clear?"

"Clear."

"Morrisseau! Wu!" Flores slung her carbine over her shoulder. "Get on it!"

The entire group had made it across now, and they pushed themselves against the gate and the retaining wall of the fort's glacis, minimizing their exposure. Two of them ran toward Flores, who opened a small keypad just to the side of the gate.

Jack flinched as another shell exploded, watched as Wu and Morrisseau took apart the panel. Morrisseau, small and wiry, pulled a cable from inside the panel and handed it to Wu, who knelt down and pulled small a computer pad from his pocket. He connected the cable, his features lit up by the glow from its screen.

"Shit!" One of the marines cursed as another shell detonated, much closer than before.

"Any day now, Captain." Jack shouted over at Flores, who was saying something he couldn't hear over the din to Wu. Then she turned around, gave a thumbs up.

"Prepare to breach!" Jack motioned to the others around him, and they arranged themselves on either side of the gate. Flores and Private Hartnett, one of the marines, took up the front positions, pulled grenades from their belts.

Jack arranged himself behind Flores and looked back at Wu, who was hunched over his pad.

Wu raised his hand.

A second later, the door began to slide open, the loud grind of the gate's motor audible even over the artillery.

Before the gate had opened six inches, Flores and Hartnett tossed their grenades through the crack and looked away. Jack did the same.

Explosions. A flash of light lanced out across the ground from the gap in the opening gate. Screams.

"Go! Go!"

Jack heard Flores' shout, saw her vanish into gate, and followed.

Smoke assaulted his lungs and stung his eyes as he took in the details. A wide corridor. The mangled body of an enemy on the floor. Blood spattered on the walls. Bits of glass and metal from grenade fragments and exploded light bulbs. Two more enemies stumbling out of the guardhouse, covering their eyes and waving pistols around.

Flores and Hartnett knocked them over, silenced their surprised screams with bayonets. Jack caught movement to his left, saw another enemy clambering to his feet a few yards down the corridor. Jack aimed his rifle, thought twice, and then ran toward him, knocking him back down to the ground with his rifle butt. Looking anywhere but at the man's face, Jack pushed the point of his bayonet past the poor bastard's desperate hands and into his chest. He planted his foot on the enemy's torso, withdrew, and punched the blade in again. The man went limp.

Fighting back his nausea, Jack withdrew his bayonet. They had to hold off from firing their weapons as long as possible. The explosion of the grenades could be mistaken for artillery, but the sharp crack of rifle fire would give them away. The farther they could get inside the fort before they had to start fighting, the better.

Jack looked behind him. The rest of his troops were flowing in through the fully opened gate. Flores was running toward him with Private Fletcher in tow. They stopped beside Jack, breathing hard.

"Alright, Fletcher," Jack clapped the private on the back. "Get us to the command center. Shortest route."

Fletcher nodded, then ran off down the corridor with Flores. Jack waved to the rest of the group, and then followed. The corridor continued, then opened onto a large, brightly lit bay, which was empty except for a jeep Jack recognized as Colonel Neville's. Just beyond, the corridor ended, and a staircase rose up and to the left. The concrete walls echoed with their footsteps, a stark contrast to the noise outside, which had faded to a muffled rumble.

The group came to a halt as Flores and a handful of marines and rangers crept upwards, clearing the landing at the top.

"So far, so good." Lieutenant Arnot appeared at Jack's side.

Before Jack could respond, Lieutenant Squires walked by and muttered, "Don't jinx it."

No kidding.

Fletcher signaled that the landing was clear, and Jack ran forward, taking the stairs two at a time. At the top of the landing, he found Flores, Squires, Fletcher, and a few others with their backs against the wall, ready to move around the corner. Jack made eye contact with them, moved into position, and began creeping around the corner, clearing the corridor beyond one pie-slice at a time.

Then he saw them, and the corridor exploded into gunfire.

"Send all our forces to the west tunnels. Keep them out!" Tom shouted at the messenger, who stood at the bottom of the stairs leading up into the command center. The telephones only serviced the bunkers, turrets, and guardhouse, and without a radio, they'd resorted to sending runners back and forth to the various lines of defense in the fort.

The runner nodded and sprinted away.

Damn it!

The enemy attack force had seemed to retreat, and when their artillery had started again, Tom had given in to the Supervisor's suggestion, ordered the turrets down, and sent out most of the fort's garrison to catch the retreating Alliance forces. He wasn't about to let them melt into the woods again, and if his people could catch them fleeing and packing up their cannons, they could wipe them out for good.

But he'd kept back a couple hundred troops. The Supervisor had called it an unnecessary precaution. Then someone had heard an explosion down at the main gate, probably a shell strike. The guardhouse hadn't answered the telephone, so he'd sent some of his people to investigate. They'd run headlong into an Alliance attack force. Unknown strength, unknown numbers. And no way to call back the unit running after the other Alliance force. To make things worse, judging from the targeting scanners, the enemy warship was doing a number on the fleet.

Tom turned on his heels, strode over to Jordan. "Are you ready to fire?"

Jordon nodded, wincing at the distant sound of gunfire echoing down the corridor — and getting closer. "We'll have target lock in a moment."

"Begin the launch sequence."

"Enemy vessel destroyed," Isabelle said as another one of the enemy warships split in two, spewing fire and atmosphere into space as it began to drift into the planet's gravity.

Four down. Sixteen to go.

Kim gripped the armrest of her chair, took a deep breath. This was going better than she could have imagined. Out of effective range of the enemy fleet, the *Verdun* was tearing her adversaries apart with her main guns. Every time the enemy ships attempted to close the distance, the *Verdun* would blast one of them apart and the others would retreat, try to re-shuffle their formation.

If this continued, they would have the enemy fleet demolished in no time.

"It's only a matter of time before they decide to rush us and accept whatever losses they take in the process." Holsey's voice broke into Kim's thoughts, articulating her own concerns. "Once they're in close, they'll run circles around us. Our advantage will disappear."

Kim swiveled her chair around, took in Holsey's grim expression. At least someone else here was sharing Kim's cynicism. All the rest of the bridge crew seemed to be enjoying the fireworks show of the exploding enemy vessels.

"I agree." Kim spun back around. "Mr. Stetler, begin plotting a trajectory away from the planet."

"Away from it, Ma'am?" Stetler looked back over his shoulder at Kim, his brow furrowed.

"Correct. If the enemy fleet rushes us, I want to maintain our gravitational advantage as long as we can. We'll turn it into a running battle if we have to, but we can't let them get close."

"Aye, ma'am." Stetler bent over his controls and began working.

The bridge lit up again as a volley of shells from the *Verdun* split another enemy ship into pieces.

"Enemy vessel destroyed," Isabelle confirmed. "Enemy target lock. Recommend evasive maneuvers."

Chills skittered down Kim's spine. "What the hell?"

She swiveled around in her chair. "Fowler, report!"

Fowler was shaking his head, sitting straight in his chair. "Someone on the planet is pinging us with an EM beam."

The bottom fell out of Kim's stomach. "From where?"

"From a set of structures in the mountains near the fort." Fowler swallowed hard. "It's an illuminator. They'll have positive lock in—"

Kim interrupted Fowler. "Holsey, have fire control direct the secondary guns to load time-fuse shells. Put all anti-fighter and anti-ordnance turrets on alert and feed in the coordinates of the fort. I want an effective flak screen. Keep the main guns on the fleet. Keep them busy!"

Kim heard Holsey pass on her orders to fire control, looked over at Baudouin.

"Chief, give the defensive fighters the coordinates as well. Tell them to prepare for a missile strike. Lieutenant," Kim looked down at Urquhart's back. "Increase our speed to maximum, get us in a higher orbit. I want as much—"

"They've launched! Missile incoming!" Fowler shouted over the rumble of the main guns firing again.

"Flak screen, now!" Kim looked down at her screen, rifled through camera views until she found one facing toward the planet. The deck plating beneath Kim's feet vibrated as the secondary turrets opened fire, throwing a curtain of small explosions against the bright disc of the planet beyond. Kim strained her eyes to pick out the missile, couldn't find it.

"Impact in one minute!" Fowler yelled.

Where is the damn thing?

Kim spotted a bright spot in the top right corner of her screen. It was growing larger every second, an orange-red splotch against the blue of an ocean below. She zoomed in, made out the dark shape of the missile within the fiery halo of its engines.

She had only a basic familiarity with these missiles from training. After all, ground-to-space missiles were the Army's concern, not the Navy's. She knew that they were huge, had their own ordnance deflection system, and were very hard to take down.

She knew enough to fear them.

The missile was passing the enemy ships now, and Kim's insides tensed. Huge didn't begin to describe it.

"Twenty seconds."

She saw the *Verdun's* defensive fighters swoop past it, peppering it with fire. Their rockets and bullets missed — it was so damn fast! — or warped around the missile, exploding uselessly in space.

"Come on, take it down!" Urquhart called, a hint of fear in her voice.

"The flak will do it," Stetler responded.

Kim hardly heard them. She watched as if spellbound as the missile approached the flak screen. It was coming straight toward them, unwavering, then began to break up.

"See!" Stetler said, and Kim heard a thump as Stetler smacked Urquhart on the back. "Told you."

Kim felt a wave of relief, then her heart plummeted into her feet.

It wasn't breaking up. It was separating.

The missile blossomed, its nose splitting apart and releasing what looked like a tight coil of smaller rockets, each of them about the size of one of the *Verdun's* fifteen-inch shells. The rockets spread out from each other, their own engines sputtering on, racing toward the *Verdun* even as the main body of the missile continued forward. There were at least a hundred of the damn things. They were passing into the flak screen, and Kim watched as the main missile body and some of the smaller rockets were caught and exploded by the hail of fire from the *Verdun* and the fighters trailing them.

Not good enough.

A cloud of rockets emerged from the screen, only seconds between them and the hull of their target.

"All hands, brace for impact," Isabelle announced coolly.

Kim saw some of the rockets begin to warp around the *Verdun* as the ordnance deflector bent their trajectories—she pitched forward, caught hard against her safety belt. A machine-gun blast of explosions merged into a roar that filled the air. The lights flickered, and she heard someone scream.

Kim shook her head, looked down at her static-washed screen.

"How bad?" Kim spun around in her chair, checking on each of the bridge crew in turn. At least none of them seemed to be hurt, except for Stetler, who was shaking his bloodied left hand, a shattered screen next to him attesting to what had caused the injury.

"The MOD deflected most of them," Fowler said. "We have some impacts amidships, near the gaps in our defenses from our previous engagement. A couple sections are reporting fire, and we have one area that has decompressed. There's minor damage across the ship from the explosions of the rockets that were bent off course. They've opened a couple more gaps in our MOD coverage."

Kim shook her head. One missile had caused all that?

"Baudouin, dispatch damage control teams to the affected areas," Holsey called from over Kim's shoulder. "Captain?"

Kim turned around, saw a trail of blood coming down from Holsey's eyebrow.

"They're going to chew away at our deflector until we lose coverage. If we take a full strike without the deflector, we're cooked."

"Agreed." Kim faced the bridge crew. "Fowler, what were the speed readings on those warheads? Can we outmaneuver them?"

"No Ma'am. And we can't outrun them without faster-than-light capabilities."

"Could we withdraw from the area?" Stetler asked.

Kim shook her head. No way were they going to retreat. Not yet.

"Ma'am?" Fowler's voice cracked as he called out again. "They've still got target lock on us."

"There's no knowing how many of those things they have." Holsey's voice was soft so that only Kim could hear it. "Maybe we should withdraw."

Kim weighed the options for a second longer. If they ran, they'd be back hiding in that gas giant, waiting for the enemy fleet to regroup, reinforce itself, and come after them — and that's assuming they could outrun the next missile. There was no way they could ever reach the nearest Alliance station during their lifetime without their main engines.

"We make our stand here, Commander." Kim swallowed, her mind made up. "Hard over, Ms. Urquhart. Charge down on the enemy fleet. Get us among them."

"Ma'am?" Stetler turned around, cradling his injured arm.

"You heard me. Chief, have the fighters regroup and close in around us. We'll be fighting in tight quarters. Load all secondary guns with anti-armor warheads. Stetler, keep us moving within the fleet. I want them confused."

"Aye, ma'am."

Kim felt the ship's inertia shift beneath her as the *Verdun* banked and descended on the enemy fleet, a stream of shells preceding it and exploding among the enemy ships that were rushing up to meet it.

Like a pack of wolves.

"They may be able to maintain target lock even when we're among that fleet," Holsey said.

"But we won't make it easy for them." Kim adjusted her safety belt. "And besides, I'm hoping these ships will lend us a hand in absorbing some of those missiles."

"They're launching another one!" Fowler called out.

Kim gripped her armrests, felt the air close in around the bridge as everyone's nerves tensed together. "Maintain your course, Mr. Stetler. Get us into that fleet."

Chapter 28

Gordon ignored the stream of cusswords spewing from Lieutenant Garrett's mouth as the air above the forest roared and a blinding light streamed down through the branches, bringing a brief moment of daylight to the inky night. The light faded away, and Gordon strained to see his feet in front of him.

Another missile had launched from the silos behind the fort.

"Son-of-a-bitch! Mother fuck! Cunt-smacking asshat—"

"Save your breath for running, Lieutenant."

Truth be told, Gordon had a few choice words in mind as well. But they wouldn't help anything now. They had to give the attack force time to take the fort. And that meant taking care of the enemy army trailing a few dozen yards behind them.

Ward, Garrett, and Gordon had met the rest of Garrett's platoon in their rush through the woods. They'd worked to stay just ahead of the enemy force, turning now and again to fire into their ranks or send a grenade their way, keeping them sufficiently pissed off to maintain the chase. The ground was sloping up now as two thickly wooded hills rose up in the darkness on either side of them, forming a sloping valley. It wouldn't be far now.

Thank God, because Gordon couldn't handle much more of this. His legs burned from the exertion, and his abdomen felt like it was crushing inward from the pain of his barely healed wounds. Under normal circumstances, this operation would have been a strain. But with his injuries from the Triangle? He'd been in bed so damn long that he'd clearly fallen out of shape.

Focus, Gordon!

Gordon concentrated on his breathing and on threading a path through the trees and brush that grabbed for him in the darkness. The woods were thinning out, yielding to tall, silky grasses. He stopped in his tracks, waved for a couple of Garrett's troops to join him while the rest ran past, and fired a few shots into the darkness. Screams. The crack of rifles. Muzzle flashes. The whiz of bullets through the air. The shriek of shells passing overhead. The rangers copied Gordon, firing a few shots before resuming their sprint through the woods. Gordon coughed, tasted blood, and ran after them.

The ground rose ever more steeply, straining Gordon's already tired muscles. The air opened up around him as the last trees gave way to a huge open meadow. To the left and right, steep, rocky slopes reared up, their jagged tops dark against the sky. Ahead, the ground continued to slope upward toward a patch of boulders strewn across the meadow, the black wall of the forest behind it.

"Come on! We're nearly there!" Gordon shouted, as much to himself as to the others. Corporal Ward, more burdened than the rest of them under his radio set, was slowing down. Gordon planted his hand firmly on the man's back and pushed.

"Whose idea was this?" Ward gasped.

"Shut up and run."

The buzz of bullets in the air increased. Without any more trees to conceal them, Gordon and the others were much easier targets than before. Clods of dirt kicked up in front of him, to the sides, all around him. One of Garrett's troops screamed, clutching her arm, and fell forward. Gordon barely broke his stride as he hauled her to her feet and pulled her along with him. An explosion to the right. More sprays of dirt. Corporal Ward stopped in his tracks and fell over.

"Go!" Gordon pushed the wounded ranger on, stopped to help Ward. He pulled the man upward, saw a gaping hole where his face had been.

"Fucking son of a bitch!" Gordon took off running again, wincing at the angry swarm of bullets in the air.

"Save your breath for running, sir." Lieutenant Garrett's voice drifted back to him, almost lost under the scream of ordnance passing overhead. The explosion of the shells as they struck the fort behind them were a distant rumble now.

Gordon bit back his remark, peering ahead of him in the darkness. They were only a few yards from the boulders now, and Gordon could just make out the sandbags of the positions in front of him, the glint of starlight on steel. Only it wasn't just starlight. Gordon glanced upward, saw faint flashes and streaks of light falling across the sky like clusters of shooting stars. They were telltale signs of a battle in orbit, of wrecked ships burning up as they fell toward the planet. Could it be from the *Verdun?*

Gordon shook the thought from his mind, put every last ounce of energy into reaching the positions ahead. Just a few more yards. Another ranger fell in front of him and lay still. Gordon jumped to avoid tripping on the man's body, held back his anger. The enemy would get theirs in just a moment.

Gordon saw Garrett and the remaining members disappear into the shallow trench ahead of him, and then jumped down into it as well, grateful to be out of the crackling air, to not be running anymore.

"Glad you made it, sir." Lieutenant Rankin was beside him, her hand on his shoulder. "We're in position."

Gordon coughed again, felt as if he was about to throw up. He looked up at Rankin, whose face was dark against the fire-streaked sky. "Light these fuckers up."

"Copy that."

As he stood back up and rested his rifle on the sandbags that capped the trench's parapet, Gordon heard the order pass down the line, heard a radioman speaking it into his handset. Gordon took aim into the dark mass of approaching soldiers. A wave of noise assaulted him as the weapons of the Alliance soldiers opened fire.

They had prepared this position well. Rifles and heavy machine guns flashed from their breastworks up on the rocky hillsides to the either side of the valley, sweeping the enemy with enfilading fire. A second later, the pop of mortars, positioned on the hilltops and behind the trench, broke through the din of gunfire. Explosions blossomed across the valley floor, casting the toppling, tumbling, running bodies of the enemy into light for an instant. To Gordon's right and left down the trench, the rangers opened fire. Rifles, light machine guns, and heavy machine guns scorched the air with the fire of their reports. Tracers sliced through the air, and a flare arced into the sky from one of the hilltops. Gordon could see the enemy, who were filling the valley and rushing forward and to either side, no doubt trying to storm the Alliance positions. Even as they fell in droves, more of them poured into the valley from the forest below.

There are so damned many of them!

Whatever happened, they were going to hold the Legion here. They wouldn't yield this position, and they wouldn't let the enemy retreat back to the fort. They would succeed, or die trying.

Gordon knew which of those two he preferred. He lined up his rifle's sights, tasting blood in his mouth again, and fired.

"Get him to the rear and get back into the fight!" Christine yelled at Hartnett as she dragged a wounded marine — Private Douglas — back from the corridor junction.

Not that it mattered. It was so damn loud that she doubted anyone could hear. Individual gunshots, shouts, and explosions all blurred into a continuous wave of sound that assaulted her ears, pushed against her sinuses, and rattled her bones. An entire battle bottled and crushed into the concrete box of the fort's cramped hallways. Even the noise cancellation of her headset was not enough to stop the din.

Christine watched Hartnett drag Douglas back down the corridor to the right, past the line of marines and rangers who were scrunched up against the concrete wall, ready to storm around the corner and face death. They hadn't made it far into the fort before running smack into its defenders. Christine couldn't guess how long they'd been fighting now, pushing the enemy deeper into the fort, demolishing their defenses barricade by barricade, locked door by locked door, but she knew it was longer than Wilcox wanted. They were taking too damn long. After the last barricade, they'd forced the bulk of the enemy force onto the top level, where the command center was located. Sending Lieutenant Colion and his platoon to secure the lower level, Wilcox had ordered the attack to press forward — only for the marines on point to run into a hornet's nest of gunfire at this T-junction.

Christine kept her back firmly against the concrete, the hard press of steel against her spine reassuring her of her armor's protection. The alarming lightness of the magazine pouches on her belt, however, was not so comforting. She had already expended half of her ammunition, despite her efforts to conserve it. If this fierce resistance continued...

Well, she always had her bayonet.

She looked ahead and to the left, at the splatter of concrete being chipped away as bullets dug holes into the wall. Directly across from her, the corridor continued and turned another bend, heading toward the big artillery turret. It was empty, as far as she could tell. Around the corner, the hall led into the superstructure of the fort, going past the upper barracks block, and to the command center. There was also, apparently, an army there.

"Captain? Captain!" Wilcox's shout was almost inaudible.

Christine looked to see him walking toward her along the line of waiting soldiers.

"What's going on up here?" Wilcox scrunched against the wall next to Christine, one hand around his rifle, the other holding the brim of his helmet.

"They're set up pretty good around there, sir." Christine flinched as small bits of concrete were blasted from the corner of the wall, bouncing off her shoulder pad. "Just how good, I don't know. Douglas got hit coming around the corner, Hartnett was able to drag him back, and we took cover."

"Get us moving again as soon as possible."

Christine looked past Wilcox at Néri. She waved to get his attention, then made her hand flat and tilted it back and forth. Néri knelt down, rummaged in his musette bag, and pulled out a small mirror with a short, plastic handle. He passed it down the line of soldiers.

"Old trick of yours?" Wilcox handed it to her.

Christine nodded. "Whatever works, works."

She scooted close to the edge, wincing again as another round struck near the corner. She held her left hand out, slowly moving the mirror past the edge of the wall and angling it so she could see the reflection of the space beyond.

"Those busy little bastards." She shook her head.

On the small, dirty face of the mirror, she could see what looked like a wall blocking the hallway. It was about six feet tall, and had netting strung between it and the ceiling, no doubt to keep grenades from being thrown over it. Moving the mirror back and forth, she realized that the wall wasn't continuous. Rather, it was a barrier jutting out from the corridor's left wall, leaving a space just wide enough for one person to walk at a time. Behind it by a few yards was another barrier, this one jutting out from the right side. Both had loopholes built into them at about waist height, and judging by the muzzle flashes coming out of them, there were machine guns set up back there. Christine gasped as the mirror shattered. She tossed the broken tool to the ground and looked at Wilcox, who had been joined by Lieutenant Arnot.

"They've built overlapping stone barricades back there," Christine shouted, holding up her flattened hand to illustrate the idea.

"What?" Arnot's brow furrowed. "Overlapping?"

"One barricade goes across most the corridor from one side," Christine continued, doubting whether or not Wilcox and Arnot could hear more than every other word. "A few feet behind that, another one blocks the corridor from the other side. You have to run a zig-zag to get through them. Get past one, and the other is still there. Each one covers a section of the hallway."

And there was no way of knowing how deep they went. Fighting through a maze of them would be a tall order.

Arnot nodded, looked at Wilcox. "Our portable loopholes on the Verdun are like that."

"They must have built this themselves," Christine added. "The fort didn't have these before."

"Will rockets do the trick?" Wilcox looked between Christine and Arnot.

Christine shook her head. "I wouldn't risk it. Could cave the ceiling in and block the way." The absolute last thing they could afford was to slow the attack down.

"What about grenades?" Arnot asked.

Christine considered for a second, trying to remember the exact specifications of the fort's construction. It was hard to think at all in that damn noise.

"I think grenades are fine," Christine said finally.

Wilcox's mouth tightened as he seemed to consider the options. "There's no way but through it. See if you can suppress their MGs and get a grenade or two back there. Arnot, Flores, make it happen. I'll hold back the other two platoons as reserve." Wilcox headed back down the corridor, speaking in his headset to relay what was going on to Squires and Perez.

Christine nodded, waved Néri over. "Sergeant, get one of the LMGs up here."

She turned to Arnot, pointed directly across the corridor to the empty hall beyond. "Lieutenant, if we can put some fire on the loopholes, do you think you can get across to the other side?"

They'd have an easier shot at breaking through these barricades if they could un-ass themselves from this bottleneck and get another angle on the enemy loopholes. If they could knock one out, they'd open a gap in the area covered by those machine guns, and they'd be able to get closer.

"Yes, ma'am." Arnot turned and walked back down the corridor, peeling the men and women of his platoon off the wall and readying them for action. Christine shifted to let Krouri and Accardo past her with the machine gun. They unfolded the weapon's bi-pod, knelt down behind the corner of the junction. Christine felt a tap on her shoulder. She turned, saw Néri beside her again, a smoke grenade in his hand. Christine took it.

"Sergeant, get the platoon ready to move. I want Meyer's squad around that corner as soon as that first machine gun is down. They'll move in fast and tight against the left wall."

"Yes, ma'am." Néri moved back down the corridor to relay Christine's orders.

"We're ready!" Arnot appeared next to Néri.

Christine pulled the grenade's pin, leaned out over Krouri and Accardo, tossed it around the corner, then tucked herself back into cover. A small flash. A bang, lost amidst the gunfire. The noise lessened, and smoke stung Christine's nose.

She slapped Accardo's helmet, and he pivoted the barrel of his machine gun around the corner. He opened fire, spraying staccato bursts toward the loopholes.

"Lieutenant, go!" Christine made sure that Arnot's eyes met hers and that he understood the order before pressing next to Krouri and training her carbine around the corner. She could only barely make out the barricades through the thick, white smoke. She guessed where the loopholes were, and sprayed fire toward them, first the left one, then the right one.

The enemy fire had all but stopped now, and Christine could see the shapes of Arnot and his platoon moving past her and across the corridor out of her peripheral vision.

The enemy machine guns opened up again, no doubt deciding that the stream of marines across the hall in front of them was reason enough to brave Accardo's bullets. Christine heard a scream, glanced over to see a couple of the marines fall over. Another stopped to try to drag them across, and fell as well, pressing a hand to his stomach. He tried to crawl, jerked again as a round hit him, and lay still. Christine bit her lip and, seeing Accardo spray fire toward the right-hand loophole, took careful aim at the muzzle flash of the enemy machine gun on the left. She steadied her weapon against the concrete, fired. The flash disappeared, then, a few, long seconds later, started up again. Maybe she'd hit and some other fucker had picked up the MG. Maybe she'd made the guy duck for a second. Either way, the rest of the marines were across.

She pulled back into cover and looked over at Arnot, who was barking orders to his marines. Christine caught his eye. He gestured with a fist, holding it like a grenade, and pulling off an imaginary pin. Christine nodded and knelt down next to her machine gunners, careful to not interfere with Krouri as she supported a belt of ammunition from her olive-green ammo can and into the side of Accardo's weapon.

"Accardo!" Christine slapped his helmet again to get his attention. "Duck back in here when you see the grenades fly!"

Accardo nodded, sending another burst of fire into the barricades.

She looked over toward Arnot's platoon in time to see a grenade fly from the hands of two marines and around the corner. Accardo and Krouri pulled quickly back, and Christine stepped backward to make room for them.

The grenades detonated in quick succession, and bits of shrapnel flew through the air and peppered the bullet-scarred wall. The enemy machine gun fire resumed.

"Damn it!" She looked over at Arnot, who made a fist, then bounced it off his other hand, which was held flat. She understood. The grenades had missed and rebounded off the barrier, exploding uselessly in front of it. There was nothing to it but to try again.

Accardo moved to get his machine gun back in position, then suddenly hunched backward again. Had he been hit? No, he was looking around at her, trying to say something that got lost in the noise.

Christine put a hand on his shoulder, but something caught her eye. A grenade bounced and rolled to a stop a few feet from her. She started toward it, but Néri was already there, using the stock of his submachine gun like golf club and sending it skittering back at the barricades.

Christine pulled Néri back into cover as the grenade exploded around the corner.

"Come on," Christine shouted to Accardo and Krouri. "Let's take these guys out!"

She was tired of these damn barricades.

Accardo got back into position, opened fire. Christine trained her carbine around the corner and fired a few shots at the loopholes just in time for a few grenades to come sailing toward the barricades from Arnot's position. She saw the grenades disappear into the gap between the first barricade and the second, heard muffled shouts. She ducked back into cover, tugging Accardo along with her.

The grenades detonated behind the barricade, a muffled blast, and Christine peered around the corner. A few of the bricks from the first barricade had been blasted out of place, and its loophole was dark. To the right and behind it, the other barricade was silent, though it was impossible to say whether the crew behind it was dead or simply stunned. Either way, they had to move fast.

She looked across the corridor, caught Arnot's eyes again. She slapped the top of her helmet repeatedly with her opened palm.

Give us suppressing fire.

Arnot nodded, and turned around to yell orders at the other marines. A few seconds later, Arnot and his troops were peppering the barricade with fire from their rifles and moving a light machine gun into position.

Christine looked for Sergeant Meyer, found him, and motioned him to move his squad forward. She dropped her carbine to low ready as they filed past — Henrikson, Clos, Harris, Miller, Meyer, Simmons, Young, Lazaar, Sassano, and Francis — keeping close to the wall and out of the arc of the remaining enemy machine gun, which had sputtered back to life.

Christine bit her lip. She hated not being at the front of the attack, not having direct control over what would happen to her troops next. The squad had come to a halt in front of the destroyed loophole. They couldn't move around the end of the wall because they'd be running in front of the other, intact machine gun. Christine watched as Henrikson pulled a pair of wire clippers off of his belt and started cutting away at the netting strung above the first wall. Miller handed Henrikson a grenade, then reached past Henrikson and stuck the tip of his bayonet through the hole in the netting, holding it open. Henrikson armed the grenade and tossed it through the hole, no doubt trying to get it around the second wall.

BANG.

The enemy machine gun choked and ceased firing again, and Sergeant Meyer's squad vanished one by one around the corner and through the gap between the barricades. Sporadic gunshots. A shout. A machine gun chattering.

Dammit! What was going on?

A second later, Harris came around the corner, dragging Clos' limp body. He made it to the junction and laid Clos down next to the three marines who had fallen minutes before. Clos was completely still, and Christine couldn't tell if she was dead or alive. Either way, she was out of the fight. Christine's chest tightened, and she dashed forward to stand next to Harris, keeping an eye on the silent loopholes. It was strange to stand in the middle of the hallway that had been so filled with enemy fire only moments ago.

"Private? Private! What's going on?"

Harris met her gaze, and Christine's stomach fell as she recognized the resignation on the young man's face.

"More barricades on the other side, spaced out between the entrances to the barracks rooms. We're setting up positions to suppress the next loopholes."

Christine felt the press of her ring against the stock of her carbine. These bastards were going to make them pay for every inch of ground they took. How long would it take them to get through this? Could they even do it? She chased away her mounting dread, straightened up, raised her chin.

"Get into those barracks. Use them as cover to leap frog forward and get good firing positions on the barricades. We're coming in behind you." Christine looked back at Néri. "Sergeant, get Wilcox up here. Arnot!" Christine turned to face the marine lieutenant. "We're pushing forward."

CHAPTER 29

"Where the hell is the Supervisor?" Tom paced around the command center, his gaze scanning the personnel manning the various stations and consoles. He hadn't seen the man for at least five minutes, and now was not a good time to vanish. Now was the time to be a leader and model calm for their people.

"They've broken through the first set of barricades on this level! They're pushing down the main corridor!" The breathless runner wiped sweat off his head, his eyes as big as saucers against his dark face.

Tom let the news sink in. The Alliance soldiers were closing in. He was running out of time. The battle was all but lost. He looked around the room again, taking stock of everyone there.

"You, you, and you." Tom pointed at Eugene and two others working to fix the radio. Grab rifles and get to the barricades."

If they didn't repel this attack, there'd be no need for communications.

Tom turned on his heel and walked to the silo control station. "Fire again. Do not let up on them."

"They're among the fleet," Jordon glanced back at Tom, shaking his head. "Our last shot hit some of our own ships. I can't get a clear lock, and we can't risk—"

"Keep firing!" Tom spun Jordan around in his seat. "Do you know what will happen if that ship breaks through? We've killed Alliance soldiers. Do you know the penalty for treason? Do you want to die? Rot in prison somewhere?" Tom's frayed nerves were exploding.

There was no way out. They were backed into a corner, waiting for death from above or from the rifles of the Alliance soldiers tightening the noose around them. And why was Smith missing?

Jordan stammered. "N-No, but—"

"Fire!" Tom spun Jordan back around. "And don't stop until that ship is destroyed. Our fleet will make way as best they can."

Jordan shook as he punched the controls, activating the launch sequence for another missile.

Kim fought back a wave of nausea as she was bucked sideways against her safety harness, the nylon strap biting into her through her uniform jacket. The bridge blacked out for a second as the overhead lights dimmed and flickered. The smell of burnt plastic and hot metal stung her nostrils.

"Turret six has lost electrical power. They are attempting to make repairs." Fowler shouted over the muffled booms of enemy ordnance exploding around the ship. "We're losing ordnance deflector coverage on our port side. We managed to block most of the warheads with the enemy ship to starboard."

"Mr. Stetler, keep us moving! Holsey, have fire control concentrate on the closest ships. Give us some breathing room in here, and screen our port side."

Kim scanned the holoports around the room, her own screen having flickered out minutes ago, some part of its wiring cut somewhere. Two of the ports were out, but Kim could see the flaming hulk of another enemy warship listing to starboard, between the *Verdun* and the planet. At least these missiles were doing more damage to the enemy fleet than they were to their intended target. That made two enemy ships killed by friendly fire and one by the *Verdun* herself since they'd plunged into the hostile fleet.

Eight down, twelve to go.

Whether or not they'd get that twelve was anyone's guess.

The flashes from enemy shells and rockets detonating in the space around the *Verdun* threw the bridge into brief moments of extreme brightness, as if they were facing a crowd full of sparkling cameras. Many of the shells were being deflected, while the fighters were screening quite a few of the rockets. But at this close range, more than enough were getting through. The *Verdun* was slowly being chewed to a pulp.

The deck lurched again, and something hot seared the back of Kim's neck. She turned, saw the action table erupt into sparks and flames.

"Just fixed the damn thing," Holsey shouted.

"Geonor's going to be pissed," Kim shouted back, then looked down toward the radio console. "Baudouin, get fire crews up here."

Baudouin looked over, shook her head. "Damage control reports that they're all out, ma'am."

"We'll handle it ourselves, then." Kim unbuckled her harness and got to her feet, just as the ship lurched again and a dull boom filled the air.

"They got a direct hit. Secondary turret eight is on fire. The crew is evacuating, fire control teams attempting to suppress." Fowler's voice held a note of panic.

Kim held back her own fear and worked her way around the bridge to a fire extinguisher, leaving the rest of the bridge crew to concentrate on their tasks. Pulling it from the wall, she walked over to stand next to Holsey and unleashed a stream of white flame retardant onto the burning table. The flames hissed and went out, sending up billowing clouds of smoke that stung Kim's eyes.

"I suppose this is when you tell me that there's no way we can survive this. That I've doomed us all." Kim said to Holsey as she gave the action table another spray down for good measure.

"No, ma'am."

Kim turned to meet Holsey's gaze. What was the emotion she saw there? Anger? Regret?

Something worse, something she'd never expected from a battle-axe like Holsey.

She saw resignation.

"We both knew there was only one way through this, and one likely outcome. I can take that." Holsey held out her hand.

"Captain, another missile incoming from the fort."

"Thanks, Commander." Kim handed Holsey the extinguisher and strode to her chair. She snapped the harness shut, wincing as the strap touched skin made tender from being jerked against it.

Kim looked around the holoports, cleared her throat. "Mr. Stetler, I see three sponges twelve degrees to starboard. See if you can keep them between us and that next missile."

"Aye, ma'am."

"Enemy vessel destroyed," Isabelle announced. Kim looked around, saw an enemy ship to port breaking into pieces as the *Verdun's* shells ripped through it.

This fight was not lost. Not yet.

But then she lost sight of her dying enemy as the deck jerked again and the ports flickered on and off.

"Another hit," Fowler shouted.

"Step on it, Mr. Stetler." Kim gripped her chair's armrests, caught sight of the small, bright shape of the missile shooting toward them from the planet. She squirmed in her chair, helpless before the slow ballet of spaceships playing out before her. They were drawing close to the trio of enemy ships, whose shells crackled and flashed around the *Verdun*, burst beside it, above it, below it, dug into its metal skin. The deck vibrated beneath Kim's feet, and she was thrown hard against her harness again, but she kept her eyes on the missile.

"All hands, brace for impact," Isabelle said.

The missile was separating, its nose unleashing its multitude of warheads. Then Kim lost sight of it as an enemy ship passed in front of it.

Kim blinked, was thrown to one side, then the other. The bridge lit up as the enemy vessel split open. The other two ships were turning to face the *Verdun*, their gun turrets rotating around to fire.

"Nice flying, Stetler!" Urquhart called out, her voice small against the continued noise of explosions.

"If the enemy could pilot worth a damn, we'd be lost," Kim agreed.

Stetler didn't say anything, but wiped his forehead with his sleeve. He was keeping their opponents confused, disorganized, turning in all the wrong ways.

"We've got another one incoming," Fowler called.

Kim's insides tensed. "Let's do this again. Keep with these other two ships. Don't let them run—"

Kim's sentence was cut off as the *Verdun* shook again, and the bridge flickered in and out of darkness once more.

The enemy force was charging again, shouting, firing wildly, stumbling over the mounting piles of their comrades' bodies. Gordon shook his head, raised his rifle again to pick out another target in the darkness. He found one, dropped him with a center-mass shot.

Won't they give up already?

He'd hoped that, faced with high losses and their own lack of training, these revolutionaries would surrender quickly. Instead, they'd taken cover wherever they could in the valley — behind rocks, small rises in the ground, even the occasional downed tree — and settled in for a fight. These poor sons-of-bitches were more motivated than any troops Gordon had ever seen before. A hungry belly and a chest full of desperate anger had been enough to sustain them through repeated attempts to rush the Alliance trenches at the head of the valley — and through the horrific casualties they suffered each time.

As dumb a strategy as these mass charges were, they might actually pay off. At this rate, the Alliance troops would run out of ammunition sooner than they'd be able to kill or wound every enemy soldier. They needed bigger guns.

Gordon bit his lip as he lined up another shot, fired. With all the small-arms fire in and around the valley, he could barely make out the sound of the shells from the pack howitzers flying overhead. They were still sending the occasional shell toward the fort every couple minutes, trying to add to the confusion of whatever garrison had been left there and help Wilcox and the others with their job. He hated doing anything that would jeopardize the attack on the fort. If that fort didn't fall, if it kept shooting off its missiles…

For all you know, the Verdun *is already gone, jarhead.*

Gordon shuddered, dropping another opponent with a shot to the chest. He couldn't use the artillery. Not yet.

What do you think will happen to Wilcox's team if these guys wipe you out and get back to the fort?

Gordon didn't get a chance to answer the question, a shout to his left interrupting his thoughts.

"Reloading!"

Gordon glanced at the machine gunner to his left, who was flipping open the weapon's top cover while the assistant called for a new box of ammunition from the runner.

"Keep them back! Pour it on!" Gordon pumped the trigger, sending shots into the bristling darkness, heard the rhythm of rifle shots from up and down the trench increase. With the machine gun out for a few seconds, the enemies were sure to make ground toward the Alliance position. The troops dug in on the sides of the valley were protected by the small cliffs that prevented the enemy from running up to them. The trench was the weak point in their defenses, and it wouldn't take long before the enemy figured that out.

Gordon felt the bolt of his rifle lock back, lowered it from his shoulder, and reached for a fresh magazine, but a raw shout snapped his attention back up in time to see a group of at least fifteen enemy troops rushing toward him, close enough now to see clearly in the darkness. Several of them fell to the fire of the rangers, but the rest pushed forward. In a few seconds, they'd be in the trench.

Gordon felt out his ammunition pouch, found nothing, felt for another.

"For fuck's sake!" In one fluid motion, he dropped his rifle and tore his Colt from its holster, clicking off the safety. At this distance, there was no aiming. He emptied the magazine as quickly as he could point the weapon and pull the trigger. Each shot was a kill.

Not good enough.

Gordon stepped to the side as an attacker jumped into the trench beside him. He swung his pistol and cracked it across the back of the man's head, pitching him forward. Gordon spun around in time to dodge a rifle butt swishing past his head. He let his opponent's momentum carry him off balance and struck out with a kick to the man's leg, tripping him. Gordon holstered his pistol as he ducked down and pulled the stunned man's rifle from him. He punched the butt down into the back of his opponent's neck once, twice. Gordon heard a snap, dropped to one knee, and racked the bolt on the enemy's rifle, ready to shoot down any more of the attackers who'd made it into the trench.

He saw Private Willard's body leaned against the back of the trench as if taking a moment to rest, his hands laid over several jagged holes in his armor. Private Heinkel was lying still on his side, a knife sticking out of a gap in his breastplate. The rest of the rangers seemed to be faring better, shooting or beating down the last of the enemy troops who'd rushed them.

The machine gun stuttered to life again, and Gordon let out a tense breath. The moment of vulnerability had passed — until the next reload.

"Fix bayonets!" Gordon pulled the magazine out of his opponent's rifle, dropped it, and recovered his own weapon. "Take whatever ammunition you can off the enemy."

Gordon repeated the command to fix bayonets into his headset, then dropped to one knee again to see to his own weapon.

He loaded his rifle, then slid his bayonet out of its scabbard and fitted it to the end of the weapon. The next time those bastards made it to the trench, he'd be ready for them. But it would take more than a knife on the end of a rifle to keep him and his troops alive. Gordon nodded to himself, his decision made.

He spat out the blood in his mouth, the quick motions of hand-to-hand fighting giving him a painful reminder of each and every one of his old wounds.

No stopping now. Push it.

Gordon jogged down the narrow trench, past the rangers who were once again firing their rifles into the oncoming enemy. Mortar shells were bursting among the attackers in the valley again, though at a slower pace than before.

No doubt the mortars were starting to run low, too.

Gordon spotted Corporal Li and his bulky radio pack ahead, hunched over slightly as an enemy grenade exploded in front of the trench. He reached Li and dropped to kneel, breathing hard and trying to massage his aching chest through his armor.

"Corporal, get Ames on the line."

Li fired one more shot toward the enemy, then squatted down next to Gordon.

"Aye, sir. What am I telling him?"

"Instruct them to fire on the valley, known point zebra. Blast these bastards apart."

Li glanced over the lip of the trench, then looked back at Gordon, his eyes wide. "At this distance, sir? Any shell falling short will—"

"Get them on the line, Corporal."

Li shook his head, but he unlatched the radio's handset and began calling in fire coordinates.

Gordon didn't like the distance either, but—

The sky lit up again as another missile sped upward, streaking fire behind it as it arced toward the burning debris falling from space, painting the northern sky with so many shooting stars.

There was no other choice. They had to hold this valley until the team finished inside the fort. With any luck, that wouldn't be long.

"Son of a bitch!" Garrett's voice cut through the roar of weapon's fire. "They're coming again!"

Gordon stood up, saw the massive wave of people running toward the trench in the dying light of the rocket's engines.

Then again, any amount of time could be too late.

You live or die here. Nothing else matters.

Gordon sighted his rifle and fired.

The wall of sound inside the fort was unreal. It assaulted Tom's every sense, surrounded him, crushed him beneath it. Every gunshot, every scream was captured and amplified in this damn concrete maze the Alliance had built. If only he could just let the bastards have it.

At least the enemy artillery had stopped pounding the fort. Though at this point, Tom doubted it mattered, and he'd take the muffled boom of the enemy's shells over the roar of his rifles and machine guns.

"Have you seen Smith? Have you seen the Supervisor?" Tom zigzagged through the barricades, squeezing past soldiers running the other way, toward the barricades on the opposite side of the command center and the main group of Alliance troops. Their faces were tight, closed, and Tom's mind flashed to the lines of workers he'd seen outside the factories of home.

You were supposed to save them. What have you done?

Tom reached the end of the barricades and the corridor beyond. A pair of his troops was emerging from a nearby munitions storage closet, hauling a pair of ammunition cases between them.

"Have you seen Smith?

Without breaking his stride, one of the two men wordlessly stuck his thumb back over his shoulder. Tom pushed past the soldiers, ran down the corridor, and reached a staircase down to the lower level in time to see Smith reach the bottom and disappear out of sight.

Tom bounded down the stairs, turned, and saw Smith running down the hallway toward a T-junction. Stacks of supplies and half-empty crates of ammunition were lined against one wall. The oppressive sound of fighting was echoing from down the hallway to the right. To the left was the corridor to the hanger.

"Supervisor!"

Smith stopped in his tracks, spun on his heels.

"Where are you going? Our people need you in the command center. They need you to be strong for them."

Smith looked over his shoulder in the direction he'd been running, looked back at Tom. He licked his lips, which then broke into a grin. The Supervisor stepped toward him, hands out to either side.

"Tom! Thank goodness! There's still time. Come with me. The Alliance has another force clearing this level." The Supervisor spoke quickly, spouting out words almost faster than Tom could follow them. "We don't have the barricades down here. Our force won't last long. Don't worry about your things. We'll have quite enough supplies in our—"

"What the hell are you talking about?"

Tom's words stopped the Supervisor in mid-stride, though the man's greasy smile remained as wide as ever. He was silent for a moment as a set of troops ran past the two men and turned right at the end of the hall to join the defenses.

Finally, Smith cleared his throat. "There's no need for a man of your talent to die here, Tom. We have other battles to lead, other ways to help *our* movement."

Tom shook his head, a ringing that had nothing to do with the deafening noise filling his head.

"You're running away! Coward!" Tom spat the words at the man in front of him, wishing he could break every one of those perfectly white teeth.

"Tom," The Supervisor stepped forward again, his palms toward Tom in a gesture of surrender. "I know this fort has captured your attention, but there are more important things to do. Other fights to win. The Legion will be fine without this planet."

"You mean this — what did you call it — this great, strategic outpost? You yourself said—"

"Tom, things have changed. It's a new situation we're in. I'm merely adapting to it."

Tom shook his head. It was so obvious now. The way the man had never taken any part of this mission seriously. Having that small tender brought to the fort for his private use. Tom slowly moved his hand toward the holster at his hip.

"You never thought we would succeed here, did you?" Tom angled his pistol hip away from the Supervisor, fought to keep his voice even. "I don't think you even *wanted* us to."

The Supervisor stopped again, and put his hands to his sides. Tom noticed one of them come to rest next to his bulging pant pocket.

"Tom. Tom, Tom, Tom. Tom, you misunderstand me."

"Do I?" Tom took another step back, his muscles coiling, tensing. "Then why are you abandoning us?"

"You take this too personally." The Supervisor chuckled, his eyes darting between Tom's face and holster. "I know you care about your people. Who knows, many of them will probably survive to be captured. But we're not abandoning them. We're saving ourselves for their sake. To make sure their sacrifice meant something."

"Save the bullshit, Smith, if that's actually your name." Tom's finger ached to feel the trigger under it. He slowed his breathing, readied every nerve for action. "Why are you here, and who do you work for, really?"

The Supervisor's smile dissolved.

They drew and fired at the same time. A bullet whistled past Tom's ear, and he stepped to the side and fired again from the hip. His shot went wild, and the Supervisor sprinted away. Tom raised the pistol to fire, but broke his aim to tuck behind a stack of ammunition boxes as Smith spun around and fired. The bullets thwacked into the steel cases, and Tom sprang up again to shoot.

"Dammit!"

Smith had vanished around the corner toward the hangar.

Tom shot to his feet and took a few running steps down the hall before stopping in his tracks.

Let Smith run. Tom wasn't going to leave his people without a leader, not now, and not for a scumbag like the Supervisor. If there was any chance of succeeding against the Alliance forces, Tom needed to be in the command center, where he was most useful. If he survived this fight, he'd find Smith.

Find him, figure out who he really was and what his angle in all of this had been.

Tom shoved his pistol back in its holster, then turned and dashed back the way he'd come, taking the stairs two at a time and sprinting down the corridor toward the barricades. He passed the munitions closet, saw the long, olive-green tube of a rocket launcher.

Yes, he'd find Smith. Find him, and kill him. But first, he had to keep this fort out of the Alliance's hands long enough to shoot down the enemy warship. And he'd find a way, if only to live to wipe that smile off Smith's face for good.

Tom leaned inside the closet, hefted the launcher into his arms, picked up a case of rockets, and shuffled toward the command center, his tall frame bowed under the weight of his new burdens.

CHAPTER 30

Jack ran, his rifle clamped in his hands, bayonet forward, the strange, garlicky smell of burning phosphorous filling his nose, his lungs, his head. He rounded the corner of the last barricade, leaving the cluster of troops waiting their turn to follow his lead. The air sighed and buzzed with bullets that knifed through the thick, white cloud in front of him. He could just make out the shape of a barrier that blocked off most of the corridor directly in front of him, and, to the left, the outline of the entrance into the last barracks room.

He turned toward the barracks, accelerated his pace, picking out the sounds of fighting coming from inside.

Gunshots.

Screams.

The thud of boots running behind him.

He plunged forward, entered the room. Suddenly, as if a veil were lifted from his eyes, he broke through the wall of smoke. He almost skidded to a stop as he took it in. Most of Captain Flores and Lieutenant Perez's platoons were there, struggling with at least as many of the enemy fighters. Hand to hand. Bayonets and rifle butts. Firing at point-blank range. Splintered bunks. Flipped-over furniture. A half-dozen enemy troops were behind a stack of tables in the corner, firing indiscriminately into the turmoil and toward the entrance, toward Jack.

Jack dodged to the left, heading for the edge of the massive room and a good angle on the assholes in the corner. He hit the wall, scooted forward against it to reach the concealment of a stack of rations crates. But just as he was raising his rifle, he saw someone running toward him out of the corner of his eye.

He stepped to the side, letting his opponent slam face first into the wall. The man staggered back, swinging a knife blindly through the air. Jack jabbed the butt of his rifle into his opponent's midsection. He gasped, stumbled, and toppled into the crates, hitting his head again as he fell. Jack lowered his rifle and sprayed a couple shots into his enemy's torso. The man jerked and was still. Jack knelt behind the crate, glanced back toward the entrance of the room, and saw Lieutenant Arnot and some of his platoon emerging from the smoke. They started toward the brawl in the center of barracks, but Jack waved, caught Arnot's attention.

"Lieutenant! Over here!"

Arnot and his troops dashed toward him, knelt down.

"Sir?"

"They're enough guys in the brouhaha. Help me take these bastards out." Jack pointed at the enemy troops in the corner, who were still shooting frantically into the room.

Jack straightened up, rested his rifle on the top of the crate, and sighted in on one of the enemy soldiers.

Jack fired, winced at the blast of Arnot and the other marines' rifles.

The enemies dropped one by one. The last two turned, tried to shoot at their killers, but fell before they could fire.

Satisfied, Jack turned toward the fighting, which was continuing even over the bodies of those who had already been cut down. Jack saw a ranger beat to the ground by the rifle butts of two fighters. He saw a marine stabbed from behind through a crack in his armor.

With a yell, Jack charged into the crowd, Arnot and the others behind him. He almost tripped on a marine who hit the ground in front of him. One of the enemy troops stepped over the marine, raising a rifle over her head like a club. Jack's temper flared, and he lunged forward, driving his bayonet into the woman's ribcage. She dropped her rifle and reached for the bayonet, grabbing onto the end of Jack's rifle, and pulled on it as she sagged to her knees. He twisted his weapon, then kicked the woman to the ground as he withdrew his blade. Seeing that Arnot was helping the marine to his feet, Jack looked for someone else to fight and threw himself into the brawl.

His nerves buzzed white-hot in his skull. Thought, reasoning, evaporated away. He kicked, punched, slashed, stabbed, and crushed. He lost track of the individuals he killed, the combat blurring together as rage and adrenaline filled him, consumed him. He wouldn't let these bastards kill any more of his troops, or kill his shipmates on the *Verdun,* even if he had to rip each one to pieces with his bare hands. He knocked down an enemy and pounded at his skull with the butt of his rifle, again and again.

"Sir!"

Jack could barely hear through the fog in his brain. He kept slamming the butt of his rifle down into the red mess of his opponent's body.

"Sir! Wilcox, he's down."

Someone grabbed him, and he spun to hit the person with his elbow, only to find himself looking into Flores' brown eyes.

"He's down, sir. Relax."

Jack stared back at Flores, fighting to control his breathing.

"It's all right. You got them." Flores' voice was calm, even.

Jack swallowed and nodded, his thoughts clearing. He looked around. Bodies were heaped on the ground, and the surviving marines and rangers were helping one of the platoon medics see to their wounded and taking up positions by the entrance in the dissipating smoke. Jack was glad to see only a handful of marines and rangers on the ground next to the heaps of the enemy. He spat onto the body of his mangled opponent and nodded at Flores again, who let go of him.

"Henrikson!" Flores shouted toward the door. "What is Squires' situation?"

Henrikson dashed into the room, a shock of red running down his face, his helmet missing. "Ma'am, they're suppressing the command center and the barricades on the other side of the hall. They've got one hell of a cross fire going."

"Good." Flores turned to look at Jack again. "Are you ready to finish this, sir?"

Jack wiped the blood off the buttplate of his rifle and onto the pants of one of the dead enemy soldiers, rage still clinging to the edges of his consciousness.

"Yes." Jack's voice was hoarse, a whisper. He cleared his throat and tried again. "Yes. Let's see what we're dealing with."

Jack stalked out of the room, leaving Flores, Perez, and Arnot to get their platoons back in order. He slung his weapon over his shoulder, waving his arms in front of him to sweep the remaining smoke out of the air in front of him. Back in the corridor, Squires' troops were taking cover against the wall that blocked most of the hallway to the left or tucked between the barricades that they'd come through to the right. The wall was like the barricades they'd defeated, reaching most of the way to the ceiling, with heavy netting filling the gap. There was a doorway at the far end of the wall, big enough for only one to pass at a time. Squires was next to the door, mirror in hand. Gunfire spat and roared from the other side of the wall, and bullets were passing through the netting and striking the ceiling over the Alliance troops, sending little fragments of concrete raining down on them and tinkling off their helmets.

Jack came to a stop next to Squires and looked down at the mirror he was holding out past the edge of the wall. Jack could see the hallway beyond, which looked to be open for fifty yards before hitting another set of overlapping barricades. In the middle of the open corridor was a gap that led onto a narrow staircase. In front of that was a low wall of sand bags, abandoned. Muzzle flashes from the barricades at the end of the hallway told Jack that they were occupied.

"Lieutenant, does that staircase go to the command center?"

"Yes, sir." Squires straightened up and tucked the mirror away into one of his equipment pouches. "Unless it's been destroyed, it's closed off by a set of heavy doors. We'll need to set charges to get in."

That would mean crossing that open area while the enemy barricades fired on them. Jack shook his head. They'd be left with no choice but to fight through the enemy barricades on the other side, to repeat the hell they'd just pushed through yard by yard.

"We're ready to move when you are, sir."

Jack turned to see Flores standing next to him, her platoon clustered next to Squires' troops along the wall.

"Get suppressing fire set up, Squires. Same drill as before. Flores, get your platoon ready to move on the command center. I want someone familiar with the command center going in. Arnot, your marines will assaul—"

Jack was cut off, pushed sideways slightly by the rocket launcher strapped to the back of one of Squires' troops, who was standing to make room for the light machine gun crew.

"Sorry, sir," the soldier said, adjusting the launcher on his back.

Jack grabbed the soldier's sleeve, an idea hitting him.

"Private—" Jack spied the name tag on the front of the ranger's armor. "Private Grady, get that thing loaded."

"Are you crazy?" Flores stepped forward. "That could collapse the corridor."

"Not to mention our eardrums," Squires added.
"How much ammunition do your troops have, Captain? How many grenades?" Jack let go of Grady's sleeve. "Do you think we can sustain another attack through barricades like that?"

Jack looked between the incredulous faces of Flores and the lieutenants, who had clustered around him now, their hands crossed in front of their chests.

Flores pursed her lips. "We don't have a lot. But killing ourselves with that thing isn't going to help."

"We're not going to die here," Jack said. "There's just enough distance between us and those other barricades, especially if we use the cover we have. I think it's an acceptable risk."

Jack could see Flores working the situation out in her mind, could see that she didn't like it one bit. Finally, she nodded.

"All right, sir. We'll make it happen."

Jack tapped Grady's shoulder, and the private took the launcher tube off his shoulder and set it on the ground. Another soldier helped him pull a rocket out of his bulging pack and set it inside the tube.

"Clear the hallway!" Squires shouted down the line. "Clear the backblast area."

The marines and rangers did as they were told, backing up into the barracks room or threading their way back between the barricades they'd taken earlier. Finally, Jack was left with Grady, Squires, and Flores standing next to him against the wall. Grady squatted at the edge of the doorway, then flinched backward as a bullet struck the edge. Flores stepped next to him, trained her rifle around the corner and fired twice. The machine gun fire stuttered out.

She stepped back. "You've got a couple seconds while they clean their friend up."

Grady leaned out again, took aim. "Firing."

Jack felt the hot air wash back from the launcher, its roar muffled by his hands over his headset. An instant later, the shock of the rocket's explosion washed through the air, compressing Jack's sinuses painfully.

"Give me another one," Grady said, looking over his shoulder. "I hit the barricade."

Flores knelt down, pulled another rocket out of Grady's pack, and stuffed it into the tube.

"You just missed so we could lighten this backpack for you." Flores grinned.

Grady smiled back and leaned out. "Firing!"

Jack covered his ears again, felt the blast of the weapon and its rocket once more — and then it was unbelievably quiet. No gunshots, nothing. Jack held out his hand and took Squires' mirror. He scooted to the edge, poked the mirror out past the edge of the wall.

The end of the hallway was filled with smoke and dust, but where the barricades were before, Jack could just make out a jumbled mess of concrete slabs and sand completely blocking the corridor. The rest of the hallway was intact, though cracks had appeared in the ceiling, streams of sand trickling through them. The stairs to the command center were still abandoned, though a few of the sand bags at its base had been knocked askew.

Jack handed the mirror back to Squires. "Captain, take your platoon in. Arnot, you'll follow. Squires, I want you to lead Perez and his platoon back down to the level below this one and link up with Lieutenant Colion's platoon. It won't take the enemy long to figure out that they can circle around if they go down to that level and around."

The little space behind the wall was packed full as Squires and Perez moved their troops through it and back through the barricades. Flores and Arnot lined their soldiers up against the wall, readied them to move. The silence beyond the wall was unbroken.

Had the enemy left the command center abandoned? Rigged it to blow?

But then a low, sustained rumble carried faintly through the air, seeming to come out of the walls themselves.

"What the hell is that?" Arnot asked. "Is that our artillery?"

"No," Flores shook her head as the sound gradually faded out. "That's one of the missiles firing."

The missiles

Jack cursed under his breath. If the missiles were firing, that could only mean the *Verdun* was in trouble. Were they too late?

Jack looked for Captain Flores, found her, and held her gaze for a moment. She nodded.

"Alright, Fifth Platoon! We're going to rush that command center all at once." She stood out from the wall, facing her troops. Jack was struck by how much smaller the group had become. How many had they lost? A third? Half?

"Secure the silo station first, or destroy it," Flores continued, stepping over to the doorway. "Let's bring this home. Come on!"

Flores sprinted around the corner, and her rangers followed her. Jack let a couple troops pass him before he ran after them. He stepped out into the hallway and charged for the stairs. Flores and the rangers in front were nearly there.

Then a tall man emerged from the command center and stood at the bottom of the stairs, rocket launcher in hand.

Oh God!

"Back!" Jack shouted. "Get back!"

He turned, ran back toward the wall, dragging the closest rangers with him. He opened his mouth to shout at Arnot, who had appeared at the edge of the barrier.

The entire world shattered. A fiery hurricane threw Jack to the ground, and wasp stings peppered his legs, his shoulder, his neck. Someone screamed, followed by the thud and crack of tumbling concrete, the hiss of sand. The rotten-egg odor of explosive and the choking rasp of cement dust smothered Jack where he lay.

He blinked, tried to shake his head to make his ears stop ringing. He pulled himself to his feet, looked around. The corridor had collapsed ten yards in front of him. Perhaps half the rangers of Flores' platoon were dusting themselves off, picking themselves off the ground. Arnot and his marines were filing out from behind the wall and helping their comrades, guiding the wounded back toward the rear. The others?

Jack looked at the pile of rubble, saw legs and arms sticking out from underneath it. Flores? Jack stood there, reeling from what had happened, trying to find a solution.

"Sir, let me help you to the rear."

Jack turned and saw Arnot standing next to him, concern written on his face.

"No. We're getting through."

"You got shrapnel splinters all over you." Arnot put his hands on Jack's shoulder.

"No!" Jack shook Arnot off, bent down to grab his rifle.

"Sir, we'll start digging, but there's nothing you can do to speed it up. Take care of—"

"Henrikson!" Jack spotted the ranger standing with his hands on his knees, covered in dust. "Is there any way around this?"

Henrikson shook his head. "These are the only corridors into the command center."

Jack cursed, wanted to throw himself at the rubble, kick it, hit it.

"That's not entirely true."

Jack looked to see Fletcher pulling himself up, Arnot lending him a hand.

Jack walked over to Fletcher, put a hand on his shoulder. "Tell me everything, and tell me quickly."

CHAPTER 31

*C*hristine was grateful for the sun in her face. It hid Ryan's expression from her, gave her an excuse for the tears trying to gather in her eyes. But the sun would be gone soon, hidden behind the superstructure of the huge troopship in the bay, the ship that would take her to her new billet on Kensington. A first-class ticket to nowhere.

"It's not as if you're falling off the edge of the galaxy," Ryan was saying. "I know you'll write to me as often as you can."

Christine shifted, straightening the stiff service dress uniform she was wearing for the journey.

"Maybe there's no need for me to." Christine looked at the ground, stared at her polished black shoes in front of Ryan's worn, brown ones. "Maybe it's better for both of us if we let go now."

There was a long silence. Christine hated the words that had come out of her mouth, wished she could pull them back. But facts were facts. She'd be gone on Kensington for years, too far away to return for leave, surviving off messages and the occasional photograph. It didn't take a genius to know how much that would hurt. Christine had already been through that with her parents, living letter to letter, planning for some next time, only for it to never come. She wouldn't do it again, and she wouldn't put Ryan through it.

She felt Ryan's hands on her shoulders. "If I wanted to let go, don't you think I'd have done it by now?"

Christine shook her head, looked up at Ryan, blinked back tears against the sun. "Tell me that when you haven't seen me in six months."

Ryan's grip tightened on Christine's shoulders. "Babe, you forget who you're dealing with. I don't think this is about distance. I think this is about your parents."

Christine brushed off Ryan's hands, stepped back. She looked for something to say, to throw back at him. All she could come up with was, "Drop it."

Ryan crossed his arms across his chest. *"You're afraid something will happen to you, or to me, and so you're hoping I'll take the opportunity to chicken out of this and protect you from losing someone again."*

"You really think you'll last two years apart? And wherever they send me after that?"

"Yes."

"Yes?" Christine almost laughed. "Just like that?"

"Yes. And I have proof. Hold out your hand."

Christine gaped at him. If this was a joke, it wasn't funny.

"Come on. Hold it out."

Christine sighed and stuck her hand out, palm up. Ryan dug into his pocket, pulled something out of it, and placed it on her hand. She stared at it, and gasped.

A ring! It was plain gold, no diamond. But she didn't want any of that nonsense anyway. You can't wear a rock with a uniform.

She looked up at Ryan, expecting the sun to help her save face again, but finding it completely hidden by the troopship. Ryan's grey eyes were fixed on her, his lips curved slightly into a smile.

"Christine, I can't say that I don't wish you had a different job, something that kept you closer to me and out of danger. But I know that I'm happier with you than I've ever been with anyone else. And maybe I can't have you with me as much as I want. But what I can have, I want. I'd rather spend the occasional leave with you than spend a lifetime with someone else."

Christine's ears rang, her pulse kicking up. She wanted him to stop and take that ring away. She wanted him to kiss her and slip it on her finger.

"Christine Flores," Ryan said, kneeling in front of her. "Will you marry me?"

She couldn't breathe. She was fighting for air, fighting to answer him, to shout the 'yes' that came leaping from her chest. But there was no air in her lungs, no sound came out—

Christine's eyes flicked open and focused on the concrete floor in front of her. Panic gathered at the cloudy edges of her brain. Where was she? What was going on? She heard a moan, realized it was coming from her own mouth. Sharp pain stabbed at her side, but when she tried to gasp, she couldn't breathe in. She tried again, struggled desperately to pull air into her aching lungs. She felt her side, trying to locate the source of her agony, felt a huge dent in her armor.

She shook her head, trying to clear it, and rolled onto the dented side, her hands finding the clasps for her armor. Her fingers were stiff, clumsy. Christine cursed under her breath, biting her lip against the pain, against the crushing weight of the armor.

The armor opened and fell away from her, and air rushed into her body. She rolled onto her front, her hands on the ground in front of her face. She didn't know how long she stayed like that, focusing on breathing in and out, on remembering where the hell she was. The details faded in gradually.

The smells of smoke and burned explosives.

The dim flicker of a single, damaged light fixture.

Her carbine lying a few feet to her right with its bayonet fixed.

The jumble of debris blocking the collapsed corridor a few dozen yards in front of her.

The stairway just ahead and to the right, surrounded by a ring of toppled and split sandbags.

Kensington. The fort. The attack.

"Son of a bitch!" She coughed.

That man, the enemy with the rocket launcher. She'd seen him appear at the staircase, had tried to shoot him down. But he'd popped out and fired in an instant, and Christine had dived for cover, trying to drag a couple of her rangers with her.

Her platoon!

Christine pushed herself to a sitting position, looked around, and saw another mess of concrete and sand filling the hallway a few yards behind her. She could see an arm sticking out from under the rubble, and there was Lazaar's head and shoulders peeking out from the debris, as if trying to crawl out from under it. A curl of smoke rose slowly from his smashed radio backpack, and a pool of blood was spreading from his mouth.

Had they all been killed in the collapse? And what about Wilcox and the others?

Christine's thoughts were interrupted by the low grumble of another missile launching outside. She sat for a minute, listening to the noise, her mind sorting through possible courses of action. If any of the attack force had survived, they'd find a way around or dig through. She could wait for them and then move in with sufficient force to take the command center.

Who are you kidding?

At this rate, she'd be surprised if the *Verdun* wasn't a heap of scrap before help arrived.

She pressed her thumb against her ring, balled her hand into a fist around it.

She scooted toward her carbine, pulled it into her hands, and ran her gaze over its length. No damage she could see, except for a few scratches. She dropped the magazine, looked at the witness holes in its side. Only two shots left. She placed the magazine on the floor and patted her ammunition pouches. They were all empty, except for one. That meant twenty-two shots. Christine pulled the fresh magazine from its pouch, slapped it into her carbine, and tucked the nearly empty one away. She continued her inspection of her equipment belt, found two grenades. But where the hell was her pistol? The holster and its magazine pouch had been torn from her side, probably by whatever had dented her armor. She looked around for the weapon, couldn't find it in the low light.

Probably under all that rubble. She'd have to do without it. She reached up, felt her bare head. She'd have to do without her helmet, too, and its radio headset.

Christine stood, biting her lip as pain shot through her side again, irritated at how wooden her legs felt. She shook herself, willing the last blur of her unconsciousness to fade away, to regain her senses. She'd need them now.

She crept toward the staircase, her carbine at low ready. She stepped over what was left of the sand bags and pressed herself against the wall beside the stairs. Raising her weapon to her shoulder, Christine pied off the corner. The staircase was empty. Above, the entrance to the command center glowed, the room far brighter than the flickering dimness of the corridor. She could hear voices from inside, but couldn't quite make them out. At least the command center's doors seemed to have already been destroyed.

Thank God for small miracles.

Christine concentrated on climbing the stairs as quietly as possible, placing her feet between the pieces of rubble that littered it. A waist-high, sandbagged barricade was at the landing at the top of the stairs, a rocket launcher propped up against it. Reaching the barricade, Christine tucked herself into cover and peered into the room. There were at least thirty people in there. A cluster of them stood by an open panel on the left, back end of the room. They had their weapons trained on what looked like a hatch in the floor. Others were scattered around the various computer stations. And there was the tall man who'd fired the rocket launcher, leaning next to the silo control console while a young man sat in front of it, tapping the controls.

"Missile on target," the young man was saying. "Warhead separation in six seconds."

Christine set her carbine down, reached for her belt, and pulled a grenade off. She ripped the pin from it, and held the striker closed in her hand as she readied her muscles for the throw. She'd kill the guys at the silo station, then deal with the others when they bunched up into cover. This would be easy. She could do this.

She raised herself over the barricade, swung her arm, and tossed the grenade — just as the rocket launcher man looked over his shoulder.

The grenade landed with a metallic clunk right in front of the tall man, who kicked it to the side. It rolled and landed next to the group of soldiers at the hatch.

"Take cover! The Alliance is here!" The tall man pulled the young guy at the silo controls with him, and everyone scattered for cover.

"Dammit!" Christine ducked back behind the barricade. She heard the grenade explode, screams of agony. Then she was up again, firing at the people rushing around the command center, diving behind tables, flipping over chairs. Her first shot went wide, but then she dropped two targets and folded back into cover.

Gunfire crackled from inside the room, and bullets sizzled over the top of the barricade. She crawled a few feet, hoping they wouldn't expect her to pop up in a different spot. She waited for a couple shots to whiz past, then straightened up again, her sights already finding their next target. She moved methodically, knocking down an enemy with each bark of her rifle.

A man dashing for cover behind an overturned metal table.

A woman hiding behind a chair.

A pair of them running toward her, rifles firing from the hip.

Another one drawing his pistol.

Christine ducked down, scooted over a few more feet, then came up. The room looked empty, except for the two, bullet-dented metal tables at either end of the room. Christine sprayed a couple shots at the tables, then tore the last grenade from her belt and lobbed it toward the table on the right. The grenade sailed through the air and dropped behind it. Christine ducked again, heard the explosion, more screams.

"It's only one soldier. Rush her! Go now!"

Christine looked back over the barricade in time to see a dozen people un-tuck themselves from behind desks, tables, and consoles and run toward her.

Christine sprayed shots at them, but they were so close. She felt the bolt lock back on her empty rifle with three of them left. They covered the last few feet between them and leapt over the sandbags.

She lowered her bayonet and stepped to the right. One man went sailing past, lost his balance, and toppled down the stairs, the crack of bone on cement almost lost against the shouts of the other two. One of them jabbed a rifle butt at her, but she deflected the blow, sending the man off balance. She pivoted on the spot, her side screaming in protest, and slammed the buttstock of her carbine into the other one. The man dropped his rifle and grabbed his face. Christine kicked him in the midsection, and the man fell down the stairs. She turned, ducked the swing of her remaining opponent's weapon, and thrust her bayonet up and into his stomach. He screamed, and Christine withdrew her blade. The man slumped to the ground, tried to point his rifle up at Christine. She sidestepped and punched her bayonet into him again, once, twice, three times. She freed her blade, and ducked back behind the barricade. She dropped her empty magazine, replaced it with the one from her belt.

Only two shots.

She rested for a moment, breathing hard, pain washing over her from her injured side. A broken rib maybe? No time for bullshit.

She was up again. One of the enemies had run over to the silo console. Another had stood up from behind the table and was spraying shots at her with a pistol. She dropped him with one shot, then turned to the man at the console and took his head off with the other. Christine sagged behind cover, letting the empty magazine fall to the floor with a clank.

How many more of them were there? Only a handful at best. She massaged her side, biting her lip. The pain was getting worse. She looked over at the body of the man she'd bayoneted, saw his rifle lying next to him, and the rifle of another one of her attackers nearby.

Why aren't you paying attention?

Cursing her pain-muddled brain for not thinking to do it earlier, she reached out and dragged the weapons over to her, then unloaded them. Between the two of them, there was a full magazine. Fighting an enemy with Alliance equipment had certain perks. She held her own weapon steady, loaded it, and peered over the barricade again.

Yes. She could do this. As long as she kept the silo console covered—

Gunshots burst from behind the table on the left, and another man ran toward the console.

"Lock the controls on fire! Send another one!" The shout came from the rocket launcher man, who was standing up from behind the table and shooting a pistol in her direction. Christine aimed, took down the man at the console, then turned on the rocket launcher man.

BANG.

A gunshot from the right made Christine flinch, and for a second she thought she'd missed, but rocket launcher man tumbled over backward. She spun, saw the source of the other gunshot, a man hiding near the radio console.

She ducked as the man fired again, then came up and sent three shots his way. He screamed, fell, tried to stand, and was still.

Silence. Christine stood, panning her carbine back and forth, looking for any sign of movement. She stepped forward, pivoting as she entered the room to check the corners. Nothing. She looked ahead, saw the silo console in front of her. Taking one more look around the room, she ran forward. When she reached the console, she shifted her weapon into one hand, freeing the other to fly over the controls. First, she powered down the silos on standby. Then she shut off the targeting system. She paused.

She was alone here. If the enemy broke through first, or if Wilcox and the others never came… She didn't have keys to lock it down again. There was only one option. She raised her weapon over her shoulder, readying herself to smash the buttstock into the screen, break the controls to pieces.

BANG.

She staggered sideways, pain blossoming across her abdomen. Someone had punched her, come out of nowhere.

She turned, saw the rocket launcher man, his shoulder soaked with blood, stepping toward her, pointing a pistol at her.

Not punched. Shot.

She tried to level her weapon at him, to fire back.

BANG.

She gasped, felt her knees buckle from beneath her, heard her weapon clatter to the floor, and pitched sideways.

"Captain!" Fowler's surprised voice carried over the chaotic din on the bridge.

Kim looked over at the Ensign, winced as the floor shook and another booming sound shook the air.

"I don't know how, but target lock is gone."

"Gone?" Holsey's voice called from over Kim's shoulder.

"Yes, ma'am. It just stopped."

Thank God, because that last shot had done a number on them. The MOD was just about hosed, and the enemy ships were getting better and better at matching Mr. Stetler's tricks.

"Mr. Stetler, get us out of this fleet, maximum possible speed. Order the remaining fighters to screen our exit. All gun batteries keep them busy, distract them from hitting our engines."

"Aye, Captain."

"This could be a trap," Holsey said, her sentence broken up by the hiss of her fire extinguisher. The action table had lit up again. "Are you sure we should give up our cover?"

"It could be," Kim agreed. "But if we can get out of here and gain some distance, we may be able to limp away before they spring it. But I'm betting it's not."

Kim turned, saw Holsey's skeptical expression as she set the extinguisher down next to her. "What else could it be?"

"Wilcox and Osterman are on that planet, Commander. And I'll take a chance that he's behind this."

"One hell of a chance." Holsey frowned, crossed her arms. "We don't even know if they're alive."

"You don't know them like I do." Kim turned to look around at the remaining holoports. The enemy ships, no doubt eager to make distance from the *Verdun,* were allowing them to pull away, sending sporadic shellfire toward them as they sped the other direction.

It *was* one hell of a chance. But at this point, Kim would take what she could get. With some distance to use her main guns effectively, the *Verdun* could finish this fight fast. And if it were a trap?

"You have a lot of faith," Holsey said. "But between that and nothing…" She trailed off, but Kim was not paying attention. She was watching the image of Kensington, growing gradually smaller in the holoports, and wishing she could see down, past the rain of burning, destroyed ships, past the clouds and air and concrete, down into the fort, where Jack was busy saving her ass.

She was certain he was there.

"Keep them tied up, Mr. Wilcox," Kim whispered to herself. "Just a little longer."

Tom gaped at the silo control screen, at the target icon representing the Alliance ship. It was moving off, increasing the distance between it and what was left of the fleet with every passing second. And by the looks of it, the warship was taking advantage of the distance to pound the fleet to pieces again. There were fewer than half of the Legion's ships left up there, and they wouldn't last long against the enemy's big guns.

Luckily, they wouldn't need to.

The Alliance vessel was in the open now, an easy target. Tom sat down at the silo station, the pain in his mangled shoulder unbearable, hot, sticky blood trickling down the length of his arm. He glanced over at the Alliance solider, who was groaning softly and writhing on the ground, then set his pistol down on the console next to him. He ripped a piece of cloth from his shirt and pressed it into his wound, trying to stop the bleeding.

He'd been too conservative, firing one shot at a time. His error had allowed the ship to use his fleet as a shield.

Anger and regret coiled his chest, mixed, burned hotter. His missiles had killed so many of his own people.

So much bloodshed.

But he wouldn't let it be for nothing. The Legion could still hold this outpost.

He wouldn't underestimate the Alliance ship again. This time, he'd fire everything they had left. He would not give it the chance to hide again.

It was coming down. Now.

Marcus Hillman took a second to look out his Stallion's cockpit at the massive shape of the *Verdun* pulling up and away from the mess of debris and enemy ships. One of its thrusters was stuttering on and off, wisps of atmosphere and smoke trailing behind it and freezing in the vacuum of high orbit. The *Verdun* had taken more than its share of damage. Now they'd make these bastards pay for it.

He keyed his mic. "Viper Squadron, Viper One. Let's keep these ships from following the Verdun. Go for their engines. Work in pairs."

"Copy."

"Get some, sir."

"Let's make 'em cry!"

Marcus saw Viper Six take position just behind his left wing, nodded to the pilot through the glass. Now that they weren't having to screen the *Verdun*, they could put these Stallions to their intended use — wrecking enemy ships.

He nosed his fighter down, pointing it toward the bright ball of the planet below. The enemy ships were slowly forming together, pulling against gravity to chase the *Verdun*. Marcus accelerated down, weaving to avoid the rounds spitting at him from the hostile fleet. A bead of sweat trickled down his temple as he shot between two of the ships, Viper Six just behind him, the auto turret on top his fighter whirring as it shot down rockets streaking toward him. His peripheral vision cleared of the huge, tan shapes of the ships beside him, and he shoved the controls over. He turned, his momentum drifting him past the engines of the closest target. He opened fire, knew from the pair of rockets that shot past him that Viper Six was still on his wing. Gratification bloomed within him as explosions rippled across the enemy ship. One its engines stuttered, died, spilled burning atmosphere behind it. The ship began to list, causing the others beside it to break formation.

No time to gloat. Marcus put out on a burst of speed, moving back under and around the enemy ship just before the cloud of fire the enemy had fired at him and Viper Six reached their position. One of the destroyers was breaking from the pack, racing upwards toward the *Verdun*.

"Viper Six, Viper One. Let's get that ambitious one over there."

"Copy," she replied.

Marcus brought the Stallion around, was pushing it toward his next victim when his computer's target lock warning flared to life for a second.

"What the—?" He tapped on the controls, his jaw clenched. The damned fort was sweeping for target lock again, and the *Verdun*, all off on its own now in higher orbit, would not be hard to find. "Son of a...." Marcus trailed off. They'd need to act fast.

"Vipers, regroup on my position. Prepare to engage enemy missiles."

CHAPTER 32

Christine fought to stay conscious, to keep her mind sharp, in the present. She saw her father's face in front of her, shook her head, realized her eyes had been shut.

"You've made it, girl. You've made it out of here."

The man, the one who'd shot her, the rocket launcher man, was sitting at the missile console. Spots danced across Christine's vision, and she heard herself groaning from the crushing pain in her chest.

"Maybe it's better for both of us if we let go now."

She wasn't sure how much later, but Christine opened her eyes again. The man was holding a cloth to his wounded shoulder.

Christine felt annoyance snake through her. She'd missed. She hadn't been good enough. She hadn't.... She shivered. She was cold, colder than she'd ever felt. She tried to reach over, to staunch her wound with something, but the pain of moving tore another moan from her throat.

"Congratulations, Lieutenant. I know how much this commission must mean to you given the circumstances."

Dammit! She'd fluttered out of consciousness again. She bit the inside of her mouth to suppress her pain as she slowly rolled onto her side, the extreme agony of the movement almost making her pass out. She could see her weapon just next to her. If she could only get to it! Just one shot in this bastard's back and it would be over. She could rest then, find something to stop the bleeding.

The man was putting down his bandage, starting to punch the controls. She could see the screen for the target lock had come back on, the man scrolling through different targets.

No way in hell.

Christine pulled herself across the floor, every inch torture. Her hand closed on the weapon's stock. She dragged it toward her. It was so damn heavy! When had it ever been so heavy?

She was still for a second, breathing hard, her pulse pounding rapidly in her ears. She tugged again, felt the weapon slide across the coarse cement floor. She reached out her other hand to grab the carbine about the handguard.

A boot came down on the weapon's barrel, pinning it to the ground. Christine blinked, looked up, saw the man standing over her, the pistol pointed at her head.

"All you had to do was give up and stay still," the man was saying. "I want you to know, I don't want to do this."

Christine tried to kick at his feet, to trip him, to fight back. But her legs were so heavy. She was freezing, freezing solid.

"You… can piss off… asshole." Christine spat the words at him, wishing they were bullets. No way would she give up for this dick.

She saw the man's finger move to the trigger.

"Stop!"

Christine thought for a moment that the man had shouted at her, but no.

The man was turning, shooting to the side. Gunfire shattered the room, assaulted Christine's ears. She saw the man's pistol lock back empty, saw a decision flash across his face, saw him dive for the console controls.

But then someone was there, pushing the bastard aside. Wilcox? They tussled for a moment. Christine tried to help, tried to do something, couldn't move.

Wilcox pushed the man backward. He tripped over Christine's legs, toppled to the ground. Wilcox leapt over her, bayonet forward. She turned her head in time to see the man pick up another pistol lying on the ground next to one of Christine's victims. But Wilcox was there, knocking the pistol out the man's hands and driving his bayonet again and again into the man's torso. The man gasped, gurgled, and stopped moving.

Christine heard the fall of footsteps, the clamor of shouted commands. She couldn't turn her head, but she looked out of the corner of her eye, saw some of her platoon helping Arnot and a stream of marines out of the access hatch at the back of the room.

They'd done it. The realization washed through her. The fort was theirs.

She looked back at Wilcox, who was still standing there, looking at his opponent. He turned to face Christine, his face softening from rage to something else, something worse.

Was that concern? Concern for her? Did she look that bad?

Fear lanced through her, but she tried to smile. "You... You found the back door?"

The slightest grin tugged at the corners of his mouth. "You didn't think I'd get lost, did you?"

G ordon needed a second, just a second to rest. Let the enemy charge again, but not before he caught his breath. He slumped down onto an open space on the floor of the trench, careful to slip between the bodies lying there. He kept his weapon in hand, bayonet pointing in the air. He could hear the long whistle and ear-splitting noise of shells exploding in the valley below. They'd shelled the bastards, shot practically every round they had at them, and still there were more. There had to have been at least two thousand men and women in the enemy force to start with. Gordon couldn't begin to guess how many of them could be left. The fact that the Alliance troops only had the ammo to shoot at them whenever they charged probably explained things. Soon, they wouldn't even have that. Only the artillery would save them at this point.

"Sir!" Lieutenant Garrett's call interrupted Gordon's thoughts.

Here we go again.

Gordon used the butt of his rifle to push himself to his feet, groaning at the ache in his chest. He tasted blood again, spat it out. He didn't bother to check his ammunition. It had been gone for a while now.

Gordon looked over the lip of the trench and saw—

"What the hell?"

In the flickering light of a flare, he could see enemy troops emerging from cover, from behind piles of bodies, and running back down the valley. There were still a lot of them, at least two or three hundred, but, by God, they were retreating.

"They're giving up!" Garrett's tired shout was repeated down the line.

Gordon's heart leapt — and then fell.

They would return to the fort, they would trap the attack force, and everything would be lost. Then again, since the fort hadn't fired any new missiles in a few minutes, Wilcox's group had probably succeeded. That, or the *Verdun* had already been destroyed.

"Mr. Garrett, prepare your platoon to attack. Signal the other platoons to move in after us. Get Li to repeat the signal over to the artillery."

Gordon turned, saw Garrett's expression fall.

"Understood, Sir." Garrett turned around. "Corporal Li! Li, get over here!"

Gordon looked for the radioman, couldn't see him. Had he been hit?

"Li!" Garrett called again, his voice all but drowned out by the now useless shells falling in the valley.

"Here!" Li emerged from down the trench, walking slowly, radio handset to his ear.

"Corporal, you ain't paid by the hour. Hurry—"

Li waved his hand to silence the lieutenant.

"Copy that, Sparrow Two." Li looked up, a huge grin spreading over his face. "Sir, you won't believe it. Tac-Two!"

Gordon's hands flew to his headset, adjusted it to the Tac-Two channel in time to hear the last snippet of radio traffic."

"...Take cover and do not approach the enemy. Sparrows out."

Sparrows? Could it be?

Not believing the voice on the radio, Gordon listened for the sound, heard it. Faint, growing louder, but there, even under the explosions of the artillery.

"Corporal, tell the arty to cease fire."

A few seconds later, the shells stopped, but the valley was far from quiet. The sound filled the air, rumbled through Gordon's chest, brought ragged cries of joy from the rangers in the trench and up on the hillsides.

The Verdun's *Fighters!*

And there they were, strafing the forest where the enemy force had run to, the rapid stream of tracers from their machine guns lighting it up, rocket fire blossoming among the trees.

Gordon let himself slide down the trench, suddenly feeling as if he could fall asleep right there.

Of course, they'd need to move in to mop up any survivors and take any prisoners they could find, but for the moment, he was glad to let the flyboys handle it. For the moment, he could rest.

M arcus cheered as the glowing salvo of shells from the *Verdun* struck home. Two of the massive charges hit the lead enemy ship amidships, splitting it in two, the sudden decompression of air causing the pieces to spin off like deflating balloons. The other ships were turning, trying to scramble out of the way.

"No, you don't." Marcus tilted the control stick, pointed his bird toward one of the ships on the edge of the fleet. It was trying to pull away, sneak out of the group. "Vipers, let's keep this herd together. Hit the ships pulling toward the flanks. Cyclone Squadron has the bottom." With one squadron having left the battle to go relieve the ground forces, and most of their ammunition expended, the remaining Alliance fighters would need to coordinate their maneuvers carefully.

Marcus waited just long enough to see that the rest of his squad mates had joined him before he accelerated and shot toward the fleeing ship. The distance between them shrank, and his cockpit lit up, the warm glow of another exploding enemy casting his controls into high relief.

He fired his payload, watched the enemy ship crack apart as the squadron unleashed burning death upon it.

This battle was as good as over.

" I t's bleeding through. Grab me another bandage."
Jack followed the medic's directions and pulled a blue-and-white package out of the trauma kit, ignoring the sting of his own wounds. He tore the package open, and handed a soft, white gauze pad to the medic, who placed it on top of the soaking red bandages already on Flores' wound. The medic pressed in, and Jack winced, imagining the pain Flores must be in. But Flores didn't flinch, or cry out. She was muttering something, her eyes opening and closing. She was slipping away in front of them, and he couldn't do a damn thing about it.

He looked around the command center, at the marines rebuilding the sandbag barricades at the entrance and piling the bodies of the enemy in the corner of the room. None of the rangers were there, though. Squires' platoon was with Colion and Perez's units, securing the rest of the fort, clearing out the last pockets of resistance, searching for where the fort's garrison was imprisoned.

And Flores' soldiers?

They'd seen their leader's wounds and been rooted to the spot, looking down at her where she lay.

"She won't survive a trip down the back access," Sergeant Néri had spoken up. "We need to unblock the main corridor and get her to the infirmary. Let's get to work, Fifth Platoon."

Tired as they were, bleeding from their own scrapes and minor wounds, they'd moved as one into the hallway, attacking the pile of rubble with entrenching tools, the butts of their rifles, their bare hands. They were still there, the thuds and bumps of their efforts audible inside the command center.

But by the frown the young medic was wearing on his thin face, Jack knew it wouldn't make any difference.

They were too late.

You stupid son of a bitch!

Jack cursed himself. If he'd been faster, if he'd moved just a little more quickly. Hadn't stopped here, said that there...

He'd climbed out of the access hatch, hauled himself off the ladder from the cisterns, and seen that bastard standing over Flores, ready to blow her head off. He'd tried to shoot his opponent down, but his shots had missed. He and the man had run out of ammo at the same moment, and the man had dashed for a console — the silo console, Jack now knew. After losing so many under his command, Jack had enjoyed knocking the man down, ending his life with his bayonet. He'd thought for a minute that Flores was okay, that he'd saved her. But then he'd seen the holes in her side and known he'd failed...again.

It's the Triangle all over again.

Flores had been cogent at first, asking after the other platoons, the progress taking the fort, but she had drifted away from them. It was unbelievable how many of the hostiles Flores had taken alone. A whole platoon's worth of them. Then again, that surprised Jack less than the fact that she'd been hit. He'd seen people die before — some of them had even been friends. But Flores wasn't supposed to one of those ones. She had always seemed so untouchable, so confident. It shook him to see her like this.

"Sir," the medic said, softly, meeting Jack's eyes.

Jack held the man's gaze for a second, shook his head.

No way in hell!

"I'll get you more bandages." Jack rummaged through the kit, blinking hard. "And here's more clotting powder." Jack tore open the packages, handed them to the medic, who took them — and placed them on the floor.

"Sir, unless you've got a couple pints of blood to replace what we've already used, and an IV drip—"

"Don't you fucking say it!" Jack stood, paced on the spot, running a bloody hand through his sweat-soaked hair. "Don't you dare. You stick with her." Jack pointed at Flores, his voice rising.

"Sir," the medic murmured again. "There is nothing for me to stick with."

Jack stopped, stared at the medic. In the man's eyes, eyes that had seen more death than any eyes should, Jack saw certainty.

He nodded, and the medic stooped to pick up his kit, then walked away. There were others to treat, others to try to save. Flores? She wasn't his concern anymore.

Jack wouldn't leave her.

He knelt down, looked for her hand. Her left hand was balled up at her side, but her right was open, laying on her chest. She looked so still. Was she already dead?

Jack picked up Flores' hand, held it in his own. It was cold, but he could feel the faintest pulse at her wrist.

She stirred, and her eyes opened. She looked up at him, and her brow knotted.

"Sir, you... crushed. The... hall collapsed. How're you...?" She spoke slowly, pausing to take shallow, rattling breaths.

Jack shook his head, painted a smile on his face. He'd already told her this a few minutes ago.

"We got through. We did it, Captain. You stopped them. We have the fort."

Flores closed her eyes, let out a little sigh. Then she frowned again. "Pla…platoon?"

"They made it through. They'll be back in a minute to take you to the infirmary." Jack glanced out the doorway, hoping against hope that one of the rangers would burst in and say that the hallway was clear. But the sounds of work still echoing from the corridor told him that wouldn't happen.

Flores nodded, coughed. "Néri… Keep them … order. Don't… Let… Get… lazy."

"Sure thing." Jack wiped his eyes with a free hand. "You've done a good job with them, Flores. They're damn fine rangers."

Flores tried to laugh, but settled on a cough. Blood trickled out of her mouth. "Tell…Mom and Dad. They'll… wanna know."

Weren't her parents dead?

Jack hid his reaction to her increasing delirium, gave her hand a squeeze. "You bet they will. They're proud of you, Captain. Damn proud."

Flores' head lolled to the side, and for a second, Jack thought she was gone. But she coughed again, then looked up at him. Her eyes had a glaze to them, and Jack felt as if she were looking right past him, through him.

"Ryan?" She smiled faintly. "Y…you know… you could duck… out of that sun. Let me… See you. Just… ask me… already."

Jack looked above his head, saw a light fixture directly over him. The glare must be in Flores' eyes. But who was Ryan?

Jack shifted himself, looking up at the light to make sure he was out from in front of it. "Uh…" He began, not sure who he should pretend to be. "Is this better?"

He looked back down at Flores, whose gaze was fixed in front of her. "Captain? Flores?" Jack squeezed her hand again. "Christine?"

She was gone.

Jack stayed there, holding her hand in his, holding it tightly, as if it would save him from the raw surge of emotion that welled up from his chest, closed his throat, filled his head, stung his eyes.

He looked down at her other hand, still closed tightly around something. Not letting go of her right hand, he gently took hold of her left. He carefully turned her wrist and eased her fingers open so that her hand was palm-up in his.

And in it was a single, gold ring.

CHAPTER 33

Heat. It shimmered in waves over the trees and the metal forest of the bristling docks, fighting with the cool breeze coming off the water, and soaking through Kim's uniform jacket and into her skin. Over the past two months, heat had become synonymous with Kensington in Kim's mind, and, she imagined as she shielded her eyes against the sun, always would be.

The planet's rainy season had dragged on for a few weeks, washing every operation on Kensington with thick, dark mud, but at least it had offered the occasional cool respite from the sticky, humid warmth. But now the rain was behind them, and the oppressive heat saturated every moment spent outside the *Verdun's* climate-controlled interior, an unbroken chain of blinding, blistering days and sweltering nights.

Today, though, Kim didn't mind. It was worth the discomfort, if only to find a moment alone, the first in a long time.

The activity of the past few months had been demanding of captain and crew. After reducing the enemy fleet to ashes, the *Verdun* had landed the rest of its marines, who, with the help of the rangers, had begun the long task of clearing all remaining enemy forces from the surface of the planet.

The fort had been first, its labyrinth of barracks, munitions bays, and storage rooms requiring a full two days to completely secure. Then, based on intelligence obtained from one of the few enemy soldiers taken alive, the Alliance forces had located the *Barracuda,* set down in a natural bay sixty miles north of the dockyards. Guarded by only a few hundred disorganized troops, the destroyer had been easy to liberate, and casualties had been mercifully light.

Kim breathed in the sweet, dry scent of trees curing in the heat, of earth, of sunbaked clay, let it carry out the memory of the stench that had filled the

Barracuda. Had she not seen the horrors within that ship with her own eyes, she wouldn't have believed them possible. The followers of the so-called United Worker's Legion had forced the *Barracuda* crew and the personnel they'd captured on the train and at the warehouse complex to sit in their own filth, down the hall from where the rotting bodies of their slain comrades had been piled. Some of them, including Commander Agrum, the ship's executive officer, had barely been alive when the Alliance forces had liberated them. Kim's nausea at the reek hanging inside the ship had been nothing compared to her reaction when she'd seen the jury-rigged instruments of torture that the enemy had devised to wring the *Barracuda's* command codes from her crew. Whatever compassion Kim had had left for her enemy, a human enemy at that, had evaporated in that moment.

Despite their travails, the men and women of the *Barracuda* hadn't cracked, and, thanks to the concentrated efforts of Commander Cadogan and his medical crew, were recovering well. The same could be said of the many other personnel wounded by enemy action on the ground and aboard the *Verdun.* Physically, at least. Kim suspected that few of the servicemembers who had served through the Battle of Kensington, as some of the crew were calling it now, were completely unhurt, be they marines, rangers, or Navy crew.

Some were hardly themselves anymore.

Lieutenant Commander Wilcox, once affable and talkative, barely spoke to anyone anymore, unless it was to deliver a report or give instructions. Kim hadn't pushed him to talk about it, not yet anyway. She'd known enough from the after-action report of his experiences on the planet to know he needed time and space.

"When I got to Captain Flores, she was beyond help," Wilcox had said, his eyes staring at a point on the wall behind Kim's head. "She died shortly thereafter. Without her... I doubt we'd have climbed out of that access hatch alive."

"You did everything you could, Commander." Kim had tried to reach him, to let him hear her pride in him. "Your attack against the fort was remarkably successful, given the tactical limitations of the resources you and Major Osterman had at your disposal."

"I intend to recommend Captain Flores and Major Osterman both for commendations," Jack had continued, as if Kim hadn't said a word. "The officers and enlisted personnel of our marines and the ranger company will figure prominently in my report as well. Permission to be dismissed?"

Kim had peered up at him, searching for something, anything to say. Nothing had come to her. "Granted. Dismissed, Commander."

Yes, two traumatic encounters in a row had taken their toll on the *Verdun's* crew. At least they had a heavy workload to distract them. Once Kensington had been secured, the *Verdun* had limped through the solar system, stopping at the communications relay stations that the Legion had destroyed to cover its invasion and cut the planet off from the rest of the Alliance. The *Verdun's* sorry condition and lack of spare parts for the wrecked relay drones had complicated the crew's repair efforts. Thankfully, the *Leclerc* had arrived a few days ahead of schedule and taken over the operation, allowing the *Verdun* to finally land and join the *Barracuda* for repairs.

The fact that Lieutenant Geonor and his team were still standing was a testament to the stubbornness and tenacity of engineers everywhere. Between the old damage from the Frontin and the *Verdun's* new wounds, the list of necessary repairs had been staggering, the most Kim had seen for one ship since the worst battles of the war. Rumors had circulated among the crew that the *Verdun* would be planetside for a year, maybe two.

"We better get ready to go camping in the woods," Stetler had chuckled at one staff meeting.

"I know how to pitch a tent," Urquhart had offered.

"You're welcome to do so." Osterman had grinned, still pale from the pain of his re-aggravated wounds. "I'll stay in a nice bed indoors for a while, with a real toilet."

"Let's do what we're here to do and cut out the chatter." Wilcox's quiet voice had silenced the room.

For a while, Kim had started to believe the rumors herself, that the *Verdun* would be trapped forever. But now, with the help of Kensington's facilities and liberated personnel, who had cut their recuperation short to join in the repair efforts, Geonor and his people were almost finished patching the ship's Keahey drives back together. A day or two more, and they'd be underway.

"She'll still need an overhaul at a shipyard," Geonor had said, handing Kim the day's progress reports. "But we'll be able to get her there so long as we don't try to break any speed records."

Soon, Kensington would be far behind the *Verdun*. None too soon for Kim's tastes. Yet she didn't want to leave without taking a moment to enjoy some real, non-recycled air, no matter how hot it may be. Kim squinted at the shoreline, at the buzzing activity of cargo tenders moving between the *Verdun* and the docks. She glanced over at the rocket-scarred hull of the *Barracuda*, baking in the sun a few hundred yards to the *Verdun's* port side. She didn't expect she'd be doing much besides moving between her quarters and her office for a long time.

Her work wasn't close to being done.

Casualty reports, after-action reports, promotion requests, citations for valor… All of it came through her. She was the paperwork funnel. It wasn't that she minded the task. She'd always been the type to enjoy organization, the finality of submitting a finished piece of work. It was soothing, something regular to hold on to.

No, the paperwork would be fine, with one, painful exception. She hadn't even begun to write the condolence letters. Sure, she could spread some out to direct supervisors and other officers who'd known the deceased better, but there were plenty waiting for her attention.

Of the three hundred men and women in the ranger company, eighty-two had given their lives, most in the attack on the fort. The three platoons of marines that had been stranded on the planet alongside the rangers had lost a quarter of their ranks, thirty-one people in all. Some seventy-eight members of the *Verdun's* crew had joined their marine comrades. Among all the Alliance forces, more than two hundred had been wounded, some severely. How many of those people could have been saved agony and death agony if she'd made a different choice here or there?

The fact that more than two thousand of the enemy had been killed and more than four hundred captured — the numbers increased daily as bodies kept turning up — didn't make Kim feel any better. These people, fellow servicemen and women, were gone forever, and it fell to Kim to inform their families of this fact.

But not right now. Right now, there was time, time to look at something besides a computer screen, to stand instead of sit at her desk, to let the blast furnace air chase away the grief that had struck so many around her. There was time to look anywhere but at the decisions she'd made, the consequences of her command. Kim heard the whistle of the freight train announcing its departure from the dockyards to the warehouse complex. She couldn't see the train through the buildings and equipment of the docks, but she looked toward the dense forests hugging the sides of the hills and gullies that marched in rugged succession toward the fort and the high mountains beyond, a landscape that didn't give a damn about the Alliance forces here, or Kim's condolence letters.

The man-made components of Kensington had changed so much since the *Verdun* had first arrived. Once the *Leclerc* had restored communications to the system, it hadn't taken long for the general staff to react to the news. Two more cruisers and three destroyers had arrived in orbit, ready to repel any further attacks on the planet. A huge troopship had arrived, bringing with it two full infantry regiments, a company of Seabees, additional personnel for the fort, and enough machine guns, cannons, and equipment to restore and rearm every bunker and battery on Kensington. The bustle of activity — rebuilding roads and narrow-gauge rail between the various emplacements, repairing the damage to the fort, re-stocking the missile silos — was in stark contrast to the middle-of-nowhere calm that had surrounded the nearly abandoned station beforehand. But nature — the forest, the water, the broken terrain — hadn't changed at all. Kim wasn't sure if that indifference scared her or comforted her.

What did comfort her was the quick response her superiors had made to address the problem of Colonel Neville. A new officer for the fort, a Colonel Sally Weir, had arrived to replace Neville, who'd been relieved of command and sent away once he'd been cleared by Cadogan's medical staff, along with all of the enemy prisoners. Kim had appreciated the justice of pairing the colonel with the enemy. She doubted Neville would be in command of anything once the board of inquiry read the reports she had prepared with the help of Wilcox and Captain Squires. Had it not been for Neville's incompetence, the fort likely never would have fallen, and the Battle of Kensington would have been over much more quickly and with fewer losses.

Weir seemed to be a solid officer and a good leader.

"I'd like to prioritize getting the Verdun in space again, Captain," Weir had said when she'd first come aboard to take operational command of Kensington from Kim. "Your engineering staff will continue to have whatever support they need from my work crews. Headquarters is eager to have you back home."

Kim didn't doubt that. Having been at the front lines during the battle, the *Verdun* would no doubt face endless debriefings to learn about the Legion. Then Kim would sit before an inquiry to examine her role in Derek's Triangle and on Kensington in detail. The upside of the days that would be spent in meetings would be gaining more information about what was happening elsewhere in the Alliance. Had the UWL struck anywhere else? Where exactly had it come from? The rumor mill on board had been busy non-stop, predicting massive rebellions, huge civil wars, and, as always, Milipa plots, but there had been very little in the way of concrete information. It seemed for the moment that Kensington had been the Legion's first and only target. Kim hoped it stayed that way.

She looked down the length of the *Verdun's* hull, at the work crews dotting it here and there. They were packing up equipment, walking toward access hatches in small groups. That could only mean—

"The Barracuda will be lifting off in fifteen minutes." Commander Holsey's voice interrupted Kim's thoughts, made her jump. She hadn't expected anyone would think to look for her here.

"We'll need everyone inside while their lift thrusters are running," Holsey finished.

Kim glanced sideways at her, saw her step to the railing and lean forward against it. Holsey closed her eyes, then knotted her brow.

"Does it always have to be so damn hot?" Holsey took in a long, slow breath.

"It's horrible, isn't it?" Kim looked down at where the water met the *Verdun's* hull, making little white waves as it lapped against the ship's blue-grey skin.

"The worst." Holsey took another deep breath.

Kim did the same, filled her nose with the smell of salt water, of hot metal under sun. For a moment, neither of them said anything, but stood side by side in silence. They'd have enough time for the *Verdun's* perfectly regulated temperatures and scentless, sterilized air later.

"Command asked again if you're ready to send the death notices out." Holsey drummed her fingers on the metal railing.

Kim shifted. "Ah. I expect they did."

"I don't think I need to remind you that delaying these letters will only make things harder on the families of the deceased."

Kim shook her head, annoyance flashing through her. "Sending them now or later won't change a thing, Commander. It won't bring them back. I…" Kim hesitated, wondering how much of her real feelings she could share. "I need time."

"Respectfully, ma'am, that's the most selfish thing I've ever heard you say."

Kim spun around, found Holsey's blue eyes fixed on her.

"You're out of line." Kim stood up straight, squared herself to Holsey, who remained leaning against the rail.

Holsey shrugged. "That's my prerogative at times, remember?"

"There's been a lot of work to do." Kim crossed her arms over her chest. "I have not been stalling, if that's what you think."

"Bull." Holsey pursed her lips, looked back out at the water. "You could have delegated your other jobs. Writing these letters should have been your first task as soon as the planet was secure."

"There we go again." Kim hated the rising edge of emotion in her voice. "You critiquing my choices. I suppose you're here to tell me about the list of ways I screwed up this time around—"

"Captain, I—"

Kim ignored Holsey's attempt to interrupt her, paced back and forth along the railing. "You want to tell me when we should have retreated, stood and fought, made a different call?"

"Ma'am, you—"

"That's not worth a damn now. It won't change anything. I did—"

"Everything I would have done."

Kim stopped cold, gaped at Holsey, who was looking toward the shoreline now.

"Well," Holsey said, turning to face Kim. "Almost everything. No one's perfect. But I'd have told you if I thought you were screwing up."

"Oh." Kim had nothing better to say.

That was not what she'd expected from Holsey.

"Ultimately, this all falls on you." Holsey stood, faced Kim. "You're in charge. You make the calls. Sometimes, they're bad ones. Okay. But you live with them. One way or another, you find a way to live with them."

Kim laughed, a harsh, sarcastic sound even to her own ears. "Okay, sure. Easier said than done. When you have to tell people their loved one died because of your choices—"

"That has nothing to do with it." Holsey shook her head, crossing her arms to match Kim's posture.

"Oh really? Then what's the problem?"

"You are."

Kim glared at Holsey for a second, looked for something to shoot back at the commander's impassive face, found nothing.

"Look at what happened in the Triangle. Look at this mess. It's not like these losses will be the last. You need to learn to let it go. For the crew's sake — and for your own."

"For me?" Was that concern in Holsey's eyes?

Holsey ignored the question. "The crew needs you to be decisive, whole. You can't do that by beating yourself up each time we fill up some body bags."

Kim's throat tightened. "It's not that easy."

"Tough. It has to be. Putting off your responsibilities to the families of the dead isn't going to solve your problems. To be honest, that's the kind of self-centered shit I'd expect from you."

Kim leaned back against the railing, looked over at the *Barracuda*. The ship's lift thrusters had started to hum, the noise building with each second.

"I'm so happy to hear I meet your expectations. If you have so little faith in me, why'd you come down here? The view?" She and Holsey had gotten along so well in the past few months. Clearly, she'd been mistaken to think the woman's attitude toward her had truly changed.

Kim met Holsey's gaze, and for a moment, they did nothing but stare at each other.

Holsey uncrossed her arms, took a couple steps toward the door, then stopped and looked back at Kim over her shoulder.

"If all I'd wanted was the view, I'd have gone to the starboard side. The Barracuda isn't that pretty." Holsey stepped through the hatch and out of sight into the comparative darkness of the launch control room.

Kim looked after Holsey for a minute. The din of the *Barracuda's* thrusters was overpowering now, pushing aside the noise of the waves and the whistle of the breeze. Kim turned to look one more time at the shoreline and the vast cloak of forest beyond. Then she walked inside, and sealed the hatch behind her.

CHAPTER 34

"Get that last crate in there. Keep it tight."

Jack watched as Chief Petty Officer Austin, one of the *Verdun's* logistics specialists, shouted commands to the group of sweat-stained crewmembers scrambling about the dock. They were attempting to fit one final crate into a steel cargo container, the last container. The last of hundreds, thousands of containers the *Verdun* had taken on in the past few days. Spare parts. Medical supplies. Food. Fresh uniforms. Toiletries. Candy bars for the commissary. Once this last load was aboard, the *Verdun* would be clear to take off and head toward a full repair and refit. More engineers fussing and working on the ship while the rest of them sat on their thumbs and did paperwork and PT. Certainly, he'd have enough to keep him occupied, but not doing what he wanted to do. No one had any answers about the Legion, how widespread it was, where it had started. Jack wanted those answers. He wanted that, and he wanted to take the fight to them. No sitting around and waiting while others did *that* job. If it meant asking for a transfer, Jack would find a way to stay engaged against the enemy.

Jack glanced over at the tender, bobbing slightly in the water as it lowered its crane arm toward the pier. Two of the crewmen were leaning on the container, talking and laughing. They didn't see that the arm was moving toward them. Jack was about to yell something when the tender emitted a light toot from its horn. The men jumped out of the way and waved at the tender's cockpit.

"Chief Austin, keep your crew's heads out of their asses." Jack fixed Austin with his gaze, massaging his temple with one hand, trying to push down his flaring nerves.

"Aye, sir." Austin turned to his crew. "Look alive there. No getting out of work now with a trip to Commander Cadogan."

The crewmembers laughed, then began securing the crane's spreader to the container's locking points. Some of them cast glances in Jack's direction.

Let them look. They weren't responsible for keeping this crew from killing themselves in stupid accidents. There'd be enough death when they went into action again. Until then, Jack would be damned if he'd let the crew get lazy and land themselves in the infirmary because they weren't paying attention.

Jack's temper rose in his chest, and he turned away, struggling to regain composure. He looked out, past another tender that was floating toward the pier, past the *Verdun*, its grey-blue hull washed red-gold from the late afternoon sun, and to the ocean, rolling gently toward the shore, reflecting the turquoise of the sky. He focused on the soft, in-and-out sound of the waves, so much like slow breathing. Jack fought an absurd impulse to jump in the water, to let it wash his emotions and this blasted heat away.

"Sir, last patrol reporting in." Lieutenant Arnot's voice broke Jack's train of thought.

He turned, saw Arnot standing a few feet behind him. Arnot's platoon was filing down onto the pier, mingled with some of the rangers. The *Verdun's* marines had continued to supplement the rangers on their foot patrols until replacements could arrive. Given everything those troops had been through together, and considering the experience the marines had already gained in woodland fighting, Captain Morden and Colonel Weir had figured it would be better to keep them together than try to familiarize the newly arrived infantry regiments with the rangers' operating procedures.

"Very good, Lieutenant. Get your squads loaded up as soon as that second tender is here."

Arnot nodded, wiped sweat off his forehead, and then gathered up his troops against the edge of the pier.

The container was up in the air now, swinging out and over toward the tender, which leaned slightly to one side with the weight of the load. The rangers were milling about next to the marines, shaking hands, exchanging contact information. One of them broke from the group and walked toward Jack.

"Captain Squires." Jack grinned, his dark mood scattering for a moment. "Fancy seeing you down here. Big responsibilities and all."

Squires stopped in front of Jack, slung his carbine on his back, and felt the new, matte-black coronet rank pins on his collar, less of a liability to camouflaged troops than the normal gold. "We higher-ups still have to get out sometimes."

"Congratulations." Jack held out his hand. "I'm sorry I missed the promotion."

As the senior remaining officer among the rangers, Squires had been the natural choice to help lead the company until the new command platoon arrived.

Squires took Jack's hand and gave it a light shake. "Not a lot of time to sit around and celebrate, sir." Squires tipped his helmet back slightly and adjusted the weight of the weapon on his shoulder.

"Regardless, you deserved it." Jack smiled.

"Yeah." Squires looked at the ground, and Jack could see some emotion soften his expression. "It... It should be hers, you know?"

Jack nodded. "You're right, it should be."

Squires looked up, met Jack's gaze.

"But it's not," Jack continued, hearing a slight quaver in his voice. "And you've got to do the best with it you can. She'd have been proud it was you."

Squires nodded, and, for a while, neither of them spoke.

"Our new command platoon arrives tomorrow," Squires said at last. "We'll have our own major and command staff."

Jack knew this would be big news for the rangers. From what he'd gathered, the company had been without its own command staff or support elements since around the time Neville had been given command of the fort. Now that Kensington Station was no longer a forgotten dump, the brass had finally decided to give the rangers the personnel they needed.

Too little, too late.

"Good," Jack said, grinning again. "Then you can be done with all the paperwork and get the hell back to your platoon."

Squires smiled conspiratorially. "Yes, sir."

Another silence passed between them. The first tender was folding away its crane now, and the second had arrived at the pier. Arnot was herding his troops onto the craft, waving them aboard with obvious impatience.

"Come on, boys and girls. Let's get back to the air conditioning."

Some of the marines laughed. Others stopped at the tender's doors to take one last look around or to wave at the rangers again.

"Good luck, Captain Squires." Jack held out his hand again.

"I… I have something for you." Squires rifled through his pockets. "If I can find it, that is. Aha!" He pulled a small envelope out of the breast pocket of his uniform and handed it to Jack.

Jack turned it over in his hands. "Going away present?"

"Just something she would have wanted to give you."

Jack held Squires' gaze for a moment, then opened the envelope and pulled out a thin cloth patch. He turned it over and saw—

"Your ranger patch." His throat tightened.

The shield-shaped patch, showing crossed rifles against a background of mountains and with the word "ranger" in capital letters across the top, was embroidered in subdued shades of black, grey, and olive green. Only a number three, in the sky over the mountains, representing the company's number, was in red.

"The one on the dress uniforms is nicer," Squires was saying. "All kinds of colors. But we didn't have any extra."

Jack looked up. "Thank you."

"No, sir, thank you." Squires saluted.

Jack returned the salute and held out his hand.

"Waiting on you, Commander!" Lieutenant Arnot called out from inside the tender. The first tender was already grumbling back to the *Verdun* with its cargo aboard.

Squires took Jack's hand, and they shook again. Then Jack walked over to the tender and stepped inside. Sweet, cool air enveloped him, and the hatch hissed shut. The engine started, and Jack could feel the craft pushing through the water and moving away from land. He turned to look out the window and saw the rangers walking back up the pier and between the warehouses toward the wall of the forest.

"I am *not* going to miss sweating my balls off there," one of the marines was saying.

"I'm sure we all agree," Arnot replied. "We had to smell your raggedy ass."

The tender filled with laughter.

Jack looked back at the men and women sitting and standing around the cabin. They were smiling, leaning back in their seats, their eyes closed. For many of them, it had been an unbroken string of grueling patrols and harrowing combat ever since the *Verdun* had been forced to abandon the landing party two months ago. It would be good to have everyone back aboard and safe, if only for a while. Kensington would finally be someone else's problem. At least Jack knew that Squires and Colonel Weir would do a good job with it.

Jack turned back to the window and raised his hand to wave at Squires, but the rangers had already melted into the forest and were gone.

K im stepped over the mess of spare parts, tools, power cables, and debris in the corridor as she passed a trio of crewmembers repairing a jagged hole in the bulkhead. The acrid smell of their welding torch and the odor of hot metal choked the air. They looked nervously at her, tried to move some of their equipment out of the way.

"Sorry, Ma'am."

"You're fine, Shipman. As you were." Kim walked on, stretching her aching shoulders as she went. She'd been glued to her seat with casualty reports for… hours, days? She'd completely lost track of time. Kim had made it through quite a number of them before Holsey had asked her to come take her shift on the bridge. Kim had wanted to keep working — indeed, she'd put Holsey on the bridge so that she could make it through as many letters as possible — but something in the commander's voice had told her to take the request seriously. After cleaning herself up a bit and putting on a fresh uniform jacket, Kim had transmitted the first batch of condolence letters. In a few days, a week at most, they'd reach their destinations.

For those families, nothing would ever be the same. There would be before and after, but at least they'd know.

Kim flattened herself against the wall to let another repair crew pass by, dragging a cart full of metal sheeting behind them. She walked on, then turned into a stairwell and climbed toward the bridge. She enjoyed the motion after being in that damned chair and that blank, empty room for so long. One thing was certain, when they reached the shipyards at Craterton, Kim was going to requisition some furniture for her room and make it a real captain's office. If she got to keep her job, that is.

Command had been very clear that Kim's first task would be to face a board of inquiry. The *Verdun* had found herself in two disastrous situations in a row. First, the encounter with the Frontin at Derek's Triangle, and now the so-called Battle of Kensington. The ship had been damaged severely, the crew had suffered heavy casualties, and all in the beginning stretch of Kim's first command of a vessel. Boards of inquiry were common for events like the ones the *Verdun's* crew had been through. Captain Knight had endured his share of them. But the tone of the command staff's message was obvious. They were concerned, to use their own careful language. Very concerned.

Kim supposed she ought to feel nervous, but right now, she had other things to worry about, and too damn much to do. She'd worry about feeling nervous later.

She reached the top of the stairs, returned the salute of the marines on duty in the guardroom, and stepped into the bridge. Isabelle announced the change of command. Everyone was at their stations, including—

"Mr. Wilcox, happy to see you on the bridge again." Kim smiled.

"All stations reporting ready for translight, ma'am." Wilcox's voice was flat, though Kim could see the faintest upward curve at the edges of his mouth.

"Colonel Weir wishes us smooth sailing." Baudouin looked up and over at Kim. "We're clear to depart Kensington space, ma'am."

"Very well." Kim sat down in her chair, took another look around. "Ms. Urquhart, plot a course for Craterton. Mr. Stetler, best possible speed."

Urquhart turned around, and Kim almost did a double take at her expression. The normally chipper lieutenant was wearing a frown. Come to think of it, everyone on the bridge was looking at Kim, their faces drawn, tight.

"Ms. Urquhart, is there something—"

"We can't go to Craterton, Captain." Holsey interrupted Kim. Kim swiveled around to look at her.

"Why not?"

Holsey's face was tight, grave. "We received word ten minutes ago that... that Craterton has fallen."

"What?" Kim stood up, a spike of adrenaline lancing through her.

"The Legion took control of the facility by surprise," Holsey continued, her tone flat. "We've been ordered to Port Souville."

Souville was in the opposite direction from Craterton, deeper in the Alliance's interior, one of the nation's capital planets. If they were being sent there, it must mean that the Alliance was truly in crisis.

Kim felt dazed, sat back down in her chair. "How far has this thing spread? Did they mention that?"

"They said new reports are still rolling in, but a dozen worlds have been confirmed."

Kim looked at Holsey for a moment, then glanced around the room. All eyes were on her, and she could see the same fear, the same mounting panic in their expressions that she felt.

But now was not the time for that.

"Your orders, ma'am?" Urquhart's voice was quiet, strained.

"Best speed to Souville. And I want radio discipline. Run silent." Kim looked at Wilcox, who nodded slightly, as if he had reached the same conclusion, as if he knew what she was about to say.

Kim stood again. "Order all hands to heightened alert. From this point, we will assume we are in enemy territory."

"Even within the Alliance?"

Kim looked down at Urquhart's surprised expression.

"Lieutenant, the Alliance is at war — with itself."

The bridge was silent for a moment before the crew gradually resumed their jobs. Kim sat back in her chair, and looked up at the bright disc of Kensington through the holoports. Despite everything they'd done, despite everyone they'd lost, they hadn't escaped the most terrifying prospect of all.

Civil war.

Also by W.P. Brothers

Line of Battle Series

First Command

Outpost

Legion – Coming 2018

About the Author

W.P. Brothers grew up in Colorful Colorado, where he filled his childhood with made up heroes, villains, and incredible adventures in space, on the sea, and on smoky battlefields. A life-long fan of science fiction, his other passions include military history, fine cooking, competition shooting, and hiking and camping in the beautiful Rocky Mountains.

Connect with him at www.wp-brothers.com, and sign up for his mailing list. You can also join the conversation with other fans of the Line of Battle Series on Facebook at www.facebook.com/AuthorWPBrothers/.

www.ingramcontent.com/pod-product-compliance
Lightning Source LLC
Chambersburg PA
CBHW020238180626
46810CB00006B/2252

*9 7 8 0 9 9 7 7 3 9 4 3 5 *